Lessons in Lemonade

KATHRYN ANDREWS

Lessons in Lemonade
Copyright © 2020 Kathryn Andrews
Published by Kathryn Andrews LLC
www.kandrewsauthor.com

ISBN: 978-0-578-23309-3

Cover design by Heart to Cover, LLC
Editing by C. Marie
Proofreading by Lawrence Editing
Formatting by Allusion Graphics, LLC (http://www.allusiongraphics.com)

Dedication

To the readers, thank you from the bottom of my heart.

Lessons in Lemonade

Prologue

From Your Mouth to God's Ears

Jack

I'VE THOUGHT A lot about *the* day.

The unavoidable fateful day.

The day all professional athletes know is coming . . . the day it's going to end.

Unfortunately for me, deep down in the very fiber of my being, I know for me, that day is today. It's here, it's finally arrived, and on a day I thought we would win it all. Instead, I lost everything.

It's as if I should have known—like a premonition, for lack of a better description—because with every dream, every thought, every scenario, I always come back to this one specific end: injury.

To be more specific, in my dreams it was the one-way-ticket-to-retirement injury—a knee injury.

At the moment I don't know which is greater: the pain in my knee or the pain in my heart.

As an athlete, we all know any day could be the day. Should it come to pass, we're trained to bury the pain, reflect, and feel grateful for all the days, seasons, and years we've been given—only now that I'm here in this empty locker room thousands of miles away from home while my teammates are out there playing the most coveted game of our lives, I can't.

"You hanging in there?" asks Dr. Leffers, our team orthopedic physician.

I look up to find a concerned expression set deep in the wrinkles across his forehead, and I don't respond. There's nothing to say.

"You'll be all right," he says confidently, nodding then giving me a closed-mouth smile.

"From your mouth to God's ears," I mumble on an audible exhalation.

He frowns at whatever he sees on my face, purses his lips tightly, taps me fondly on the shoulder, and then walks away. He puts his phone to his ear, mumbling something, and I glance down at my leg. It's wrapped tight from mid-thigh to mid-calf and has ice packs strapped all over it. They've given me a heavy dose of a pain reliever, but it's not touching the sharp, debilitating pain in my chest.

A roar from the sixty-thousand-plus fans just past these walls slips down the hallway and vibrates anything not tied down. I don't know if the cheers are for my team or not, and I can't help but feel bitter that this is where I am, that this is how my life has suddenly turned out. Every day, every minute—hell, every second a bead of sweat dripped off my body was leading up to this, to this game. I should be with my team. I should be on the field, helping lead them to victory. I should be winning my first Super Bowl, but I'm not.

They're out there, and I'm in here.

I made it a little over seven minutes into the first quarter of the game of my lifetime, and that's all I got. That's all I'll ever get.

Closing my eyes, I put that last play on repeat. I knew both of those defenders were there. I didn't know how close the guy coming from behind was to me, but I knew he was coming. Was it going to be a tricky catch? Of course it was, but this is the Super Bowl, and if there's ever a time for big, risky plays, it's this. That said, if I ask myself if the benefits outweighed the risk, the answer is resoundingly no.

Would I have done anything different? No. I certainly wasn't going to drop the ball or let him throw it away with the potential of a fumble—or worse, a pick six—and yet, this is suddenly my reality.

My whole life, ever since I put on my first set of pads and laced up those cleats, I've dreamed about playing in and winning the Super Bowl. Every sacrifice, every decision, every ounce of my heart—it was all for this, for this sport, for the love of the game. As I sit here now, staring around the unfamiliar red and black Washington Wolves visitors locker room, I feel more defeated than I ever have in my entire life.

Shifting my hips, I resituate myself and lean my head against the back of the bench. After they brought me in and moved me here, one person raised this end to act as a recliner while others undressed me and the medical staff began to examine me. One removed my shoes, leaving my socks. Another literally took a large pair of scissors and cut off my pants, leaving me in my compression shorts, and a third had me pull off my pads. Once the jersey cleared my vision, I wasn't prepared for the sight of my knee. Yes, I knew from the pop on the field that I had an ACL tear, but what I wasn't expecting was for it to look deformed. What should be the straight line of my leg is now angular, crooked, and that means only one thing: a dislocated knee, the most feared knee injury for an athlete.

When I gasped, the medical staff took that to mean I was in pain and forced me to lie back. In actuality, visions of my future were flashing before my eyes: surgery, pain, six to twelve months of physical therapy, and not even a fifty-fifty chance of returning to the job I love.

Who am I kidding? At thirty-two, there is no chance. There is no returning.

Time passed as they wrapped me up, fielded the questions being fired at them by unwelcome people who had made it into the locker room, and then just as quickly as they all blew in, the majority of them headed back out to the field to see what happened next. Dr. Leffers stayed behind, and his assistant brought me my gameday bag. I tossed on a hoodie, he helped me slip on a pair of athletic shorts, and I stared down at what has become my reality.

"Sir, can we get you something to drink?" a young guy asks as he warily approaches me.

"No, thank you," I tell him. Just the thought of ingesting something has my stomach rolling. I know it would come right back up.

He nods, his face solemn, and resumes his duties.

People are moving quickly and quietly around the locker room, coming and going, but no one says a word to me. They're keeping their heads down, doing their jobs: cleaning, rearranging for halftime activities, and putting out food. There's everything from sandwiches to cupcakes on the table, though I don't know who they think is going to eat it. At halftime, adrenaline is high, and appetites are not. Then again, it's not like I'll still be here to see it.

Shaking my head, I grab the towel in my lap, run it over my face, and close my eyes. They burn from the thousand pounds of disappointment strapped to my back, and I can't help but mourn the memories, the wins, the years I'll never have. It's a loss we tell ourselves we're prepared for, only I find I'm not. I'm devastated. I'm angry. I'm at a complete loss for what happens next, and I have to remind myself to breathe because the weight of this reality is crushing me.

From behind me, the internal locker room door opens, and I twist to see who it is. I'm expecting security so I can be escorted—well, I should say, *transported* out. I don't want to be in here when the team is; my emotional state can't take the avoidance from people I consider family or the pity looks I'll be given. I've been a captain for the last four years, a leader, and being helpless in front of men who look up to me, this shift in the dynamic—it's not only confusing for them, it's mortifying for me. I won't do it. Besides, injuries also make people superstitious, and I can't have that, nor do I want to be a part of that.

I also can't have just anyone operating on me. I need someone I know, someone the team knows.

Dr. Leffers called one of his partners, and although I'm certain the surgeons here are fine, I just want to be cut open by one of our own, in my city, with our people. One of the team's on-call private planes is currently waiting on standby to take me home, where I'll be met by familiar faces and a hospital I know.

Home.

I can't get there and away from here fast enough.

But as my eyes skip to the person behind security, what I'm not expecting is to see another familiar face walk through the door—someone I didn't even know was here in Seattle, a person I'm not prepared to see but am so grateful for. Emotions flood me from every direction, my breath catching in my throat, and with that, the last of the very thin armor holding me together cracks.

I couldn't stop the tears even if I tried. Instead, I squeeze my eyes shut, cover my face with the towel again, and as she wraps her arms around me and runs her fingers through my damp hair, I openly cry.

Ham-Wich

Ingredients:

1/3 cup butter, melted

2 tablespoons prepared mustard

1 small chopped onion

1 tablespoon poppy seeds

1 package of Hawaiian Sweet Rolls

6 slices of ham

6 slices Swiss cheese

Directions:

Preheat the oven to 350 degrees.

Remove all rolls from the package in one piece and place on a cookie sheet. Slice horizontally through all 12 rolls at once. Remove the top and set aside.

Combine butter, mustard, onion, and poppy seeds. Spread 1/2 of the mixture across the lower half of the rolls.

Place the slices of ham across the rolls so all 12 are covered. Repeat with the Swiss.

Return the top half of the rolls to complete the sandwich.

Spread the remaining sauce across the top.

Heat for 15 minutes and remove.

Run a knife through the lines of the rolls to make 12 mini sandwiches.

Chapter 1

When Life Gives You Lemons

Meg

Seven months earlier

EVERY DAY MY heart is at war with my brain, and every day the brain wins out.

I've learned over the last couple of years that there's no point in allowing emotions to drive us, our behaviors, or our decisions. They make the most rational person irrational, and I find that's no way to live.

Heart—everything happens for a reason. Brain—no, sometimes bad things just happen.

Heart—good things come to those who wait. Brain—no, good things come to those who hustle, work for it, and never give up.

Heart—if only I was a little bit prettier, taller, funnier, he'd like me more. Brain—no, you are gorgeous inside and out; if he can't see what a badass you are, he's not worthy.

Sure, there's the romantic side of me that wants to believe there's some truth to wishes made on coins tossed into a fountain, candles blown out on a cake, and shooting stars—after all, the idea of these originated from somewhere—but the truth is, it's all fake and there's no such thing as luck. Those are just dreams of the heart. The only thing that matters is what we can give each day and to make a promise to ourselves, originated from the brain, that we'll live life to the fullest.

Hence why I've adopted the expression *When life gives you lemons, make lemonade* as my life motto.

Lemonade. Lemon martinis. Lemon pound cake. Lemon bars. As a chef, they all work, and depending on my mood—sweet, salty, bitter, or sour—I've been known to make all of them.

Just the thought of ooey-gooey pound cake has my stomach growling and me looking at the caterers as they put the finishing touches on the food stations around the tasting room of Wolff Winery.

Shelby, my soul sister, and I are here for the wrap party of the latest issue of Food Network's *All About the South* magazine. In this edition, the magazine focused on farm-to-table local foods, and Shelby was hired to provide the magazine with restaurant recommendations across the southeast. Along with that, she was paired with Zach Wolff here at Wolff Winery to create food pairings for his wine. She spent a few weeks on site in the spring, working with Zach on the recipes, being filmed, and basically loving every minute of it.

Including him.

That's right—they fell in love. I mean how could she not? It's my first time here, but this place is magical, like right out of a fairytale magical, including the castle, which is the main structure of the winery. How crazy is that? A castle, here, in the middle of nowhere northern Georgia, complete with east and west wings, a ballroom for functions, a library, a sitting room, a dining room, a tasting room, and—well, it's just exquisite.

And also overwhelming.

Needing a moment to myself before the chaos fully begins, I slip out past some of the few guests who have already arrived, heading to the back porch overlooking the rows and rows of full leafy vines at the base of the Smoky Mountains. As much as I love a good party, there's a reason I choose to be in the kitchen. I'd rather be lost in a recipe or creating something new than have to entertain and make sure everyone is happy and good to go.

A bee buzzes by before it lands on a planter hanging over the railing. I take a deep breath in and slowly let it out as I watch it dip in and out of a tall stalk of lavender. The lavender here is plentiful, and the bees make the most delicious lavender honey, another element in the winery's overall charm, and that reminds me I need to grab a few jars before I leave tomorrow.

"There you are—what are you doing out here?" Michelle asks from behind me. She's standing in the doorway, looking concerned, so I smile brightly. I hate it when people are uncomfortable or unhappy because of me. Michelle works here at Wolff Winery, for Zach, and is quite possibly the sweetest person I have ever met.

"Nothing. It's just so pretty. I know it's almost noon, but I thought I'd step out for a minute to soak up some of this country air." And a minute is really about all I got. I live in

Charleston, which is only five hours away, but the air here feels and smells so different. It's nice to be able to take it in while I can.

She moves to stand next to me, and I grin down at her cowgirl boots. While I am always in heels, and I do mean always, she's always in boots. At least we're consistent.

"It is beautiful here," she says, staring out over the property. "Some days I pinch myself, expecting to wake up, because this has to be a dream."

I know what she means; it's how I feel when I'm standing in my restaurant's kitchen.

Glancing back inside, she takes a few steps away and toward the party. "New people have arrived, and Shelby is looking for you."

"Tell her I'll be there in another minute. And thank you."

She nods in understanding and leaves me.

I didn't expect to feel this way today, and the quicker this passes, the better off we'll all be.

The hum of an engine catches my attention and I watch as a small tractor makes its way across the back of the property, heading toward the barn. When Shelby was here, she talked about how the people work from sunup to sundown, and even today with the party about to be in full swing, they still aren't stopping. They never stop. I can't even imagine how hard it must be to run a place like this, but it's been in Zach's family for years, and well, if you tasted his wines, you'd see he was born for this.

Now, this will soon be Shelby's home, too, as she's decided to explore new ventures away from the restaurant and away from Charleston.

The restaurant we started together three years ago.

Don't get me wrong, I am elated for her; I'm just also feeling a little sorry for myself. We met in college and I've loved having her by my side for almost ten years, but all good things must come to an end eventually. I'm over the moon for all the exciting opportunities that are coming her way in this next chapter of her life.

As for me, I'll be all right. I always am.

Remember the lemon martinis?

Tasty, right?

And strong.

I've always known working for Food Network was her dream, and I've done a great job over the last two years reminding myself of this as she's begun taking on projects for them and making a name for herself. She is amazing, and it was only a matter of time before they realized it, too. Now that I've allowed myself to wallow for these five minutes, I shake out of it, pull my shoulders back, and suck in a deep breath of the lavender-scented air.

Today is her day, and I am officially one hundred percent here for her, just like she has always been there for me.

Walking back into the main tasting room, I find her standing next to Zach, and my heart fills with joy at how stunning they look together. She's wearing a pale pink dress with a pair of tall sparkly Gianvito Rossi heels, and he's wearing a gray suit with the top button open on his dress shirt. She looks couture, he looks *GQ*, and they are smiling at each other like lovestruck goons.

I clear my throat, startling them, and they both turn to look at me. They hadn't even realized I had joined them.

"Sorry!" Zach says as he holds out his hand. "We haven't properly met yet. Hi, I'm Zach." His smile is so large and genuine I falter briefly. No wonder she fell under his spell; when he turns on the charisma, it's impossible not to feel light-headed.

"Meg. Nice to finally meet you," I respond, slipping my hand into his. He towers over me, but then again, most do. On my best day, in my tallest shoes, I'm only five-foot-five. "This is quite a place you have here, Zach." Behind him, sunlight pours in through the arched ornamental windows that line the front wall.

"I think so," he says proudly as he releases my hand and looks around.

I do the same, taking in more of the details of the tasting room. It's exquisitely put together, and with its arched ceilings and massive columns, it matches the overall baroque feel one usually sees in European castles.

"Shelby was a lucky girl to get to spend two weeks here. A castle that has endless amounts of free wine—I can't think of anywhere better." I wink at her, and we share a knowing, heartfelt look honed over years of friendship. Then I turn back to Zach with a stunning smile of my own.

He laughs, and in my peripheral vision, I see Shelby take in a deep breath. She's happy that the two of us are getting along. I'm not surprised that we are. She loves him, and I know I'm looking at her future, one I'm so happy for. She deserves this more than anyone I know.

"Actually, I'm the lucky one," he says affectionately. He pulls his hand out of his pocket and reaches over for one of hers. Bringing it to his mouth, he kisses the back, and she sighs with hearts in her eyes. Peas and carrots, I have heart eyes too.

Love might not be in the cards for me, but it sure looks good on them.

"Zach!" From behind him, he gets slapped on the shoulder, and we turn to see two new guys have approached us.

"Hey, Shelby," says the tall drink of water with dark hair and deep chocolate eyes as his gaze drops to their connected hands. He grins and gives Zach an *I told you so* look before turning his attention to me.

Electrical charges start firing, and I feel shocked.

Neither of us moves or says anything, and I can feel all four of them looking at me. This guy . . . his expression slowly brightens as if he's just found the best piece of candy in the candy shop, and I narrow my eyes in a way that says, *Don't even think about it.*

He smirks, completely unfazed by my unspoken warning.

"And hello, gorgeous," he says smoothly, shifting to face me a little more after the silence between us and the stare-down has stretched into awkwardness.

I'm not normally thrown off by meeting new guys—in fact, I'm known to be a bit of a maneater with my anti-forever policy—but for some reason I can't get my brain and my tongue to work together right now.

"I'm glad y'all could make it," Zach says, breaking the silence after I don't respond. Then he turns toward the second guy, who has yet to say anything.

Tearing my eyes off of Mr. Dark Adonis, I find Mr. Blond Adonis, another handsome addition to the room. Seriously, why is it that the beautiful ones always flock together? Where do they even find each other?

"Absolutely," the blond answers, giving him the tiniest hint of a smile.

Wait a minute . . . Tilting my head, I get a better look at the blond. He looks familiar, but I can't place why, and it's then cool air washes over me. I know it's because the dark-headed one has stopped looking at me.

Confused by the sensation, I quickly glance over to find him focused back on Shelby.

"We're glad the timing worked and we could come up. Wine and some of Shelby's cooking"—he raises his brows hopefully—"how could we turn it down?"

Hold up, just a second—has she cooked for him before? When? I didn't even know she knew guys like him. Wait, did I say him? Ugh. I meant them. Has she cooked for *them* before?

She shakes her head and laughs. "Meg and I brought the cobbler"—she glances at me—"but the rest of the food was prepared by others from the recipes for the pairings. Although I didn't personally cook the food today, I promise you won't be disappointed."

She leans forward and squeezes his arm briefly before pulling back. It's a friendly gesture, one that confuses me. When did this happen?

His face falls a little and he says, "I don't know about that," as he shoves his hands in the pockets of his ridiculously gorgeous tailored navy pants. Yes, I can spot fashion yays and nays a mile away, and this guy is all yay.

"Well, if you like my cooking, you'll love Meg's even more. She is a way better chef. You should drop by our restaurant in Charleston next time you're out that way and have her cook for you."

Two things occur to me at once. First off, she's still calling it "our" place even though it'll soon not be, and this makes my heart swell and ache at the same time. Secondly, she's essentially inviting this guy over and volunteering me to cook for him! I shoot her a *what the heck* wide-eyed look, and she just grins conspiratorially.

"Is that so?" dark-headed guy says as he turns and looks at me. I try to neutralize my expression, but as he grins, dimples pop out, and inwardly I groan. Dimples are my weakness— only, I don't want to have a weakness. I also don't want a man, any man. I kind of want to ignore him, which is why the glare on my face drops into a scowl.

Blond guy chuckles next to him, picking up on my indifference, and that's when I notice someone from the magazine has approached Shelby and pulled her attention away.

"Come on, sunshine, how about the three of us leave these two to do some work, and you and I can get to know each other better." He holds his hand out, but I just stare down at it like it's plagued.

Frowning, I look at Zach and Shelby, and as much as it pains me, I do the right thing. They are here to work, and they need to start circulating the room.

"Fine." I relent, but instead of taking his offered hand, I cross my arms against my chest.

Of course all that does is force his eyes down my body, and a blush burns through me. Seeing my resistance and my discomfort, he smiles even bigger, deepening his dimples, and drops his hand.

"Fine starts with an F, and did you know there are only two Fs needed to satisfy a man? Food and fu—"

"Oh my God! Don't even say it," I snap, glancing toward the blond for backup. He just grins and shakes his head like there's no use fighting it, but I've got news for him: I'm not even going to enter the ring. I've made promises to myself, and not even this guy will have me breaking them.

Together the three of us turn and head for the bar. Wine—I need wine. Lots of wine. "You do realize we just met, right?" I toss over my shoulder.

He laughs then looks down at me with a smolder so intense I expect smoke to rise up from his feet. Holy. Moly. This guy is something else.

Placing his hand on my lower back, he guides me through the people. Heat sears through the thin fabric of my dress, and his hand is so large it covers almost the whole span of my back.

"Technically, we haven't met, but I'm real glad that's about to change," he says with his mouth lowered next to my ear. The warm air sends a shiver through me, and I begin a mental chant of, *Not today, Satan. Not today. You will not be affected by this guy.*

Sliding up to the bar, the three of us each tell the bartender what we'd like, and I use the opportunity to take in more of his features: strong jaw, high cheekbones, tanned skin, *perfect.* If I could growl, I would; instead, I reach for my white wine and take a large gulp. I've always been a white drinker; I blame it on the heat of the south. I like light, crisp, cool, refreshing, and I know I shouldn't, but I do find it ironic that this guy picks a cabernet sauvignon—bold, rich, and full of complex layers.

"So, you must be one of the three legs of the tripod," he says cheerfully, not even acknowledging that his friend is standing next to us.

I almost spit out my wine and look at him skeptically. "How do you know about that nickname?"

"James, of course." He sips his wine, looking pleased as punch to have thrown me off.

While we were in culinary school, which is where Shelby and I met Lexi, one of our teachers dubbed us the tripod. We were inseparable and still try to spend time together whenever we can.

"You know James? Wait, do you know Lexi, too?" I look back and forth between the two of them.

A sly smile slowly stretches across dark-haired guy's face. "James, yes. Lexi, no. I just know of her, but Bryan here grew up with both of them."

Just hearing Bryan's name has the flow of air in my lungs halting. Turning to face him, I take him in from head to toe and start involuntarily nodding.

"Bryan Brennen. I knew I recognized you from somewhere."

He shrugs his shoulders and gives me a warm smile back. So this is Lexi's Bryan. Well, I'll be.

"But you don't recognize me," says tall-dark-and-handsome, bringing himself back into the conversation.

"No. Should I?"

"Jack. Jack Willett. I play football with this guy." He holds out his hand and I once again look down at it as if it's offensive, but I still slide my hand into his. Again with the large hands, only this time the warmth is touching me directly, skin on skin. Realizing I like this more than I should, I snatch my hand away and wipe my palm against my dress.

"Meg Dukette." I nod at Bryan, letting him know it's nice to meet him, and then scowl back at Jack. Around us, more and more people have sidled up to the bar, pushing me closer to him, and I'm overwhelmed by his nearness.

"So, Shelby seems to think I should visit you in Charleston. I love food, and well, if you're as good as she seems to think you are, I might just have to make a trip."

My jaw drops.

"Speaking of food," Bryan chimes in, "I'm going to go find some. Either of you want anything?"

I shake my head, and Jack answers, "Not yet, but thanks." Bryan wanders off, and I can't say I blame him—he wasn't exactly being included.

Looking back at Jack, I see his eyes are already on me, and my stomach drops just a bit as sparklers light and fizzle underneath my skin. I haven't physically reacted to a guy like this in so long, and I'm almost confused by the sensations.

"So, about that dinner," he says, his voice lower, deeper. I hear the double meaning behind it—he isn't subtle—and maybe in another life I might have gone with it, but not in this one. I don't date people who are or potentially will be in my inner circle. Like, ever. Those I do go on dates with are mostly strangers, guaranteeing it won't become too awkward when I don't go out with them a second time. Which I never do.

Looking up at him—he towers over me by almost a foot—I laugh to myself as I think about the height difference between us if I were to take my shoes off. My eyes would barely be staring at his nipples. *Wait—no! Why am I thinking about his nipples? Just no, no, no.*

"You're more than welcome to come any time. We love all our paying customers."

He chuckles. "What if I'm paying, but it's for you and me, and someone else does the cooking?"

"I don't date," I blurt out.

"Ever?" he questions, tilting his head to the side.

"Well, I do, but not people I know." As if that will make any sense to him.

"But you don't know me," he taunts, one side of his mouth curving up.

"I do now." I attempt to take a step back from him but end up bumping into the person behind me. Jack reaches out and tucks his hand around my elbow to steady me. There he goes with the hands again, and there I go liking him touching me more than I should.

Humming, he twists his lips to the side while he thinks, and then his eyes light up. "Well, I'm down for skipping the dinner and going straight for dessert, if you know what I mean."

Yeah, I know what he means, and as tempting as it might be, that's not my style.

"Not gonna happen, cowboy." I shake my head and my arm so he'll release it. He does.

"Cowboy—does that mean you're into role-playing?" He wiggles his eyebrows, and a laugh bursts out of me.

"No. No role-playing. Ever." Although, him in a Stetson hat and nothing else—I bet it would be a sight . . . a glorious sight. "Persistent much?" I ask.

"Can't blame a guy for trying." He shrugs, those dimples making another appearance.

He lightly taps his glass against mine, and we both take a sip of wine.

"Does that approach usually work for you?"

He doesn't say anything, just continues to smile. He licks the wine off his lips, and unfortunately I watch every move. Also unfortunately, I have my answer.

This guy is nothing but trouble, and considering the fact that he's friends with Zach and James, I have a feeling I'll be seeing him around here and there, which is why I settle on understanding it's definitely for the best that we're going to be friends—just friends. He may be too handsome for his own good, but I find the silver lining, the lemonade to this new acquaintance: he seems like a funny guy who will make me laugh, and I love laughter in life.

"Well, if we're not having dinner together, tell me about this restaurant of yours. What kind of meal would you serve me?"

Oh brother.

Lemon Bars

Ingredients:
For the crust:
  1/2 pound unsalted butter, at room temperature
  1/2 cup granulated sugar
  2 cups flour
  1/8 teaspoon kosher salt

For the filling:
  6 extra-large eggs at room temperature
  3 cups granulated sugar
  2 tablespoons grated lemon zest (4 to 6 lemons)
  1 cup freshly squeezed lemon juice
  1 cup flour
  Confectioners' sugar, for dusting

Directions:
Preheat the oven to 350 degrees F.

For the crust, cream the butter and sugar until light in the bowl of an electric mixer fitted with the paddle attachment. Combine the flour and salt and, with the mixer on low, add to the butter until just mixed. Dump the dough onto a well-floured board and gather into a ball. Flatten the dough with floured hands and press it into a 9 by 13 by 2-inch baking sheet, building up a 1/2-inch edge on all sides. Chill.

Bake the crust for 15 to 20 minutes, until very lightly browned. Let cool on a wire rack. Leave the oven on.

For the filling, whisk together the eggs, sugar, lemon zest, lemon juice, and flour. Pour over the crust and bake for 30 to 35 minutes, until the filling is set. Let cool to room temperature.

Cut into triangles or squares and dust with confectioners' sugar.

Chapter 2

Keep 'em Coming, Ladies

Jack

"I SWEAR, PIE is one of the greatest foods of all time," I mumble to Reid, who's watching Bryan walk to the training room showers after announcing that he's heading off to his childhood hometown to accept an award. Actually, it's the key to the city.

How hilarious is that?

Bryan is our quarterback for the Tampa Tarpons, and he's also one of my best friends. He's the least flashy person I know in our profession, and yet in the last month he's gone on the Paul Miller show for a one-on-one interview, which aired in primetime on National Sports Network, and now he's doing this. Granted, it's deserved—he's donated a lot of money to the town and the youth sports programs they have there—but in general, the guy is all business, no pleasure. In fact, it's like pulling teeth to get the dude to even smile. He has what we've officially dubbed as RDF—resting douchcanoe face.

Reid glances back at me and the fork hanging out of my mouth as he goes about packing his practice bag. "It doesn't matter if it's pie, cake, ice cream, cookies, doughnuts, whatever. As long as it's in front of you, you'll eat it—even though you shouldn't." He frowns.

"What do you mean? We practiced for an extra hour today—I've earned this," I say as I shift the two pie boxes under my arm: grasshopper and cherry, both now my dates for dinner tonight.

Reid is my other best friend. When he transferred to Tampa, he moved in across the hall from me in our condo building. It's made working out, commuting to practices and games, and life in general not so lonely.

"What do you mean what do I mean? You know as well as I do all that sugar is not good for you." He eyes me knowingly while completely passing judgment.

Athletes tend to be very strict on the whole "my body is a temple" mentality, but I work hard daily, possibly harder than anyone else. Think about it: Bryan is just doing the three-step drop and then throwing the ball while I'm continuously sprinting out twenty, thirty, sixty yards. As such, I don't feel guilty when something like pie lands in front of me, because the way I see it, I earned it.

"You're just jealous because I got to them first." I grin, licking the fork clean and dropping the boxes back on the bench to take a photo of them: me with the fork in my mouth, the team logo visible on the wall behind me.

His look is incredulous as he goes back to shoving things in his locker. "I can assure you, jealousy is the furthest thing from what I'm feeling. Are you ready? I need to get home— Camille is waiting for me."

Camille is his wife. They recently got married—well, remarried—and much to my dismay, they are moving to Davis Islands, where they bought a home on the water.

"Yep, just gonna post this real quick to say thank you to all the fans."

"You do realize they aren't your fans, right? Those pies were for Bryan." He throws his bag over his shoulder.

"Don't care," I tell him, because I don't.

While Bryan was doing the interview, he did a round of this or that, and one of the questions was cake or pie. Clearly, the answer was pie, and I think it's hilarious how many pies have been coming in to the front office. Staff loves it, players love it, everyone loves it, except maybe Reid and Bryan, and we all know Bryan isn't going to say a word about them, so I will. I caption the picture and post it.

Reid rolls his eyes as I grab my things, and we head out to the parking lot to my brand-new black Ford F-150 Raptor, which I didn't feel bad about buying at all. I've been very cautious with how I've spent my money. I know I can't play football forever, but after many years of holding out, I finally gifted this truck to myself.

"How's the packing going?" I ask, my arm draped over the steering wheel. We've been driving for ten minutes, and he's been quiet while texting but looks up to answer me.

It sinks in that this is one of our last commutes together, and my happiness over the pies wanes. I'm sure another teammate will move in across the hall—the condo is owned by a former Tarpons player—but it won't be the same. I'm going to miss him, and Camille, too.

"Well, Camille has done most of it. I feel bad, but she's got it under control. Sunday she plans on being at her house in

Savannah with the movers to direct what she wants moved, and then Monday morning they'll be here to get the things from the condo. The goal is to have everything moved in by late Monday night."

"That's exciting, man. I'm happy for you guys." And I really am. I'm sad for me, but they are awesome together, and the house they bought is incredible.

"Thanks. She's happy, and right now that's all I really care about."

Reaching over, I slap him on the shoulder. "Such a good husband you are."

He rolls his eyes and shakes his head.

"How can I help?" I ask, because there's no way I'm going to sit back and just watch this happen. When you're a friend of mine, you're a friend, and I always try to go above and beyond when I can.

"I'm not sure. Like I said, she's got people all lined up for each aspect, so I'm even wondering what I'm supposed to be doing. I appreciate you offering, though."

"Food—I'll bring the food. Oh, how about arroz con pollo?" I ask as we cross over the Hillsborough River, and I glance toward downtown. I love the view of the city, along with Spanish chicken and yellow rice, one of my favorites.

Reid chuckles and again shakes his head. "Are you going to make that?" He looks back at his phone in his lap and fires off another text.

"No way. I'll have Eric make it."

Eric is a guy I found through the culinary program here at The Art Institute of Tampa. He wants to be a full-time personal chef, and well, I need to be fed. He wasn't starstruck, didn't ask to meet any players or get tickets to any games, so we hit it off perfectly.

"Why doesn't that surprise me?"

"It shouldn't. You love his food just as much as I do."

He laughs, shoving his hand through his still wet hair. "Yeah, I do."

Ten minutes later we pull into the condo building, and Zeus is waiting behind my front door for me as he hears us walk down the hall. His big tail is thumping hard on the floor and, like usual, I can barely get the door open before he's on me.

"Hey there, big guy! How's my boy?" I scratch ferociously behind his ears and rub his sides. There is nothing better than owning a dog. We never had one when I was growing up, but now that I have, I can't see me ever not having one again. The love, the loyalty, the companionship—it suits me perfectly.

He circles around me and nuzzles me hard with his head.

"Yeah, I missed you, too," I tell him.

Zeus was a spontaneous addition. I had honestly never even thought about having a pet—we do travel a lot during the season—but I was out for a run on Bayshore Boulevard, and I stopped in at the grocery store to pick up a few things for lunch. Outside, in a box, were three black puppies with a sign that said *Free*.

One look at Zeus and it felt like lightning struck through me, an electrical charge that shocked me, and I knew he was meant to be mine. That's how he got his name, too—Zeus is the god of the sky. He controls the lightning and the thunder.

Of course, I had no idea how to take care of a dog. I took him to the vet, who couldn't be certain what breed he might be or how big he was going to get, but I didn't care. At the pet store I had the salesperson help me buy all the things he thought I might need, I got a book about caring for a dog and found a dog sitter for when we're gone, and the rest is history.

Reid told me I was out of my mind, but I saw the way he looked at Zeus; he loved him instantly, too.

Now, over a year later, he's eighty-five pounds of all black fur with just a tiny patch of brown on his chest, lean muscles, and floppy ears, and he's just the sweetest boy.

Moving past him, I walk to the kitchen, drop my bag on the counter, and put the pies in the refrigerator. I do understand what Reid is saying about the sugar and unhealthy ingredients, but I just can't help myself. Everyone's got their weaknesses, and it just so happens pie is mine. Well, any sweet for that matter. I have the biggest sweet tooth.

From across the room, the sounds of Bryan's name being spoken on the main sports channel catches my attention. Yes, I leave the television on for Zeus when I leave. I don't want him to be lonely.

"Rick, I do think this is the year for Brennen and the Tampa Tarpons. They have every tool in their arsenal to make for the perfect season and go all the way."

"I have to agree with you, Darren, and based on what we've seen just from the start of this season, the rest of the conference better watch out."

On the replay screen between the two hosts is a pass Bryan made to Reid, another to me—the best wide receiver in the country, if I do say so myself—where I ran for an extra thirty-two yards, one of our defense crushing the offensive line of the Giants and sacking their quarterback, and one of our kicker completing a fifty-six-yard field goal.

Man, do I love highlights like this. It's like reliving the adrenaline of the moment all over again and showing all my boys in action. Of all the teams I've played with over the years, this group of guys is by far my favorite. It feels less like a team and more like a family, and I'm picking up all the feel-good vibes everyone is throwing down.

Grabbing a glass of water, I hear my phone ding as I chug. Rummaging through my bag, I find it and see there's a text from Billy inviting me over to his house for dinner (his wife Missy is cooking Mexican) and an Instagram notification. Dinner with them? Hell yeah—she makes the best guacamole. I fire off a text thanking them and saying I'll come over, and then I open the app. There's a comment from Meg on the photo I just posted, the one of me eating a bite of pie in front of the stack of pies at the training facility, the caption saying: **Living high on the hog. Keep 'em coming, ladies.**

Her comment says: **Living high on the hog—more like being the hog. Oink oink, Jack. *pig emoji***

Ha, funny girl! A grin splits my face and I shake my head. She's been giving me shit ever since I met her over the summer, and honestly, it's become one of the highlights of my day.

Immediately after the wrap party at Zach's winery, I found her on social media and turned on post notifications so I would see her through the noise. I followed the Instagram page for her restaurant, and she tagged herself on one of the photos, which is how I found her personal, private page.

Her feed is one hundred percent the girl I met at the party. It's bold, full of color, and has a ton of pictures of her with her friends and cooking food . . . all in high heels. I don't know how she does it, but I'm damn sure glad she does. Her legs are phenomenal, which I had to comment on, and so began the banter. Not a day has gone by where we haven't poked fun at each other for one thing or another.

Did I want more with her? Absolutely, but she friend-zoned me pretty quickly, and well, I'm okay with that. You can't win them all, and really I'm glad it didn't happen, because I'm enjoying our exchanges way too much.

Responding, I add: **Word is, eating chocolate-covered bacon is all the craze, and this pig's got something you can dip in chocolate and eat.**

Smirking to myself, I shove my phone in my pocket and grab Zeus's leash. He runs to the door and sits like a good boy, waiting for me.

In my pocket, my phone buzzes with a new notification. Pulling it out, I see it's Instagram again; Meg must have replied. When I open the app, there in the notifications is her response: the green puking emoji. I can't help the laugh that bursts out of me.

Arroz con Pollo

Ingredients:

1/4 cup dry white wine
Pinch of saffron threads
4 bone-in skin-on chicken thighs 6 ounces each
Kosher salt and freshly ground pepper
1 tablespoon extra-virgin olive oil
1 medium onion finely chopped
1 red bell pepper finely chopped
2 teaspoons minced garlic
1 bay leaf
2 cups chicken broth plus more if needed
1 cup short-grain rice such as Calasparra, Arborio or Calrose
2 tablespoons chopped parsley optional
3/4 cup frozen peas thawed

Directions:

Preheat the oven to 375 degrees F.

Combine wine and saffron; let stand until ready to use.

Season chicken on both sides with salt and pepper. Heat oil in a large pan over medium-high heat. Cook chicken, skin side down, until browned, 4 to 5 minutes.

Flip, and cook until golden brown; transfer to a plate.

Drain any excess oil, leaving 1 teaspoon of oil in the pan.

Reduce heat to medium and cook onion, red bell pepper and garlic, stirring often, until tender, 5 to 7 minutes. Stir in wine-saffron mixture, 3/4 teaspoon salt, 1/2 teaspoon pepper, and the bay leaf.

Cook until wine is almost completely evaporated, 5 to 10 minutes. Add chicken thighs, broth and rice; bring to a simmer.

Cover the pan and place it in the oven. Bake for 30 minutes.

Remove the pan from the oven. Stir the peas into the rice.

Top with parsley and serve.

Chapter 3

Should I Go All In or Fold?

Meg

I'M GOING ON a date tonight—well, in about ten minutes now—and surprisingly I'm super excited about it. Not just a little bit excited, but *a lot* excited. Actually, I think I'm more excited about what we're doing, but the guy seems okay, too.

I met him on a new dating app I joined, and he appears to check all the boxes for having a good time. His profile says he's a college graduate, works in finance, likes to travel, loves to try new food, and loves sports. I mean, if his personality doesn't suck, our interests are lined up pretty closely, and I can't see me not having a good time.

As for what we're doing, it's the final night for the scarecrow contest. That's right, scarecrows, and we're going to stroll through the Battery and check them out before we sit down for dinner.

The competition is hosted by the Junior League of Charleston. It's a hundred dollars to enter, and each establishment gets to decorate their own scarecrow and display it. The money is being used to provide food bags to families in need over the holidays, and I can't think of a better use for it. The whole city has gone crazy with scarecrows, and it's drawn in visitors from all over.

The competition kicked off the night of the harvest moon, it closes the third week in October, and the scarecrows are displayed until each business chooses to take theirs down, which will most likely be soon after Halloween. The contest winners will be announced in tomorrow's Sunday newspaper, and ribbons will be awarded throughout the day.

Of course, our scarecrow is a chef.

Taylor, being the awesome new front-of-house manager that she is, found us a six-foot scarecrow online and then decorated her to look like me. When I first saw it completed and staked in the bushes outside, I couldn't help but laugh. She put a brown curly-haired wig on it, it's wearing an OBA apron with high-heeled boots, and it's holding a rubber chicken in one hand, a large plastic knife in the other. I've posed next to it for more pictures than I can remember, we've been tagged on social media more in the last month than we have in the last four, and sales have gone up thirty-two percent this month over October of last year.

I can only imagine how positive this has been for the city.

At the moment, though, I need to decide on this gravy—a new sausage biscuit gravy, that is.

My restaurant, OBA (short for Orange Blossom Avenue), serves breakfast and lunch during the week, and on the weekend we have a special brunch menu. As for at night, generally we're closed, but it seems more and more we've been booking private events for Friday and Saturday nights.

I'll never complain about the private events. The menu is set ahead of time, so it's easy for us to prepare and serve, and I get to charge a nice amount per person.

Now, what makes us unique is that we do have a lot of classic dishes on our menu, but we also have a bunch of originals, too, to keep patrons coming back for more. Plus, everyone who comes in gets a bag of madeleine cookies to take with them when they leave.

Of course, over the last couple of years, our menu has included biscuits and gravy on and off, but each time we change it, I try something new. Today, I tested four different sausages: a spicy chorizo sausage, a browned maple sausage, a chicken and pancetta sausage with rosemary, and a seafood sausage. I'm leaning toward the seafood sausage, and then with each biscuit open-faced, we can top it with lump crab meat and serve with a garnish of cantaloupe.

Beside me, the door to the kitchen swings open and Taylor breezes in, her eyes lit up with humor. That wasn't even ten minutes, more like five, but I'm excited to get out of the kitchen tonight. Bonus points to him for being a few minutes early.

Taylor joined us here at OBA a couple of months ago after I realized how hard it would be to do it all with Shelby gone. She's bubbly, just out of college, loves being around people, and is insanely organized. She's perfect for the job.

"Oh no—I know that look," I tell her, a smile pushing past my lips.

"Yep, tonight is going to be so much fun for you." She grins, her eyes crinkling a little in the corners.

This year, for my New Year's resolution, I set a goal to go out on a date with someone new every month. Though I have no interest in finding a life partner, I do enjoy meeting new people, and I realize that over the last couple of years, I've spent too much time behind this kitchen door and not enough out living life. Also, like Taylor Swift, I use each experience as an inspiration to create a new monthly dish.

"Are you being sarcastic?" I ask, moving over to the sink to wash my hands.

"Just wait and see." She swings the door open, and a medium-height guy cautiously saunters in with wide eyes. His gaze roams around the kitchen and then lands on me.

"You're a cook?" he asks, as if this displeases him.

In all fairness, I left my career off my profile so I can see how this might throw someone off, but what's wrong with being a cook?

Taylor lets out a surprised sound next to him and quickly rolls her lips between her teeth.

"Chef would be a more accurate term, but yes, I'm a cook." I remove my apron and lay it on the counter. Taylor will hang it up for me with the others after we leave.

"Huh." He presses his lips together then decides to look me over from head to toe. His eyes halt on my legs and heels then shoot back up to my face.

Taylor is still standing in the doorway, and even without looking at her, I know she is trying hard not to laugh.

"And you make enough money off cooking to make a living?"

Okay, that's a little forward of him to ask, but I'll go with it. After all, first impressions don't necessarily need to be lasting impressions. Maybe he's nervous, or has terrible social skills?

"Yep, I do. I'm ready when you are." I gesture toward the dining room to get him moving.

He turns, takes a few steps, and then tosses over his shoulder, "You look beautiful." As if my profession has all of a sudden been forgotten. The kitchen staff behind me murmurs.

"Thank you. You don't look so bad yourself." And he doesn't. He has light brown hair, a bit of a baby face in that his skin is smooth, and he's wearing dark jeans with a white button-down shirt and nice shoes.

Taylor winks at me as I grab my purse from the office desk and Scott and I head out the front door.

"Ha, look at that—your scarecrow looks like you," he comments, stating the obvious.

My mind drifts to Jack, the guy I met at Zach and Shelby's over the summer. When Taylor first posted our scarecrow, I mimicked its pose and Jack made a similar comment, but more along the lines of me finally exposing my long-lost twin sister. Over the next two weeks, on additional posts, he also teased that he couldn't tell which one of us was the scarecrow and how I need to stop scaring the scarecrow. He was definitely more original, and he's always funny. The guy regularly makes me laugh, and I already know he's going to have a field day with tonight's date.

"So, you're a cook," he says again, only this time he's nodding approvingly.

"Yeah, something like that," I answer as I start walking toward the heart of the Battery.

"How long have you worked there?" he says, looking over at me. I can feel his eyes roam over me again and I can't tell if it's making me feel slimy or not, but I already know this is over just as it begins. I mean, if he doesn't understand the difference between a chef and a cook, he'll never understand me—not that I was looking for long-term anyway.

"Since it opened," I tell him, not glancing his way. A vision of Shelby and me standing outside after we flipped the wooden sign in the window to open for the first time flashes in my mind. We hugged each other tight, and I knew right then the restaurant would do great things.

"Nice. It says a lot about a woman when she can keep a job consistently."

I stop walking. "I beg your pardon?" There's fire in my tone; I can't help it.

He tries to ignore my ire and keeps on walking. "You know what I mean," he says sheepishly, stuffing his hands in his pockets.

"I don't think I do." My hands fall to my hips.

He lets out a sigh and turns to face me. "Sorry, that came out wrong. My last girlfriend was constantly trying to find herself and changed careers like four times while we were together."

"Oh. Well, I don't think it's a bad thing to want to find yourself," I say defensively.

"Yeah, well, you weren't the one paying for it," he says bitterly.

"Ah." Now his comment makes more sense. I'm definitely thinking it's his social skills (or lack thereof) creating the weird vibe.

We begin to walk again, and conversation stays minimal as we're both a little uncomfortable now.

The weather is cooler and the humidity has receded, which is nice. We must walk for a solid mile up and down the blocks, and with each new scarecrow, the tension lightens. Most scarecrows are typical with a plaid shirt, jeans, and suspenders, but some went all out to match their stores like we did. There is an old man scarecrow smoking a cigar, sitting in a rocking chair, and playing chess out in front of the smoke shop. Child-sized scarecrows are decked out and playing in front of a children's clothing store, and there's even one on its knees praying in front of St. Mary's Catholic Church.

Eventually we decide we've seen enough and dip into an Italian restaurant not far from where we started at OBA. The head chef has been here for years and makes the most delicious gnocchi. She sneaks out from the back to say hello, and we talk a little business but mainly keep it to pleasantries.

"So," Scott begins after we've ordered. "Do they ever host any sporting events where you work? Like the World Series, the Kentucky Derby, things like that?"

Where I work. I snicker on the inside at how he hasn't put two and two together yet.

"Ah, no. OBA is more of a low-country chic bistro. Its Southern fare and quaint setting attract locals and tourists, and the menu is known for intertwining fresh farm-to-table ingredients from the local market with a strong mix of coastal and French influence. Think crab cakes, oyster stew, jambalaya, she-crab soup, shrimp and grits, fried green tomatoes—things of that nature."

He looks bored by my description then asks, "No chips and queso or chicken wings?"

"No, that's really not our brand."

"Those are my kind of places. I'm a pro sports bettor," he announces while leaning back in his chair. He smirks at me like I should be impressed by this.

Taking one from his playbook, I ask, "So, you're a gambler?" I know it's a low blow, but I couldn't help it.

He frowns. "We don't really call ourselves that."

"I see."

In the spirit of the once-a-month dates, I ask him questions about what he does. Although he and I aren't going to work out, I make the best of the dinner and let him talk about what he loves. It's not my thing as it all seems a little risky and uncertain, but he's passionate about it, and well, I am definitely learning something new today.

By the end of dinner, we acknowledge that we're just going to be friends, and while I drink wine and he drinks beer, he whips out a deck of cards and we play a few rounds of Texas hold 'em, seven-card stud, and poker. That's right, he carries a deck of cards and two rolls of pennies in his pocket.

Pulling out my phone, I sneak a picture of the cards splayed across the table then post the image to Instagram with the caption: **My date tonight is a pro sports bettor. What do y'all think—should I go all in or fold?**

By the time I finally walk through my front door, there's a comment from Jack, and I'm smiling before I even read it.

Jack: As long as he's betting on me, the odds are ever in his favor.

I reply: **Who are you, Effie Trinket?**

Jack: More like Peeta and you're my Katniss.

Me: In your fictional fantasy dreams.

Jack: *wink face emoji*

For Scott's dish, I'm reliving a trip Shelby and I took to Vegas a few years ago, where we stopped in at a place called Dirt Dog. Its menu consisted of street food, including crazy hot dogs and fries, and it was so super delicious. As such, the dish will be an elote hot dog with garlic fries.

Elote Hot Dog with Garlic Fries

Ingredients:
For the lime mayonnaise:
4 tablespoons mayonnaise
1 teaspoon lime juice
¼ teaspoon smoked paprika
⅛ teaspoon ground cumin
Pinch of chili powder

For the hot dogs:
4 hot dogs
¾ cup corn
4 hot dog buns
1 tablespoon butter, melted
Chili powder or smoked paprika
¼ cup crumbled cotija cheese
1 tablespoon cilantro leaves, chopped
Lime wedges, for serving

For the street corn:
4 ears corn, cut off the cob
2 teaspoons olive oil
1 clove garlic, minced
1/2 teaspoon chili powder
2 tablespoons mayonnaise
1/2 cup crumbled cotija cheese

squeeze of lime
2 tablespoons chopped cilantro
pinch of salt

Directions:
For the lime mayonnaise:
Stir together the mayonnaise, lime juice, smoked paprika and ground cumin. Add the chili powder to taste.

For the street corn:
Heat a medium skillet over medium-high heat. Add the olive oil and garlic and sauté for 30 seconds or until fragrant. Add the corn and chili powder and cook for another two minutes, stirring frequently.

Add the two tablespoons of mayo, a squeeze of lime, and a pinch of salt and stir to combine. Add the cilantro and cotija and stir again to combine. Remove from heat and set aside.

For the hot dogs:
Grill the hot dogs.

While the hot dogs are grilling, char the corn and prepare the buns. Char the corn in a small skillet over medium high-heat, stirring occasionally, until it's lightly browned. Remove from the heat.

Brush the tops of the buns with the melted butter then lightly sprinkle with either chili powder (spicy) or smoked paprika (not spicy) depending on whether your preference. Toast the buns.

Put a hot dog in each bun. Divide the lime mayo between the hot dogs. Use half the cotija cheese to sprinkle over the mayo, reserve the other half. Divide the corn between the hot dogs then top with the remaining cotija cheese. Garnish with the chopped cilantro, lime wedges and a dusting of chili powder and/or smoked paprika.

Garlic fries
Ingredients:
- 1 bag frozen french fries
- 6 cloves of garlic, very finely minced
- 1 teaspoon Kosher salt
- 2 tablespoons canola oil
- chopped parsley for garnish

Directions:

Cook the fries according to the directions on the bag.

When the fries come out of the oven, put them in a large bowl.

A minute or so before serving the fries, put the garlic in a small fry pan with the oil.

Heat on medium and cook for 15-30 seconds, not long enough to brown the garlic, just long enough to take mute the raw garlic flavor.

Toss the fries with the garlic oil mixture and salt.

Serve hot and garnish with parsley if desired.

Chapter 4

Catching Fireflies

Jack

THANK GOD FOR the cold front that hit Tampa yesterday. Well, when I say cold front, I mean the rainstorm that brought the humidity-free, eighty-degree weather. I love living in Florida, I do, but sometimes we just need a break. Fortunately for us, it happened the weekend of the team family picnic.

The picnic has always been one of my favorite events. At practice we are all focused and split up into offense, defense, and special teams. We all work out in the gym at different times so we don't see each other all that often, and at our weekly offensive dinners, it's only a small group of us. So, unless it's game day or we have an event like this one, we are never all together, and I love it when we are, especially when the family vibes are flowing hard.

The picnic is hosted in the stadium, and the north end zone has been completely transformed for the event.

There are white tents, covered tables and chairs, balloons, flowers, a disc jockey—you name it, it's there, along with the people: people laughing, people hugging, people just being themselves. Man, I love this team and these people.

We are a little over two months into the season—an undefeated season, that is—and I have a feeling that this year, we are definitely going all the way. I can sense it deep in my bones.

Walking around, I stop and say hello to my friends and their families. It's great to see so many kids here running around on the field and tossing the ball. I can't imagine what it would have been like to grow up in an environment like this one, especially if you love the sport.

"Hey, Jack!" I hear from behind me, and next thing I know a ball is flying toward my head. A little boy about the age of eight is grinning at me with a crooked smile, and I can't help but tuck the ball under my arm and hold out my other to pretend I'm blocking fake oncoming tackles. The boy jumps up and down delightedly as I toss the ball back, and then he runs off to play with someone else. I haven't given much thought to having kids, but I've always thought they'd be in my future somewhere down the line and we would play catch just like this. Girl or boy, we'll play together, because that's what dads are supposed to do.

Heading over to the food and drink tent, I grab a bottle of water and, off to the side, I spy the thing I've been wanting most just arriving.

"Well, butter my biscuit, if it isn't the third leg of the tripod," I say as Bryan and a woman I assume is Lexi due to her Firefly Kitchen T-shirt walk under the tents dragging a large flatbed dolly with thermal boxes on top.

She pauses and turns at the sound of her and her friend's nickname then smirks at me. "Let me guess—Jack?" she says, giving me a once-over.

"The one and only." I throw my arms out. "And you're Lexi." I wink at Bryan before wrapping her up in a giant bear hug and grinning. Lexi laughs and returns the hug while the scowl on Bryan's face says he would strangle the lights right out of me if he didn't love me so much.

Pulling away, I reluctantly release her, and she giggles.

"Meg was right about you," she throws over her shoulder as she moves toward the tables assigned for dessert, not realizing that just the sound of Meg's name being tossed my way has sent this weird and unexpected spear of excitement or something through my chest. "Come on, Jack," she continues, "make yourself useful. Help us unload these pies." My mind has gone foggy as she reaches for the first box and unhinges the door to open it. I'm trying to maintain my composure at the thought of Meg talking about me to her friend. *Me.*

"Meg mentioned me to you?" I ask curiously, looking at Lexi as if she suddenly has the answers to solve the mysteries of the universe.

"She might have a few times. You sure love to get her all riled up."

I certainly do.

An involuntary smile breaks free, and that's when I spot Bryan watching me closely. He tilts his head a little as if trying to read between the lines, and I decide it's best to change the subject. He already knows we banter on social media; if he thinks there's any interest in her beyond that, I'll never hear the end of it. So, I pretend to get distracted as the sweet smell of home-baked pies hits us.

"Pie," I mumble, breathing it in and successfully redirecting the conversation.

One of the event staff sees us and runs over. "Oh, hi! We were expecting you, and I can take it from here." She smiles warmly at Lexi.

"Are you sure? I don't mind," she says, wiping her hands on her pants and taking a step back toward Bryan.

"Absolutely. Y'all just enjoy your afternoon and eat lots of food. I hear the shrimp salad is to die for."

Shrimp salad . . . my stomach grumbles.

"Okay," Lexi says hesitantly, glancing between the girl and Bryan.

"Come on, they've got this, and I want to introduce you to a few people," he says, holding out his hand. Her eyes drop as she shyly slips her fingers into it, and they walk away from me and the food, toward Billy and his wife Missy.

It's then that I take a closer look at my friends, and I realize everyone has someone but me. Usually this doesn't bother me—I'm perfectly fine being on my own—but today, something about it suddenly makes me feel off, like I'm missing something.

Remaining by the desserts, I wait patiently for the staff member to hand me the first slice. I know everyone here welcomes me with open arms—after all, it is a group event—but have I become the third, fifth, seventh wheel?

"Here you go, Mr. Willett," the staff caterer says as she hands a plate my way. My mouth waters as I see it's strawberry rhubarb, and the discomfort I just felt dissipates.

I don't know why I love food so much; I just do.

Well, I take that back. I love food so much because as a kid, it was when my father was home and we were a family.

See, I was an unexpected addition late in my parents' lives. My father had just celebrated his twenty-fifth year in the army and was promoted to general, and my mother was his doting wife. They never planned on having kids, but then along came me and their lives were changed.

We didn't move around a lot, but we did move. I grew up under strict but loving conditions, and really the only time I saw my father was when he joined us for dinner. We had dinner every night. Even when I started playing football at ten, he would come home early and we would eat before I headed out for practice.

Much to his dismay, I didn't follow in his footsteps and head off to West Point. Instead I went to USC, the University of Southern California. I don't know why, but the military never appealed to me the way it did for him. I have nothing but an insane amount of respect for those it calls to, but it just wasn't me.

My father has since retired and they now live in Arizona. He spends his days playing golf, and I'm not sure what my mom does. I try to make it out to see them a couple times a year, but they're so regimented in their schedules, I know after a few days they're ready for me to go. There's no question that they love me; they've just always lived a very different life.

Which is why I'm ninety-nine percent sure I'm heading to Georgia for Thanksgiving.

Last month, Zach sent out an invitation for several of us to travel north and spend it with him and Shelby, and I would be lying if I said the only reason I'm interested in going is the food. Meg was on the invitation, too, and when I asked Zach on the sly who all was coming, he mentioned that she was.

Pulling out my phone, I contemplate sending her a direct message. Neither one of us has opened that line of communication yet, but I think, *What the hell—why not?*

Me: Your friends are nicer than you.

I laugh to myself because from the few interactions we've had, I know this will get her fired up.

Now that I've finished the pie, I head over to the rest of the food and make myself a plate.

"I've got my eyes on you, Jack," says our offensive coordinator from a few tables over. He complained about me eating all of Bryan's pies and his eyes have narrowed now as he takes in my plate, but I don't care. As a high-performing athlete, it takes a lot of calories to keep me fueled. Yes, eighty-five percent of my diet is clean, but he knows I still need to consume between four and five thousand calories a day.

Picking a table that overlooks my friends, I sit down and place my phone next to my plate. It lights up with a message, and I can't help but grin.

Meg: What's that supposed to mean? And why are you messaging me?

She's always so quick to respond or leave a comment . . . I love it.

Me: Just met Lexi (her pie is delicious), and because I can.

Meg: You stay away from her. You're not her type.

Yeah, I know I'm not her type. From the few minutes I've spent watching her this afternoon, it's easy to see the poor girl definitely has eyes for Bryan—not that the feeling isn't mutual, because it is. He was more nervous about seeing her today than I think he was last year when we entered the postseason.

Me: Type . . . hmm, am I your type?

Meg: Not in a million years.

This has me laughing as I take a bite of food. The girl was right—the shrimp salad is delicious.

Me: You're wounding my already fragile ego.

Meg: Lies. There's nothing fragile about you.

Me: I think you should come find out just how unfragile I am. *wink face emoji*

Meg: Gross. That's what your groupies are for.

Groupies . . . yeah, the novelty of those wore off years ago. Now I find even the idea of it is a hassle. They are all about posting pictures on social media and tons of tagging, and it takes forever for these things to go away. Honestly, I'm just not interested anymore.

Me: A gentleman never kisses and tells.

Meg: You're not a gentleman—you're a hopeless flirt.

Me: Only with you.

Meg: *palm on forehead emoji*

Which is true. For whatever reason, I can't seem to stop myself when it comes to her. I know we're just going to be friends—she made that more than clear at Zach's over the summer, which I think has me more excited than much of anything lately—but it's just so much fun provoking her.

Meg: Seriously, though, how's the picnic?

Me: How do you know we're at a picnic?

I shovel the last of the food from my plate in my mouth.

Meg: I talked to Lexi.

Me: You should have come as her assistant, then we could have hung out.

Stretching my legs out in front of me, I lean back to let the food settle and chug down half my water bottle in one go.

Meg: Because that wouldn't have been awkward.

Me: Why would it have been awkward?

Meg: Because I'm not family, and I barely know you.

Looking up, I glance at all the people standing around laughing and talking. The organization has well over five hundred employees; add in their dates, spouses, and some children, and there are a lot of people here.

Me: It would have been fine. Actually, it would have been better than fine, and you could have gotten to know me.

She doesn't have a comeback to that (not sure what she would even say), and there's a lull in our conversation. A few people stop to say hello as they pass by, but for the most part I'm content just sitting here people watching. Seeing my friends happy makes me happy.

I spot Bryan and Lexi, his arm wrapped around her shoulders and hers around his waist. They are laughing with Reid and Camille, and I can't resist snapping a photo and sending it to Meg. If Lexi told her she was coming, I'm sure she's wondering how things are going with Bryan. I think all of us were interested to see how the two of them would interact today, and they look good, at ease. Meg responds immediately.

Meg: You have no idea how much this picture just made my day.

Me: Good, I'm glad. I'll let you make mine at Thanksgiving.

Meg: Wait! You're going to be at Zach's, too?

Me: I am. I'm looking forward to tasting your food.

Meg: Jack . . .

Me: I mean it! I love food. Like really love food.

There's a pause, and then it shows me that she's typing.

Meg: All right, then for you I will make something special.

Me: Special—see, I knew you loved me.

Meg: *eye roll emoji*

A bit later I put up my post for the day, a picture of a few of us on the field. The stadium is blurred in the background, and Reid, Camille, and Lexi are laughing as I've scooped Lexi up and tossed her in the air. Bryan, not so much, but the look on his face had me throwing my head back and howling with laughter. Poor dude's got it bad. I've captioned it **Catching fireflies**, as her shirt is visible and shows her company name, Firefly Kitchen. I added a few hashtags about the event for Lexi, and it takes no time at all for Meg to comment.

Meg: Keep your paws off my girl.

To which I reply: **Volunteering?**

Meg: *green puke face emoji*

Three weeks and counting till Thanksgiving. It can't get here fast enough.

Strawberry Rhubarb Pie

Ingredients:
Crust:

2 cups all-purpose flour, plus additional flour as needed, up to 1/4 cup

1/2 cup cake flour (recommended: Soft As Silk)

3 teaspoons sifted powdered sugar

1/2 cup butter-flavored shortening (recommended: Crisco)

1/4 cup salted butter

Pinch salt

1 egg

2 teaspoons vinegar

1/4 cup ice cold water

Filling:

2 1/2 cups chopped red rhubarb, fresh

2 1/2 cups de-stemmed, washed and cut strawberries (in larger pieces)

1 1/2 cups sugar (1 1/4 cups for high altitude)

2 tablespoons minute tapioca

1 tablespoon all-purpose flour

1/2 teaspoon lemon zest

1/2 teaspoon lemon juice

1/2 teaspoon ground cinnamon

1 teaspoon vanilla extract

3 tablespoons butter, cubed small

1 egg white beaten with 1 teaspoon water
Large granule sugar

Directions:
Crust Preparation:
Using 2 pastry blenders, blend the flours, sugar, shortening, butter and salt. Whisk the egg, vinegar and water in a 2-cup measure and pour over the dry ingredients incorporating all the liquid without overworking the dough. Toss the additional flour over the ball of dough and chill if possible. Divide the dough into 2 disks. Roll out 1 piece of dough to make a bottom crust. Place into a pie dish. Put dish in refrigerator to chill.

Preheat oven to 425 degrees F.

Filling Preparation:
Mix well in a large bowl the rhubarb, strawberries, sugar, tapioca, flour, zest and juice of lemon, dash of cinnamon, and vanilla, and pour out into chilled crust.

Dot the top of the filling with the butter.

Brush edges of pie crust with egg white wash.

Roll out the other piece of dough and place over filling. Crimp to seal edges.

Brush with egg white wash and garnish with large granule sugar.

Collar with foil and bake at 425 degrees F for 15 minutes. Decrease temperature to 375 degrees F and bake for an additional 45 to 50 minutes, or until the filling starts bubbling.

Chapter 5

Elephant in the Room

Meg

I WOULD BE lying if I said I wasn't a little bit excited about seeing Jack this weekend. When he finally confirmed he would be spending Thanksgiving at Zach's, I may have sacrificed all holidays for the rest of the year to make sure Taylor and Lee, my sous chef, would cover for me on Black Friday. Yes, I know our morning rush gets a little crazy after the late-night shoppers, but when are we not crazy? Business has been good, real good, and I have complete confidence in my team.

Team . . . team makes me think of the Tarpons, and immediately my mind drifts back to Jack and the picture he posted last week. It's one of him midair, at least three feet off the ground, and he's catching the ball over his head. His long, lean body is stretched out, and his arms and hands seem to go on for days. It's a great action shot of him, and he captioned it: **Jack Attack.**

I know that's a nickname that has followed him for years, and I know that because I might have looked him up on the internet once or twice.

Name: John Robert "Jack" Willett

Birthdate: July 12

Astrological sign: Cancer

Profession: Wide receiver for the Tampa Tarpons

Height and weight: 6'2", 221 pounds

History: Second-round draft pick from USC by the Denver Stallions, two years later traded to the Tarpons

College degree: Communications (This doesn't surprise me—his personality is bright enough that he would make a great sportscaster one day.)

Family: Single, only child to General Mack Willett and Cindy Willett

Favorite candy: All, but primarily Swedish Fish

Least favorite food: Actually not a food, but a beverage—coffee (Tried his mother's once and that was it. Never again.)

Favorite thing to do in the offseason: Golf with his dad and snowboard

I mean really I could go on and on. The information about him feels endless. There are pictures of him going back twenty years to when he played on a little league team, pictures of him with friends over the years, and even a picture of him in a suit standing next to his father, who's in full military uniform, and it looks like they're at a funeral. It's like his whole life is showcased for the world to see, and I find it a little intimidating. I also hate to use the word starstruck, but in a way I am. I don't know why; it's just such a different life than I've known.

Winding through the mountain roads at the base of the Smoky Mountains, I roll down my window. There's a hint of fall in the coolness of the air and on the leaves of the trees and bushes. Although it's only a five-hour drive, I feel as if I'm somewhere completely different and far, far away from Charleston. The feeling is welcome, too, as I haven't really taken any time off in months.

Excitement flutters in my stomach as I turn down the driveway of the winery and get my first glimpse in months. It's so beautiful and rustic with its fairytale castle, and I'm continuously in awe that this is where Shelby lives now.

I park in the circle drive and breathe in deeply as I climb out of the car. Someone is already up and burning leaves, and the smoke smells so good. Carefully, in my new Prada heels, I walk on tiptoe across the gravel and to the front steps.

Helping myself, I walk through the front door of the winery then wander through the foyer and into the tasting room. It's empty—obviously, since it's a holiday and they are closed—and I call out, "Hello?"

"Back here," a male voice answers from the west wing.

The door that leads toward Zach's private part of the estate is open, so I head in that direction and spot Jack as he appears in the hallway just outside of what most would call a living room, even if the size is comparable to the square footage of my house.

As he approaches me with his signature grin, I can't help but take him in, his long legs closing the distance between us. He's wearing a thin ivory sweater with the sleeves pushed up that makes his dark features pop, a pair of worn-looking jeans that intimately hug his legs, and trendy brown boots that complete the look perfectly.

Cheese and crackers, I forgot how handsome he is in person. The photos online are incredible, but the real deal feels amplified by a thousand.

"Hello, Meg," he says, coming to a stop in front of me. I'm hit with sandalwood and citrus, and it smells so good. He slips his hands into the front pockets of his jeans, and his deep brown eyes sparkle as they peruse me from head to toe then land back on my face. I can feel heat climbing into my cheeks, and I remind myself that we are just friends— no matter how good-looking he is, no matter how attractive those dimples are, and definitely no matter how well he's executing the smoldering look. We are just friends, and thanks to the promises I made to myself years ago, we will only ever be friends.

"Jack." I smile back, the moment feeling a little surreal. This is the guy I've been bantering with online for months, almost like a pen pal, and now here he is, standing in front of me.

"Come here," he all but demands, closing the last bit of distance between us then wrapping me in his arms. His smell intensifies as it floats around me, and I pick up scents of warm dryer sheets, a sporty-spicy body wash, and comfort . . . pure comfort. My eyes drift shut as I lean into him, returning the hug, and ask, "What? Are we friends now?"

"Best friends," he deadpans.

"Ha, since when?" I ask, wishing I could stop time and just stay here longer than past the moment it becomes awkward.

He chuckles, and the vibrations under my cheek have me tightening my embrace just a little bit. "Since the moment you met me."

"Is that so?" I'm now grinning along with him.

"Yep, I decided," he states, pulling back.

"What about our current best friends?" I pop an eyebrow up.

"They won't mind. You and me—it's brilliant."

How do I answer that? And do I even want to?

He remains silent for a moment, his eyes drifting over my face like he's trying to memorize it, and then he asks, "How was the drive?"

"Easy, relaxing." I reluctantly pull away from him and take a step back to create some space. "I'm usually up early in the mornings because of the restaurant, so this was nothing."

"Well, that's good." His hand drags down my arm and lingers at my wrist before he finally breaks the contact between us.

"Will you help me bring some things in? My car is just out front." I point my thumb over my shoulder.

"If you mean help you bring in all the food, that's a definite yes." He smiles, and I exhale at the sight of it.

Together we turn and walk back toward the tasting room, through the foyer, and out the front door. The cool air clears some of the Jack-induced fog in my brain, and I glance over at him. Even with my heels on, he's so much taller than I am, and I realize I like it. I like it a lot.

"How was the flight?" I ask as we head toward my car. My feet wobble a little as my heels stick in the gravel, and he reaches for my elbow.

"Short. It didn't take me hardly any time at all once I landed in Atlanta."

His hand is warm, and I have the odd sensation of wanting him to reach for my hand and slip his fingers through mine. I don't remember the last time I held a guy's hand, but with him I think it would be nice.

"That's good. I'm surprised Bryan didn't come with you."

He looks over at me and his eyes brighten as he smiles. "Not this time. He's too busy driving to Lexi's today."

"What?" I stop and turn to stare at him. Lexi never mentioned him coming over for the holiday, so I don't think she knows.

"Yep. Poor guy's whipped and couldn't stay away." He says this as if it isn't a world-changing revelation.

"I don't think she knows," I say, more to myself than him, but he shrugs anyway.

"Well, she's about to."

A breeze blows by and ruffles the top of his hair. The sides are kept short, but it gradually transitions to being longer on the top. It's styled and looks perfect with his face.

"Huh."

Moving again, I walk to the trunk and pop it open, and Jack groans next to me.

"Damn, how did you drive all the way here with these delicious smells swirling around the car? I would have pulled over, found a fork somewhere, and dived in."

His eyes are scanning over the dishes and the box of uncooked food. After we closed yesterday afternoon, I decided to get a head start and went ahead and made a butternut bisque soup, mashed potatoes, and a few desserts.

"And that's the difference between you and me—I have self-control." I grin at him, and he groans again.

From the entryway, a squeal pierces the air as Shelby sprints down the front steps toward us and throws herself into my arms.

"Oh my God, I'm so happy you could make it. I was practically holding my breath in fear thinking something would happen and Taylor would back out."

"Back out? No way. Worst-case scenario, I closed the restaurant tomorrow. I wasn't missing this for the world. Life is short."

She pulls back and looks at me lovingly. "Yes, it is."

"Ladies, as heartwarming as this is, there is food in this car, and I need to be fed."

We both turn to look at Jack. There's a small crease between his brows, and his gaze bounces back and forth between the two of us as if we're preventing him from being somewhere important.

"Oh my God. Really?" One hand lands on my hip, and I glare at him.

He looks at Shelby and me, and then his signature smirk drops into place. "You said you would cook for me. That makes you my new best friend, as stated earlier, and you must take care of me."

"What? You're delusional. You decided we were best friends, not me. Keep it up and you'll be lucky if I even give you any leftovers." I try to say this seriously, but as he's now grinning at me, I can't help the smile that creeps onto my face, too.

Beside me, Shelby looks at the two of us, and I can see the questions forming in her eyes. I don't have any answers for her, other than the obvious—that we're just friends.

"Ugh. Would you just stop," I say to him, now fully grinning myself.

"I'm not doing anything." His happy expression forces those butterflies to return and dance around.

"You are, and you're the one who's just standing here. For someone who wants food so bad, you could be halfway to the kitchen with those bags by now."

He looks at the bags, realization dawning on him, and he says, "You're right."

"Say it again." I lift my chin a little higher and cock one eyebrow.

He smirks, shakes his head incredulously, and then grabs the bags and heads back across the drive, up the steps, and into the house, leaving Shelby and me just standing there. I wouldn't be female if I didn't appreciate the way those jeans fit across his backside, and boy do they fit nicely.

"What was that?" Shelby asks, turning to face me.

I can't look at her, so I say, "Nothing," reach into the car, grab my overnight bag, and slam the trunk shut.

Being back in the kitchen with Shelby, us working side by side while laughing, drinking iced coffee, and catching up—so far this is the best Thanksgiving I've had in a long time. It reminds me of how we used to be years ago, when we were just starting and all of our time revolved around being in the kitchen. Yes, mine still does, but life is different now, and we're rarely together.

Occasionally, throughout the morning, Zach pops his head in to smile at Shelby and give her a kiss. Michelle offers to help, but she ultimately slips out as she knows we need this time together, and Zach's parents, who have just gotten back from yet another European vacation, choose to sleep in, having requested they be told when it's time to eat. Retirement is suiting them well. As for Jack, he's steered clear, and I can't help but wonder what he's doing.

Looking across the kitchen, I smile as, dish by dish, the meal slowly comes together: roasted turkey with gravy; lemon-glazed honey carrots; roasted sweet potatoes, Brussels sprouts, and apples; a jellied cranberry sauce; balsamic-glazed green beans; oyster stuffing; and a few others. There will be leftovers for days, but to me that's the sign of a perfect holiday meal, and I'd always rather have too much than too little.

People often assume cooking is my passion, but it's not; it's sharing. When you share, that's when the magic is created. After all, food is love, and more memories than not are made around the table. There have been many days when I've stood and stared out the kitchen door window to the dining room of OBA. Couples old and young, families, friends, laughter, and occasionally tears—it all happens as the seconds of time and life tick by, and it all happens with my food in front of them. I love giving these moments, no matter how small they might be.

"Well, don't the two of you just look so cute in your matching aprons." Jack's deep voice echoes across the room, pulling me from my thoughts.

He's wandered into the kitchen, and I do a double take because I keep being struck by how handsome he is. He walks right up behind me and looks over my shoulder to see what I'm making. The closeness, his heat, his essence—it engulfs me, and I'm unable to maintain control over myself, my heart rate picking up.

If I just leaned back a little bit, I would be lying against him . . .

Wait!

No.

Seriously, why do I keep reacting to him like this?

Ugh.

Friends.

Just friends.

Again, I can feel Shelby's eyes on us. Jack doesn't seem to notice or to care, so dismissing the thoughts I just had, I take one from his playbook and decide I'm not going to either. Leaning over, he sticks his finger into the mashed potatoes, brings it to his mouth, and then licks it clean.

"Did he just do what I think he did?" Shelby asks.

"Sure looks like he did." Both of us have stopped what we are doing, she's turned to face him, and I turn to glare up at him.

"What? I wanted to taste it!" he declares innocently, licking his lips and grinning. Dark eyelashes swoop down over his eyes. From this angle, they look even longer than normal and result in him looking even prettier than before.

"Haven't you heard of a spoon? That was gross. Everyone here is going to eat these potatoes, and now you've contaminated them with your dirty digits," I scold.

"My hands aren't dirty. See?" He holds them up, and I'm momentarily awestruck by how large they are.

"Hands. Stay. Out. Of. The. Food," Shelby tells him.

He takes a step back and throws them up a little higher like he surrenders.

"Fine, no more finger-sticking." His eyes sparkle a moment later as he realizes what he's said, and he smirks at me while I shake my head.

Next thing, he picks up my iced coffee and takes a sip of it. His face scrunches up, and inwardly I relish already knowing he doesn't like coffee. He sets the glass back down and shakes his head. "That is not good."

Shelby laughs next to me. "Yes, it is. You're just being a menace, so you deserved that."

"I'm not being a menace, I just wanted to come in here and see what y'all are up to." His eyes zero in on the completed dishes and widen just a bit.

"You know what we're up to. Are you offering to help?" I ask him.

"Help?" He looks back at me and then around the kitchen at the mess we've made. He runs his hand over the back of his neck, frowning, and of course I notice how the sunlight pouring into the kitchen illuminates him. "I can help if you need me to, but I'm not sure what I would do."

I glance at Shelby, and we both bust out laughing. His obvious discomfort is cute, but there's no way we are actually letting him help us.

"Don't worry, we've got this," she says.

Instant relief floods his face as he looks at the two of us. "Okay, but I would have. Seriously, though, what's up with the matchy-matchy?" He waves back and forth between us, and I look down to see what he's talking about. Shelby and I are wearing matching Thanksgiving aprons I happened across in a boutique one day while walking through the Battery.

"Aprons are kind of our thing," I tell him, smoothing mine down.

It started with my grandmother. Sure, I had aprons growing up, but when I went off to culinary school, my grandmother gave me hers. It's green and white and has sort of become my good luck apron. I wear it when I'm working on a new dish, or just feeling nostalgic for her. She used to love to tell me an apron is just a cape tied on backward, and I've never forgotten it.

After that one, Shelby and I started collecting really cute ones from places we'd travel to, pretty ones we'd see in stores, and holiday ones. When we worked together, all of them hung on a single wrought iron coat rack we repurposed at the restaurant, and now Shelby has her own here in the winery kitchen. I point toward it and his gaze follows, spotting it in the corner, and then he looks back at me.

"Huh," he says, dropping his eyes and staring at the fall leaves and pumpkins across my chest.

Instantly, the back of my hand smacks his stomach—his flat, hard stomach.

"Ow! What was that for?" he howls, rubbing the offended area.

"You know what. Eyes up here." With two fingers, I point from my eyes to his.

"You're the meanest best friend I've ever had." He frowns. Then, whipping out his phone, he puts it in selfie mode and takes a picture of him and me before I can ask what he's doing. As a parting shot, he flashes us a devilish grin, sticks his finger back in the bowl, and swirls it around before walking out the door.

"Tell me he did not just do that," Shelby says in horror.

"I think he did." I try to hide the grin that follows him, but I just can't.

Ten minutes later, my phone buzzes in my back pocket with a new notification. Jack posted the photo of us in the kitchen, tagged me, and added the sweetest caption wishing everyone a happy Thanksgiving, thanking all of his followers, and expressing gratitude. Then I reach the end where he says he's also thankful for his best friend's pumpkins, and heat radiates up my neck and across my face.

I'm going to kill him.

At one o'clock, we sit down to eat. The table is decorated with bursts of fall in orange, yellow, and brown. The candles are lit, music is playing in the background, and the wine is poured. Food is steaming and spread out from one end to the other, and even I can't stop my mouth from watering. It is the perfect feast fit for my friends.

"Shelby, this turkey is delicious. You did a great job on it," I tell her as I take another bite. Murmurs go up around the table, everyone busy eating instead of talking.

"It's the turkey brine. Zach's mom gave me the recipe." She winks at Mrs. Wolff. "She assured me it would be juicy and everyone would love it. She wasn't wrong."

"The recipe was my mother's, and she handed it down to me. I'm happy you like it. We can keep it going year after year for Thanksgiving."

"Sounds good to me. Taste of my childhood right here," Zach says, his mouth full.

I look over at Jack's plate—he's sitting next to me—and it's overflowing. A chuckle escapes me, and he glances in my direction.

"What?" he asks, chewing and smiling at the same time.

"Nothing." I shake my head then flick my eyes down to his plate, back to his face.

"I like food," he declares, as if that should explain everything.

"We can tell," Zach says. Laughter breaks out around the table.

Keeping his eyes on me, he says, very matter-of-factly, "If you cook it, I will eat it."

My cheeks heat, and I know they've tinged pink. There's not a whole lot anyone can say that will make me happier than this. A quote I once read from Julia Child comes to mind: "People who love to eat are the best people." Maybe Jack is best friend material after all.

"You have to tell us about this month's date," Michelle says, putting her fork down and taking a sip of wine. "We saw you post about the meal, well, dessert of the month, pineapple fruitcake."

I can't help but groan. My friends have enjoyed hearing about my monthly dating escapades this last year.

"It didn't take y'all long to ask. I was wondering when it would be brought up." I dip the tip of my spoon into the gravy and decide it would be better with more pepper.

"This month's date?" Jack asks as I reach over him for it instead of asking him to pass it.

"She made a resolution to go out with a different person every month this year, and last week was November's." Kyle grins; he's Michelle's boyfriend, and he also works here at the winery.

"Why?" Jack turns to look at me closely as I season the gravy and put the pepper down.

"Because, people are interesting and life is short. You never know who you're going to meet, or what you'll learn. Who knows, maybe next month I'll meet my new best friend." I cut a bite of turkey and dip it in the gravy before bringing it to my mouth. I give him a big tight-lipped smile, and he frowns.

"That position is not available."

"You're right, it's not," Shelby chimes in from across the table, and the two of them glare at each other.

I finish chewing the bite and swallow. "I should have known the night was going to be a disaster the minute Taylor swung the kitchen door open and I saw him. He was wearing a black T-shirt with the NASA logo, only under it was the tagline *Never A Straight Answer*. Pineapple fruitcake was served on the Apollo 11."

The guys around the table chuckle.

"This story just got better already," Zach's dad says cheerfully.

"Yeah, have you ever heard of modern flat-Earthers?" Everyone shakes their head no. "Apparently, there's a whole society out there who believes the Earth is flat."

"You're kidding," Jack says, humor lighting up his face.

"Nope. Let's just say it made for some interesting conversations."

"Tell us more," Michelle requests as she adds another helping of stuffing to her plate.

"Well, outer space is not real, and we've never walked on the moon. It's all a conspiracy by the government, the photos taken are fake, and while most will agree that they think the Earth is disc-shaped, some believe it's diamond-shaped."

"Wow, I have no words," Shelby says, and I nod in agreement.

"I know. I should have canceled—my left foot had been hurting since we got back from the race and I had just worked all day in the kitchen—but hearing him talk about this was so far out there, I was humored to sit there for another two hours. Besides, as it was my resolution, I'm not quitting now when I'm so close to the end."

"Good for you," Michelle says supportively.

"My left foot is still killing me." I wince. "Next year, we need to find a pair of heels where we can slide in a built-in arch support."

"Wait, did you say heels? As in you ran that race you posted about in heels and not tennis shoes?" Jack asks with raised brows.

"Yep! This was our fifth year running it." Shelby and I lock eyes again across the table, and the love between us shines bright as our dinner guests remain silent, letting us have the moment.

"I think I'm missing something here," Jack interrupts. "Why in the world would you choose to run a race in high heels? I mean there are so many races out there—that one just seems like torture on top of the torture of running."

The table falls silent again as all eyes turn toward me. Cue the elephant in the room. It's not that I mind talking about it—after all, in many ways it defines who I am—but I know the big C word makes a lot of people uncomfortable.

Jack follows the lead of my friends and turns to look at me, too. He lays his fork down and his forehead wrinkles in confusion.

Looking up at him, I'm proud as I tell him, "We run this race because they support me, and it supports ovarian cancer."

"Oh, did someone in your family have it?" he asks.

I want to look away, but I don't, not yet. This is my story, and it's an amazing one. "Sort of—I had it. I was diagnosed with ovarian cancer when I was twenty-one. I'm in complete remission, and we do our part to give back, even if it's just a small part."

He shifts in his chair and looks at me, like really looks at me. I briefly smile and hold his gaze, but I end up looking back at my plate and resume eating. Everyone follows suit.

Up until now, I really liked the way Jack looked at me, and I don't want to see the shift. I can't see the shift. Shelby, bless her, breaks the silence and starts rambling on about the money the winery raised this year and her poor feet.

The thing is, people don't understand. It's like once they hear you've had cancer, you'll always have it, despite the fact that they also need to hear the cancer is gone. They need to hear that I'm cancer-free. Otherwise, they aren't sure how to talk to me, treat me, or really interact with me. It changes things. It's like I suddenly become fragile, and I don't want to be fragile. I just want to be normal and live my life as if it's normal, even if my version of normal is different than others'.

Turkey Brine

Ingredients:

1 12- to 20-pound turkey, *not kosher, saline-injected, or otherwise pre-salted*
3 oranges
3 lemons
1/2 cup fresh sage leaves
2 bay leaves
1 tablespoon whole peppercorns
5 large garlic cloves, peeled and smashed
4 quarts water
250g kosher salt (1 cup Morton, or 1 3/4 cup Diamond Crystal, or 3/4 cup table salt), plus more if needed

Directions:

Prepare the turkey for brining: Remove the turkey from its package and pat dry. Place the turkey in a large pot, brining bag, or other container large enough to keep the turkey submerged.

Prepare the brine ingredients: Strip the peels from the oranges and lemons using a vegetable peeler. Try to remove just the peel, leaving behind as much of the bitter white pith as possible. Roughly chop the sage leaves. Make sure the bay leaves, peppercorns, and garlic cloves are measured out and ready to go. (Save the leftover oranges and lemons for stuffing the turkey during roasting!)

Prepare the brine concentrate: Bring 1 quart (4 cups) of the water to a boil in a large saucepan or stock pot on the stovetop. Once boiling, add the salt and stir until dissolved. Add the orange and lemon peels, chopped sage, bay leaves, peppercorns, and garlic. Let the water return to a boil, then remove from heat.

Cool and then dilute the concentrate to make the turkey brine: Let the brine concentrate and flavoring ingredients cool until no longer steaming, then stir in the remaining 3 quarts of water. (If your pan is too small, you can do this in a pitcher or other large container.) Check the temperature of the brine; it should be room temperature or lukewarm.

Pour the brine over the turkey: Make sure the turkey is submerged, though it's ok if the boney tips of the legs stick out the top. If needed for larger turkeys, prepare additional brine solution (1/4 cup of salt dissolved in 4 cups of warm water) in order to cover the turkey. If the turkey is floating, weight it down with a plate or other heavy object.

Brine for 12 to 24 hours: Cover the turkey and keep refrigerated during brining.

Remove the turkey from the brine and rinse: When you're ready to begin roasting your turkey, remove it from the brine and rinse it with cool water. It's ok if the water is tinged pink. Pat dry.

Roast the turkey as usual: There's no need to salt the turkey before roasting, but otherwise, roast the turkey as usual following your favorite recipe. If desired, stuff the cavity of the turkey with leftover sage and the peeled lemons and oranges from preparing the brine. Roasting time may be shortened; begin checking the temperature of the turkey halfway through roasting.

Chapter 6

Whisk Me Away

Jack

CANCER.

As if I wasn't already in awe of this girl, she just moved herself to up-on-a-pedestal status. I knew she was strong, ambitious, and kind, but this kind of strength and life experience adds to what I already know about her, and I'm kind of speechless.

Of course I have a ton of questions I want to ask her, but considering I am the only one at the table who didn't know, questions will have to wait—assuming she'll even want to answer them.

After dinner, we move into the living room, we each find a comfortable place to crash, and we watch football—hours and hours of it. With a full stomach and the sliding glass doors open to let in the cool air, it's the perfect day, which bleeds into the perfect night.

We all stay up way too late drinking wine, eating dessert, and laughing. I can't remember the last time I laughed so much and felt so content in one place. I don't know if it's because it's a holiday and holidays pull out the sentimentality in us, or if it's that I'm with her. Either way, there is nowhere in the world I would rather be than right here, with these people.

Shelby decided since it's just for one night, both of us would be better off in the main house versus down in the cottage, so she's prepared Meg's and my rooms in the east wing. It's where I always stay when I come to visit, so I lead the way when we all decide to call it a night. It still cracks me up to say east wing, but this place is huge.

"I'm happy you enjoyed the dinner today," she says, looking over at me with her clear smoky gray eyes as she detours for the sitting area.

"Are you kidding? If I could have gotten away with it without being made fun of for the rest of my life, I would have licked the plate and then crawled out of the room. I was so stuffed."

She smiles, and something in my chest pinches. I like making her smile.

"Just whisk me away with your magic wand. Pun intended . . ."

Her smile grows even more as she releases her hair from the mess it's in on the top of her head. Dark curls tumble down around her shoulders, and then just as quickly as it's down, she's swooped it back up.

"What was your favorite thing?" She takes a seat on the couch, pulls a throw blanket over her lap, and pats the spot next to her. The sitting room isn't large. There's a couch, a coffee table, and two chairs on the other side. One wall is a bookshelf filled with all sorts of things, on the other is a fireplace, and the outer wall has windows overlooking the back of the property and French doors to the porch.

"The bread pudding with bourbon sauce," I answer easily, sitting down and picking up a remote from the table to turn on the fireplace. It flares to life, and warmth immediately spreads throughout the room. I should be heading to bed as I'm one of those who desperately needs sleep and I have an early flight, but who knows when I'll see her again. I like her company too much to miss out.

"Really? I thought you were a pie guy," she says, giving me a sly grin. Thoughts of the social media photos where she commented and made fun of me come to mind, and I smile back at her.

"I'm an everything guy, but that bread pudding was something else." And it was. I also know she made the pudding, not Shelby, and while I'm with her, I'm going to do my damnedest to make her happy. I see I've done so as her eyes light up.

"I'm glad you liked it. I almost didn't make it thinking you would just want pie, but we made it in the restaurant this week and it was well received."

"So you finally admit you were thinking about me," I tease her.

She rolls her eyes. "How could I not? Every day this week you were harassing me and demanding to know what I was making that day."

"It gave me something to look forward to, and boy did I. Can you blame me?" I stretch my arm out across the back of the couch. "And I didn't just like it—I loved it. It was melt-in-my-mouth delicious." Her smile grows a little larger. "Thank you for cooking today, by the way. I appreciate it, and I appreciate being included."

"I have an open door policy for my table. You are always welcome at it."

I don't respond, just soaking in the details of her face, and pink slowly tinges her cheeks. Without thinking I reach over to tuck a piece of loose hair behind her ear, and her head tilts my way an infinitesimal degree.

Damn, she's beautiful.

"Tell me about your restaurant. How did that happen?" I ask her.

The muscles in her face relax and she shifts to face me more, pulling her legs underneath her then letting out a deep breath. She doesn't look excited to talk about it, more resigned; my guess is that this story is somehow tied to her previously being sick and she knew this conversation was coming.

"Meg," I say quietly, and her eyes rise to meet mine. "We don't have to talk about anything you don't want to. Ever."

"I know, but I knew this was coming. And I don't mind, it's just . . ."

"Just what?"

Across from us, the fireplace lets off a crackling sound.

"It always changes things." Her eyes break contact with mine and look down at her hands. She's scrunching the blanket back and forth between her fingers, and after all these months of her firing off fun jabs and insults, it's strange to see this moment of vulnerability in her. Given what I know of her, her *take charge and live each day to the fullest* mentality, I didn't expect this.

I bump my shoulder into hers, bringing her gaze back my way. "I can't see how anything you tell me is going to change the way I feel about you." There couldn't be anything more true than that statement. I pretty much think this girl walks on water.

"I hope not." She gives me a pressed-lip smile.

Stretching my fingers, I loop them around a few strands of her hair that didn't make it into the messy bun and roll them between my fingers. Her hair is so soft, and if I was allowed, it's possible I would bury my face in it and breathe her in.

"As I mentioned at dinner, I was twenty-one when I was diagnosed with ovarian cancer. My parents had moved to Fort Myers, Florida, when I graduated from high school, and I'd moved to the college dorms. Fortunately for me, I was on track to graduate early, so after the surgery, when the chemo started, I found myself living with my aunt, my mother's older sister. I already had a great relationship with her, but this experience took us to a whole new level. She was amazing, and just the person I needed."

"Your parents didn't come home to help you?" Irritation at this settles into my muscles.

"They visited, but it was okay that they didn't stay. I had it in my mind that if they fussed, things were dire, but if we moved forward with business as usual, all would be okay. And my aunt . . . well, she's a rock star like that.

"During the treatment, there's a plan. Everything becomes regimented, scheduled. We knew what we had to do, and it was like checking boxes and moving forward: surgery, chemotherapy, radiation, reassessment, then oral chemotherapy. And then suddenly it was done. All over. At least that's what they told me, but I didn't feel that way. I felt lost. Like, I'd survived this thing, and suddenly I was expected to throw myself back into normal society and live amongst people who didn't know, didn't understand.

"Anyway, my aunt helped me push forward with a new plan. She knew Shelby and I had talked about culinary school. On the sly, the two of them applied for me, and then the next thing I knew, Shelby and I were packing up and heading out. It was smart of them to keep me going. Believe it or not, there are a lot of dark places one can go to after something like surviving cancer. And when we were done with culinary school, my aunt handed me a check and said, 'Go make me proud.'"

"Wow. I hope to one day meet this aunt of yours. She sounds amazing."

"She is. You would have liked my grandmother, too."

"Would have?" I ask her.

"Yeah."

Meg looks across the room, not really at anything in particular, just lost in thought. Given this moment, I take in the details of her profile, even though it's cast in shadows: full eyebrows, long curved eyelashes, smooth-looking skin, and earlobes that are attached versus dangly and pierced with diamond studs. The spot under her ear, on her neck, is open and inviting, but not for me. Internally I sigh, hoping to suppress some of the attraction I feel for her.

"Where's your aunt today?"

She looks back at me. "She's two hours south of Charleston, over on Hilton Head. She loves to golf."

"Golf?" My brows shoot up, and she grins. "A woman after my own heart."

"You golf?" she asks, but somehow I feel like she already knows.

"With my dad, yeah. It's become our thing. Besides, it's a game, and I love to play games."

"Yeah, my aunt loves it. I'm not very good it at, although I've tried. Every chance she gets, she's on the greens, which is why I don't ever see her leaving the south. She loves it there."

"Cousins?" I ask.

"Yep. My cousins both decided they preferred the mountain life and moved to Denver, so it's just me and her mostly."

I find myself wanting to say, *And me.*

"What about you? How did you get into playing football?" she asks as she reaches for one of the throw pillows on the end of the couch and pulls it into her lap.

"Do you want the media told story, or the real story?"

"Is that even a question?" Her eyes sparkle, and considering what she just shared with me, I know it's truth time.

I chuckle, and she hugs the pillow.

"My dad worked a lot. He was never big on showing emotions, but one thing he loved was football. I know he loves me, but in my ten-year-old mind, if I played football, he would love me more. What boy doesn't want to be adored by his dad? So, that's how it all started, and well, I was good at it. I've never looked back."

She hums as she thinks, twisting her lips. "If you weren't playing football, what would you be doing?" She lays her head to the side and on my arm, which is stretched out across the back of the couch.

"Oh, isn't that a loaded question? If you weren't cooking, what would you be doing?" My fingers tangle more in her hair.

She grins. "I asked you first."

"Honestly, I don't know. I know I should have thought about it, or I should be thinking about it—after all, this can't last forever—but I've been smart with my money, so when the time comes, I'll have space to figure it out."

I've been real smart with my money, and fortunately for me, so far I've been able to play for ten years. I have a good chunk of change set aside, saved, and invested. Wherever I land next, I'm going to be just fine.

"I think I'm fortunate that there's never going to be a situation where I won't be able to cook. Even if I didn't have the restaurant, I could have my own catering business, or work as a chef for someone who believes in my vision. You know?"

"Have you ever wanted to live anywhere other than Charleston?"

"No. It's my home. I'm a Southern girl through and through. I can't imagine ever being anywhere else."

I've never been to Charleston, have never had a reason to go—at least not until now. The only college near there is The Citadel, and the closest professional football team is the Carolina Wildcats up in Charlotte.

"I've never really been attached to one single place. Don't get me wrong, I love living in Tampa, and right now it is exactly where I'm supposed to be, but Tampa will most likely not be my forever city. I can't tell you where it will be, but I'll cross that bridge when I get to it."

"Hmm," she responds just before letting out a huge yawn. I'm reminded that it's super late and both of us have to get up early to head home.

Scooting closer to her, I wrap my arm around her shoulders to draw her in. We both stretch out our legs and fall into a comfortable silence. She lays her head against me, and I rest mine on top of hers. I already knew being friends with her was going to be awesome, but I didn't expect to feel this level of comfort with her.

Pulling out my phone, I set my alarm just in case and snap a picture of our feet with the fire blurred in the background. Somewhere along the way, we've lost our shoes; my socks are navy with turkeys on them—yes, they were a big hit today—and hers are cream-colored, thick, and fluffy-looking.

She lifts her head and opens her eyes at the sound of the click. "What are you doing?"

"Taking a picture for tomorrow. Look." I turn the screen toward her. "It's a nice photo."

She stares at the image for a few moments and is silent. Then she lays her head back down, closes her eyes, and says, "It is a nice picture."

Bread Pudding with Bourbon Sauce

Ingredients:
Bread Pudding:

   1 loaf French bread, cut into 1 inch cubes (16 oz.)
   4 cups milk
   3 large eggs, beaten
   2 cups sugar
   1 cup raisins
   3 tablespoons butter
   2 tablespoons pure vanilla extract

Bourbon Sauce:

   $\frac{1}{2}$ cup butter, softened
   1 cup sugar
   1 large egg, well beaten
   2 tablespoons Bourbon

Directions:
Bread Pudding:

   Preheat over to 325 degrees.
   Combine bread and milk in a large mixing bowl; set aside for 5 minutes.
   Add eggs, sugar, raisins, butter and vanilla; stir well.
   Spoon mixture into a greased 3 quart casserole.
   Bake, uncovered, for 1 hour or until firm.
   Cool in pan at least 20 minutes before serving.

Spoon into individual serving bowls; serve with Bourbon Sauce.

Bourbon Sauce:

Combine butter and sugar in a small saucepan; cook over medium, stirring frequently, until sugar dissolves.

Add egg, stirring briskly with a wire whisk until well blended.

Cook over medium heat 1 minute.

Remove from heat, cool slightly; stir in bourbon.

Chapter 7

Ho Ho Ho!

Meg

IT'S IN THE fifties today, and the weather is overcast with low-hung dark clouds and a steady breeze. I imagine for most it's not the most ideal weather for Christmas Day, but I love it. Somehow it makes the lights twinkle brighter, the poinsettias appear bolder in color, and delicious flavors like peppermint and fir linger in the air. It may be damp outside, but that makes it even cozier and more nostalgic inside. I can't imagine it being more perfect.

Well, almost perfect. It would be nice to have someone here with me, but I'm good by myself. As an only child, I always have been. It's relaxing, and I'm free to do exactly what I want. I'm still wearing my pajamas, I don't have a stitch of makeup on, and in the background the Hallmark Channel is on. Candles are lit around the house, and I'm doing my favorite thing: cooking.

My mother hated cooking on holidays, which is why we always found ourselves at my grandmother's. Well, I'm pretty sure most would say she hated cooking every day, but to her, holidays were a day off, a day to relax, and she didn't think slaving in the kitchen for hours over food that would take ten minutes to eat followed by cleanup was any way to spend a day off. While I do see her point, I also think it's the food that helps make holidays so memorable.

Just think about it . . .

For Thanksgiving, it's turkey, stuffing, and all the pumpkin things. For Christmas, it's prime rib, homemade eggnog, and all things peppermint. For Easter, it's ham, sweet potato casserole, deviled eggs, and hummingbird cake. On Valentine's, there's chocolate fondue with strawberries and other sweets, and for the Fourth of July, there's barbeque . . . My point is, with holidays come food, and even though I'm by myself, I can't imagine not making any.

Next to me on the counter, Jack's name flashes across my phone screen, and a smile splits my face. Since Thanksgiving, we've moved from just commenting on social media posts to texting daily. Conversations are always light and funny, and usually there's a photo from something random that happened that day. Mostly his are related to football, food, and his dog Zeus—who, by the way, is the cutest thing ever—and mine are about the restaurant, holiday things around town, and food. The food ones drive him crazy, and I'd be lying if I said I didn't send them on purpose to taunt him a bit.

Swiping, I answer the call, put it on speaker, and say hello.

"Ho ho ho, Merry Christmas, Meg!" His voice booms through the phone, all loud and happy, and something inside my chest squeezes.

After pausing just to make him hesitate with confusion, I say, "Are you calling me a ho?"

"What? No!" He starts stammering, and I start laughing.

"I'm just kidding. Merry Christmas, Jack." My smile is so big I'm certain he can feel it through my words.

"Funny, very funny," he teases, and I can feel him grinning through his words, too. "What are you doing?" he asks. There's no noise in the background, and his voice comes through loud and clear. Glancing at the clock, I see it's still midmorning for him in Arizona.

"Perfecting my own beef Wellington recipe." I look down at the plastic wrap where I've evenly spread the duxelles mixture on top of the prosciutto. The trick to making the perfect duxelles is to use fresh thyme and shallots instead of a regular onion. I sprinkle some salt, pepper, and a few more pieces of the chopped thyme.

He groans as I pick up the sheet pan and move it to the refrigerator. I can't help the spark I feel at his blatant desire to eat my food.

"Who are you making that for?" he asks, subtle but also not at the same time.

"Myself." I wonder if it bothers him, the thought of me cooking for someone else, but then again it shouldn't—we're just friends. "You'd think I would take the day off from cooking, but I can't seem to help myself."

"I could be there in a few hours to help you eat that." There's a hint of hopefulness in his voice.

"I thought you were visiting your parents."

"I am, but . . . beef Wellington," he says on a moan, as if that explains it all.

Happiness trickles through me, because deep down I

think he's serious. If I asked him to come here, he probably would. His picture from yesterday was of him boarding a Wheels Up private jet, which tells me he's a member. That seems to be the new thing for athletes and such lately, getting them where they need to go quickly and without the hassle of commercial airlines.

"If you ever make it to Charleston, remind me and I'll make it for you." I pick up the room-temperature beef and move it to my work station.

"Really?"

"Sure, whatever you want." Rolling it into a cylinder, I tie it in four places to help it hold its shape while I brown the outside, and then I drizzle olive oil over it.

"Where's your aunt? She didn't feel like driving up?"

I sprinkle the meat with salt and pepper then gently place it in the pan to begin searing all the sides.

"Actually, she decided to brave the cold and went to Denver to see my cousins Jayce and Ethan. Jayce has a new baby, and she's been itching to head back out there to see her. She's staying with each of them for a week before she heads back."

"Well, that's great for her, but I don't like you being alone on Christmas." His voice has dropped in tenor.

I look around my house and smile at the ambiance I've created. How can I be sad about being alone today when I've been blessed with all this? It's my place, my space, and that makes it my perfect holiday.

"I don't mind. Besides, it's better than the alternative where I'm not here at all." I meant this to come out light and chipper, but silence stretches between us as he doesn't say anything. "How's Phoenix?" I ask, suddenly feeling the need to change the subject.

"Pleasant. My dad and I played a round of golf this morning, stopped for brunch in the clubhouse, and now we're back at their house. He's taking a quick nap and I'm on the back porch staring out at the Phoenix Mountains. There's a trail over on Camelback I'm thinking about hitting up later today."

"That sounds nice. Is it a hard trail?" A picture of Jack hiking up a mountain fills my mind. Blue skies, clay colors, trails, a long-sleeved T-shirt, shorts, a small backpack that holds snacks and water, and a nice southwesterly breeze that sweeps through his hair. I know I shouldn't imagine him this way, but he is gorgeous, and I can't help but appreciate the vision.

"Yes and no. I've done it before, so I'm used to it. It's only about three miles, but the view is gorgeous."

My vision changes, and now he's standing at the top with one foot propped on a rock, his hands on his hips, staring out at the view in front of him. I laugh inwardly and say, "You'll have to send me a picture later."

"You know I will, and I expect one of the beef Wellington in return."

"Of course." I flip it over, and the sizzle sounds so good. "What is your mom making today?"

He chuckles. "If you mean what she picked up premade from Fresh Market, I think there's some mashed potatoes and a green bean casserole in there."

"No!" I start laughing.

He laughs with me. "Yep."

"I'm so sorry. Now I'm kind of wishing you could ditch them and come here to have a real meal."

"Why do you think I was so excited at Thanksgiving?" he

asks.

"That's just sad, Jack."

"Tell me about it."

Picking up my spoon to baste butter over the meat, I accidentally drop it on the floor, and as I bend over to pick it up, a flash of light pink and yellow hits my peripheral vision. Folded over the back of one of my kitchen chairs is an apron from Jack that showed up to the restaurant for Christmas. It was obvious he had wrapped it for me; to say I was shocked is an understatement, but there really isn't a more perfect gift for me.

"Thank you again for the apron. I love it," I tell him as I rinse the spoon off in the sink and move back to the stove. Tilting the pan, I scoop up the butter, pour it over the meat, and repeat.

"You already thanked me, and it's nothing. I saw it, thought of you, and well, you did say over Thanksgiving how much you love aprons."

The thoughtfulness from this guy over the last couple of months hasn't gone unnoticed by me. In little ways, he always goes out of his way to make sure he's at least said hello once a day, he comments on my photos, and recently, he's started texting me good night.

"I guess I did. Where did you find it?" Feeling satisfied with the browning of the beef, I remove it from the pan, cut the ties, and set it aside to cool a bit.

"I can't tell you all of my secrets," he says. "What would be the fun in that?"

"You kill me." Moving to the refrigerator, I grab the sheet pan with the prosciutto and a bottle of Dijon mustard.

"But in the best way, right?" Do I detect a little vulnerability in his voice? No, can't be. Jack is the type of person who knows just who he is and is perfectly okay with it.

"Always. When do you fly home?" Using a rubber spatula, I smear the Dijon all over the meat.

"Tomorrow morning. We have light practice tomorrow night and then a full practice again the next morning. At least our game is at home this weekend."

"You're playing the Broncos?"

"Yep. We already beat them once, so we're feeling pretty good about it."

"They have a cute quarterback."

"Meg . . ." Jack basically growls in warning, and I laugh.

"What?" I feign innocence. "There's no way you don't agree with me. I mean, look at him."

"Looks can be deceiving. The guy is an asshole," he states very matter-of-factly.

"That he might be, but his arms . . ." I drawl out. What is it about a guy's arms that's such a turn-on? From their shoulders to their hands, long, defined, and muscular, and so inviting.

"I have nice arms, too," he says.

"Fishing for compliments?" I grin, knowing he doesn't need compliments from me. He's very proud of the way he looks.

"No, just stating the obvious. Tell me about your December date, and how does corned beef hash factor in?"

Placing the beef on top of the duxelles, I use the plastic wrap to help me tightly cover it with the prosciutto. "It was actually really nice." I tuck the ends in and twist the plastic wrap to hold it in place in the shape of a log.

"Nice—girls only use that word when they're trying to be polite."

"No, really. It was nice, nicer than a lot I have been on this past year." My mind drifts over the last couple of guys I've met: all interesting, and there's someone out there for them, but it's definitely not me.

"Are you going to continue these dates next year?"

"I think so, but I'm not going to worry so much if I miss a month."

Despite some of the guys being complete weirdos, it has been fun to put myself out there and meet new people. You would think I meet them daily in the restaurant, but I barely come out of the kitchen.

"Back to food. Tell me the story."

Lifting the pan, I take the meat and put it back in the refrigerator so it can settle and hold its shape. I'll leave it there for at least thirty minutes.

"I'm certain you're thinking it's because he's Irish, but that's not the case. He's a middle school history teacher. Currently, they're talking about the Lewis and Clark expedition, and apparently they ate a lot of protein, from bison to elk to pork, and even dog."

"Well, that's disgusting."

"I suppose it is what it is if you're hungry, but they also had potatoes. I'm not sure if they made a hash or not, but seemed like something I would have cooked—salted meat to make it last and chopped-up potatoes."

"Did he kiss you good night?" he teases, certainly not expecting the answer I'm about to give him.

"He did actually." I never bring guys back to my home— they don't need to know where I live—so he walked me back to the restaurant, thanked me for a nice night out, and leaned in to lightly brush his lips across mine.

There's a three-second pause.

"And?"

"It was nice." And it was. There was nothing aggressive or unwanted about it. It was sweet and appropriate for a pleasant night out.

"There's that word again." He chuckles.

"Well, it's true. It was nice. I haven't been kissed in a while." A guy earlier in the year kissed me, but none since then.

"I'm always available if you get the itch." His devilish tone has me shaking my head.

"Stop it."

"Just sayin'. Will you go out with him again?"

"I don't think so."

"Well, that's just sad. I almost feel bad for the poor guy." There's a creak in the background, like he's shifting in his seat.

"Why? I've told you before—I'm not looking to find a boyfriend." I move the pan and other utensils to the sink to wash.

"Then I don't understand . . . why do you keep going out with these guys?"

"I like meeting new people."

"And you can't do that without the pretense of dating them?"

I see what he's saying, and he does have a point.

"It seemed like a good idea at the time."

"Well, let it be known I think it's a terrible idea."

"Noted."

Two minutes after the phone call ends, a picture appears on my screen. Jack has removed his shirt and is flexing his bicep to show off his arm—just his arm. I can't help but laugh, and he's right . . . can I just say eye candy times ten? It's a good thing he doesn't live closer, because I could easily see myself getting lost in those arms.

Three hours later, a notification pops up that Jack has posted a new photo. It's a selfie of him at the top of the mountain, only it's not quite how I imagined it. He's wearing a green T-shirt that says *Mr. Christmas*, and the goof has a Santa hat on. The caption says: **If I can't have beef Wellington, at least I can have this view. #blessed #wishyouwerehere**

Beef Wellington

Ingredients:
For the Duxelles:

    3 pints (1 1/2 pounds) white button mushrooms
    2 shallots, peeled and roughly chopped
    4 cloves garlic, peeled and roughly chopped
    2 sprigs fresh thyme, leaves only
    2 tablespoons unsalted butter
    2 tablespoons extra-virgin olive oil
    Kosher salt and freshly ground black pepper

For the Beef:

    One 3-pound center cut beef tenderloin (filet mignon), trimmed
    Extra-virgin olive oil
    Kosher salt and freshly ground black pepper
    12 thin slices prosciutto
    6 sprigs of fresh thyme, leaves only
    2 tablespoons Dijon mustard
    Flour, for rolling out puff pastry
    1 pound puff pastry, thawed if using frozen
    2 large eggs, lightly beaten
    1/2 teaspoon coarse sea salt
    Minced chives, for garnish

Green Peppercorn Sauce:

2 tablespoons olive oil
2 shallots, sliced
2 cloves garlic, peeled and smashed
3 sprigs fresh thyme, leaves only
1 cup brandy
1 box beef stock
2 cups cream
2 tablespoons grainy mustard
1/2 cup green peppercorns in brine, drained, brine reserved

Directions:

To make the Duxelles: Add mushrooms, shallots, garlic, and thyme to a food processor and pulse until finely chopped. Add butter and olive oil to a large sauté pan and set over medium heat. Add the shallot and mushroom mixture and sauté for 8 to 10 minutes until most of the liquid has evaporated. Season with salt and pepper and set aside to cool.

To prepare the beef: Tie the tenderloin in 4 places so it holds its cylindrical shape while cooking. Drizzle with olive oil, then season with salt and pepper and sear all over, including the ends, in a hot, heavy-based skillet lightly coated with olive oil - about 2 to 3 minutes. Meanwhile set out your prosciutto on a sheet of plastic wrap (plastic needs to be about a foot and a half in length so you can wrap and tie the roast up in it) on top of your cutting board. Shingle the prosciutto so it forms a rectangle that is big enough to encompass the entire filet of beef. Using a rubber spatula cover evenly with a thin layer of duxelles. Season the surface of the duxelles with salt and pepper and sprinkle with fresh thyme leaves. When the beef is seared, remove from heat, cut off twine and smear lightly all over with Dijon mustard. Allow to cool slightly, then roll up in the duxelles covered prosciutto using the plastic wrap to tie it up nice and tight. Tuck in the ends of the prosciutto as you roll to completely encompass the beef. Roll it up tightly in plastic wrap and twist the ends to seal it completely and hold it in a nice log shape. Set in the refrigerator for 30 minutes to ensure it maintains its shape.

Preheat oven to 425 degrees F.

On a lightly floured surface, roll the puff pastry out to about a 1/4-inch thickness. Depending on the size of your sheets you may have to overlap 2 sheets and press them together. Remove beef from refrigerator and cut off plastic. Set the beef in the center of the pastry and fold over the longer sides, brushing with egg wash to seal. Trim ends if necessary then brush with egg wash and fold over to completely seal the beef - saving ends to use as a decoration on top if desired. Top with coarse sea salt. Place the beef seam side down on a baking sheet.

Brush the top of the pastry with egg wash then make a couple of slits in the top of the pastry using the tip of a paring knife this creates vents that will allow the steam to escape when cooking. Bake for 40 to 45 minutes until pastry is golden brown and beef registers 125 degrees F on an instant-read thermometer. Remove from oven and rest before cutting into thick slices. Garnish with minced chives, and serve with Green Peppercorn Sauce.

Green Peppercorn Sauce:

Add olive oil to pan after removing beef. Add shallots, garlic, and thyme; sauté for 1 to 2 minutes, then, off heat, add brandy and flambé using a long kitchen match. After flame dies down, return to the heat, add stock and reduce by about half. Strain out solids, then add 2 cups cream and mustard. Reduce by half again, then shut off heat and add green peppercorns.

Chapter 8

This One's For You

Jack

IT'S CLOSE TO midnight as I find myself walking down to the small boat dock behind Reid's house under a sky full of twinkling stars. The smell of saltwater and fresh grass permeates the air, but it's cool, not cold, and there isn't even a trace of humidity lingering.

Looking out across the water to the houses lining Bayshore Boulevard, each one lit up in all its splendor, I chuckle as I wonder how much these people pay monthly for electricity. It's not that I would mind owning a large home one day; I'm just not sure I see the purpose of it being *that* big.

As I take a sip of my beer, my shirt sleeve pushes up under my jacket, and I use my fingers to pull it back down, straightening the platinum football cufflinks my mother gave me one year for my birthday.

It's New Year's Eve, I'm dressed in a black tuxedo (per Camille's request), and I'm so happy with life right now, everything feels damn near perfect. My friends and family are happy, my team is undefeated, and well, between Meg and Zeus, I'm just smiling all day.

Turning around, I lean against the dock railing and look back up at Reid's house. I'm proud of him, too; he's really done well for himself. Don't get me wrong, I miss him being across the hall from me like crazy and I think poor Zeus went through a slight phase of depression, but he's got this amazing life he's started with Camille, and only every now and then do I find myself a little bit envious.

Speaking of Camille, distinct laughter floats my way and I find her, Lexi, Missy, and a few other women deep in conversation. They've just raised their fruity champagne punch glasses and I watch as they clink them together, toss their heads back, and swallow. I tried the punch when I arrived—way too sweet for me, perfect and girly for them.

Seeing Lexi, I can't help but think that Meg would have liked it here, and again my mind drifts to her and I wonder what she's doing. She posted a photo earlier of herself laughing, and she was so gorgeous I felt my chest tighten. She had on a short fitted dress that was silver and sparkly along with a pair of killer red heels. Her lips were also red and she kept her hair down, letting it spill over her shoulders and down her back. On top of her head, she had one of those cheap *Happy New Year!* tiaras. Obviously she was headed out somewhere, and I found I was uncomfortable wondering who she might be with.

I left a comment, like I always do, but this time I didn't say anything, just put three flame emojis. After all, she looked smokin' hot, friends or not.

"What are you doing down here?" Reid asks as he comes to stand next to me.

"Just taking it all in, brother. Taking it all in." I clap him on the shoulder and squeeze hard. Behind him, Billy and Jonah follow and step up to join the conversation. We look sharp tonight, and I decide Camille wasn't wrong to make us dress up. It's nice and a change of scenery from our regular workout attire.

"I think he's hiding." Billy smirks, eyeing me with a knowing expression.

"From who?" Jonah asks, flipping his head back and to the side a little to move the hair off his forehead.

Turning, all four of us stare up at the back of the house, and I reply, "See that girl standing next to Missy? Shoulder-length straight blonde hair and big pink lips."

"Yeah," he responds, his brows rising slightly as he drinks her in.

"Missy invited her and apparently pushed her my way thinking I would like some company tonight when I'm just fine on my own."

"Hold up, bro," Billy says, raising a hand. Of course he's going to come to his wife's defense. "In all fairness, she really likes that girl. They're friends, and she knew you were going to be alone tonight. As you're always up for a good time, she thought y'all might have one together. Her intentions were good."

"I'm not arguing with you there, man, but maybe she should have run it by me first. All I wanted was a low-key night with my friends. I'm not interested, and the girl isn't getting the hint." I can't help the frown that overtakes my face as we watch her break away from the group and look around like she's looking for someone specific. I want to slink back into the shadows so she doesn't find me.

"I'm interested," Jonah says eagerly, facing us again and looking excited by the prospect.

"Really?"

Jonah, who is younger, newer to the team, and one of our starting tight ends, never partakes in willing girls, so I'm kind of surprised but insanely relieved. He nods, and I graciously wave my hand in her direction. "Then go for it. Have a ball."

"I think I will." He grins as he raises his bottle toward us, tips it in a solo cheers, and then walks back up toward the party. The three of us stand there silently and watch as he approaches the girl. Both of them start smiling at each other, and I feel like I'm off the hook. I think my shoulders loosen for the first time since I arrived and she was dropped in front of me.

Billy chuckles then turns back to our little group.

"You guys talk to Bryan tonight?" My eyes skip over from Jonah and land on Bryan. He's standing with Lexi, but he isn't saying anything. His back is straight, he's got one hand in his pocket, and the other is white-knuckling his drink. He's been like that for the last two hours. Of course he's being cordial, but it's like he's just going through the motions of being here and his mind is definitely somewhere else.

"I did briefly, but he's got the look," Reid says, taking a sip of his beer.

"He does. Dude needs to relax, but something is definitely going on in his head," Billy says.

Yeah, and I know what it is. He's unhappy with his performance from yesterday's game—well, the last couple of games—but man, does he need to let it go.

"I think you should talk to him," Billy suggests. Of course he does. Everyone else is afraid of him, at least when he gets like this, and I somehow always get volunteered.

"Or maybe he just needs his girl to work it out of him," I state, thinking that's the best solution for him. Since Lexi has come into the picture, he's been less serious, happier, but then again, with that slight change in his personality, the sharks have come out to feed. The media has had a field day talking about his performance, his relationship—hell, all aspects of his life. For someone like him, this is just about the worst thing to happen.

"Speaking of girls, it's time for me to go find mine," Billy says.

"Me too," comes from Reid, and together they head back up to the party.

Alone on the dock again, I move to take a seat on a decorative patio chair that's been set on the lower level. Leaning back, I prop my feet up on the accompanying one and pull my phone out of my jacket pocket. Suddenly feeling overwhelmed by the need to know what Meg's up to, I scroll to her contact and fire off a text: **Out on the town tonight?**

I don't expect her to reply; in fact, as much as I have the urge to know the answer, a huge part of me hopes she doesn't. I want her to be out and having fun, living her life, but she does reply, almost instantly.

Meg: Not really. Taylor had people over to her place. I told her I would come, but I have to open in the morning so now I'm on my way home.

Relief floods me in a way I know it shouldn't. I also know I shouldn't have been jealous over some random guy she kissed this month, but I was. It's my own fault for asking her, and there's definitely something to be said for the idea that ignorance is bliss.

Me: Well, you look beautiful.

Meg: Thank you. Lexi mentioned a party at Reid's house—are you there?

Hearing her speak about my friend as if he is hers warms a place in the center of my chest, and I can't help but rub it.

Me: Yep. Wish you were here, though.

And I do. I had the best time with her over Thanksgiving, and it would be fun to show her off to my teammates.

Meg: Sounds fun. I probably could have talked one of your teammates into being my date.

Wait, what? Uh, no—not a chance in hell.

Me: What am I, chopped liver?

I try to keep my response light, because although she isn't mine, just the thought of her with someone else has me grinding my teeth together.

Meg: No, silly. You're my friend.

Me: Correction: best friend. But friend or not, I make a great date.

Although I have seen how she is with her dates over the last few months—one and done. As far as I know, she hasn't repeated with any of these guys. I actually feel bad for the poor schmucks. She's a great girl, and I can only imagine how being tossed aside has bruised some egos.

Meg: But then I'd have to kiss you at midnight.

Me: And that's a problem . . . why? I'll have you know I'm an excellent kisser.

Meg: I'm sure you think you are.

Me: Ouch. You're wounding me with your inaccurate assumptions.

"Good evening, ladies, gentlemen, and teammates," I hear loud and clear over the partygoers. I stand and tuck my phone in my pocket as that's my cue to head back up. Chuckles ripple across the crowd as people gravitate closer to the stage Reid and Camille are standing on.

"I'll keep this short as it's almost midnight, but Camille and I wanted to say thank you to all of you for coming tonight and spending New Year's Eve with us. We know y'all have many places you could be and you chose here, so thanks again. As we ring in the new year, I would be remiss if I didn't give a shout-out to the one that's ending. After all, some amazing things happened." He looks over at Camille, and whistles rip through the air. "I can't imagine this next year being better than the last, but I welcome it with open arms." He bends down to kiss her and then pops up, grinning. "I mean, how many seasons have we gone undefeated?!"

The guys roar, and I can't help but smile at my teammates, my brothers.

"I'd like to make a toast, so raise your glasses. As we head into this year, I hope it brings each of you good luck and happiness, and may all our dreams come true."

Someone coughs, "*Super Bowl*," and the crowd cheers through laughter.

"Happy New Year, everyone!"

We all raise our glasses, and after Bryan's clinked his with Lexi's, he turns to face me. He knows I've been keeping an eye on him tonight. He hasn't said anything, but between him trying not to scowl all night and overhearing some of the comments that have been made, I know he's struggling.

"You know it's just noise, right?" I say to him, catching his eye.

He doesn't answer me, but he knows I can read his nonverbal cues. Admitting it to me would mean he believes it's true, and it's not. This is just how the game is played.

"I'll be on the field at ten tomorrow morning. Think you'll be ready by then?" I ask him, my question more about his mental state than his physical. He needs the negativity gone, and our team needs our quarterback back and focused on what's next, not what's passed.

"I'm always ready," he tells me definitively.

"That's my boy!" I again knock my drink with his and grin as we down the rest of these bottles in one swoop, eyeing each other as we do.

Around us, champagne glasses are distributed as people start counting down. Deciding I want this moment to be with Meg even though she isn't here, I hold up my phone and take a portrait photo with the focus on the bubbles, my teammates and the patio lights blurred out in the background. Posting it on social media at 12:02 a.m., I caption it: **This one's for you. Happy New Year.**

Almost instantly, a notification from her pops up with the clinking champagne glasses and wink-kiss emojis. It may as well have been the real thing, because in my chest, that's what it feels like.

Champagne Punch

Ingredients:

- 16 ounces pomegranate juice
- 12 ounces cranberry juice
- 3 tablespoons cinnamon syrup
- 3 tablespoons lemon juice
- 8 ounces citrus vodka
- 1 (750-milliliter) bottle Champagne or sparkling wine
- 12 ounces ginger ale
- Garnish: pomegranate seeds, seasonal fruit, mint, rosemary, or citrus slices

Directions:

Gather the ingredients.

Place a frozen ice ring or large chunks of ice and some of the fresh fruit in a punch bowl.

Add all of the ingredients except the wine and soda and stir well.

Slowly add the ginger ale and Champagne.

Garnish with pomegranate seeds and other seasonal fruit, mint, rosemary, or citrus slices.

Ladle into individual serving glasses, including a few fruits in each.

Serve and enjoy!

Chapter 9

Goodness Gracious

Meg

I CAN'T BELIEVE they made it to the Super Bowl.

I can't believe I'm *here* at the Super Bowl.

When Lexi called last minute and told me we were going, there wasn't one second of hesitation. The ticket was offered, I called Taylor—who was almost as excited for me as I was about getting to go—and packed a bag, and then I boarded a plane to Tampa. There, I met Lexi, and together we flew to Seattle with just our backpacks, no plans, and an anxious giddiness.

At the airport, we hopped in a cab and took it straight to the stadium. Because we were heading from east to west, the timing couldn't have worked out better if we'd tried.

The last time I was at an event like this was when Lexi and I went to watch her brother (and secretly Bryan Brennen) play in the College Football Playoff National Championship game. Yes, that game was insane, but so far this one is nothing like it.

For starters, the average age of the attendees is older, but also, this time I'm here to cheer someone on, someone that's for me. Well, sort of for me. Actually, I take that back—definitely for me. As he keeps claiming we're best friends, this is definitely something one best friend does for the other, and with how much our friendship has grown since Thanksgiving, there's nowhere I'd rather be.

I'm so excited for him. He's been talking about this game nonstop for months, and now here we are—or I should say now here he is playing in the game of his dreams. I couldn't possibly be any happier for him, and I'm over the moon that I get to share in this experience with him.

Arriving at the box—yes, Bryan gave Lexi box tickets, not just regular tickets—a girl I instantly recognize as Camille from Lexi's photos squeals when she sees us enter and jumps up for hugs. The energy in the box is palpable, and I find my heart is racing with adrenaline for Jack and his team.

"I'm so glad you guys could make it! And I'm so happy to finally meet you," she says to me, beaming from ear to ear. "I mean it feels like we've already met. I think I'm the last to meet you, and Jack talks about you nonstop, so this is just the best! He's going to be so happy." Her blonde hair is slicked back into the perfect ponytail, and her blue eyes are so large and bright. She's genuinely happy to meet me, and that only ratchets up my excitement to be here for him.

Nerves flutter a little at the idea of that. I hope he'll be happy to see me. Jack mentioned last week that he could get me a ticket if I wanted to go to the game, but at the time, Lexi wasn't going, and coming all this way by myself didn't sound that fun.

"I'm happy to be here. I'm so proud of them." I glance down toward the field where the teams are warming up, and I scan over each one to find his number. When I do, my heart thumps hard in my chest. It's been ten weeks since I've seen him—ten weeks too long.

"I'm so proud, too, and I'm so anxious. I should have been prescribed something for this because it's almost too much." Camille shakes her head and then rubs her hands together.

Looking her over, I can't help but think, *She's so Southern.* People have commented on my accent over the years, but hers wins hands down.

"Y'all come grab something to eat. I know once the game starts, the food will be forgotten, and well, we're gonna need all the energy we can get."

She's right. I've never been one to sit still at a sporting event, especially if I know people who are playing. I'm full-on expecting to lose my voice today from the cheering.

Together, the three of us wander over to the food as the team clears the field to make way for pregame activities. I'm actually hungrier than I thought, and we fill our plates with cheeseburger sliders, salad, and other snacks while a few more people come over and introduce themselves. I was worried I would feel intimidated here with the other wives and higher-ups from the team, but I don't. I feel great.

Better than great—I feel amazing.

Settling into a seat, I soak in the energy, the chatter, and the scene before me. No matter how long Jack and I are friends for, whether it's months or years, it truly is something extraordinary to be here to watch someone else's dreams come true.

One after the other, the teams are announced, fireworks, flames, and smoke shoot out over the tunnels, and the teams run onto the field. As they each line up on their respective side, the music in the stadium cuts off and an announcer calls for everyone to stand for the national anthem. A male country singer walks out, assumes his position in front of the color guard, and sings so beautifully it leaves chills all over my skin. At the end, the Blue Angels fly over, the roar of their engines echoing fiercely around the stadium. The feeling is electric, and I'm on the edge of my seat with excitement. Well, not literally, since I'm standing—there's no way I could be sitting for this.

Needing a photo, I run down to the edge of the box and have Lexi take it to show me in my Tarpons gear with the game about to start behind me. I know he won't see it until later, but that doesn't mean the support is any less important. I caption it: **Watching my best friend play in the game of his life. #gotarponsgo**

I chuckle at my use of the phrase 'best friend.' I know he'll appreciate it, and today I need to give him everything I have. He deserves it.

The captains meet for the coin toss then the game is underway before we know it. Just four quarters and sixty minutes to determine the once-in-a-lifetime outcome of this game.

First down. Second down. Third down. Punt. Repeat.

Both teams move the ball back and forth down the field but never enough to get into field goal range, and although neither team has come close to scoring, you wouldn't know that by the way the fans are cheering.

"What hotel are y'all staying at?" Camille asks a little over halfway through the first quarter.

"Funny you should ask that," Lexi responds, grimacing just a little and wiping her hands down the legs of her jeans.

"What do you mean?" Camille now looks at both of us, and I just shrug my shoulders.

"This was really last minute, and I looked at hotels around the stadium while we were on the plane, but they were all booked," Lexi tells her.

"Oh, well, Bryan and Jack are rooming together like they usually do, so I imagine y'all can crash with them," she says cheerily, as if this solves the problem.

"We'll see," Lexi says, returning her attention back to the game. She is also here to support someone, only I'm not sure when they last talked. Bryan's been busy in the postseason, and that's affected them. Still, no matter what, this is one of those situations in life where you put all the drama aside and you show up. You show up for your person, because that's the right thing to do.

"Or, you can fly home with us tonight. My dad brought the plane." She smiles brightly, and I can't help but smile with her.

"Your dad owns a plane?" I ask her.

"Yep. Rarely leaves home without it."

"Huh," I answer, not sure what to say. Just then, Bryan steps back five paces, shuffles his feet, and then moves up into the pocket, firing the ball thirty yards downfield toward Jack. Collectively, everyone in the box sucks in air and holds their breath to see if the pass completes, which it does just as two linebackers take him out. The crowd erupts with elation and then it instantly dies.

Lexi's hand flies over and grabs my arm, hard, and the entire box falls dead silent as we stare down at Jack, who isn't moving.

Oh my God.

On shaky legs, I move closer to the edge, brushing her off and clutching my chest. My heart has been cleaved in two, half nosediving into the lowest part of my stomach, the other climbing up into my throat. I feel like I'm about to choke.

"Come on, Jack, get up," I whisper to myself. Only . . . he doesn't.

The team's medical staff rushes onto the field, Bryan runs to him and drops to his knees, and we all watch and wait. Slowly, he begins moving a little, but what he's not moving is his left leg. The television behind us cuts to a commercial as they assess him on the field; meanwhile, on the jumbotron, they show the replay of the tackle in slow motion, and the entire stadium gasps and groans for the pain and devastation we all know has just befallen Jack. The angle at which his knee was hit, the direction the bottom of his leg bent—there is no coming back from this, at least not any time soon.

My eyes swell with tears.

More and more people rush onto the field. He's on the Wolves sideline, which is far from us, and it's hard to see what's happening. The spidercam—the one that runs up, down, and horizontally over the field—has moved as close as it can to them, but still it's not enough. A transport cart flies out of the closest tunnel, and the crowd is quiet as we all watch a worst fear for an athlete come true.

My athlete.

The tears break free as they begin to spill over. My heart is breaking for my friend.

Quickly they immobilize his knee, help him stand, and load him onto the cart. Being the standup player that he is, he waves to the fans to show he's okay, and the stadium roars in support of him. He throws a towel over his head, hiding his face, and then he's gone.

Panic settles into my muscles. I need to move. I need to help him. I need to do something. Frantically, I start looking around the box as the game below us continues, and I find Lexi and the other wives staring at me.

"I have to go." I look at Lexi, and then at Camille and their friend Missy, waiting for one of them to help me. They have to help me.

"Goodness gracious, yes. Yes, you do," Missy finally states, jumping into action, and that crashing panic begins to slightly recede. Missy heads straight for the stadium staff member who's been assigned to our suite, and together they arrange for security to come get me and escort me down. I'm so fortunate we were in this box and these people know why I'm here; otherwise, this would never be happening.

The walk is long, much longer than I expected, even with the elevator ride down. There's silence between the security guard and myself; really, what is there to say? I feel as if I'm marching to my death, the roaring of the crowd from just beyond the walls echoing down the concrete hallways. With each step closer to him, my heart pounds harder.

Part of me wonders if I should be going to him. Is there someone else here at the game that he invited? Does he even want someone by his side? Would he want *me* by his side? After all, who am I to him? Mostly, outside of Thanksgiving, we're just internet friends.

"No," I say to myself. I have to push all this aside. The worst that can happen is he says he doesn't want me there, but if by some small miracle he does, the possible disappointment I might feel at the rejection pales in comparison to what he needs. I would want someone to come for me, and who knows if anyone else is.

Finally we reach the visiting team locker room. When the security guard steps out of the way and I see Jack sitting all alone on one of the training benches, my heart calls out to his. Sure there are people in the room moving around and two of the Tarpons medical staff are standing on the far side to give him space, but what I can't tear my eyes off of is my fallen knight. Damp hair, minimal clothes, and the most distraught, devastated expression I have ever seen.

His eyes flare at the sight of me, and the muscles in his face relax with an intense level of relief at having someone come. Every bit of nervousness I felt on the death march coming down here instantly disappears, and all I see is him.

Putting one foot in front of the other, determination to wrap him up and make this all better pounds through my veins. As I reach him and slide my arms around him, he tucks his face in the crook of my neck and leans into me in such a devastating way, and I know with certainty coming down here was the right thing to do. Against mine, his chest begins moving up and down inconsistently, letting me know just how much disappointment his poor heart can't restrain any longer. With my own tears freely flowing, I run my fingers through his hair and hold him tight.

Pickled Red Onions

Ingredients:

- 1 red onion, thinly sliced (use a mandoline if you have one)
- 1/2 cup apple cider vinegar
- 1 tablespoon granulated sugar
- 1 teaspoon whole cloves (optional)
- 1 1/2 teaspoons salt
- 1 cup hot or warm water

Directions:

Slice the red onions as thin as you can. I use a mandoline.

Stuff all the red onions in the jar of your choice. A bowl will work too.

In a measuring cup, combine apple cider vinegar, salt, sugar, and warm water. Stir to dissolve the sugar and salt. Pour this pickling mixture over your sliced onions, making sure they are immersed in the liquid, and let them set for an hour. After an hour, cover and store in the fridge for up to three weeks.

Chapter 10

Sight for Sore Eyes

Jack

WITHIN MINUTES OF Meg arriving and me having a meltdown that's worthy of an award, Dr. Leffers is back with two others following him, and through the double doors comes a flatbed cart to transport me out. The doctor gives Meg a brief, curious look—I'm still clinging to her like she's my lifeline—but then it's gone and he's all business.

Most knee dislocation injuries for athletes result in artery and nerve damage as well, and I have to block out the possibilities of this as they examine me one more time. During the exam, they use a portable ultrasound machine to watch the blood flow in the popliteal artery, the one that runs behind the knee, and all signs point to undamaged. *Thank God.* Otherwise I would have been rushed to a hospital here to prevent amputation of the lower leg. Additionally, they kept poking at the peroneal nerve to see if it had been compromised, and it doesn't appear that it has. The consequences of that could be temporary paralysis like drop foot, or even worse, permanent paralysis.

"Are you sure you don't want to go to the hospital here? I would feel more comfortable having it looked at in greater detail to rule out some of the other complications we examined for." He wraps his stethoscope around his neck and frowns down at me. I lean farther into Meg, and her arms tighten around me.

"Blood flow is fine?" I watch his face for any tell that might express that it's not. He gives me none.

"Seems to be." He shrugs his shoulder a tiny bit.

If he thought for one second there were complications beyond ligament tears, he would have already put me in an ambulance. I know him; he errs on the side of caution versus let's wait and see.

"Then I want to go home," I tell him matter-of-factly.

The doctor lets out a deep sigh, nods, and positions himself next to the team's head athletic trainer to help me off the table and onto the cart. I show Meg where my things are, she grabs my bag, which the sports trainer packed for me, and the three of us hang on as we're taken through the emergency vehicle tunnel to an SUV that's waiting outside.

"So, Jack," Dr. Leffers starts after they've positioned me in the car. "We've arranged for a vehicle to pick you up at the executive airport in Tampa, and from there you will head straight to the hospital, where Dr. Watson will be waiting for you. I don't foresee there being any problems or delays, and if all goes well, by this time tomorrow, you should be home in your own bed recovering."

I give him a nod. "Sounds good. Thanks, Doc."

The words are like acid on my tongue. I'm thankful he's helping me, but I'm not thankful that I'm in this situation in the first place. I'm sad, frustrated, and extremely pissed off.

He wishes me well, lets me know he'll be following up with Dr. Watson, and says he'll see me in a few days. The door closes, and silence descends like a vacuum. I'm closed off from the game, from my teammates, and with every mile further separating me from them, my soul feels more lost.

The entire commute to the plane is silent. Meg is in the front seat due to me needing the full back to extend my leg, but she glances my way a couple of times, and once she reaches back and rests her hand on top of my uninjured knee.

I know there are things I need to say to her, mainly that she doesn't have to be here, doesn't have to come with me, but selfishly I want her by my side, so I refrain from giving her the out.

As we board the private plane, I'm helped by staff waiting to assist me, and after I'm seated with my leg stretched out in the aisle, Meg boards and sits across the way, in the opposite rear-facing seat so she can look at me. It's the first time in the last hour I've taken an actual detailed look at her, and she's a sight for sore eyes. It's then I see she's wearing my number.

My number.

Not just a team T-shirt to support the Tarpons, but one with my name across her back to support me. I know that's what fans do, buy gear with our numbers, but still, on her it looks like I'm hers and feels like she's mine. An unexpected sense of pride waves through me, and I catch my breath, swallowing down even more emotions trying to push their way to the top.

The door to the plane closes, and the single stewardess gives us her spiel. I reach over to hold Meg's hand, neither of us saying anything, just looking at each other.

"Thank you for being here," I tell her once we've taken off, rubbing my thumb across the back of her hand.

She shifts in her seat so she's better facing me and gives me a small smile. "I was only there for you in the first place. Where you are is where I want to be."

Her words touch a place deep in my chest. I want to smile back, I do, but I can't seem to get my lips to rise. She's so beautiful.

"I didn't know you were coming. When we talked about it this week, you said no." I look at her earnestly.

"I know. It was a last-minute decision by Lexi, and well, she invited me to be her plus-one, so I jumped at the opportunity. I felt regret about missing your game, and it hadn't even happened yet. I wanted to be there. So, when she called going into the weekend, the only thing to say was yes."

"I wish you had told me," I tell her. My parents weren't interested in coming due to the weather, which is the stupidest thing I've ever heard, so I didn't think I was sharing the experience with anyone other than the team.

She shrugs her shoulders.

"I thought about it, but you needed to focus, and I just figured I would see you afterward." She smiles warmly, but her eyes tell me differently. She thought she'd see me afterward, after we won. Then again, it's what we all thought. At takeoff, the Wolves were leading, and right now, I just can't bring myself to log into the plane's Wi-Fi and look.

"Where were you sitting?" I ask curiously.

"In one of the team-provided boxes with Lexi, Camille, Missy, and others. It was a great seat, plus we had warming lamps, which was a really nice perk."

That's good. I'm glad she was with them and she was warm. The average temperature in February in Seattle is forty-nine, but today it was a little colder.

"Are you in a lot of pain?" she asks, her eyes scanning over my splinted leg.

"Not at the moment. They gave me a ton of painkillers." I'm actually starting to feel really tired. With the combination of the medicine and my adrenaline wearing off, it's left me lethargic and sluggish.

"Then you should be eating something." She sits up in her seat as if this gives her purpose. I think in these situations, it's natural for the significant other—not that that's what she is, but close enough—to want to help, to be moving, doing, useful, so even though I'm not hungry, I agree.

"Probably." I lean my head back on the headrest. Her hair was down when she first walked into the locker room, but now it's up. The blanket she tossed over her lap twists as she finds the call button, ringing for the stewardess, and requests that some food be brought over. Underneath, her foot pops out, and I take in the tall black boots that are wrapped over her tight jeans and up to her knees. Damn, those are hot. I wouldn't be a red-blooded male if I didn't wonder what she would look like in those boots and nothing else.

Settling into silence, we both stare at each other until the food comes. It isn't much, more just snacks, but I decide she was right about me needing to eat as the pineapple banana bread goes down easily and calms my upset stomach.

"What are you thinking about?" she asks, nibbling on some cubed cheese.

"How my whole life, all I ever wanted was to play in the Super Bowl." Letting out a deep sigh, I drop eye contact with her, the ache of disappointment in my chest intensifying.

"Well, it might have been a little shorter than you would've liked, but you did get to play," she tells me, trying to put a positive spin on it.

I can't help the snort that escapes and end up mumbling, "I guess." In my dreams, it was for a full four quarters and we won at the end.

Wishing I hadn't brought it up, I change the subject. "You went on a date earlier this week." It's not a question, just a statement.

"I did." She opted for a bottle of water instead of a drink, and I watch as she picks it up and brings it to her lips for a sip.

"I saw you post the new dish on OBA's page, an aged cheddar and apple German pancake. Tell me about it." I'm hoping she reads between the lines: *Tell me a story, keep me distracted.*

"He was nice, but not what I was expecting." She moves the food tray away from her and props her feet up in the seat across from her.

"You met him online?" We've talked about her dating before, but we've never talked about the specifics of it.

"Yep. I'm so busy, so that's where I've connected with most of my dates this past year."

"Hmm. Where did he take you?"

I would be lying if I said the idea of strange dudes prowling the internet and creeping on her profile sat well with me. I get that sometimes there are love connections made, but mostly it seems like a shady way for people to catfish.

"Well, not that there's really anything wrong with it, but he took me to Italiano's."

I blink at her, and it takes me a second to register what she's said. "Wait, the large chain restaurant?"

"Yep." She pinches her lips shut and nods once. "In a city like Charleston, he took me to an inauthentic place."

How unoriginal. Sounds like something my parents would do because it's the easy choice. They rarely try new places, preferring consistent and boring.

"Did he know you own your own restaurant?" I'm appalled for her and the story has just begun.

"Nope. I don't tell them that, but I do have the guys meet me at the restaurant. As far as they know, it's where I work, so that should say something about my food preferences and be their first clue about the type of places I frequent."

I've never been to her restaurant, but I've looked at enough photos and reviews online to know it's unique and original. Seems to me he should have switched to a different place once he saw OBA.

"Was he at least nice?" I ask, running my hand through my hair and feeling frustrated for her. Already I feel like the guy has more slashes in the con column on his pros and cons list.

"He was, and I tried really hard to overlook where we were and what he ordered—which, by the way, was chicken parmesan. That's not a problem in itself either, it's just so predictable. It's boring even for a restaurant like that. But, wait for it, though . . . then we went to a biergarten, and the bouncer checked our IDs at the door."

I can feel my brows pull down.

"He mumbled his birthdate, and I did the math in my head—it made him fifty-one. Fifty-one. I don't have a problem with older men, but he told me he was thirty-five. And before you say anything"—she holds up her hand—"no, he didn't look over fifty. His hair must be dyed, because it wasn't gray, and well, he just looked the age he said. Clearly he gets away with it, but he lied, and the twenty-plus-year age gap is too much for me. That's essentially father range, and just no, thank you."

A small chuckle comes out of me. I'm surprised, given our current circumstance, and I think she is too as a tiny smile slips over her lips.

"Well then."

"I know, right?" She shakes her head then leans over to remove the tray in front of me and stacks it with hers.

"How did you get out of there then?"

"Once we got inside, he ordered us a beer at the bar, and I just asked him. At first he looked surprised, and then he got an attitude about why that mattered, and that's when I called it a night. He didn't say anything as I kindly thanked him for dinner and left."

"That explains the aged cheddar." I smirk at her, and she grins in return.

Silence falls over us again, and eventually the heavy weight of my eyes has them drifting shut. At the sound of movement next to me, I crack them open and watch as Meg unfolds a blanket and drapes it over my chest and lap. A whiff of her perfume floats my way, the same smell that engulfed me in the training room, and my gaze falls to her neck. She's so tiny, her skin so smooth, and I find that if I could, I would absolutely lean into her again.

As she settles back into her seat, I let out a deep breath, and the exhaustion of the last hour and a half sinks in. Disappointment is a funny thing. It taints the soul with a good mixture of ache and numbness, and today it's been handed out in spades. While I am so grateful she is here, I feel that disappointment with her a little as well. I know she let that guy in December kiss her, but I've often wondered if she ever allows for more. I know it's none of my business what she does, even if I don't like it, but that doesn't change the fact that deep down I wish she were kissing me.

Pineapple Banana Bread

Ingredients:

    3 cups all-purpose flour
    2 cups sugar
    1 teaspoon baking soda
    1 teaspoon ground cinnamon
    $\frac{3}{4}$ teaspoon salt
    1 cup chopped walnuts (optional)
    3 large eggs, beaten
    1 cup canola oil or 1 cup vegetable oil
    2 cups mashed very ripe bananas
    2 teaspoons vanilla extract
    1 (8 ounce) can unsweetened crushed canned pineapple, drained

Directions:

Preheat oven to 350& lightly grease & flour 2 8-inch loaf pans.

In large bowl, combine flour, sugar, baking soda, cinnamon& the salt.

Stir in walnuts.

In separate bowl, mix eggs, oil, banana, vanilla& pineapple until well combined.

Add wet ingredients to dry ingredients, stir just until moistened.

Pour equal amounts into pans.

Bake about 50 to 55 minutes or until toothpick in center comes out clean.

Cool for 10 minutes on racks; remove from pans and continue cooling.

Chapter 11

Fine and Dandy

Meg

EVERYONE HAS A number, a number that's their favorite, one they love, or just one they gravitate toward, and for me that number is one. I like being number one at things, always have. I was first chair cello when I was in school and graduated in the number one position at the top of my class as valedictorian, but it's also about being the kind of friend where I'm the first one people call when they need help. So, it wasn't surprising when I learned about numerology and discovered my number is one. I laughed to myself and soaked up the attributes that go along with it: independence, leadership, trailblazing, entrepreneurship, creativity, and originality.

Then, ironically when I was twenty-one, I went to one routine doctor's appointment, had one image scan, one blood draw, and that turned into one diagnosis.

Ovarian cancer.

From there, everything changed, and for the next six months I lived one day at a time.

Back and forth to one hospital, where there was really only one emotion I lived with every day . . . fear.

If I'm being honest with myself, I still live with fear.

It shouldn't come as a surprise to anyone that being in a hospital, even though it isn't for me or one I'm familiar with, still causes me anxiety. I'm doing my best to not let it show, but I know it's there whether he sees it or not. He probably doesn't, but I'm surprised by how hard it is to keep it buried away.

He finally fell asleep on the plane, and I think I got a little bit of a rest, but mostly I was wide awake with the knowledge of where we were heading. It's a good thing this is a different hospital, because I'm certain my reaction would have been infinitely more noticeable had it been mine.

Just remembering the sights, the smells—mainly the antiseptic one—the room temperature, the people, the noises . . . all of it has me cringing and my insides protesting. But, being the best friend I'm supposed to be, I'm mentally sucking it up because he needs me.

And he does.

I'm not sure if he would ever admit it or not, but the haunted look in his eyes has only increased with each state we pass over, his grip on my hand only strengthened. I wondered about the pain medicine wearing off, but he never said anything. It was when we landed that the driver told us he was sorry about our team, said he was really pulling for them. Jack mumbled a thanks in return then leaned his head back against the seat and closed his eyes.

The Tarpons lost the Super Bowl.

What an overall disappointing experience.

I had been hanging on to the hope that they would win and that would help his disposition, but the news just made things worse as he further retreated into himself.

When we eventually arrived at the hospital, they didn't take us to the emergency room; instead they put Jack in a wheelchair and escorted us to a private room. There was a flurry of activity to get him admitted and prepped for surgery, during which he didn't say much, just mumbled kindly to those who were helping him and stared at me as if I were his lifeline.

"All right, Mr. Willett, let's get you changed and then I'll get that IV all set up in your hand," says the nurse assigned to him. She's an older lady, and she's been unwaveringly kind since we arrived.

"She'll help me," he says to her, and that's when I see her holding a hospital gown. She gives me a pitiful but understanding look, lays it on the foot of the bed, and slips out of the room. Everyone has looked at us pitifully. It's unnerving for me; I can't imagine how it is for him.

He and I are both quiet as we stare at the blue and white checked gown.

"You know you don't have to stay for this." Fingers squeeze around my hand, and I glance down—I had forgotten he was still holding it—then I look at his face. "I'll be all right, and you heard them—I'll be home just after lunch," he says quietly, his voice rough. It feels like this is the first thing he's said to me in hours.

"I know I don't have to stay, but I want to. There's nowhere I'd rather be right now than here with you." I squeeze his hand in return and nod at him encouragingly.

Dark shadows have further settled in underneath his chocolate-coated eyes, and his skin, which is usually golden and tanned, has paled. He looks like a different person, but not at the same time. I miss my happy, funny guy.

"I do appreciate it." He gives me the tiniest of smiles, and I smile back large enough for the both of us then move down the bed to grab the gown.

"Come on, let me help you," I say in a slightly cheerful tone.

He lets out a deep breath then leans forward, reaches behind his head, and pulls off the Tarpons hoodie he's wearing. His dark hair sticks up straight, there's a light smattering of scruff across his face and neck, and I'm presented with the most beautiful man I have ever seen. I know now is not the time, but it's hard not to notice how perfectly sculpted he is from the prominent line of his collarbone down to his trim waist.

I want to curl into him and have his arms wrap around me, and without thinking, I reach up and run my hand from his shoulder down over his warm skin. He grabs my wrist, stopping it over his heart. Our eyes lock, and flutters make themselves known within me. In another place at another time, this might be a charged moment, but here it's just an intimate understanding between two people sharing an unfortunate experience.

"It's gonna be all right. You know this," I whisper.

"There's nothing I can do about it now," he says, frowning, accepting the fact he has no control over this situation.

"Nope. Now we just ride the wave until we get to the shore."

"I guess so."

With his other hand, he reaches for my waist and brings me closer. Leaning over him, I place my forehead on his and watch as his eyes slip shut, his nostrils flaring as he breathes in and out.

This guy . . . he's so tragically, devastatingly handsome. My heart clenches in my chest, and being this close to him, I forget how much I hate hospitals and decide it's really nice getting to be affectionate with him. All it took was two simple interactions, Thanksgiving and this, and he's familiar to me in a way no one has ever been.

Minutes pass until I feel the need to shake off the tender way my heart is reacting toward him, and I pull back, smile, and hold up the gown. He slips his arms into it, and I tie it behind his neck. From underneath the gown, he yanks on his shorts, which I pull down and carefully slide over his legs, and then he flips the side of the gown up and looks at the compression shorts.

"I think you're going to need to cut these off."

I think he's right.

Looking around the room, I find a pair of surgical scissors next to the sink then carefully cut up the thigh of each of his legs. He pulls them off, hands them to me, and I throw them away as he not so subtly adjusts himself under the gown.

"All set now." I grin to attempt to keep the mood light. It doesn't work; he just stares blankly, clearly lost in his own thoughts.

Overhead, the air conditioning kicks on, and a hum settles around us. I climb up on the edge of his bed to sit, and he shifts a little to give me more room.

"What if I never play again?" he asks, his voice so somber.

The vulnerability in him is so palpable and so real it's creating a thickness around us, and I just want to blow it all away, want to clear the air and thin it out so he can breathe a little easier.

Reaching over, I lay my hand on his arm and gently run it up and down. "Then it's time for a new adventure. You'll be all right—no, you'll be better than all right. You'll be just fine and dandy." I push optimism and confidence his way, smiling to try to ease his aching heart. I know right now he feels like there's no silver lining and nowhere to go, but I have faith that eventually he'll pull through.

Instead of responding, he sits up, his hands find my waist, and he yanks me closer then lays his head on my shoulder. My arms wrap around him, and I hold him to me until it's time for him to go. His eyes lock onto mine when he's about to pass through the door, and they're pleading for this not to be happening, even though it is. I stand strong and reassure him I'll be here when he gets back, and then he's gone.

God, this sucks.

I'm left standing in the room with the nurse, and she turns to look at me. I'm clutching his hoodie, and she pats me on the arm.

"Don't worry, dear, he'll be fine."

"I know. Thank you."

And I do. After all, it's just a knee surgery. Maybe a complicated one based on what they find, but in no way life-threatening . . . just life-changing.

"Of course you know you're welcome to stay here to wait for him, but if you get hungry, you should head on down to the cafeteria. I promise the food isn't all that bad, and since it's breakfast time, you should definitely get the hash brown casserole. It's delicious." She gives me a wink and then she's gone, too.

Anxiety drips back in now that I'm alone. It's silent except for the noises coming from beyond the door, and I eye the chair in the corner. It's eerily similar to the ones in the chemotherapy infusion centers, but at least there the room was large and there were several patients present. Here, I'm left alone with my thoughts, and I don't like it. Then, as if the universe understands, sunlight breaks through the cracks in the blinds and floods the room, reminding me that I made a choice years ago to always look on the bright side instead of falling down the rabbit hole.

Settling into the chair, I begin thinking about all the good things in my life, the simple things that bring me joy, starting with his hoodie. I slip it on; it swallows me in size, and it smells so much like him I want to drown in it. It's a little bit of sweat, but mostly a sporty scent mixed with citrus, and it smells so good. I instantly feel better already.

I may not be able to control what's going on around me, but I can control what I choose to focus on, and right now, I can't think of anything better than him.

My best friend.

Hash Brown Casserole

Ingredients:

1 (2 pound) package frozen hash brown potatoes, thawed
1/2 cup of butter softened
1 teaspoon salt
1/2 teaspoon black pepper
1/2 cup chopped onion
1 can condensed cream of chicken soup
2 cups of shredded Cheddar cheese

Directions:

Preheat oven to 350 degrees F. Spray one 9×13 inch pan with non-stick cooking spray.

In a large bowl, combine the potatoes, butter, salt, pepper, onions, soup and cheese. Gently mix and pour into prepared pan or dish.

Bake in the preheated oven until browned, about 35 minutes.

Chapter 12

It Is What It Is

Jack

THERE ARE FLOWERS in my home.

Not from any of my friends or the team, but from Meg. Hell, the team knows dudes don't want flowers; we want shit that's going to make this go away as fast as it can. They sent over a schedule for when I should be in the training room to meet with the athletic trainers and who'll be helping me maintain the rest of my body, along with a phone number for a chef who will bring me meals for two weeks when I'm ready.

But the flowers . . .

They are yellow and bright, a complete contrast to the muted gray, navy, and white tones of my condo, and I find my eyes are continually drawn to them. I'm angry at their colorful cheerfulness, as if all of this is the flowers' fault.

I hate that I'm mad, too. It's such a contradiction to how

I thought I would feel when my career approached this crossroad, yet I can't help it. I'm not ready.

The knee surgery ended up lasting three and a half hours. Multiple ligaments needed to be repaired, and they lied when they said I'd be home by lunch. Turned out it was closer to dinner, and I felt awful that Meg was stuck at the hospital all that time waiting for me. Of course, the first thing I asked when I woke up was if I will ever play again, and Dr. Watson just frowned and said he didn't know, told me athletic abilities return differently for everyone, but he had full confidence I would heal up nicely in no time. The pessimistic dark cloud that had moved in sometime over the last twenty-four hours read between the lines: he doesn't think I'll be returning to the career, the sport, the life I love.

In addition to that, I'm also not ready for Meg to leave, and she will be first thing in the morning. I understand, though; just because my world stopped doesn't mean everyone else's did. Aside from the day she flew out to the game, she's been with me for two days now, making a total of three, which is one and a half past how long she thought she would be gone. She had plans to fly back to Tampa after the game with Camille and Reid and then be off to Charleston first thing the following morning. I'm certain her restaurant manager Taylor has had about enough.

Hearing a noise in the kitchen, I tear my eyes off the flowers and shift them to her. The anger I feel dissipates a bit as I mentally take pictures to store away for later. I like having her in my house and among my things more than I should. Upon walking in, she had Zeus wrapped around her finger immediately, and she easily made herself comfortable, maneuvering around as if she's been coming here for years.

It was nice to watch, even through the haze of the medicine. She was like a little tornado as she took charge and whirled around from one thing to the next.

"Can I get you anything?" she calls over to me. Without her shoes on, she is short—like really short. Her head and half her chest barely peek above the counter, and another day at another time, I would most definitely make fun of her. Not today, though; I just don't have it in me.

"Nah, I'm good. I just want you to come sit with me." Like a security blanket, I want her near me all the time.

"Okay, just give me a few minutes and I'll be right there." She smiles at me then spins around. See: tornado.

I watch as she opens the oven door and bends over to check what's inside. A big part of her whirling has been making me food that will sustain me for quite some time. Right after we got home from the hospital yesterday, she inspected my kitchen, and then using an app on her phone, she placed a large grocery order to be delivered. She's been cooking nonstop and packing my freezer. I told her it wasn't necessary, but she looked at me as if I was crazy. She and I both know how much I like food, specifically how much I like her food.

"It smells delicious," I tell her as she walks over, pushes Zeus to the floor, and sits down on the couch next to me.

"I hope it will be." She smiles warmly. He places his head in her lap and she pets him; I wish she were petting me. It feels so good when she has her hands on my arm, my back, or in my hair.

"What is it?" I ask.

"Church supper spaghetti. It's not the healthiest dish with the cheese and noodles, but if you eat a salad with it, you'll be all right."

Color hits her cheeks as she looks at me, and I look at her without commenting in return. Her face is scrubbed free of any makeup, her hair is plopped on top of her head, and aside from how beautiful she is, the evidence of the last several days is present under her big, gorgeous eyes, like I imagine it is under mine, too. She's helped me so much, and I'm incredibly grateful, even if my mood doesn't reflect that.

"Tell me a story?" I ask, just wanting to hear her voice.

"What kind of story?" She pulls a blanket over her lap as Zeus curls up at her feet, and she tucks an escapee piece of hair behind her ear.

"It doesn't matter. Anything about you."

I want to know this girl, like really know her.

"Hmm. Let's see . . ." She looks up and over toward the windows as she thinks, and then, surprising me, she says, "When I was going through chemotherapy, I lost my sense of taste."

Shaking her head to herself, she looks back down at me, smiling a little, and I know my brows have risen.

"I'd loved food for so long, and I had known for years that whatever career I ended up in would somehow revolve around food, so shortly after the chemo started and that happened, I kind of lost myself for a while."

"Is that normal, and how long was it gone?" I don't move, don't reach out to comfort her; she wouldn't want it because she's moved past all this, but still.

"Yes, it is normal, but at the time I didn't know that. At first things just started tasting differently, and then I lost it. About fifty percent of people have taste changes. They don't know why but think it has something to do with damage to the taste buds. All in all, I had issues for eight to nine months."

"That's a long time."

"Yeah. Shelby and I had already been accepted to culinary school when this happened, and even though there was sufficient time for me to go through treatment and come out the other side, it was still hard. Nothing like explaining to teachers and other students that, while my hair had just started growing in so it was obvious what'd happened, I was there to be a chef but had no sense of taste."

"That sucks. I'm sorry."

She shrugs one shoulder. "I remember the moment when I got the first tiny hint that my taste was coming back. Shelby and I were in Stocks, Soups, and Sauces, a first-semester class where they were teaching classical and contemporary methods. It was a béchamel, one of the five mother sauces. In it is whole milk, flour, butter, onion, and spices. We were tasting it, and I could very distinctly detect the flavor of whole cloves and salt. Salt! My heart started racing with the realization and I started crying, which alone was embarrassing enough, but I was so excited I burst out to the entire class that I could taste it and everyone cheered." She smiles to herself and looks back up at me tenderly. "That was a good day."

"Sounds like it. Since I've known you, you haven't talked much about what it was like having cancer."

She glances down at her hands then brings her head up to look me straight in the eyes. "What's there to really talk about? Bad things happen to people all the time. Divorces, illness, a lost job, a sudden death of a family member, car accidents—you name it, but once it's done, it's done. Time to learn from it and move on."

"Have you moved on? It hasn't been all that long."

"Most days, yes, but I'd be lying if I said the fear doesn't linger. Even though the cancer is gone and I've been told I'm cancer-free, I'm not free. My wounds have healed, that last cycle of chemo is completed, there's no more radiation and I've rung the bell . . . one would think I'm free, but I'm not. It's on my mind constantly with every ache, every common cold, every scan, every poke. It's been over seven years since the words 'full remission' were said to me, but I'm still dealing and I'm still healing. Despite what people think, it continues long after you've been told you're cancer-free."

"You still go for scans?" My heart rate picks up a little at knowing she still has to get checked out, at knowing there's a need for it and there's an actual possibility the cancer could come back.

"I do. Blood work, too. They've slowed down over time, and I only go in once a year now."

"Is it scary?"

Her lips press into a flat line, and then she answers, "Yes." She doesn't elaborate; she doesn't need to.

"I'm sorry you went through that." I truly am. She's here with me, and more than anything I wish I could go back in time and be there for her.

"It is what it is. Things turned out all right in the end. Could've been worse." She gives me a small smile, only I can't smile back. I don't want to smile back.

Suddenly my anger is back, only this time it's twofold. I'm mad for the situation I'm in, and I'm rip-roaring mad for what she went through.

Why? Why her?

I know this is a question loved ones always ask, but it's truly how I feel. What was the point of it? Why did she have to experience that? I know I'm being completely irrational as this happened a long time ago, it's over, and she's fine, but to me it feels like it's happening now.

Reaching up with her thumb, she gently rubs the wrinkles that have taken up residence between my eyes. I know my face is frozen in a permanent scowl, but I can't help it; I'm not happy. As much as I loved her story, loved her sharing that with me, it may as well have been another log tossed onto the fire of my already outraged mood.

"You need to rest. You know the more you sleep, the faster you'll heal." Her pale gray eyes trail over my face as she takes in each point of tension, and her thumb slides to the outside of my eye and down over the rough stubble of my cheek.

It feels so good, but I don't answer her. There's nothing for me to say. She sees the storm brewing inside me, only now it's grown in response to what life has tossed at us both.

I hate this. I hate how things have turned out for me, and I hate how life has treated her. It's not fair; none of it is. Yes, I know she's fine now, but the rational side of me can't catch up to the irrational side, and my emotions are strung so tight I feel like I'm going to burst from the inside out.

And then at her words, I do.

"Lie down," she says tenderly, patting her lap.

She is the needle to my balloon, and just like that, I pop.

Letting out the deepest breath known to man, I shift my hips on the couch to scooch down and lie backward, placing my head in her lap. At this point I would crawl into her lap if I could, even though she's half the size of me.

From above, she leans over, presses her lips gently but firmly to my forehead, and kisses me.

My eyes burn with the telltale sign of tears, and I curse the unwanted emotion. I feel like I've hit a new level of rock bottom, and I can't find it in me to give a fuck. Instead of fighting the tears, I close my eyes and let them leak out.

She softly runs her fingers over the lines of my face and through my hair. It's soothing and apparently the key needed to unlock my insides. I know she's doing her best to understand, but can anybody really? I'm fucking brokenhearted, and I don't know where to go from here.

Church Supper Spaghetti

Ingredients:

1 pound ground beef
1 large onion, chopped
1 medium green pepper, chopped
1 can (14-1/2 ounces) diced tomatoes, undrained
1 cup water
2 tablespoons chili powder
1 package (10 ounces) frozen corn, thawed
1 package (10 ounces) frozen peas, thawed
1 can (4 ounces) mushroom stems and pieces, drained
Salt and pepper to taste
12 ounces spaghetti, cooked and drained
2 cups shredded cheddar cheese, divided

Directions:

In a large skillet, cook beef, onion and green pepper over medium heat until meat is no longer pink. Add tomatoes, water and chili powder. Cover and simmer for 30 minutes. Add the corn, peas, mushrooms, salt and pepper. Stir in spaghetti.

Layer half of the mixture in a greased 4-qt. baking dish. Sprinkle with 1 cup cheese; repeat layers.

Bake, uncovered, at 350° for 20 minutes or until heated through.

To give Church Supper Spaghetti a new flavor twist, use Italian, Mexican or Cajun diced tomatoes in place of the plain diced tomatoes.

Chapter 13

Well, I'll Be

Meg

IT'S BEEN TWO weeks since I left him, two weeks where I've felt like the worst human ever because he is there and I am here. He needs me—well, he needs someone, and from snooping around and talking to Camille and Lexi, I know he isn't getting it. He's holed himself up in his condo, he's refusing to see his friends, and he's all alone. I'm surprised by how much this is bothering me, but I just can't seem to help it. I know he will pull through this, know his knee will heal, but I'm still worried about him.

I'm also bothered by how different from the Jack I knew he quickly became. There's definitely something to be said for seeing a person at their worst, and he was at his. I don't mind his worst, though. In many ways, he resembled a broken bird, perhaps a very large bird but nonetheless one who'd had its wings clipped and its very essence somehow stripped away. The guy I've come to know, the one who laughs, jokes, and is always up to no good—he is gone, and in his place is anger, melancholy, and silence. It was eerie to be near him and for him to be so quiet.

Of course I've called to check on him, but conversations are short, his voice flat and dull. He doesn't say much, but then again I guess there really isn't much to say. He's stuck in his condo and having to wait to sort through what happens next.

Feeling the need to take care of him from afar, using the same packaging Lexi does to ship pies, I overnighted him a few dishes last week. I know he's perfectly capable of ordering his own food, but I want him to know I'm thinking of him, too. Of course he sent me a text to thank me for the food, but not much beyond that.

There are also no social media posts from him. Every day I find myself looking, multiple times a day, waiting for the buzz of a notification, but his last post was from the day of the game where he put up a picture of him in his jersey adorned with the Super Bowl patch. The caption: **Dreams do come true.**

Fans have commented nonstop wondering how he is and looking for an answer, but he isn't giving them one. It's not that he has to—his private life is his and his alone—but like his fans, I'm sitting here holding my breath and wondering too. He also hasn't commented on any of my posts. He does like them, but the banter from my friend is gone. I feel like his spirit has died.

And with it, so has mine.

Ridiculous, I know. After all, we've only spent a handful of days together, but I can't help it. He's so sad, and there's nothing I can do about it to make it better. I even canceled my date that was scheduled for this week. I just couldn't bring myself to go. I keep reminding myself that soon enough this sucky period will be over, that life does go on, but in the meantime I feel weary, run-down. I know I just need to recharge a little and then I'll be back at it.

Speaking of recharging, the restaurant has been slammed the last couple of weeks. I know we are in season with the snowbirds heading south, but still, we are booked solid just about every single day with a few private functions thrown in here and there. I hate saying the business has been a good distraction because I'm grateful and love how much people want to eat at OBA, but it is. If only I could come up with a distraction for him.

The kitchen door swings open and Taylor breezes in, holding up a piece of paper and waving it.

"Guess what I've got?" she singsongs, grinning from ear to ear.

"I'm not sure, but you're very excited, so I'm sure you'll tell me," I sing back at her.

My hands are covered in corn fritter batter. Instead of flattening them, we like to roll them into balls before we drop them into the oil for frying. Served in a paper bag, they are one of our bestselling items.

"It's the official list of who's who for the Charleston Wine and Food Festival, and guess whose tickets for brunch on Sunday have sold out?" She's beaming.

Behind me, the noise in the kitchen softens as heads pop up from different stations to hear what she has to say.

"No way. Us?" I wipe my thumb and index finger on a towel next to me then take the paper from her. Looking down at it, I see there is an updated alphabetical list of those who are participating, and there next to OBA is stamped 'Sold out.'

I can't believe it. I'm in delighted awe.

"Yep!" She rocks up on her toes and clasps her hands together behind her back.

"This is amazing, and such great news . . . much-needed great news," I mumble, mostly to myself, but she hears me. I'm still staring at the list, spotting the predictable places that are chosen to participate every year, and I can't help but feel pride for those of us who are the unexpected wildcards.

Her look turns briefly sympathetic at my admission, but the joy of being on the sold-out list shines through. Taylor has done an amazing job managing the front of the house since Shelby left, and she should be just as proud as I am.

When we first threw our name into the hat last year, I don't think we expected the committee to pick us as we're still fairly new to the Charleston food scene, but then they did. Our idea was simple as we are mainly a brunch place, but nothing goes better with brunch than a sparkling beverage, so that's what we pitched.

Located in the heart of downtown Charleston, OBA, short for Orange Blossom Avenue, is housed in a historic building with floor-to-ceiling windows, exposed whitewashed brick walls, vintage chandeliers, and a covered courtyard filled with fruits, vegetables, plants, and herbs used by the kitchen. You'll enjoy a menu featuring unique and delightful Southern dishes that will give you all the goodness without the guilt. Each course will be paired with a specific delicious selection of bubbles for a meal guaranteed to be as light and fresh as your surroundings.

Before we knew it, a photographer showed up to take photos of the restaurant and a few signature dishes, and then we were listed on the festival's website. Our event was announced in the lineup, our blurb was featured, and through a link posted underneath, attendees could purchase tickets. We made a promise to ourselves that we wouldn't consistently check it for updates, and with everything that's been going on with Jack, I kind of forgot and had no idea.

When I lower the paper, Taylor and I stare at each other, grinning. Words don't need to be said as we both understand the enormity of this. The Charleston Wine and Food Festival is one of the premier culinary festivals in the nation. We have no idea how many critics, journalists, and bloggers have purchased tickets, but this one meal has the potential to be defining for us for quite some time. If we nail it, the sky's the limit, but if we bomb it, there's no telling how long it will take for us to dig ourselves out of the hole.

My heart feels like it's going to burst as Taylor gets called back to the front, and the staff behind me slips out of the trance and returns to work. Walking to the sink, I wash my hands and allow the excitement to override the fear.

Fear—such a stupid emotion. What do I have to fear? As long as I have all the ingredients, I can make anything work, and if for some reason I don't, I'll improvise. We've got this. I've got this.

Picking up my phone, I call the one person who'll truly understand what this means. She answers on the second ring, and I blurt it out before she can even say hello.

"Shelby, we sold out." I pinch my eyes shut, smiling so big my teeth are grinding together.

"Sold out what?" Her tone is excited now too, matching mine.

"The Wine and Food Festival brunch." Opening my eyes, I spot my latest glass of iced coffee on my station and reach for it.

There's not even a pause—she squeals immediately. "Well, I'll be. I knew you would," she states matter-of-factly.

"How did you know?" I take a sip and let the beverage cool me down.

"Because you are an amazing chef and OBA is quickly becoming a landmark in Charleston."

I don't argue with her. I know she's right. We've worked so hard to make a name for ourselves.

"You'll come, right? To help?" I put the glass down and pick up a large rubber spatula to run around the inside of the fritter batter bowl, pushing it into a fresh pile.

"Of course I'll be there. Zach and I both will."

Zach . . . Zach makes me think of Jack. My heart dips, and my hand stops. It crossed my mind that I should call him and tell him, too, but that expression about kicking a man when he's down takes over and I don't want to do that to him. It's not that I think he wouldn't be happy for me, but it feels a little like rubbing my good fortune in his face while he's been dealt a hand of misfortune.

Shaking my head, I decide I won't call him, and I refocus on the job in front of me, and on Lexi and Zach. Zach and his sangrias—a couple of those would be perfect! Light, refreshing, and a way to highlight his wines to a large, influential audience. I could also use some of his lavender honey.

"That makes me so happy." My heart sighs at knowing she'll be here. "I think I need to place an order for some honey," I tell her, and she starts laughing.

"I'm on it. How many jars do you need?"

Golden Corn Fritters

Ingredients:
- 1 1/4 cups self-rising cornmeal mix
- 1 1/4 cups all-purpose flour
- 1/4 cup sugar
- 1 teaspoon salt
- 1 cup milk
- 2 large eggs, slightly beaten
- 1/4 cup (1/2 stick) butter, melted
- 1 (15.25 ounce) can corn, drained
- Vegetable oil, for frying

Directions:

Heat oil to 325 degrees F.

In a medium bowl, combine cornmeal mix, flour, sugar, and salt. In a small bowl, combine milk and eggs. Add milk mixture to cornmeal mixture, stirring well. Stir in butter and corn.

Pour oil to a depth of 2 inches in a Dutch oven, or use a deep-fryer. Drop by tablespoons into hot oil. Cook 2 to 4 minutes, or until golden, turning once. Drain on paper towels.

Chapter 14

Throw Caution to the Wind

Jack

I DON'T THINK I've ever told anyone this, but March is my favorite month. I know, I know, one would think it's in the fall at the start of the season, but it's not. As much as I love football, tailgating with the rich smell of charcoal, and the crispness of autumn touching most of the country, it's still a time of work for me and there's no time to slow down and breathe.

By the end of the year, we are so dialed in to finish strong that the holidays are mostly a blur, and we consistently make it to the postseason, pushing us into January. Then the season comes to an abrupt end and before I know it, February has already started and then is halfway done, which leaves March as the beginning of my new year.

March one. There's beautiful weather, and it's a great time to be outside and to refocus myself. I detox my body and heal any outstanding issues, and as any sports lover will tell you, it's the beginning of baseball season. Pitchers and catchers have reported in and spring training is well underway. A perk of living in Florida or Arizona is there's never a shortage.

Only this year, I feel as if my calendar has shifted. Hell, everything has shifted, and I feel out of sorts in a bad way. February third was the Super Bowl then February fourth was the surgery, which became day one of my new year, and since then I've been counting the days. It's not like I have anything else to do.

It's been twenty-nine days since Meg left, fourteen days since my staples were removed and the knee immobilizer changed, and one day since I got the call to head in to the front office.

Today is the day.

Today is the day I've been dreading where team management wants to meet to discuss my options. The way I see it, there are only two options: I stay on their roster, or I don't. It's the don't part that makes me nervous, because if I don't, what do I do with my life? I'd like to say life has been hard lately, but it hasn't. If anything, it's just been boring, and I'm not meant to live a boring life. I miss my routine. I miss my friends. I miss the ache, burn, and exhaustion from a killer workout. I miss taking Zeus for long walks, and if I'm being honest with myself, I really miss her.

Meg.

I know I haven't been the most social person with her lately, and that's my fault. I just feel like I'm in limbo, and until I know what's happening next, I've shut down and shut off. I don't know what to talk about, I don't want to be asked any questions I can't answer, and I certainly don't want to be pitied. I'm not saying she would, but what man wants that or to even set themselves up for the possibility?

Looking out the window as I cross over the Hillsborough River, I see the water is gray today . . . gray like her eyes, gray like my soul. Dramatic much? Yes, but I just can't help it. I'm headed to meet with my boss, and I have a bad feeling I'm not going to like what I hear. I didn't even sleep last night, because with every fiber of my being, I know what they are going to say.

Retirement.

Shaking my head, I shove out the worst-case scenario thoughts and focus on the road as I drive the remaining distance, park, and hobble in through the front doors and toward Coach's office. All down the hallway, there are pictures of the team's players in action, and I pause just for a second as I get to one of mine. It was an insane end-zone catch from a game two years ago, a split-second need to change the play, and with it the points tipped us over to win the game. I'll never forget that moment.

Letting out a sigh, I continue down the hall.

"Good morning. They're ready for you if you want to go on it," says the staff administrative assistant. Her gaze drops to my leg as I approach then quickly flashes back up as she smiles. It's a fake smile, and I can't help but grit my teeth and scowl, her acknowledgment an unwanted reminder of what this meeting represents.

Moving past her, I crutch my way into his office and sit down in one of two leather chairs in front of his desk. There are two other people waiting for me, and I push down the sensation of their stares and the silence crawling up my spine. I'm exhausted after just the walk in from the parking lot, and internally I'm swearing at how much I hate this.

His office looks like any other coach's office. There are two windows on the outside wall, to the right of me is built-in shelving with a mini refrigerator and a stocked bar, and to the left is a small table with four chairs. The left wall is complete with a flat-screen television for watching film and a whiteboard where plans and plays are discussed. Sporadically throughout the room there are memorabilia from his time playing, awards he's won over the years, and beautiful pictures of stadiums and his family.

"How's it going, Jack?" Coach says across the desk from me. He grabs one of the peanut butter and oat snack balls he's always eating from a plastic container next to him and tosses it into his mouth.

My eyes meet his and hold. There's no pity in them; for him this is just another day at the office with another injured player. If anything, he looks resolute.

"Been better," I grumble.

His lips press into a flat line as he leans back in his chair, which creaks—loudly.

"Sorry I'm late," comes from behind me as Dr. Leffers walks in and sits in the chair next to me. It's then I take a good look at the others in the room. There's my wide receiver coach and the team's head athletic trainer; I give each of them a nod as they stare at me.

Dr. Leffers turns to look at me and his brows pull down. "Jesus, Jack. You look like a vampire. When's the last time you saw sunlight?"

I frown at his assessment. He doesn't understand; it's hard to go anywhere. I'm a tall guy and my leg is essentially locked out straight. Instead of answering him, I slouch down in my chair and turn my attention back to Coach. He chuckles at whatever he sees on my face then claps his hands together to shake off the crumbs.

"All right then, let's get started."

Moving, he reaches for a folder and flips it open. My ears buzz as he reviews my contract and the details in regards to a long-term injury like this. I know everything he's saying; my agent went over it with me last week. His words are scripted—after all, organizations like this always protect themselves. This may not be their first rodeo, but it is mine.

"The most common complication of dislocating the knee includes ligament weakness and loss of motion. There's also the possibility that the kneecap may be different after it heals. As you know, complete recovery takes a minimum of nine months, and it can take up to a year. That means next season is out as well."

Next season—gone. *Poof.*

Sweat breaks out across my back with anxiety. I'm already thirty-two. By the time I would even possibly be able to return, I would be pushing thirty-four. The writing is on the wall. Why would they keep me when they could bring in someone younger, faster, healthier? Letting out a deep breath, I know what's coming, and I'm not ready. Why couldn't it have been just an ACL tear? Six to eight weeks and then I'm back at it and with the team I love.

Clearing my throat, I ask, "What happens next?"

Coach tilts his head as he looks at me, like really looks at me. "Rehabilitation. Lots of it."

"When?" I look at the doctor.

"Soon. Maybe two more weeks," he says, glancing back and forth between the coach and me.

Needing to throw caution to the wind, I lock eyes with Coach and ask, "At what point will I be ready to return to the team?"

He presses his lips into a thin line.

"For you to return, Dr. Leffers will most likely want to test your leg strength before giving all of us a go-ahead. He will compare your strength using some functional knee testing, like hopping. The goal is that it be at least eighty-five to ninety percent of your uninjured side. He will also assess your leg's endurance and your balance, and if you are having any swelling."

I know all the things he's telling me. It's a standard story they tell any of us who end up with a knee injury, but it's not the answer I'm looking for, and I rub the nervousness from my palms across the tops of my thighs.

"But you're saying there's a chance I'll be able to return?"

"Again, not next season—that would be a little too aggressive in our thinking—but as for the season after, maybe. None of us can predict how your body is going to respond, how fast it's going to heal, and what type of range of motion you're going to have at the end of the day. All we need you to do right now is take it easy until it's time to work hard, harder than you ever have, and come back to us. You will be camping out on the injured reserve list for a while. There's no guarantee or promises, but, Jack, you've meant a lot to this organization for a long time, and we're committed to giving you the time and the resources you need to recover."

My heart thumps hard in my chest and I reach up to rub it. They didn't say it. They're giving me a chance. If I could I would damn near bawl like a baby, but not here, and definitely not in front of them. For the last four weeks, I've felt nothing but disappointment, and with this tiny life raft into my future, I'm reminded that there's still fight in me. I can do this; I know I can. I just need to find my place here while I'm doing it.

The meeting lasts for another fifteen minutes or so. I can see them assessing my headspace as we talk, not that I blame them. Everyone handles injuries differently. I know they feel the presence of the cloud lingering over me, but a tiny crack of light peeked through today and I know that's a start.

Once the meeting is over, Brett, our athletic trainer, and I make our way into the training room. I'm assaulted by the smell of sweat, metal from the equipment, and laughter from the few guys who are in right now. I miss being in here with them; I miss my team. Granted, I know I'm romanticizing the kumbaya atmosphere—it is the offseason now and most people have left town—but still.

The clinking of weights, the whir of the treadmill, rap music playing overhead . . . another crack breaks through the melancholy cloud—that is until about thirty minutes into working with him when I realize teammates are moving around me as if I'm invisible. Sure, a few toss out a "What's up?" but mostly I only get nods with no eye contact. I've become that person, and people are too superstitious to overlook the fact that I need my team. I need my football family. The crack closes, pushing away the light.

Being here, doing these simple exercises, I'm not feeling invigorated or really even a sense of relief; I'm feeling frustrated and lonelier than I have in a long time. These are not moves of a professional athlete; they don't make me feel like I'll be back with my team here shortly. These are moves that remind me I'm not currently one of them.

Words from my coach filter back through my mind. *"We're postseason now, Jack. You don't have to stay here. You can go home, heal, just continue the rehabilitation and have the trainer check in weekly with progress updates."*

At the time, I immediately dismissed the idea—I'm certainly not going to Arizona. Tampa is my home. Reid and Bryan are both here, and they're like my brothers. Then reality sinks in a little as I think about how our lives have changed over the last year, theirs in particular. Both fell in love and have, in many ways, moved on. Bryan is really only here half the time now as he goes back and forth between here and his house with Lexi in the country, and Reid now has Camille. Sure, I'm always included, but I am the third wheel, and suddenly that doesn't feel so good.

If I don't have Tampa, what do I have? Where do I go? My thoughts drift to Meg, a warm flicker dancing under my skin as the idea of home and her mingle together. It's strange. I've thought about her nonstop over the last two weeks—well, if I'm being honest, for the last seven months. I've only seen her face-to-face maybe a total of five to six days, but she makes me happy in ways no one else does, or at least can right now.

With that, a plan forms, the first plan in weeks that feels good, feels right, and I welcome the new emotions coming in. I've been sitting in a fog, and finally, *finally* it's clearing a little.

Peanut Butter and Oat Snack Balls

Ingredients:

1 cup quick-cooking oats
1 cup coconut flakes
1/2 cup natural, crunchy peanut butter
1/3 cup honey
1/4 cup ground flaxseed meal
1/4 cup toasted wheat germ
1 teaspoon vanilla
1/4 cup mini chocolate chips

Directions:

In a medium bowl, combine all ingredients except chocolate chips.

Stir to combine.

Add chocolate chips to mixture and stir again, just until combined.

Using your hands, press firmly to form one-inch balls.

Place in air-tight container and refrigerate as needed.

Chapter 15

All About the Spice

Meg

THE FIRST FOUR months of the year in Charleston are my absolute favorites. Technically it's winter, but really here in the south it's spring. Every year I look forward to it, and on the first day of March, we celebrate at OBA by changing the menu and welcoming spring-inspired dishes. With the weather cool and mild, our patio fills up with guests first, and they find themselves surrounded by blooming flowers such as roses and wisteria.

In addition to the Wine and Food Festival, there's also the Festival of Houses and Gardens. It takes place the weekend after, and this year I bought two tickets to celebrate. I'm not sure who's going with me yet, but there are a hundred and fifty historic homes calling my name and saying, *Come tour us. Wander through our impeccable gardens and explore our unique architecture.* I truly love that these old homes do this. Outsiders get to wander through the historic district and glimpse the insides through the windows, observing in awe and wonder, and this allows us to step back in time and see it for ourselves.

It's while daydreaming of sweeping grand staircases and elaborate crown molding that my phone pings with a notification in my back pocket. It's seven in the morning, I've just finished making today's haul of madeleine cookies, and I've paused to slip on a pair of animal print heels I brought to wear today and to drink another cup of iced coffee. I am addicted to this coffee, which I have no qualms about admitting; it's just so good.

When I pull my phone out, my brows pull down as I see it's an Instagram post from Jack. Surprisingly, my heart rate picks up a beat as I open the app and stare down at the image. It's a picture of Zeus sitting in the grass with a beautiful old oak tree behind him. Around the tree, fog lingers on the ground. It's a beautiful photo, and I know right where this is: Lexi's back yard.

So that's where he's been, or that's where he is. I wish he had told me; then again, the last time we spoke was about a week ago. Since then it's just been short text messages about our days, the weather, boring things like that.

Part of me is happy to see he's out of the condo and with friends, but the other part of me, the part that allowed myself to believe our friendship is closer than that of others, frowns. I had no idea he was there. He didn't tell me. She didn't tell me. I feel left out, and it sucks. The caption underneath it says: **Man's best friend.**

Zeus really is; I know it—he loves that dog something fierce—but I feel the sting of rejection even though I know I'm being irrational, and I can't help but reply: **I thought**

I was your best friend. It's not original, and others have already commented that they would be his best friend too, but my feelings are a little hurt.

Oh well.

Shaking it off, I bury the rejection and focus on the positive. Bright side, right? He's out. He left the condo. He's with Bryan. And that makes me happy. I want him to be happy; he deserves it.

An hour later, my phone pings again. He's replied: **Ha! You know you are. Looking forward to lunch . . .**

Lunch? What does that mean? I answer with: **???**

Several hours later, the kitchen door swings open, and Taylor pops her head in to find me.

"Boss, you have a visitor." She's grinning hard, and this confuses me.

"I do?" I quickly think back over my schedule for the week and can't come up with anything I might have missed.

"Oh yeah you do," she says, pleased with herself.

"Who is it?" I ask, dipping the spoon into the fresh pot of soup and tasting it. With soups, it's all about the spices, and this one needs just a little more salt to be perfect.

"I didn't catch his name—I was too busy trying to roll my tongue back into my mouth." She swipes her hand over her ponytail, smoothing it down.

"What? Really?" My brows are now rising in surprise.

"Oh yeah." She knows something; she's just choosing not to tell me. I toss the spoon in the dirty dish bucket under the counter and walk over to quickly wash my hands in the sink.

Untying my apron, I place it on my work station and follow Taylor out into the dining room. There, standing next to the marble bar set against the back wall, is Jack. About ten different emotions slam into me all at once, and tears unexpectedly fill my eyes.

I walk straight to him, he wraps me in his arms, and there in front of everyone, we hug as if my life depends on it.

His warmth. His solidness. His larger-than-life size. His smell. His everything.

I'm so happy to see him.

His chest vibrates with a low chuckle, and it's then I realize he's thinner. Pulling back, I look up into his face and see the dark shadows and lines this last month has given him. My heart aches for him, and then it hits me again that he's standing here in my restaurant in Charleston.

"Oh my God—what are you doing here?" I stammer. "Not that I'm not excited to see you, because I am, but . . . gah, what are you doing here?" My hands slide to his arms. He's wearing a navy blue Henley and a nice pair of jeans that cling to him perfectly. I shake him, just a little so as to not throw him off-kilter with the crutches he's still using, trying to reassure myself that he is in fact here and I'm not dreaming.

"Thought I'd drop in and have a late lunch with you." His eyes are latched onto mine, and it's not lost on me that we are drinking in the sight of each other. I knew I missed him, but I wasn't aware I had missed him this much. From his expression, I'm thinking he's realizing the same thing.

"Lunch . . . that's what you meant." I grin, and a tear unexpectedly sneaks out. Reaching up, he uses his thumb to wipe it away as he cups my face, and I reflexively tilt my head just a bit to nuzzle closer.

"Yeah. I hope that's okay." His voice is low and rough. It sounds good, and it feels good as it rolls off my skin.

"Of course it's okay." Leaning into him, I again sink into his embrace as he drops his head and lays it on top of mine.

"I missed you," he says quietly.

"Ditto," I mumble against the softness of his shirt, and his arms tighten around me.

Minutes pass as we embrace and soak up each other's presence. I'm certain we've drawn attention to ourselves and I should have taken him to the office or into the kitchen, but I just can't find it in me to move. I could stand here with him forever, and then I start to panic. I know it's an irrational feeling—after all, he just got here—but he just said lunch, nothing more.

Tipping my head back, I look up as he stares down with his beautiful brown eyes. "How long are you staying?" I ask.

His eyes briefly dip somewhere lower on my face then jump back to mine as he contemplates his answer. "I'm not sure. I . . . uh, I had a meeting with the team's head athletic trainer yesterday, and he suggested that a change of scenery might be good for me. Then my truck just drove itself here."

He's studying me for a reaction, and the only one he's going to get is happiness.

"Really?" I'm in complete disbelief but so elated at the same time.

"Yep, really." One side of his mouth tilts up a little as I let out a sigh.

There's an edge of vulnerability to him; it's endearing, and unwarranted. How could he think I wouldn't want him here? His hand slips up my back and tangles in my hair. I can feel him rolling it between his fingers, and it feels nice.

"Are you staying with me?" I ask hopefully.

"You did say there would always be a room for me at your house."

"I did." With that the largest smile breaks free on my face, and he gives me one in return. It's so beautiful to see him smiling again; it's almost blinding. "Did you bring Zeus?" I look behind him.

"No. Bryan took him back to Lexi's a few weeks ago. He's there running free." I hear what he's not saying: it was too hard with him in the condo. I know they used to go for long walks and jogs; poor guy needs his energy expelled on the regular.

"Okay, well, if you decide you want to go get him, he's welcome here, too."

"I appreciate that. I did drop by to see him this morning, fill them in on what's going on. He's happy there for now, so he gets to stay a little longer."

"That explains your post."

"Yeah, I miss the fur beast and wanted to see him."

"I kind of miss him, too. After all, he does like me more than you."

Jack laughs, and the hairs on my arms stand up.

"I don't know about that," he says defensively.

"Are you hungry? When's the last time you ate?" Of course my go-to is food. Food is love, and I need to feed him.

Right on cue, his stomach growls, and I grin up at him.

"Well, I guess that answers that question." I slide my hand over his stomach, his very flat and defined stomach, and it growls again.

"Yeah, I ate a slice of pie this morning at Bryan's when I dropped by, but that's it."

No wonder he's losing weight. "Then you must sit down and let me feed you."

Taking a step back, I guide him over to a two-top table and take the crutches as he sits.

"So this is the infamous OBA?" he asks, his gaze leaving me and slowly trailing over the details of the dining room. I try to take it in with fresh eyes, but I'm blinded by pride. I love what I've created so much.

Exposed brick walls, wrought iron and crystal chandeliers, high-backed fabric chairs, the wall of honey, the champagne bar in the back, and chunky wooden farm tables. We have an inside dining room and an outside patio that's filled with herbs and potted vegetables. The restaurant is Southern, shabby but classy, light and airy, and it's the perfect ambiance for a delicious meal.

"Yep." I smile at him.

"I know I've seen pictures of it online, but it's so much more in person. It's bigger than I thought it would be." I watch as his eyes roam, taking it all in, and I feel exposed, as if his gaze is trailing over me. Stupid, I know, but this restaurant is my life, and here he is looking at it and forming his own opinions. What he thinks shouldn't really matter, but to me it does.

"I hope that's a good thing?" I'm seeking clarification.

His eyes come back to find mine then he wraps his hand around my hip and squeezes. "The best thing."

"Good. Thank you." He's made me so sincerely happy I could melt.

Silence again falls over us as we stare at each other. I take in how the last month hasn't been the kindest to him, and this makes me sad. Unfortunately, it's so easy to see, and I can't help but wonder what he sees when he looks at me.

His stomach growls again, breaking the moment, and we both laugh.

"I have the perfect thing. We just made a fresh pot of seafood gumbo, and there's some cornbread that'll go spectacularly with it. What would you like to drink? I make a mean iced coffee." He grimaces, and I remember he tasted it over Thanksgiving. "Oh, that's right." I grin. "Forget that. Sweet tea?"

He shakes his head. "Water's fine. Thank you."

"Of course! Okay, you hang tight. I'll be right back."

Spinning, I quickly walk back into the kitchen with my heels clicking on the floor and my heart hammering in my chest. Why is it acting so crazy? Gah, it's just Jack.

Following behind, Taylor slides up next to me as I grab a bowl and begin to fill it. "So, that's Jack?" She eyes me knowingly.

"You know it is. You knew before you told me."

She shrugs while slicing a piece of cornbread and placing it on a small plate. "Maybe. I thought you said y'all were just friends?"

"We are just friends—why?" I look over at her.

She matches my gaze, not backing down. "Sure doesn't look like it."

"How does it look?" My eyes narrow at her.

"Like it's more . . . so much more," she says dreamily.

With that, she spins around and leaves me standing in the kitchen, holding his soup with my mouth hanging open, dumbfounded.

Southern Seafood Gumbo

Ingredients:

4 tbsp. butter
1/4 c. all-purpose flour
1 small yellow onion
1 medium green bell pepper, chopped
2 celery ribs, chopped
2 cloves garlic, minced
12 oz. andouille sausage, sliced into 1/2" pieces
1 tbsp. cajun seasoning (without salt)
kosher salt
Freshly ground black pepper
1 bay leaf
1 (15-oz.) can fire-roasted diced tomatoes
4 c. chicken broth
1 lb. shrimp, peeled and deveined
3 green onions, sliced
cooked white rice, for serving

Directions:

In a large, deep skillet over medium-low heat, melt butter, then add flour. Cook, stirring constantly, until dark caramel colored, about 10 minutes.

Add onions, peppers, and celery, and stir until softened, about 5 minutes more. Stir in garlic and sausage, then season with Cajun seasoning, salt, and pepper. Stir in bay leaf, diced tomatoes, and chicken broth and bring to a boil. Reduce heat to low and simmer until thickened, stirring occasionally, about 1 hour.

In the last 10 minutes of cooking, add shrimp. Once shrimp is pink and cooked through, taste and adjust seasonings. Stir in green onions, reserving some for garnish.

Serve spooned on top of white rice.

Chapter 16

Beggars Can't Be Choosers

Jack

THE RELIEF I felt when my eyes landed on her was so visceral my entire body jolted. It's like for the last month I've been holding my breath, and only now can I finally exhale. I don't know why; the reality is we haven't been friends for very long, but seeing her walk out of the kitchen in her wild high heels and with her curly hair all piled up on top of her head and sticking out, I instantly knew with every fiber in me that it was the right decision to come here.

And don't get me started on her food.

Within ten minutes of her sitting me down at the table, it was covered with the best gumbo I've ever had, cornbread, fried green tomatoes, an order of shrimp and cheddar grits, and little cookies to top it off. I know she has a team of people working back there, but damn, all of this is technically hers, and I'm in awe. Of course, I told her it was all too much, but she just stated that her restaurant was as good as her house, and as the host, it was her job to feed me. Who am I to argue?

Once lunch was finished, she wrapped up what she was working on and beamed at the idea of driving my truck, so I let her take us back to her home. I wasn't sure what to expect there either, but as she parked on the curb in front of a little light yellow row house looking all bright and sunny, I shook my head with a wry grin. This house fits her to a tee.

"So, this is where you live?" I ask, looking around after walking up the front steps and through the front door. Just like at her restaurant, I take in every detail, and every detail is so her. The home is older, two-story—as most are in this part of town—but it isn't ostentatious. In fact, it's quite the opposite, and the decor resembles that of the restaurant: elegant but homey, and one hundred percent her personality.

"Yep. I signed a four-year lease-option contract when Shelby and I moved in. We weren't sure how the restaurant would do, but this summer it will be four years, so I have to decide if I'm staying and going to buy, or if I'm moving."

"Any reason you wouldn't want to stay? It looks like a great home. How big is it?" My eyes trail from the staircase in front of us to the left, which appears to be her sitting room and then behind it a dining room. All over the floor there are boxes of plates and piles of what look like linens, and on the table are different arrangements of flowers.

"It really is a great home," she says as she drops one of her bags on the console next to the door. "It's four bedrooms and three and a half baths. Selfishly, I want to be closer to OBA. I love to walk, but sometimes even I find it a little scary so early in the morning."

My head whips back to her. She's kicking off her heels, and she shrinks several inches to where her head barely reaches the top of my shoulder. My brows draw down, instantly not liking the direction this story is headed. "What time do you go in?"

"I try to be there by five to start baking." She glances at me all innocently before walking into the room on the right and then farther into the house, toward what I'm assuming is the kitchen. Hobbling behind her, I follow.

"Yeah, I don't think I like the idea of you walking there alone in the dark either." I know I have no ability to make any claims about what she can and cannot do, but it doesn't take a genius to know that walking around a city in the early dark hours of the morning is just dumb.

She glances at me again as she places the other bag, the one with the shrimp lasagna roll-ups we'll have for dinner in it, in the refrigerator. There's a frown on my mouth, whereas there's a smirk on hers that says, *Yeah, I don't care what you think about me walking. I'm going to do what I want, when I want.*

My frown deepens.

"That's not safe, and you know it."

Completely ignoring my concerns, she walks toward a doorway under the stairs, and my eyes trail down the backside of her. She's wearing a green T-shirt and skintight jeans that highlight her tiny little ass. I know I'm not supposed to think about how her ass would feel in my hands as she wrapped her legs around my waist, but I'm a guy . . . come on now.

"So, let me give you a quick tour," she says, changing the subject. She looks back over her shoulder and her eyes drop to my leg, the wheels turning as she assesses how mobile I am, but then she shrugs one shoulder and proceeds. "This is the dining room." We move into it, and I watch as she looks at each of the decorations on the table. "It's not usually cluttered like this, but Taylor and I have been planning for a brunch we have coming up."

"Looks like a fancy brunch." The arrangements range from large to small, with an array of items such as different flower looms, dogwood branches, and lemons.

Her cheeks tinge pink, and a small smile makes an appearance.

"It is. I don't think I told you, but we're participating in Charleston's Wine and Food Festival coming up."

She didn't tell me, and I can't help but feel the sting of rejection. I'm not sure why she wouldn't want to share this with me; we've talked just about everything over the last couple of months—well, the months leading up to the injury. I guess I haven't talked much since.

"No, you didn't tell me." I keep my voice neutral to not let her know this bothers me. "That's awesome. Isn't it like a really big deal?" I'm not a foodie and I've even heard of this festival.

"It is." She looks away from me and back to the table. "And it's our first year being invited to participate, so we are being very meticulous about the details."

"I can see that." I chuckle as I follow her gaze and look around at the different place settings and crystal glassware.

"It gets better." She looks back up at me with the sheepishness in her facial expression now gone and replaced with excitement. "We sold out."

Of course she did. Anyone who has ever eaten her food would know she is the best.

"I take it back—that's not awesome, it's fantastic. I'm proud of you." I reach out and put my hand on her shoulder. It slides down, and I gently hang on to her elbow.

She's pleased with my words as a small smile lifts her lips and long dark eyelashes sweep up and down. It's easy to see the pride radiating off of her, and she should feel this way. She's a damn good chef.

"Yeah, we've been working on the menu and who's going to be supplying what like the sparkling wines, flowers, et cetera, and I'm just so excited."

She steps toward the table, and my hand falls as she picks up two forks and holds them out for me to take. Both are a brushed dull metal, but one is silver with a long, skinny square handle and the other is copper with a thin round handle. I weigh them both and instantly like the copper one better. It feels heavier, which I prefer, and honestly I love the color. I hold it up so she knows it's my choice. She grins, takes them both, and lays them back on the table.

"When is it?" She may be sold out, but I'm certain I can convince her to make me a plate as well. I'll toss out the best friend card if I have to.

"Sunday, March twenty-second."

"That's soon." I smile, suddenly feeling a little anxiety for her. "I hope I can help you somehow."

She shoves her hands into the back pockets of her jeans. It pushes her chest out, and I want to groan out loud at the sight.

"Oh, I'm sure you will. It'll be all hands on deck. Zach and Shelby will be here too."

"That's great! It'll be good to see him." I push the sleeves of my shirt up, suddenly feeling warm.

She pauses for a second, and I know she's doing the math. Yes, I hope to still be here then. I know it's a couple of weeks away, but I already promised myself I'll stay out of her way.

"So!" She snaps out of her thoughts. "The downstairs is basically a square. The dining room connects to the sitting room"—she points to the next room over—"and the sitting room connects to the family room, which then connects to the kitchen. The stairs you saw when we entered lead up to three bedrooms, but I'm going to put you in a room on this floor."

She brushes past me, the scent of sugar and oranges trailing her, and she walks down a short hallway that leads to the back of the house. I follow.

"I'm thinking for the time being this one is probably best, even though it's smaller."

She opens a door on the right, and as I peek in past her, it feels perfect.

The bedroom is plenty large enough for me. There's a queen-sized bed in the middle, along with a dresser that has a mirror on top and a chair in the corner of the room. I brought my Apple TV with me and picked up a medium-sized flat-screen TV on the way so she wouldn't have to worry about me being in her space all the time. The dresser will hold it perfectly.

She's paused, waiting for a reaction, so I face her and say, "This room is great. Besides, beggars can't be choosers. I'm just thankful you're letting me stay."

And I really am thankful. Sure, I have friends I've made over the years spread out across the country, but the only person I want to be with right now is her.

"I told you to come visit me whenever you wanted." She reaches up, places her hand on my bicep, and smiles. "I'm glad you're here."

"I am, too."

A heavy pause falls between us and my gaze drops to her mouth. It's free of lipstick, but she's got some glossy stuff on her lips that makes them really damn inviting. Her cheeks flush pink, and she steps back into the hallway.

"Your bathroom is here, just across the hall." She opens a door that's a little down on the left. "When you're ready and you think you can manage the stairs, the bedroom upstairs has an attached bathroom. It's up to you if you want to switch or not."

"Really, this is fine." I'll be out of her way but still near her. Quite frankly, it's perfect.

"Okay." She smiles again. Damn, so beautiful. "This is my office." She waves a hand toward the French doors. "Feel free to use it if you need it."

Leaving the hallway, we weave back through the kitchen and toward another door, which heads out into the little back yard. I know it shouldn't surprise me considering food is her thing, but it still does when I see how many fruits, vegetables, and herbs she has planted around the small space.

"Well, isn't this something."

On the ground in the middle are perfectly arranged flat gray stones with a wooden pavilion over it. Underneath she has a table with chairs and a hammock.

"It's my favorite part of the house." She reaches over and touches the soil of the plant closest to her. Pulling her hand back, she rolls her fingers together before brushing away the loose pieces of dirt.

"Did you do all this?"

"Yes, but at the time Shelby was still here and she helped."

"Well, you gals outdid yourselves—this garden is something else."

"Thank you. I've spent a lot of time out here dreaming up different ideas and recipes for the restaurant. If I'm not there, I'm here, and both places make me happy."

I nod, acknowledging her, but I'm thinking back over her social media pictures for the last year. There have been a couple where she's posing with ripe vegetables or some type of flower, but I never got the impression that they were from a home garden. My level of awe of her has graduated to blatant wonderment—straight hero status.

"So, what do you want to do now?" she asks.

"Anything you want, or nothing at all. I don't want you to change your life in any way because I'm here." A breeze blows by us, and stray pieces of her hair fly around her face. She smooths them down and smiles up at me.

"Don't worry, I won't, but I am excited that you're here. I like having a roommate. The company will be really nice."

"Good." Reaching over, I tuck a loose strand behind her ear. Seriously, I could touch this girl all day every day if she would let me. "I'm going to grab my things out of the truck and get settled."

"Okay, I'll help." She walks back in the house and toward the front door like she's on a mission.

"You don't have to," I call after her.

"I want to. And then afterward we can . . . I don't know, maybe Netflix and chill?" she asks, glancing hopefully at me.

A laugh bursts out of my mouth, and she frowns at my reaction as I catch up to her.

"You know that doesn't mean what you think it means, right?"

Her forehead wrinkles in confusion.

"Though I'm definitely down if you are."

"What do you mean that's not what it means?" she asks, looking up at me curiously.

"Nothing. Come on, gorgeous."

And with that I turn and walk outside.

Shrimp Lasagna Roll-ups

Ingredients:

3 tbsp. butter
4 cloves garlic, minced
3 tbsp. all-purpose flour
2 1/2 c. whole milk
1/4 c. freshly chopped parsley, plus more for garnish
pinch of crushed red pepper flakes
1/2 c. dry white wine
1 3/4 c. shredded mozzarella, divided
1/2 c. freshly grated Parmesan
kosher salt
Freshly ground black pepper
1 lb. large shrimp, peeled and deveined, roughly chopped
Juice of 1 lemon
10 cooked lasagna noodles
2 c. ricotta

Directions:

Preheat oven to 350º. In a large skillet over medium heat, melt butter. Add garlic and cook until fragrant, 1 minute, then add flour and whisk until combined and golden, 1 minute more. Stir in milk, parsley, and a pinch of red pepper flakes and let thicken, 2 to 3 minutes. Add wine, 1/2 cup mozzarella, and Parmesan, and season with salt and pepper. Add shrimp and cook until pink, about 2 minutes more. Stir in lemon juice.

On a large baking sheet, lay out cooked lasagna noodles. Spread a thin layer of sauce in a large baking or casserole dish. Spread each with a layer of ricotta, then top with a thin layer of scampi mixture. Roll up and spoon more sauce on top of roll-ups. Sprinkle with remaining 3/4 cup mozzarella.

Bake until golden and melty, 20 minutes. Broil 2 minutes if you want the tops to look golden.

Garnish with parsley and serve.

Chapter 17

Time is Magic

Meg

I'VE NEVER MET a man who smolders as much as this one.

Yes, he's always had this dark sexy look to him, but before I could let it roll off like it amused me. Here, now, it's more. It's like he's got this untapped emotional heat burning under his skin, and every time he looks at me, I feel singed, from the moment his eyes landed on me at OBA and just about every time since then over the last couple of days. It's unnerving, it's flattering, and it's made me confused because we're just supposed to be friends. I declared it with a thick line in the sand, but every now and then I catch myself dreaming about something more. I don't know what that more is exactly, but it's always him in the thought with me.

A thought I refuse to entertain, no matter how he makes me feel.

Jack and I very quickly settle into a routine. He's still a lot more melancholy than I expected him to be at this point, but then again, this is all change and change can be hard, especially when it's a change not of your choosing.

In the mornings I make a pot of coffee on my way out the door, and he texts me sometime a bit later to say hello. After the lunch hour slows down, he comes in to eat, and then he drives me home as Taylor closes us down. Taylor loves this arrangement as she's getting to sleep in. Then at night he offers to cook us dinner, to which I laugh and tell him to sit down, and then we eat in a comfortable silence. Sometimes we eat at the island, but my favorite times are when we eat outside. Afterward, we curl up on the couch together, talking about anything and everything, and we've watched a bunch of movies and television series.

It was like this when Shelby lived here, too, but with Jack . . . I don't know. It somehow feels more right, and I would be lying if I said that didn't scare me a little.

"Okay, I'm ready for you now," I call out to Jack, who is on the couch watching *SportsCenter*.

Slowly he gets up, makes his way to the kitchen island, and sits at the end. I ladle up the first bowl of soup and place it in front of him. His hair is messy, his face is scruffy, and in his lounge clothes he looks like a favorite blanket I want to curl up in.

"Did you know before modern medicine, soup was essential to healing for a lot of different cultures?" I ask him.

"I've never given much thought to it, but yeah, I would guess so. There has to be something behind the whole chicken soup thing." He slides the bowl closer and takes the first spoonful. His eyebrows shoot up as he tastes it, and I'd be lying if I said his reactions didn't please me immensely.

"There is. Chicken contains a compound called carnosine. It slows or blocks movement of white blood cells, which lowers inflammation in the respiratory tract from the common cold."

His eyes find mine as he keeps eating the soup, listening and not responding.

"Others believed meat from a strong animal could help a weak man and protein-rich soups would help milk production after giving birth to a baby, and in China they made soup with snakes because it was supposed to help with joint pain."

The spoon pauses midair as his face turns horrified. "You didn't put snake in here, did you?"

A laugh bursts out of me. "No, silly, but try this one now."

I move over to the stove and fill the next bowl with the second soup.

"Are you going to tell me what it is that I'm tasting?" he asks, picking up the first bowl and drinking from it to finish it off.

"Nope, not until you've tasted them both. Knowing the ingredients may sway your decision based on what you think you like better versus what actually tastes better."

"If you say so." He wipes his mouth with the back of his hand then takes the second bowl, lowers his head, and sniffs it. "Smells delicious."

"It should taste delicious, too." I grin, untying the little apron around my waist. I toss it on the counter next to the sink and watch as he swirls his spoon then tastes the second soup.

Unbeknownst to Jack, he actually showed up in Charleston at the perfect time. I have been tossing around different ideas to serve at the brunch for the festival, and he's been the perfect guinea pig to try everything I've made. He never complains, seems to love everything I make, and is always ready and willing.

"So, what do you think?" I ask him.

"The first one." He leans back in his chair and licks his lips.

"Why?" I have to force my eyes up to his face.

"It's lighter, coming after the grapefruit I think it pairs better, and well, it made me feel good. Don't get me wrong, this one is fantastic, too, but that one"—he points to the bowl—"can I have more?"

And that right there is always the answer. If you can keep them coming back for more, you have a winner.

Feeling satisfied with his choice, I refill his bowl and make one for myself.

"It's asparagus and pea soup with homemade parmesan crackers."

"What was the other one?" he asks as I sit down next to him.

"Artichoke soup with fennel seed yogurt. The asparagus is easier to make, so I'm slightly relieved." I take a sip and sort through the layers of flavor. This soup actually takes me back to my grandmother's table. It's created a connection to my childhood, and I can only hope it will for the guests too.

My grandmother was something else. She grew it all and then preserved it. It was how she was raised, and in return it's how I was. I spent so many hours in the sun picking things, and it's probably why I love my own garden so much.

"The parmesan crackers are a nice touch," he mumbles, glancing at me out of the corner of his eye.

I can't help the smile that takes over as we both eat without speaking.

"Do you want anything else?" I ask once I'm done.

Getting up, I move to grab some reusable containers to put the soups in the refrigerator. Another thing I've learned about Jack is he loves leftovers, eats them cold right out of the container.

He chuckles and runs his hand through his messy hair. "No. As it is, you're already making me fat. I need to eat less. Can I help you clean up?"

"No, thanks, I've got this." I smile at him as he stands. "And maybe you should stop blaming the food and get back in the gym." My tone is teasing, but I'm not fully joking. I think it would be good for him to get back to a regular workout.

"I'm actually meeting an old friend tomorrow. He's going to help me." He takes the bowl in front of him, rinses it out, and puts it in the dishwasher.

"Really, that's great. Where is this friend?"

"The Citadel." He limps back to the couch and sits down.

"Wow." I'm surprised, although I shouldn't be. Of course he's going to go to the college gym. "You know, I've never actually been to the campus. You'll have to tell me what you think."

I watch as he reaches down to rub his knee. I don't think it hurts; it's just become sort of an involuntary tic.

"I will. I can't imagine it's anything less than perfectly adequate. My trainer back home was happy."

'Back home'—a flash reminder that here isn't. He will get better and then leave.

"How do you know him?" I ask, shoving aside the unwelcome feelings and moving into the living room to sit next to him.

"College. We played together then, and he was my first roommate." He bends over, and I watch as he takes the brace then the bandage off to bend his knee. It's the first time I've seen it since we were at the hospital and they unwrapped it after the flight. Fresh dark pink scars artfully decorate his skin.

"Wow, those are some mighty fine scars you have." I didn't expect them to be so large. What happened to microscopic incisions? I thought that was how they performed knee surgeries these days. I frown at the sight and hate that he now has these permanent reminders.

He lets out a deep sigh. "Yeah, just par for the course. I keep reminding myself that finding a football player who doesn't have a knee scar is rare, so technically I've joined the club." He gives me a lopsided grin, but it doesn't exactly reach his eyes.

"I have a scar, too," I blurt out without thinking.

"Let me see it." He shifts and turns to look at me more directly.

Feeling a little nervous and a lot self-conscious, I stand. I never show people the scar—not that they ask, and certainly never a man; it feels private, like something that's just for me. Even so, I slowly undo the button on my jeans and pull down the zipper. His face lights up and his brows rise like he's pleased with the direction of my undressing, and I just roll my eyes. Such a guy. Lowering the front part of my underwear, I reveal the seven-inch scar there between my hip bones. I've been told it looks similar to a C-section scar, but whatever, it's not. It's a cancer scar.

"It's bigger than what I was expecting, too," he says softly.

"That's what she said," I murmur, and his eyes snap up to mine just before he laughs.

"I can't believe you just said that." He's grinning, his dimples finally making an appearance, and it reminds me of preinjury Jack.

"Why not?" I take a step back and zip up my pants, trying not to feel awkward.

"I don't know, you just surprised me." His face has turned thoughtful as he watches me.

"That's me—full of surprises." I flop back down next to him and kick off my heels. I forgot I was wearing them and could have ditched them an hour ago.

"Does it bother you?" There's concern written across the muscles of his jaw. I know he wants to talk about the cancer—I've watched him try to find ways to bring it up before—he's just not sure how to.

"No. There was a tiny period of time where I wished I had my old body back, but the reality is, I'm not that person anymore. This is my new body, and because of this body I've learned a lot about myself and I'm stronger for it. No going back, right?"

"No, no going back." The tension eases as his gaze drifts over my face. "What did you learn about yourself?" he asks attentively.

"Well, for starters I learned that the body is amazing. As much as I was mentally fighting for me, it was fighting for me physically. Yes, I lost weight. Yes, I lost my sense of taste. Yes, I lost my hair. And yes, I was housing quite a large tumor that it welcomed the departure of by healing quickly. I am so much stronger than I ever thought I was. Even on the hardest days, I know I can push through it, because I already have. It's given me the confidence to know I can defeat anything."

"Hmm," he murmurs, not saying anything, just staring at me with those eyes.

A blush deepens my cheeks. I wish I knew what he was thinking, but I guess it doesn't really matter. This wasn't and isn't about him. It's about me.

"I also learned that time is magic. It's what set the tone to define how I choose to live my life now. You've teased me before about always drinking the lemonade and calling me Little Miss Sunshine, but I have to look for the good in every situation. I want to. Things may not always be crystal clear, but I know eventually the sun will come out. I choose the positive, because what's the point in the alternative?"

His face blanches and he leans back a smidge as if I pushed him. "I'm so sorry. I wasn't trying to make fun of you in any way. I admire your outlook on life. It's one of the things I love about you."

Love . . . not even going to touch that with a ten-foot pole.

"Oh, I know." I turn to face him more and pull one leg up under me. "If I thought you were being mean to me, you wouldn't be here right now." I grin at him. "I like who I am now and the perspective I've gained because of it."

He purses his lips and looks down at the couch between us. Scooching closer, he picks up one of my hands and starts playing with my fingers. I'm once again awestruck by how large his hands are. As a wide receiver, I guess they would have to be, but his basically engulf mine twice over.

"We've never talked about this." His eyes rise to find mine. "You don't bring it up and I'm not sure you would want me to, so I haven't, but I'd like to know more. I'm just trying to figure out how to word my questions without sounding insensitive or nosey about your business."

"Jack, you can ask me anything and I'll tell you." I squeeze his fingers reassuringly and give him a go-ahead smile.

"All right. Did you know you had cancer? Did you suspect it? Did you have any symptoms?"

Of course the first one is a doozy. I really do hate this question. I think Jack is ultimately just curious about me, but most of the time people ask this to educate themselves on possible markers for themselves, things to look out for. While I'm all for empowering people with knowledge, there are thousands of types of cancers and all of them can present differently.

"No, I didn't know. I was twenty-one, and no one that young thinks about cancer."

"At thirty-two, before I met you, I didn't really think about it either." He gives me a small smile, laces his fingers with mine, and then tucks a loose piece of hair behind my ear before tossing his free arm across the back of the couch.

"Shelby had started a blog where we road-tripped, eating at different restaurants, and she would write reviews. Every weekend we were out trying something new, and I noticed I had started gaining weight. Of course, I blamed it on all the food, and that's when we started running. We ran and ran, but the weight never came off, and I started getting heartburn. It wouldn't go away no matter how many antacids I ate. I ended up at the doctor for that, and the rest is history."

"Wow." His eyes widen and his brows rise.

"You can say that again." With my free hand I pull the blanket from across the couch and drag it across my lap. "The tumor was almost the size of a baseball."

His brows drop and he pinches his lips together. Tugging the blanket so it stretches across his lap too, he thinks about his next question before he asks it.

"What was the worst part of all of it?"

"You mean besides wondering if I was going to live or die?" I smirk.

He frowns, hard, but doesn't respond to my attempt to lighten the conversation.

I let out a sigh. "I know it's vain to say my hair, but I was a twenty-one-year-old college student, and losing my hair was traumatic. It was happening to me, and it placed a large blinking light over me letting everyone know I was sick. Lots of people have cancer and the outside world has no idea, but if it's to the point of needing this life-saving treatment, obviously people choose life. Still . . . I've always had this messy mop of brown curly hair. It's one of my favorite features about me, and losing it was hard."

"You do have beautiful hair, but you're so much more beautiful than your hair."

His words hit their target, and my insides squeeze. His hand moves from the back of the couch, cradles my head gently, and then slides down my neck and over my shoulder before moving back to the couch. It's the most intimately I've been touched in a long time, and he didn't even really do anything.

"I hated people saying I had a nice-shaped head, or I looked good bald, or they were certain they wouldn't look as good as me. I didn't choose the look, cancer chose it for me, and it was another reminder that all of it was out of my control."

"Yeah, I can see how that would be annoying."

"But it grew back, and like I said, I grew stronger."

"I didn't know you before, but you are definitely a force to be reckoned with." He reaches over and pulls on my earlobe.

"A force," I echo, and then a grin stretches across my face. "Like, 'May the force be with you.' I think I like that!"

He grins and shakes his head at me. Reaching for the remote, he settles back into the couch and pulls me next to him. As he flips through the channels to find us something to watch, I can't help but think he's a force too, one I might not be strong enough to fight.

Asparagus and Pea Soup

Instructions:

12 oz green asparagus
2 tablespoons butter
1 leek, chopped
1 1/4 cups fresh or frozen peas, 1/4 reserved for garnish
1 tablespoon parsley, chopped
5 cups vegetable stock
1/2 cup heavy cream
Zest of 1 lemon, 1 tablespoon reserved for garnish
Salt and pepper, to taste
Mint leaves, for garnish
Parmesan cheese, shaved for garnish
Parmesan crackers

Directions:

Remove the base of the asparagus and discard. Separate the spears, remove this tips and reserve for garnish, and chop up the remaining pieces.

In a medium saucepan, add the butter and cook over medium heat until melted. Add the leeks and cook for 5 minutes, or until they have softened.

Add the chopped asparagus, 1 cup of the peas, and the parsley. Cook for 3 minutes, add the vegetable stock, and bring to a boil. Reduce heat so that the soup simmers and cook for 6 to 8 minutes, or until the vegetables are tender.

Transfer the soup to a food processor, puree until smooth, and strain through a fine sieve.

Place soup in a clean pan. Add cream and lemon zest, season with salt and pepper, and bring to a simmer.

Bring a small pan of salted water to a boil. Place the asparagus tips in the pan and cook for 3 to 4 minutes, or until tender. Remove tips, submerge in ice water, dry, and set aside.

Ladle the soup into warm bowls, garnish with the asparagus tips, reserved peas, mint leaves, reserved lemon zest, and parmesan, and serve with Parmesan Crackers.

Chapter 18

A Month of Sundays

Jack

ALL MORNING I'VE thought about how Meg opened up last night about having cancer. I'm sure I could have asked her before now, but it's awkward and I never want to upset her.

She doesn't know that after Thanksgiving, when I first found out, I researched ovarian cancer and read as much as I could about it. We didn't discuss the specifics, what stage she had, or what kind of surgery they performed, but I guess at the end of the day it doesn't matter. She had this cancer and now she doesn't. The fact that it's considered rare, with less than two hundred thousand cases per year—it makes me angry that my girl went through this.

And yes, I do think of her as mine, even though I know she's not. Well, I think she kind of is, she just isn't ready to acknowledge what's staring her in the face. But back to the anger, something I'm trying to deal with logically.

I'm certain a lot of the emotions I'm feeling about this are more of real-time emotions, ones typically felt while a loved one is going through this, but it's real-time for me now and I'm having to internally deal with questions like *Why her?* Of course, I don't want to verbalize any of this to her; she's moved on, and I have no interest in dragging her backward to remember the scariest time of her life.

Hearing her talk about what she went through does humble me. I know I've been a sad sack since Tampa, and I've been so wrapped up in my own life and my injury; after last night, I can't help but wonder what she thinks of me. Yes, what she went through and what I'm going through are both life-changing, but thinking daily about how you might not live to see the next year is significantly different than thinking about what my next career path might be.

I know she's sympathetic, but does she think I'm being ridiculous for taking this so hard? It's not like I can change how I feel. This sucks too, and I'm sad.

Pulling into the college, I take in the sights and think about how this could have been my life: a military college. I was right to choose the path I did; I never would have been happy in this life. I needed bigger, freer, more. My personality has always been large, free-spirited, and I don't respond well to people telling me what to do. I've always known this, and it's too bad my father never has.

Meg asked me the other day why I didn't go to stay with my parents after the injury. As much as I love them, their routine is so rigid and boring it's stifling. The walls would have closed in on me and I would have gone crazy if I had to sit there with them, eating at the same time every day and watching the same television programs. For a couple of days, it's fine, but I can't do it long-term. It's not me, and any longer than a normal visit would have put me in flight mode from myself.

I also knew if I was there, I would be missing out on something over here. Whether it was here in Charleston or back in Tampa, I needed to be on this side of the country, just in case. As it turns out, Meg has her brunch coming up. I like being here with her and getting to be a part of it, even if it's just a small part like tasting food.

Food—just the thought has my stomach growling. It's going to miss all her cooking when I head back to Tampa. Then again, as I run my hand over it and feel the slight change the food has already made, maybe not. Whatever, it's worth it. I wouldn't trade this time with her for anything.

Parking the truck, I stare up at Seignious Hall, which houses the football coaches' offices, the locker room, and a top-of-the-line training room. Mentally I begin preparing myself for the world of pain I know my friend Eddie is going to put me through.

Still on crutches, I make my way into the building and into the weight room, where I scan over all the equipment. I'm happy to see Eddie is doing so well.

"Hey, man, can I help you?" A kid over by the free weights that line the edge of the room looks my way.

My attention snaps to his and I realize, while I'm lost in thought, he's looking at me curiously like he knows me but isn't sure where from. How long has he been staring at me?

"Yeah, I'm looking for Eddie Bunton."

His brows rise as he looks me up and down, his gaze lingering just a clip on my leg. Suddenly one brow pops and his eyes widen slightly. He recognizes me, and his cheeks redden. "Sure. I'll go get him for you."

"Thanks."

The kid scampers off, and suddenly I find myself nervous. I've somehow convinced myself that by coming to Charleston, between Meg and him, they're going to make all this better, he's going to make me better . . . but what if he can't?

Continuing to look around, my eyes catch on the large blue and white mural of an angry bulldog on the wall with #CitadelStrength stamped across its forehead. It's fitting for this space, and I can't help but feel nostalgic for my college days.

"Well, well. Look what the cat dragged in. I swear I haven't seen you in a month of Sundays."

Looking toward the voice, I let out a pent-up sigh as Eddie grins from ear to ear and walks straight for me.

"Eddie." I smile back, and he wraps me in a hug, patting me hard on the back.

Over his shoulder, I see the kid is lingering behind to watch. I play my role, smile at him, and give him a nod. He breaks out into a toothy grin then heads back to the wall, leaving us.

"Welcome to the Dawg Pound, my friend," Eddie says, pulling back to give me a once-over. "I swear you're even bigger than the last time I saw you."

A laugh bursts out. "Hopefully the good kind of big and not because I've been sitting on my ass for six weeks."

"Always the good kind, but now that you mention it . . ." His hand smacks me in the gut and I let out an *oof* while shoving him backward. "I'm happy you called." His expression is genuine, and I feel more hope and less doom than I have in a long time.

"I appreciate you taking the time to see me. I needed to get out of Tampa for a bit, need to try to get this"—I point to my leg—"back to some kind of normal before I return."

"I think we can do that." His smile is reassuring.

"Oh, before I forget, this is for you." Bending down, I unzip my bag and pull out a plastic container of lemon poppy seed muffins that Meg made. I hand it to him, and his brows rise in interest.

"What's this?" he asks.

"Muffins from Meg. She said to give them to you as an in-advance peace offering for the pain in the ass I'm probably going to be."

He laughs then says, "Meg," turning her name over in his head. "The reason you're in Charleston?"

I shrug my shoulders and can't help the small smile that forms.

His smile widens. "What is she? Former cheerleader? Grad student? Super fan?" he teases.

I laugh. "No. There's nothing wrong with those, but it just so happens she's a chef. She owns her own restaurant in the historic district."

"Wow . . ." he drawls, surprised. "I never thought I'd see the day, but then again, knowing your propensity to eat, she sounds like the perfect girl for you."

"It's not like that," I tell him. Although, after the last couple of days, I'm wishing even more that it was.

"Well, whatever it is, I'm glad you're here." He claps me on the shoulder.

"Me too."

"And if she feels the need to bake me more food, I won't say no."

"Don't tempt her—your whole office will be overflowing. She loves to cook." An image of her in these ankle-heeled boots in the kitchen at OBA pops up in my mind. She was wearing skintight black jeans, a yellow T-shirt, and an apron with lemons on it. Never a chef coat, always an apron, and who knows, if I'm lucky, maybe one day I'll get to see her in just the heels and the apron. I groan internally at the thought.

"I'm going to drop this in my office. You head over there and sit on the table."

The table looks like any other therapy table, but anxiety rolls through my stomach as I set my stuff off to the side and climb on.

"All right. Let's take a look at you and see what's going on," he says as he returns and starts removing the knee immobilizer. "Obviously, you know recovery is possible, but I need you to be prepared for the common outcome that the injured knee does not regain its previous capacity to absorb stress. I'm going to do my best to help you get it back, but it's going to be hard. Obviously, it'll be fine for day-to-day life, but a lot of stress is placed here"—he taps the lateral side of my knee—"so playing at the level you were before . . . I'm just not so sure."

"Yeah, that's what I'm afraid of," I tell him, not meeting his eye and voicing my greatest fear.

"But, if we take a conservative approach to rehabilitation during the early stages here, keeping range of motion limited and restricting weight-bearing exercises, I'm confident we can get you pretty close to your previous ability. No promises, but I'm in this if you are."

"I'm in it. I don't know what else to do. Football is . . ."

"I know." He squeezes my shoulder as a heavy moment of silence falls over us. "How about you show me what the team trainer had you working on at home. If you've got good leg control through those quadriceps and leg raises, maybe we can ditch the crutches and the immobilizer and graduate to a hinged brace."

"Music to my ears."

"Yeah, you won't be saying that once I'm done with you." He chuckles.

"I'm ready. The sooner I can get back to my team, to doing what I love, the better."

"All right then, let's get to work."

Most of the workouts we do together are routine, basic knee rehabilitation exercises, but then to switch it up he has me on upper body and abs, too. This time he does call me fat, punching my stomach again, and then he puts me in the hydrotherapy tank to not only get some cardio in but also to start using my knee without restrictions. It's here from the top of the machine that my phone pings with a notification.

Meg posted a picture.

Opening the app, I see her face scrunched up in the background like something smells while she's dangling a pair of my tennis shoes in front of the camera. The shoes look huge, and the caption says: **House guest.**

I'm not sure when she took the picture as she's currently at work, but it's funny nonetheless, and I laugh out loud. Quickly I type a reply: **You know what they say about a guy with big feet . . .** and I toss the phone down, grinning.

At the end of the two hours, it's the most exhausted I've felt in a long time, and the most excited.

With a smile on my face, I think, *I can do this.*

Lemon Poppy Seed Muffins

Ingredients:

3 cups of all-purpose flour

1 Tbsp baking powder (make sure your baking powder is no older than 6 months)

1/2 teaspoon baking soda

1/2 teaspoon salt

2 Tbsp poppy seeds

10 Tbsp unsalted butter (1 1/4 stick), softened

1 cup sugar

2 large eggs

1 1/2 cup plain yogurt

1 Tbsp lemon zest

Glaze

2 Tbsp fresh lemon juice

1 cup confectioner's sugar (powdered sugar)

Directions:

Prepare oven: Adjust the oven rack to the middle-lower part of the oven. Preheat oven to 375°F.

Whisk together the flour, baking powder, baking soda, poppy seeds, and salt and set aside.

In a large mixing bowl, beat the butter and sugar together, beating until fluffy (about 2 minutes with an electric mixer).

Add eggs one at a time, beating until incorporated after each one. Beat in the lemon zest.

Alternate adding flour mixture and yogurt: Beat in one third of the dry ingredients until just incorporated. Beat in one third of the yogurt. Beat in a third more of the dry ingredients. Beat in a second third of the yogurt. Beat in the remaining dry ingredients and then the remaining yogurt. Again be careful to beat until just incorporated. Do not over beat.

Distribute batter into muffin pan: Use a standard 12-muffin muffin pan. Coat each muffin cup lightly with olive oil or a little melted butter using a pastry brush. Distribute the muffin dough equally among the cups.

Bake at 375°F until muffins are golden brown, about 25 to 30 minutes. Use a tester to make sure the center of the muffins are done. Set muffin pan on wire rack to cool. After 5 minutes, remove muffins from pan.

While the muffins are cooling, in a bowl, whisk together the powdered sugar and lemon juice for the glaze. Add more lemon juice if necessary.

While the muffins are still a bit warm, use a pastry brush to brush the glaze over each muffin. The muffins will absorb some of the glaze, so you add more glaze to each muffin if you like.

Best eaten fresh and warm.

Chapter 19

Don't Get Your Feathers Ruffled

Meg

TODAY HAS BEEN a great day. I feel like I'm floating on cloud nine, and that's the best kind of feeling.

First we hosted the local news channel this morning. They are out and about doing live, on-location interviews with participants for the upcoming festival. They came in with their film crew, did a tour through the restaurant, spoke to Taylor and me, and sampled some of our more popular dishes. Immediately afterward, we were flooded with phone and online reservations.

Next, I had been waiting for a call from the florist to confirm she can make the arrangements we want for the brunch, and she can. She is having orange blossom branches shipped in, and I'm so thrilled because they are perfect for the restaurant. They represent the name, and they are so fragrant I'm certain the dining room will smell divine. Everything seems to be coming together so nicely for the brunch next weekend. The menu is set, the food and wine are ordered, and the staff have all agreed to be here. I feel on top of things, and it feels good.

Then the cherry on top of the sundae: at his usual time of dropping in, Jack sauntered in without his crutches and without the bulky knee brace. He mentioned he was seeing his friend today, but I had no idea this friend actually worked for The Citadel's athletic department. He still favors the injured leg a bit, but seeing him walk unassisted and smiling was fantastic. Even just this small change for him is like some of the clouds surrounding him have receded.

Now, I'm dressed up and headed out. There's not one cloud in the sky, and the temperature is a perfect sixty-eight degrees.

"I had no idea you were still going on these dates, and I don't understand why," Jack says to me as I bend over to fasten the buckle on a new pair of black strappy Jimmy Choo shoes I recently bought.

"What do you mean?" I glance up at him. He's standing directly in front of me, tossing a football in the air, and he's scowling hard.

"What I mean is, this whole dating thing was your resolution for last year. I thought you were done with it. Why are you still doing them?" He tucks the ball under his arm and then crosses them over his chest. He's frowning at me, and I don't like it.

I also can't tell what his problem is. He's voiced his opinion about me going on these dates before, but he was never this serious. It's almost like he's mad at me.

"I didn't go on a date last month, and I scheduled this before you got here."

"Why didn't you go last month?" he asks.

I grab my other shoe and slip it on. "I just didn't feel like it."

And that's the truth. I hated leaving him behind, and I hated how that made me feel. I was worried about him, feeling guilty for essentially bailing on him when he needed me the most, and I didn't feel like being social.

"Cancel it," he all but demands.

"Why?" I freeze and look up at him again.

He pinches his lips together and looks away from me as I stand to full height in front of him. I like being a little taller when I'm in front of him; I don't have to tip my head back as far, and it feels like a more level playing field, even if I only come up to his shoulder.

He swallows, not answering me, and I watch as his muscles shift under his shirt and tighten around the ball.

"It would be rude to cancel so close to the time we agreed to meet, and seriously, what's your problem? It's supposed to be fun, and I'll be back later, so don't get your feathers ruffled."

"Don't get my feathers ruffled." His eyes come back to mine, and they are like molten chocolate as they stare down at me. "It's not fun, it's dangerous, and I don't like it." He's leaned over a bit and is more in my face.

As I hold my head high, not backing away, a chuckle escapes me. His lips tip down even farther as I tease, "All right, Dad."

"That's not funny." His voice and his eyelids have dipped lower. It does strange things to my stomach, so I take a step back to put some space between us.

"It totally is. Jack, I like meeting new people—you know this. I find them interesting, and you never know what can happen." I turn to look in the mirror next to the door. I unbutton the top button of my shirt, decide it's too revealing, and then button it back up.

"What do you mean by that?" he asks animatedly.

Glancing up, I see his reflection is next to mine in the mirror. He's watching my hands, but as I stop moving, his eyes rise to meet mine.

Suddenly I feel guilty about going. Well, maybe my conscience has been knocking all day, but we're just supposed to be friends. It shouldn't bother him that I'm headed out with someone else, and it shouldn't bother me that I'm worrying about what he thinks.

Turning to move past him, I walk to the kitchen and pick up my purse.

"Think about it—in the last year, I found Taylor from my date in March, learned about a great new local farm from my June date, and recently the guy I met in December hooked me up with a new electrician who's been awesome."

"Wait, you still talk to the guy from December?" he asks.

"Of course I do. He's a great guy."

Jack drops his gaze to the ground and takes in a deep breath. He looks perplexed, and even kind of hurt—but why would he look like that?

"Have you gone out with him again?" He looks back up at me, and the previous disapproving expressions he was throwing me are now replaced with a wariness.

"No, but he has stopped in at the restaurant a few times to eat."

"Has he asked you out again?" He tips his head to the side, studying me.

"He has."

"So why didn't you go?"

"I told you—the whole purpose of this is to meet new people and learn new things, not to find a forever-till-death-do-us-part. People are interesting. I've enjoyed it. You know, we can make you an account too. Maybe you need to get out, meet some new people, have a little fun."

"I don't want to meet new people. I like being here with you." He reaches out and pulls one of my curls between his fingers. My brows draw down. He's not touching me, just my hair, but it feels very intimate, and the strange feeling in my stomach, almost like butterflies, is back.

"You're acting crazy, but if it makes you feel any better, I won't go out with anyone next month." I move to step around him, and he drops my hair then follows me to the front door.

When I turn to look at him one more time, his expression goes serious, and I pause with my hand on the doorknob.

"How about you go out with me instead?" He shifts the football so it's now between both hands, and he compresses it.

"We go out all the time."

"Not really," he says. "And when we do, it's casual. How about I plan something for us?"

Us.

I try not to linger on the word. There isn't an us, not in the romantic sense, even if the idea of it does sound nice. He knows where I stand, knows I just want to be friends, but as he stares at me, waiting for my answer . . . if I didn't know any better, I would say there's a trace of vulnerability in his eyes. What he has to be unsure of, I don't know. At the end of the day, I would go anywhere with him.

"I think that sounds amazing, and I can't wait." I smile, his face finally relaxes, and he smiles too.

"Good."

That one single word caresses my skin. As I wave goodbye and walk out the door, it finally dawns on me that I just agreed to go on a date with Jack.

A date with my best friend.

This date is not going well.

Instead of him meeting me at OBA, I thought it would be a good idea if we just met at the restaurant. I suggested High Cotton because they have an amazing drink called 199 that I adore. It's made with a house-made pineapple-infused orange vodka, shaken, and served in a frosted martini glass. Just thinking about it has had my mouth watering all day, and I figured even if the date is a bust, I'll at least get my drink.

Only now that we're here, he's talking and talking. He's been talking nonstop for the last forty-five minutes about healthcare insurance plans, and now my drink and my dinner have lost their appeal.

Frequently, my mind drifts to Jack and his reaction to discovering I was heading out tonight. He was surprised and bothered, and the more I think about it, maybe he has a right to be. After all, he did come to Charleston to spend time with me, and from this angle it's like I just left him there. It occurs to me that while I've moved him into the roommate category, he may not be staying all that long. I need to clarify with him, and I need to apologize.

"Our company recently switched to a PPO plan, a preferred provider organization. It's great because now I can visit out-of-network providers and they'll still cover some of the cost," he says, breaking into my thoughts while speaking with his mouth full. As if I don't know what that is. I am a business owner, and I do offer benefits for a few of my full-time employees.

I understand some topics are more interesting than others, but he has to know based on my body language that this is overkill. It would be like if I talked for just as long about lard. After all, in the south, fat is defined by bacon fat and lard.

To prove my point, I cut him off and start describing in detail different reasons why one should choose lard as their cooking oil. His face scrunches as I talk about how sustainable it is, and how it has one-third less cholesterol than butter. It's right after I finish talking about how it's higher in monounsaturated fats, which are good for cardiovascular health, and have moved on to how pasture-raised pigs are better than industrial-raised pigs that he cuts me off to ask the waitress for the bill.

Maybe he understands what I was doing, or maybe he doesn't. Either way, we're both polite and relieved in our goodbyes out front on the corner as we know this dinner is the end.

Letting out a deep sigh of freedom, I spot a stand across the street promoting carriage rides around the Battery. My night is now free, and as I walk down the block to the intersection, I think, *Why not?*

"Are you okay?" It's the first thing he says after he answers his phone. Not hey or hello, but straight to a panicked voice.

"Of course I'm okay, silly." I laugh, and in front of me the horse jerks his head away from a fly that's bothering him then neighs.

"Then why are you calling me?" he asks, his tone a little bitter.

"Because I want you to put your shoes on and come outside."

"Why?" he asks, but I can hear him moving through the house.

"Just do it and stop asking questions." I grin. I also realize I'm nervous. That's stupid, but for some reason I am.

"Fine." He hangs up.

A few minutes later, the front door swings open, and he's standing there not wearing the same thing I left him in. He's showered, his hair is damp, and he's shaved. He's wearing jeans and a black button-down shirt, the sleeves of which are rolled up, and he's stuffed his feet into black boots that are only partly laced. He looks like he's about to head out somewhere. My heart dips a little with an emotion that is foreign to me: jealousy.

Suddenly, I don't want to make an account for him on a dating site. That was the stupidest idea I've ever had. I don't want him going out with anyone else, and I think I'm starting to understand why he doesn't want me to either. We may just be friends, but I'm feeling greedy for his attention and time, as he must be for mine.

"What is this?" he asks at the same time I ask, "Where are you going?"

He looks down at his clothes and back up at me. "Food—I need some." Then he pops up one brow as if it's my turn to answer.

"I thought we could go for a ride." I hold out my arms in a *Ta-da!* manner. I'm sitting in an old-fashioned white carriage with the top down and a thick red blanket spread across my lap.

"In that?" he asks incredulously.

"Yes, and be kind." I lower my voice. "The horse's name is Baby Love Love and he can hear you."

The driver turns and winks at me, and Jack just shakes his head.

"How'd she talk you into this?" he asks the driver, who answers, "Money."

Turning, Jack pulls his keys from him pocket, including the one I gave him, and locks the front door. He heads down the front steps of the house and climbs in next to me. He smells so good, and I breathe him in, letting my toes curl in my shoes.

"You do realize this is ridiculous, right?" He eyes me as he runs his hand through his hair then over his knee.

"Yes, but fun too. You're new to Charleston, and I can't think of a more perfect way for you to tour the Holy City." Pulling the blanket up, I toss it over his leg that's closest to mine while he drags it over the other.

"What happened to your date?" he mutters.

"Eh, let's just say we're interested in different things." I scoot a little closer to him, and he looks at me curiously as the driver taps the horse and clicks his mouth. The horse moves, and we jolt backward.

"Here, I got you some of these." I reach down to my purse and grab him a paper bag of candied pecans. "Hopefully they'll tide you over until we're done, and then we can get you some food. I can make you dinner, or we can go out."

He opens the bag, and the sweet smell of roasted pecans wafts out.

"These are great, and I'm indifferent. I wanted to get out for a bit, and dinner seemed like a good reason to do so." He pops one in his mouth, and I watch him chew. He really is such a handsome guy, from his dark features to the line of his jaw. My heart thumps hard as I tell it what it already knows. I could fall for him, easily.

But not tonight. I'll worry about that another day.

"So, where to first?" Jack asks the driver.

"Rainbow Row. It's the name for a series of thirteen colorful historic houses. It represents the longest cluster of Georgian row houses in the United States," he says proudly.

Settling in, Jack wraps his arm around my shoulders and tucks me in next to him. We remain silent as he eats the pecans and the driver tells us story after story. While a lot are about the history of Charleston, he also includes a few spooky ones. He tells us about Lavinia Fisher, the first female serial killer ever convicted. She was also the first white woman ever hung in South Carolina. He pauses the carriage in front of the old Charleston jail, where visitors claim to have seen her ghost. Apparently, according to the legends, Lavinia used her last breath to yell out, *"If you have a message you want to send to hell, give it to me—I'll carry it!"*

Jack chuckles at the absurdity, and as he glances down at me, I can see the strain from earlier has left him. With his free hand, he reaches for mine, tangles our fingers together, and places them on his thigh.

The driver talks about the Gray Man, Nettie Dickerson, and even the Gullah culture and how in the early nineteenth century, old antebellum plantation homes used to paint their porch ceilings blue to represent water. The idea behind it was that it warded off haints, or haunts, as they could not cross water and enter the house.

"Is that why the inside of your porch cover is painted blue?" he asks, church bells ringing for some occasion in the distance.

"No, that's an old wives' tale trick to keep the bugs away. Wasps and other insects see the blue, think it's the sky, and take their nests elsewhere. Although, a very light blue paint would look lovely on the ceiling of OBA." I think about how pretty it would be in contrast to the whitewashed brick wall and the other colors present.

"If you want to paint it, I'll help you," he says, running his thumb over the back of my hand.

"Really?" I ask, surprised.

"Yep."

Later, after we stop for some barbecue and then end up on the couch to watch a movie, my phone vibrates with a notification. Sitting next to me, Jack posted a picture of us in the carriage in front of St. Michael's church with the caption: **Touring the Holy City in style with my favorite angel.**

When I glance up, his dark eyes find mine from his end of the couch. Neither of us says anything, but then as a small thoughtful smile curves his lips, he looks away.

Oh boy. Feelings are changing, whether I want them to or not. I just need to keep my head about me and things will be okay. He's not staying forever, and we're just friends.

I can do this.

I hope.

Candied Pecans

Ingredients:
- 1 cup white sugar
- 1 teaspoon ground cinnamon
- 1 teaspoon salt
- 1 egg white
- 1 tablespoon water
- 1 pound pecan halves

Directions

Preheat oven to 250 degrees F.

Mix sugar, cinnamon, and salt together in a bowl.

Whisk egg white and water together in a separate bowl until frothy. Toss pecans in the egg white mixture. Mix sugar mixture into pecan mixture until pecans are evenly coated. Spread coated pecans onto a baking sheet.

Bake in the preheated oven, stirring every 15 minutes, until pecans are evenly browned, 1 hour.

Chapter 20

Ain't That the Berries

Jack

LIFE HAS BEEN interesting, to say the least.

For starters, it's been a really long time since I've lived with someone. As easy as it has been for the two of us, there's also been a learning curve. I can't walk around in my underwear, as much as I'd like to. Hell, I wouldn't complain at all if she wanted to walk around in hers, but she doesn't. Sometimes I have to tell her no when she wants to cook certain foods, and that practically kills me, but I have to be careful. And as much as I like to have sports on, although she doesn't complain, I can tell she doesn't like it hour after hour. She's more of a music over TV kind of gal.

Secondly, watching Meg work has been insane. She's up at the crack of dawn, works ten hours, and then at three I bring her home, where she works on social media, deals with the business side of things, or cooks to try new recipes. She never stops. Just like at my house, she's a little tornado that's constantly spinning around and moving—in high heels—and it's overwhelming.

Third, although things are easy with us, since her last date two weeks ago, things have been different. She's still funny, kind, and great to be around, but I can see the wheels turning in her head, and I don't know what to think about that. She's more quiet than she was when I first showed up, she blushes more when I touch her, and when I'm not looking at her, I can feel her watching me. I'd like to think maybe she's about to have a change of heart about her whole let's-just-be-friends thing, but my fear is that she'll retreat instead of moving forward.

I don't get it. I really don't. Granted, I've never been interested in a girl for longer than a few weeks, so I'm not a pro when it comes to the ins and outs of a relationship, but if you like someone and are attracted to them, I feel like the possibilities are supposed to be endless. And I like her a lot.

Tomorrow, I will have been here for three weeks, and tomorrow is also the last day of the Charleston Wine and Food Festival. While I've had a grand old time wandering around the city finding something amazing to eat each day, she hasn't left the restaurant hardly at all. I get it, though; I do. This is her moment to shine, and I can't wait to stand in the background and cheer her on. I also can't wait until it's over and things calm down a bit. Call me selfish, but one day soon—fingers crossed—I'll be heading back to Tampa, and I want all the time I can get with her. That's why tonight, I'm going to cook dinner for us and she's going to put her feet up.

"Honey, I'm home," I call out as I enter the house with a bag of groceries.

"Hey," I hear from the dining room.

Kicking off my shoes, I wander into the kitchen to drop the bag, and that's when I find her sitting at the table. Her face is puffy, her eyes are red, and every bit of me goes on alert.

"What's wrong?" I scan her body for injuries. The only time I've seen a hint of tears from her was at the Super Bowl; otherwise, never—like, not ever, not even while watching a movie. So, seeing her like this now, I'm alarmed. Testosterone flares, and I need to fix this, fix her immediately.

"It's nothing. It's stupid. I'm just having a moment, but it'll pass." She lets out a deep sigh then undoes her knot of hair. Dark curls fall around her head.

"Clearly it's not nothing. You don't cry. Tell me what happened." I pull out the chair next to her and angle it so I'm right in front of her. Plopping down, my elbows go to my knees so we are eye to eye. She looks down and fiddles with the rubber band.

"The florist called twenty minutes ago to tell me the orange blossoms didn't get delivered today like they were supposed to. At the moment, I don't have any arrangements for the tables."

My brows pull down. I don't know much about decorating tables, but I do know she was extremely excited for them. A conversation from earlier in the week comes to mind where she said, *"You don't understand—this is one of the largest food festivals in the nation, and I know for a fact there are at least six big-name food bloggers who have booked a ticket for our brunch, and no telling how many others. Everything has to be perfect."*

Now I can see in her eyes that it won't be.

She lets out another sigh, one that's filled with resignation. "Ain't that the berries, as my grandmother would say."

"I'm sorry," I tell her. What else is there?

"It's fine. Only a handful of us know that's what was planned. The guest won't know the difference at all. I called Taylor, and she just sent someone to the store to buy oranges and lemons. Tomorrow morning, we're going to slice them, layer them in the vases, and then just use the greenery we bought to overflow out the top. It'll be pretty enough."

"Yeah, but that's not the vision you had. The florist couldn't provide you with anything else? She has to have something pretty. I mean between her and all the others in town, they should be able to come up with something."

"We talked about that, but with the event, the pickings are slim, and I didn't want to use overly common flowers. To me that takes away from the essence of the brunch: Southern and chic. I know that sounds terrible because I'm certain she could come up with something, but an arrangement with roses . . ." She shakes her head. "How unoriginal."

"Okay. If you're sure?" I ask, just trying to get a read on her one more time.

"I am. It's not what I wanted, but it'll be pretty. Like I said, I just had a moment. I think it's a combination of all the stress and anticipation of tomorrow, but I'm past it. On the bright side, all the food was delivered today."

I can't help but smile. Leave it to Meg to find a silver lining when she's sad.

"The food would be the most important part," I reply sarcastically then lean back in my chair. "Other than that, how did everything else go today?"

"Good. It officially doesn't smell like paint anymore, and we got everything prepped that we could. The tables are all set, minus centerpieces, and Zach dropped off all the wine."

Dumbly, during the carriage ride, I offered to help paint the ceiling blue, and she thought it was the best idea ever. She switched shifts with Taylor the next day, and she and I stayed up all night moving furniture, shifting drop cloths, and painting the damn ceiling what Sherwin-Williams calls Open Air. Don't get me wrong, it's beautiful, but it was a huge undertaking just days before this event.

"I wish they were staying here with us." I frown. I haven't spent hardly any time with my friends since the injury, and I miss them.

Zach, taking advantage of this opportunity to the fullest, decided to surprise Shelby with a large hotel room and tickets to one of the event dinners tonight. Since they spend so much time secluded at the winery, he thought it would be a nice date night for the two of them. Of course, Meg was a little disappointed that Shelby wouldn't be here like old times, but she understands.

"Me too," she says quietly. "But she'll be there first thing tomorrow, and that's when I really need her."

"So, I know you're heading to bed early, but tonight I am going to cook us dinner while you sit back and relax."

"Oh, really?" Her mood is already shifting back to normal. She eyes me suspiciously. "There is that new fuzzy robe Shelby brought me, too. It's so soft, and I could totally use some cuddle time on the couch with it."

"Hey now, I'm a good cuddler, too," I tease.

Her cheeks turn pink and she looks away. "I suppose you'll do."

With that, she heads to the living room, and I head to the kitchen. Dinner isn't fancy—I'm just grilling chicken and some vegetables—but it's work she doesn't have to do and I know it'll taste good. I also bought some peanut butter cookies for afterward. Dip them in a little milk and it'll put her right to sleep.

Laying everything out on a plate, I walk outside to turn the grill on. While waiting for it to heat up, I look around at her beautiful garden, taking in the delicious smells of the early evening air. Across the fence, my eyes catch on something in her neighbor's yard, and I'm struck with an idea—quite possibly a great idea.

Prickles of adrenaline and excitement move down my arms into my hands. Meg said she wanted unique Southern arrangements, and this just might be the solution.

First, on the sly, I call Taylor and ask her what she thinks. She loves the idea but doesn't see how I'm going to pull it off. I tell her not to worry, and she agrees to meet me an hour earlier than planned in the morning.

Next, I call Eddie. He picks up on the third ring.

"Hey, man," he says.

"Hey. Are you busy tonight?" Eddie's been married for almost five years and has a toddler at home.

"Not really, why?" The sound of clinking weights echoes in the background.

"I need some help with something, and we'll probably be out late."

"I'm intrigued. Keep talking," he says, closing what I assume is his office door as silence descends on his end.

I tell him my idea, describing what it will entail, and he's totally on board.

Hot damn.

Peanut Butter Cookies

Ingredients:

- 1 cup unsalted butter
- 1 cup crunchy peanut butter
- 1 cup white sugar
- 1 cup packed brown sugar
- 2 eggs
- 2 1/2 cups of all-purpose flour
- 1 teaspoon baking powder
- 1/2 teaspoon salt
- 1 1/2 teaspoon baking soda

Directions:

Cream butter, peanut butter, and sugars together in a bowl; beat in eggs.

In a separate bowl, sift flour, baking powder, baking soda, and salt; stir into butter mixture. Put dough in refrigerator for 1 hour.

Roll dough into 1 inch balls and put on baking sheets. Flatten each ball with a fork, making a crisscross pattern. Bake in a preheated 375 degrees F oven for about 10 minutes or until cookies begin to brown.

Chapter 21

Slow as Molasses

Meg

THIS MORNING, I choose to walk to work. Yes, it's dark out and I know Jack will be mad when he finds out, but I need the cool air and the extra time in my head to sort through my excitement and anxiety about today.

I know there's always a possibility of something going wrong, but we've planned, organized, and rehearsed the flow; the only thing left to do is execute it. Clutching the box of the place card menus under my arm, I visualize each step and each course of the brunch. I'm certain people will be pleased with what they're served, and if they're not, well, then my style isn't for them. But come on, the menu is delicious—at least that's what Jack told me as he tasted it all.

Jack.

What am I going to do about him? Letting out a sigh, I shift so my bag sits higher on my shoulder.

Every day it seems to get harder and harder to keep him in the friend zone. I knew he was charming, but I never expected him to be *this* charming and sweet. He's gotten under my skin, and although I keep reminding my heart of the promises I made to myself, I don't know what to do about it. Yes, he's still a little off from the injury, not as exuberant as he once was, but I like him. In fact, I really can't think of anything I don't like, from his face, his laugh, and his hands when they hold mine to his thoughtfulness and his sense of humor. There's a reason he quickly became my best friend, but lately I just don't know. I like him living with me, way more than I should, and I worry about how I'm going to feel when he leaves.

But this, him, these feelings—I need to think about all that another day. I can't do it right now as I need to focus on the brunch, and I know this. So, I shake my head, as if that will rid my thoughts of him, and go over in order the things I need to do first today. I have to focus on OBA.

Rounding the corner of the block, I see the lights are glowing from inside the restaurant. Taylor must already be here—seriously, the poor girl is going to need a raise after this. She's worked her butt off, and I'm so grateful.

Through the window, I see movement from several people, which confuses me, then as I open the front door, I'm met with a sight and a floral scent so wonderful my jaw drops and I freeze.

"Surprise!" Taylor yells, throwing her arms out.

As I take a few tentative steps in, the door swings shut behind me.

"I don't understand. What . . . ? How?" I look from her to Jack—which throws me off because I thought he was at home sleeping—to a guy I don't know, and then to Diane, the florist.

"Did you do this?" I ask her.

She smiles and shakes her head. "He did." She points to Jack.

My eyes whip back to him and I see that he's a little dirty, but with his hands shoved in the pockets of a nicely worn pair of athletic pants and that smolder he wears so well, he still makes butterflies take flight in my stomach.

"How did you do this?" I again look at the tables.

"You said you wanted to create a Southern ambiance, and outside of azaleas, I couldn't think of anything more Southern than these." There's a hint of vulnerability in his voice, but there shouldn't be—what he did is amazing, and I'm in awe.

The arrangements have been made, and yes, they still lined the vases with the slices of fruit, but every one of them is overflowing with magnolias. Where I had wanted orange blossom branches, he replaced them with magnolia buds and then surrounded them with the large white blooms. They are beautiful, and there are so many of them.

Tears gloss my eyes.

"They're perfect," I tell him, shaking my head in astonishment. "I don't know what to say. Thank you."

"I did have some help. Meg, this is Eddie." He points toward his friend. He looks to be about the same age, but he's smaller in stature than Jack is.

"Hi, Eddie." I smile at him, and he smiles back.

"Nice to meet you, Meg."

"And Diane and Taylor helped put them together," Jack says as he moves toward me.

"I just . . . You guys . . . Thank you. Thank you so much," I tell them, looking to each person. Everyone is pleased with my reaction, and that just makes this so much more wonderful. I'm beyond humbled that they did this for me.

"Well!" Eddie claps his hands together. "On that note, I'm heading home." He walks over to Jack, they give each other a one-armed man hug, and Jack thanks him again. "Good luck today, Meg. I can already tell it's going to be great."

"Thank you, Eddie. I really do appreciate it."

He waves to the four of us and heads out the door as Diane picks up her bag.

"If you need anything else, just give me a call." She smiles at Taylor, at me, and then lingers on Jack. "Well done," she says to him, and then she's gone too.

Silence falls over the three of us, and I turn to face Jack, completely forgetting that Taylor is in the room. All I see is him. All I want to see is him.

"I'm so happy," I tell him, walking to stand directly in front of him. Those chocolate eyes crinkle at the corners as he smiles at me and drinks me in. It's not a coincidence that I'm wearing his favorite pair of heels today. He's previously commented on them twice, and I like the way he made me feel in them. They put an extra boost of confidence in my steps, and I need that today.

"I'm glad." His voice has dropped a little, and it's rough. Just two little words, but I feel them deep in my soul. Gently, he lifts a hand and brushes back one of my curls, tucking it behind my ear.

Without thinking, I jump up and wrap my arms and legs around him. He catches me easily and holds me to him. The warmth, the solidness, the feel of him against me—I instantly melt into him, and it's the best feeling in the world.

"Taylor, give us five minutes," he says over my shoulder as he starts walking toward the kitchen.

"No worries! Take all the time you need. Well, maybe not all the time—I need to start the madeleine cookies soon." She laughs.

"Your knee," I blurt out.

He chuckles. "Not really thinking about that right now."

Stepping through the swinging door, Jack turns us and pushes me against the wall. It's just him and me, and I'm over the moon with appreciation and gratitude.

"How did you do this? Where did you get all of them?" I rest my arms on his shoulders and lace my fingers through his hair.

"If you tell anyone, I'll deny it until the day I die, but Eddie and I might have driven around all night and cut them out of trees."

I blink. "You what?"

"You wanted Southern, so we went straight to the source." One side of his mouth quirks up.

"You stole them?" I whisper.

"Stole? That's a harsh word. Besides, they don't really have any monetary value."

A vision of him and his friend climbing trees in the dark makes me giggle.

"Oh my God, what am I going to do with you?" I shake my head.

He doesn't respond, but my gaze drops to his lips as his smile grows even more. His perfect full, pink lips . . .

"You keep staring at me like that and I'm going to kiss you." His voice is thick with a longing I've not yet heard.

My eyes rise to find his, and my heart thumps hard. He's serious, and suddenly I can't think of anything I want more.

As I tighten my legs around his waist, he leans forward so our bodies are flush against each other, and he slowly lowers his head until our lips are centimeters apart. His hair has fallen over his forehead and his breath is warm as it brushes against my skin. He's giving me a moment to change my mind, but I don't, and my eyes slip shut as I close the distance between us.

Warmth like I've never known before spreads through every nerve ending at this one simple touch, his lips against mine. I'd like to say I'm surprised by the feeling, but I'm not. Secretly I've been dreaming of what it would be like to kiss him for a while now, and my curiosity is being satisfied at last.

I know this kiss should be forbidden—after all, friends don't kiss their friends—but as his lips slowly begin to move against mine, I can't find it in me to have regrets.

With my weight anchored against the wall, he moves his hands, which tremble slightly, to cradle my face so he can angle me just where he wants me. As our lips part and his tongue dips in to find mine, I hang on tight just before he devours me whole.

Seconds—no, minutes tick by as he takes his time exploring every bit of my mouth. This kiss is euphoric, the best first kiss I've ever had, and I become pliable, wanting to be what he wants, what he needs. Over and over he comes back for more, only stopping to catch his breath, until he finally pulls back to rest his forehead against mine.

His eyes are still shut, his long dark lashes lying on top of his cheeks, and beneath his shirt I can feel the fast pace of his heart as mine tries to mimic it. I find it endearing, and I would be lying if I said this moment—him, the flowers, the thoughtfulness, the sweetness, the love for my friend—didn't put a chink in my very comfortably worn armor.

"I've wanted to do that for so long," he says quietly, honestly.

"But we're just friends," I reply, not wanting to admit the same. A slight sensation of panic rises in my chest. He's my friend, and I need him to stay that way.

He pulls back and looks me in eyes. "Are we?"

I don't answer him, and he doesn't say anything more on the subject.

He lowers me, and I slide down his body until my feet hit the floor. "I'm going to run home, get cleaned up, and change, but I'll be back a little later to help you however I can. Okay?"

"Okay." I give him a small smile, the panic receding as his hand again cradles my face and his thumb rubs back and forth across my cheek.

Bending down, he kisses me one more time, and then he takes a step back. "I'll see you later," he says, giving me a wink, and then he's through the kitchen door and gone.

Holy moly.

What just happened?

Well, actually I know what happened—the best kiss, with my best friend. I clutch my chest as I suddenly feel winded, like I just ran a marathon.

I'm still standing by the wall when Taylor walks in and pops a knowing eyebrow. A blush burns through my cheeks at what she's very accurately assumed, but I can't help but think this is already the best day, and the sun isn't even up.

Sweet broiled grapefruit parfaits
Asparagus and pea soup with parmesan crackers
Fennel and citrus salad with mint
Cornbread eggs benedict
Roasted okra with tomato-glazed shrimp
Seared foie gras with aged gouda grits
Butterscotch and pecan sticky bun

Today could not have gone any better.

Granted, I started on cloud nine thanks to one very tall, dark, and handsome guy, but as the guests arrived and the first course hit the table, everything went as smoothly as possible. From being back in the kitchen and working side by side with Shelby like the good old days to having Jack and Zach both dressed in suits with no ties charming the guests and serving the different sparkling wines with each course, it was as if everyone was in a relaxed, blissed-out trance.

Then again, maybe it's the magnolias. Jack doesn't know this, but like jasmine, the smell the flowers produce binds to receptors in the nose that send signals to the brain, telling it this is the scent of romance. When diffused into the air, magnolia creates a calm and serene atmosphere. It helps relieve stress-related tension, reduce anxiety and depression, and ultimately relax the mind and body—just what we want when people sit down to dine with us.

And dine with us they did. Over and over we heard murmurs coming from pleased palates, photos were taken of the dishes, and nearly every plate of every course was wiped clean. It was a chef's dream come true.

"Something is going on between the two of you," Shelby says speculatively as she slides up next to me. We've just thanked the last guest for coming and returned to the kitchen to finish cleaning up. She pulls an elastic from her pocket and whips her blond hair up into the perfect ponytail as I grab an apron to wrap around my waist.

"Oh yeah it is," Taylor chimes in almost immediately as she exits the walk-in cooler and overhears us. Staff members are moving around us, cleaning to close things down, and politely ignoring what they've just heard. They're good like that. Taylor and I have had many conversations in the kitchen, and not once has my sous chef or any other employee so much as raised an eyebrow our way.

Zach and Jack left a little bit ago to go grab a beer together before Zach and Shelby head back to Georgia, and right this second, with the two of them staring at me, I wish I had gone with them.

"What do you mean?" I ask Shelby as my attention turns back to her. Her arms are folded across her chest and my insides take a dive because I know that look. I'm about to get a lecture, even though I don't want one.

"Sometimes you are as slow as molasses. We all saw the way the two of you were looking at each other today. I mean seriously, the sexual tension is so high and so hot I about expected the place to burn down."

"You're crazy," I tell her, feeling slightly defensive. Taylor moves to stand next to her and nods in agreement. She hasn't mentioned this morning and I don't think she will, but the two of them are ganging up on me, and I don't like it.

I mean . . . maybe there were a few heated looks between us, I can't deny that, but after that kiss this morning, how could there not be? His lips are definitely something I'm not going to be forgetting for a long time, nor do I want to, but we'll move past it soon enough. We have to.

Or do we? After all, the expression friends with benefits was coined for a reason.

"You do realize the man has it bad for you, and I'm pretty sure he has for a while, right?" Taylor says, and my benefits thought comes to a screeching halt. She turns to Shelby. "Did you know he comes here every day to eat lunch and spend time with her? As if they don't see each other enough the rest of the day when she's not here. Then when she's ready to go, he drives her home."

"No, I did not know that." Shelby turns accusatory eyes my way. "Keep this up and you're going to hurt him. Do you want that?" she asks, making me feel like I'm somehow doing something wrong.

Anger rises a little as I stare at my friends. "How would I be hurting him? He knows I don't want to date—anyone— and it's not like he's staying here forever. This is temporary. He knows it, and I know it too," I say defensively.

"He may know you don't want to date anyone, but that doesn't change the fact that you're allowing him to fall for you, and you won't commit. You don't commit. You've never committed to anyone."

I pause and think about what she's just said. She makes it sound—makes *me* sound like my promises to myself are a bad thing. She knows better than anyone why I am the way I am, and my anger now mixes with hurt.

"I'm not *letting* him fall for me. I'm not responsible for anything he does. Besides, I like my life the way it is, and you know this." I do. Things are simple, easy, and predictable.

There's no drama, and not only do I like the peace that brings, I need it.

"Yes, but we're not just talking about your life—we're talking about his, too. He's a nice guy, Meg, and it's not fair to him." She shakes her head and frowns.

Am I not being fair to him? I don't think that's the case. I hear what they are saying, and I know how it looks from the outside, but we aren't like that. We never have been. Other than that kiss, we've always been just friends. I want us to just be friends.

Come to think of it, from everything he's ever told me, he's never really done the relationship thing either, and he's also not a monk. I'm sure he's had plenty of friends with whom he had benefits with over the years, and if it wasn't a problem for him then, why would it be now? If anything, this conversation with them is giving me a little perspective about how things might be with him if I wanted them to be. He understands me, and I understand him: Charleston, Tampa, football, OBA, distance, different lives, friends, best friends. It's the perfect situation for both of us.

Taking a step away from them and toward the office, I need this conversation to end, and I need them to know I'm ending it. "You are both overthinking this. We're just friends. He knows we're just friends. There's nothing to worry about."

"Are you sure about that?" Shelby asks as she pins me with one last disapproving look.

Butterscotch and Pecan Sticky Bun

Ingredients:
   3/4 cup milk
   1 tbsp + 1/2 tsp quick rise yeast
   1/2 cup sugar
   1/2 cup unsalted butter (6 tbsp softened, 2 tbsp melted)
   2 large eggs
   20 oz all-purpose flour, by weight (4 cups, measured)
   3/4 tsp salt
   1 cup light brown sugar
   2 tsp ground cinnamon
   1 cup chopped, toasted pecans
   For the glaze:
   6 tbsp brown sugar
   5 tbsp sweetened condensed milk
   2 tbsp bourbon whiskey
   1.5 tsp corn syrup
   4 tbsp butter
   1/8 tsp vanilla extract
   1/16 tsp salt
   1/16 tsp baking soda

Directions:
   Heat the milk to 110 degrees. Place the milk in the bowl of a stand mixer along with the yeast. Add the sugar and 6 tbsp softened butter. Mix at medium speed until the butter is broken up, about 1 minute.

Beat in the eggs one at a time. Next, add the flour and salt, and mix on low for 2 minutes. Bump the speed up to medium, and beat for another 2 minutes. Shape the dough into a ball and cover the bowl with plastic. Let the dough rise for 45 minutes (it will barely rise).

Lightly flour a work surface, and roll the dough out into a 10 by 24 inch rectangle.

Mix the light brown sugar, cinnamon, and melted butter, and spread evenly all over the dough. Cut the dough into 12 strips (so each strip is 2 inches wide and 10 inches tall). Roll each strip up tightly and place into buttered muffin tins. Let rise for 1 hour.

Bake the buns in a 325F oven for 25-28 minutes, until golden on top. Plan to prepare the glaze 5 minutes before the buns are done so you can add the glaze to the buns while they're hot (that way the glaze soaks in a bit).

For the glaze: Bring the brown sugar, sweetened condensed milk, bourbon whiskey, corn syrup, and butter to a bubble over medium high heat, and cook for 3-4 minutes, stirring frequently. Remove the pan from the heat and add the vanilla, salt and baking soda. Stir for 1 minute until it has dissolved. It's now ready to be poured onto the sticky buns.

Finish the sticky buns by sprinkling the tops with the toasted pecans. Enjoy!

Chapter 22

Suits Your Fancy

Meg

ABOUT AN HOUR after Taylor and Shelby ambush me about Jack, he and Zach stroll back into OBA as we are finishing up on the final details before going home for the day. I can't help but look at him differently, and I like what I see. I also like how I feel when I look at him.

Maybe they're right. I'm not a dense person—I know he's attracted to me, know he has been since the party last summer—and I am attracted to him too. How could I not be? He's quite possibly the nicest guy I've ever known, and he's genuinely beautiful on the inside and out. That said, he knows where I stand on things, so if he gets hurt, it isn't going to be by me; it would be by himself. I've never led him to believe I want anything other than friendship from us.

And I stand behind that.

As the five of us head out onto the street to lock the door, Taylor flips her hand up in farewell before sauntering down the sidewalk toward her apartment, Zach and Shelby hug us one last time with promises to see us both soon, and then it's Jack and me left staring at each other.

He gives me one of his signature smiles, and my stomach tightens; he can't see the confusion mixed with today's adrenaline swirling in my head. He holds out his hand, silently asking for mine. Slowly, I slip it into the warmth of his, and the rightness and easiness between us soothes the war in my heart.

I'm not hurting him. He knows where we stand, and I think he's always known what we could be, because he's done this before. Maybe I should have figured this out and considered my options with him sooner.

"You ready?" he asks, a breeze blowing up off the street and ruffling his hair—hair I had my hands in earlier.

I know he's just asking if I'm ready to go home, but after listening to Taylor and Shelby talk about hot sexual tension, those two words have shaped a different question in my head: Am I ready for more? What that more includes, I don't know, but when it's just me and him, things do feel right. Things feel easy.

"I am," I say, almost shyly. His smile grows even more, showing his dimples, which I love so much.

"All right, then let's go home." He takes a step, our fingers lace together, and I fall into place next to him, thinking about the word home.

Home has always been a place, but right this second, it sure feels like him. I feel at home with him, and I like it.

Once we get there, we move to our sections of the house as if on autopilot and proceed to wash off the day. There's no question as to our routine; it's the same one we've been going through for weeks. Home, shower, change into something comfortable, cook dinner together, eat either outside, in the dining room, or on the couch, and then we curl up together in front of the television with a dessert, usually cookies since they seem to be his favorites. Although, after that kiss this morning and how I'm feeling now, I can't help but wonder if maybe tonight will be different. Do I want it to be different? Does he?

That question is answered as I round the corner to head into the kitchen at the same moment the door to the bathroom in his hallway swings open and steam floats through the air. Jack steps out and goes to turn toward his room, but he comes to a stop when he sees I'm standing there frozen. Sure, I've seen him in a towel before, but after everything that's happened today, it just feels like so much more, and a blush burns up my neck and into my cheeks.

"Meg," he says, his voice a little lower and deeper than usual. I know I should move, but I can't.

Silence falls over us for a few breaths, and the light in the hallway brightens as the steam clears. Dragging my eyes up from the shadowed dips over his hip bones to his face, I find his dark eyes even darker than usual, the lids lowered halfway. With his wet hair falling over his forehead, his straight nose, and his smooth jawline, I realize everything, just everything about him is perfect.

"Can't you be flawed somewhere?" I ask him, my eyes falling to his chest to peruse each and every muscle on display.

"I have flaws . . . you know I do," he answers lowly, watching me.

I want there to be a hint of a smile in his words, but there isn't. They are heated and a tiny bit vulnerable.

"You know, this isn't the first time you've looked at me like this, and I gotta say, I like it. I like it a lot, Meg." He takes a step closer to me and my eyes return to his. His vulnerability seems to have dissipated with the steam; these words are bold—bolder than I am.

"How? How am I looking at you?" I ask, tilting my head up to get a better look at him.

Color blooms high on his cheeks and he runs his tongue over his bottom lip. "Hmm," he murmurs, dragging his weighted gaze over the entire length of me. "Like I'm the last bit of batter in the bowl and you can't wait to swipe your finger through it then lick it clean."

Oh my.

"That's descriptive," I whisper, my heart rate and my breathing picking up.

"Isn't it, though? And accurate," he says assuredly, taking another step closer.

"It's just"—I wave my hand toward his shoulders, chest—"and the . . ."—his stomach, hips, the soft dusting of dark hair that leads down to the bulge slowly, which is getting larger under the towel. "You're perfect," I mumble in a low groan.

As if in a trance, I watch as he slowly lifts his right hand and undoes the knot of the towel around his waist. It drops to the floor, puddling at his feet. I stop breathing as I take in all of him, from feet to waist, and oh my God, Jack is naked in front of me. Naked.

A tiny noise escapes me as I'm rewarded with miles and miles of muscles on muscles and his smooth olive-colored skin. I want to look away, but I can't. Who would? From the dip just above his collarbone down to the space where his hip meets his leg, I can see the allure of being a sculptor, because he is the perfect male specimen. I know with a clarity that's almost disheartening he has ruined me for all other men.

Looking up, I find his eyes and see that he's watching me take him in. That smoldering look of his has intensified, and my heart squeezes inside my chest. He blinks, long and slow, his dark eyelashes briefly touching his cheeks, and then his gaze is aimed back at me.

"I showed you mine—you show me yours. It's only fair," he teases, the side of his mouth twitching like it wants to smile. There are questions in his eyes, but the longing is winning out.

"I don't know if I think that's a good idea," I tell him honestly, though I'm more than ready to throw caution to the wind.

"Are you kidding? It's a brilliant idea." He takes another step closer but doesn't reach out to touch me. He's letting me decide. It's my choice. His cards are on the table, he wants this, and deep down I know I do too, at least once.

I reach for the hem of my shirt, his eyes flaring just a fraction as I pull it up and over my head, leaving me in my bra and tiny pajama shorts. Some of my damp hair falls free from the top knot it's in, and I make no move to push it back. My arms fall to my sides as he looks me over just once and then says, "More."

Heat pools low in my stomach as I tug on the drawstring to my shorts and they drop to the floor. Somewhere in the back of my head I think this is probably a bad idea, but as he lifts a finger and traces it along the top edge of my bra, a shiver runs through me and I forget everything around us. I unhook the back and together we watch as it slips to the floor.

"Damn." He lets out an audible breath as his eyes fall to my chest, and that's when I see exactly what me undressing in front of him has done to him. He is hard, insanely hard and long, and I can't look away. I did this to him—me—and the part of me that wants to be a wild seductress cheers on the inside.

Feeling my insecurities slip away, I push down my underwear and step toward him as I step out of them. Lacking any self-control, I run my hands over his stomach and up his chest. He lets out a moan and tips his head back just a little but keeps his eyes on me. I know I should blink and breathe and do all those other things that are required for me to live, but I feel invincible and courageous as I run my hands back down his sides, over his hips. I push my thumbs into the space just between that delicious V and his hip bone.

"You sure about this?" his gravelly voice asks, giving me what feels like one last out. His hands clench at his sides; he wants to put them on me, and I need to feel them too.

"Seems pointless to stop now, don't you think?" I look up into his chocolate eyes and get lost.

"Just checking, because once I put my mouth on you, it's game over." He issues his warning, and I can't help but smirk in return.

"I'm pretty sure I'll be the one winning this game," I tell him, and he groans.

Leaning toward me, his hand slips behind my head, and with the self-assurance only someone like Jack can possess, he lowers his lips to mine as if it's something we've done every day for years.

One of my hands falls to his chest, landing over his heart, and the other grips his waist as he takes the final step, closing the distance between us. He's so much taller than I am, and that impressive hard length of his flattens against my stomach.

Unlike this morning, he slowly takes his time exploring, learning, and then coaxing my lips open. I freely allow him to take control as his tongue again tangles with mine, and the restraint he's been exercising slips away, now bordering on desperation.

Delicious. It's the only word that comes to mind. Well, that's not true—*mine* floats at the peripheral, too, but I don't allow myself to go there because he's not mine and never will be. At least not like that.

Time passes; I don't even know how much. I'm locked under his spell as he kisses me over and over again like a possessed man, and then I'm being hoisted in the air and pressed against the hallway wall. My legs wrap around his waist so we're now eye to eye, and I'm seeing a different side of Jack from what I saw this morning, one I never thought I would. *Sexy.*

"You are so tiny," he mumbles against my lips, never separating us.

To which I reply, "And you are so . . . large."

He catches the innuendo and chuckles as his tongue dips in, wrapping around mine, and his hands squeeze my butt then stroke up the backs of my thighs.

"Just once," I say to him, pulling back and looking him in the eye. "Friends." I nod my head, needing him to know this isn't going to change things.

"Whatever suits your fancy," he says—a little too easily— and then he brings his hands to my face, silencing me again with his lips. He's intense, just the way I imagined he would be, only I never really thought it would happen with me.

I feel him reach underneath me and stroke himself, and then he rubs the tip over me. My eyes roll back in my head at how much I want this, how he can feel how much I want this, and we're going to do this, right here, right now. Every muscle in my lower half tightens in anticipation.

"Can't wait," he says, moving his mouth to my neck, his fingers touching me while I hold on to him.

My head tilts to give him access as he licks up the column of my neck, his hot breath and his hot skin branding me.

"Your leg?" I question. I can't have him hurting himself.

He shakes his head as if that is the furthest thing from his mind, to which I reply, "Don't wait then," and lock my ankles together.

"Pill?" he asks against my lips, both his and mine now swollen and damp. I nod, because this is a conversation I'm not ready to have with him, and also because I'm unable to articulate anything else. The next thing I know, he's sliding in deep.

"*So tight . . . so soft,*" he mumbles against my cheek as he drives into me and loses himself in the feel of us. I know I should be worried about how this might change us and what this might or might not mean, but I just can't. After I lose myself the first time and he carries us the few steps down the hall to his bed, all concerns drift away as he wraps his mouth around my breast, finds every erotic zone on my body, and gives me the singular best night of sex of my entire life.

Chocolate Chip Cookies

Ingredients:
- 1 cup salted butter* softened
- 1 cup white (granulated) sugar
- 1 cup light brown sugar packed
- 2 tsp pure vanilla extract
- 2 large eggs
- 3 cups all-purpose flour
- 1 tsp baking soda
- ½ tsp baking powder
- 1 tsp sea salt
- 2 cups chocolate chips (or chunks, or chopped chocolate)

Directions:

Preheat oven to 375 degrees F. Line a baking pan with parchment paper and set aside.

In a separate bowl mix flour, baking soda, salt, baking powder. Set aside.

Cream together butter and sugars until combined.

Beat in eggs and vanilla until fluffy.

Mix in the dry ingredients until combined.

Add 12 oz package of chocolate chips and mix well.

Roll 2-3 TBS (depending on how large you like your cookies) of dough at a time into balls and place them evenly spaced on your prepared cookie sheets.

Bake in preheated oven for approximately 8-10 minutes. Take them out when they are just starting to turn brown.

Let them sit on the baking pan for 2 minutes before removing to cooling rack.

Chapter 23

Count Memories, Not Calories

Jack

THE CLANGING OF weights and the lighthearted jabbing from athletes here in the weight room at The Citadel briefly pull me from my thoughts, and I frown. It's a familiar sound, one I've listened to for the last fifteen years and one that used to bring me contentment. The gym, the guys, the sweat—it always brought me solace, but I've spent the last four hours pushing my body, hoping to clear my head and untangle the knot in my chest, and it isn't working. Nothing is working.

I should have taken her more seriously and listened when she said just once. Technically, we were together more than once, but it was just one night, one very long perfect night, and here we are seven days later and I'm not sure what to do.

I thought things would be different between us afterward, but according to her, nothing has changed, whereas for me, everything has. I already knew I had been teetering on the fence as far as what my emotions really were for her, and as much as I might have denied it to myself, the truth was glaring right at me, and now I find myself in a place I didn't expect to be by myself.

The morning after the brunch, the morning after she let me spend the entire night worshipping her body, I woke to the smell of breakfast. The restaurant is closed on Mondays, so I had been hoping to spend most of the day in bed with her, repeating the night before, but as I wandered into the kitchen and tried to kiss her good morning, she squealed, laughed, and dodged me.

I couldn't help the sinking feeling that settled into my stomach as she looked up at me, smiled shyly, and said, "Friends, remember?"

All I could answer her with was, "Right."

Of course she was her typical bright and happy self, cracking jokes about the waffles and telling me they're just pancakes with abs, but I couldn't find it in me to laugh back. I don't think I've laughed all week.

I'm confused.

No, I've never had a real long-term relationship. It wasn't something I wanted, but I'm trying with her and getting nowhere. I've given her time. I've tried to be what she needs. I'm certain she knows how good things could be between us, but for whatever reason she has indefinitely friend-zoned me, and I'm not sure what else I can do.

The question is . . . why?

All week I have watched her, much closer than I did before, to try to figure out what is going on in her head, and what I've realized is she keeps everything surface level. I'm not surprised I didn't pick up on this before; in many ways, I guess I am the same way, but with her it just seems like so much more. Or should I say less?

Yes, she is happy all the time, and one of the things I adore about her is how she finds the beautiful even in the ugly, but that's it. Other than the incident over the flowers, in the last nine months, I've never seen any other emotion from her. She's calm, easygoing, and never lets things ruffle her feathers or get her riled up. Things just tend to be smooth around her all the time. There's never any conflict, she diffuses anything that could potentially be uncomfortable, and she's just sailing through day by day.

Is it that she thinks something will change? I mean from my standpoint, things would only get better, so is she afraid of being hurt? Was she hurt before? She's never alluded to anything happening in the past, but maybe she just hasn't told me. I know she cares for me; I've had plenty of female friends over the years, and none of them have ever looked at me like she does. There's also the fact of how she was with me on Sunday night. She didn't act or look like she was just trying to get it out of her system. She clung to me as tightly as I did to her, so what is it?

It can't be the distance when I rejoin the Tampa team. That's just a tiny hiccup in the grand scheme of things, and we would figure it out, like we did before. Only this time, I would know she's mine versus wondering if she ever would be, and it's not like it would be forever. I only have maybe a few more years left in the league.

So, I'm back to my original question of why.

"I don't think it's possible for anyone to scowl harder than you are right now. What gives?" Eddie asks as he comes to stand next to me.

"Nothing," I mumble.

Looking away from him, I stare down at the pool of ice water I'm sitting in and frown. The timer reads five more minutes.

Since the day I arrived and we changed the brace I'm wearing, my knee has had swelling. In fact, I'm certain it's had swelling since the minute it was hit, and it just won't go away. Sometimes in the mornings, it's a little less, but by bedtime it's so angry at me I find I'm having to take prescription medication to reduce the inflammation.

I know it's related to mechanical stress, but my quadriceps and other related muscles are weakening to the point where I'm off balance from one leg to the other. I feel off, and it sucks. From gait and range of motion to strength and stability, none of it feels right, and it has me worried. I'm too old for this to be happening in my career. Rationally I know it's only been two months and the healing is going to take a substantial amount of time, but even I know if I can only get back to eighty percent, odds are I'm going to be replaced. Younger, faster, eager—if I were a coach, that's what I would be looking for. The team is a business, and they have to run it as one.

"Sure doesn't look like nothing. Besides, you've been quiet and stuck in your head. Look, I know you hate this, but I promise there has been gradual improvement in the stability of your knee. You know it takes time."

I know it does, but it's taking a lot of time, and I've never been one to sit still. Patience is hard for me, and between this, the possibility of losing my job, and Meg, I'm losing my mind. I don't like how any of it feels, physically, emotionally, or mentally. It's making me restless in my own skin, and I want to feel settled. Right now, I can only handle one thing at a time, and it feels like all aspects are precarious.

I don't answer him, and he accepts the silence as he claps me on the shoulder and just stands next to me.

"Damn, what did she do to these to make them so good?" He holds up one of the brownies Meg made for him.

"I think it's just the pecans, but who knows. For some reason, all her food tastes better than normal. She likes to cook for people she cares about. After the all-night flower escapade, you're officially in the inner circle. Get used to it."

"No wonder you're wanting to be in the hydrotherapy tank all the time—need to burn off all the extra calories she's been filling you with." He chuckles and takes another bite.

"Meg says we should count memories, not calories." I recite her mantra, remembering her face when we were outside a couple of weeks ago eating in the back yard. She had made us a blackened shrimp and alfredo pasta dish, and I was staring down at the plate like it was offensive when she laughed next to me. She was so relaxed, so carefree, and so beautiful. She slurped up the noodles, grinning, and I remember thinking I could do this with her forever. I guess she's right—that dish will always be associated with a memory, a memory I want more of.

"Does she now?" He smirks, thinking all is well at home with us. If only he knew, but then again knew what? That she doesn't want me the way I want her?

I flip him off, and he laughs, attracting the attention of others in the training room, including the head football coach Brick Meyers.

"Jack." He wanders over and glances at the brownie Eddie is eating.

"My office," he mumbles between bites, tilting his head. "Meg made them." Over the last week, Meg has become a legend with her goodies. Now, when people see me, they look for a plate, too.

Coach's eyes flare a bit in excitement then turn back to me. "You got a few minutes before you head out today?" he asks.

"Of course," I answer him.

They've been so welcoming and accommodating to me, and I immediately offered to help in any way I could while I was here. Coach has taken me up on this, and we've spent a lot of time reviewing their playbook, going over ideas on how to teach different technical and strategic aspects of offensive football to his players, and looking at talent videos of potential players as they head into their senior year of high school.

To tell the truth, it's been fun. When I left Tampa, I felt disconnected from my team, but here I've been absorbed into theirs, not only by the staff but also by the players, who now feel comfortable enough to come up and say hello. It's noise, and I like the noise.

"Great. Whenever you're ready, you know where to find me," he says as he turns for Eddie's office to snatch a brownie.

"Three more minutes," Eddie tells me as he glances down at the timer.

"Got it." I nod as he wanders off to see to a kid who's been dealing with a tight hamstring.

Everything takes time; I know it does. I just need to keep reminding myself to not let my heart outpace my head. Before I can change my mind, I grab my phone off the ledge next to the tub, take a photo of my legs under the water, and caption it with this: **Some things are worth the wait.**

It'll be a constant reminder for me, plus, she's a smart girl. I hope she reads between the lines.

Southern Pecan Brownies

Ingredients:
1 cup butter
1 1/2 (4-oz.) semisweet chocolate baking bars, chopped (6 oz.)
2 1/2 teaspoons vanilla extract
1 1/4 cups all-purpose flour
1 cup Dutch-process cocoa
1 1/4 teaspoons kosher salt
1 2/3 cups granulated sugar
1 cup packed light brown sugar
3 large eggs
1 large egg yolk
1 cup chopped toasted pecans

Directions:
Preheat oven to 350°F. Line 2 (8-inch-square) baking pans with parchment paper, leaving a 2-inch overhang on all sides to easily lift brownies out of pans.

Place butter in a microwavable bowl, and heat on HIGH in 30-second intervals, stirring after each, until melted (about 1 minute total). Stir in chocolate until melted; stir in vanilla, and set aside.

Stir together flour, cocoa, and salt in a large bowl; set aside.

Place granulated sugar, brown sugar, eggs, and yolk in a large bowl. Beat with an electric mixer on high speed until pale and thick, about 1 1/2 to 2 minutes. Stir in melted chocolate mixture. Using a rubber spatula, gently fold in flour mixture. (Batter will be very thick.) Fold in pecans, if desired. Divide batter evenly between prepared pans.

Bake in preheated oven until a wooden pick inserted in center of each pan comes out with a few moist crumbs and tops are set and shiny, 25 to 28 minutes. Remove from oven, and cool completely in pans on wire racks, 1 hour. Use parchment handles to lift cooled brownies from pans; cut and serve.

Chapter 21

Hanging On to Hope

Meg

THINGS ARE NOT going well.

It was stupid of me to think things would stay the same after we spent the night together. We agreed to just once, and although we've both kept our end of the deal, we've been off since the morning after, and I don't know how to get us back to what feels like normal. It's like this wall has gone up between us, and as much as we are moving through the days together like always, he now feels more like a roommate than my best friend, and I don't like it. It's almost like his behavior is a polite formality versus what it was before: open, engaging, and cozy.

I just don't understand what he wants from me.

I saw the picture he posted on social media last weekend, and it did stir emotions in me, but not the good kind. Granted, I may be taking it personally because things feel off when the reality is the photo might have had nothing to do with me, but I don't think that's the case. He knows I don't want a relationship, knows I like the way things are, so I'm not sure what he's waiting for. It makes me angry, because I feel like he's not taking me seriously, and I don't like feeling like this, especially when it comes to him. Normally I do pretty well at not worrying about what others think of me, but with him it's different.

He is different.

He's important to me—very important—and other than Shelby and Lexi, I've never had a friend like him.

Because of that fact, I'm trying to not feel completely consumed by how this shift is affecting just me, trying to be sensitive to how he feels as well. Maybe Shelby was right, but then again, he's got a lot going on right now. We'll get through this; I know we will.

"Hey, how about we get out of the house tonight?" I say as I come up behind him. He's sitting on the couch in the same spot he's been in for what seems like weeks now, and I'm not sure what to do with him. I'm starting to feel a little irritated toward his overall depressed mood, though I feel that's unfair because we all handle things differently and in our own time. But I mean . . . come on. He should be over the shock of his injured knee by now and moving toward a better mental state.

My hand settles on his shoulder, and I realize it's the first bit of contact we've had in two weeks. My fingers tingle at the warmth coming through his shirt.

"What did you have in mind?" he asks, his voice rough, his eyes glued to the sports channel.

I know he's not immune to the fact that he's a Debbie Downer. He's tried to be happy for me, especially after the great reviews we received from the festival brunch, but it's like no matter how hard he tries, he's just not. I'm certain most of it has to do with his knee and the uncertainty of what's to come, but I also know deep down some of it is because of me. I hate this.

"There's a place two miles north of Folly Beach that serves the best Frogmore stew. They're really known for their oysters, but it's not the right season, so we'll have to go back another time for those."

Another time. Oyster season is roughly six months away, and that's such a long time from now. Am I planning on him being here in six months? Is he planning on being here in six months? If—no, *when* he heads back to Tampa, that will interfere with his season, so I doubt it, and the sudden thought of him leaving has me feeling off-kilter. It's not a subject we've talked about, but we probably should soon. He isn't going to stay here forever, and I'm certain he has an idea of when he plans to head back.

"What exactly is Frogmore stew?" He looks up at me. His eyes are shadowed with stress and unhappiness, and the scruff on his face is at least three days old.

"It's another term for a low-country boil. You know: shrimp, sausage, corn, potatoes, et cetera. They also have great hushpuppies." My hand runs across his back as I move to the end of the couch and sit on the armrest.

There's a moment of silence between us as we stare at each other, and then his nostrils flare as he takes in a breath of air and says, "Sounds good."

"I think so." I give him a small encouraging smile. He reaches for the remote to flip off the television as I glance down and see he's wearing old baggy sweatpants and a

T-shirt that's seen better days. Getting him out of the house is definitely going to be good for him, so I say, "Get dressed, and we'll leave in twenty."

Mostly, the drive out to the restaurant is quiet. We decided to take his truck since he fits more comfortably in it than in my car, and he lets me drive. He's slipped on a clean shirt with a pair of jeans, and he attempted to style his hair. He looks inviting and familiar, and it creates an ache in my chest, a desire to climb over, sit in his lap, and be hugged by him. Again, I hate this place we're in now. Even so, it's going to be a beautiful night, so we roll down the windows to let the salty air blow in. I think the fresh air will be good for him, good for us. Maybe it'll lift his spirits, at least that's what I'm hoping.

After we're seated at a table on the outside deck that overlooks the low country, I bite the bullet on trying to get to the bottom of this awkwardness between us. "Do you want to tell me what's going on in your head?" I ask him quietly.

His gaze shifts to find mine and he frowns. Picking up the bottle of beer the waitress dropped off, he takes a sip before answering me, never breaking eye contact. "No, not really."

My stomach dips at his focus on me, at his non-answer, and my lips press together in a line. Of course he doesn't want to talk; he hasn't for a while now, so why did I think he would? Maybe coming out here was a mistake. Glancing past his shoulder, I look toward the horizon, which is starting to shade with the early colors of night, and I try to think of something else that might open him up without his mood continuing to pull me down.

"How's the therapy going with Eddie? You saw him today, right?" A breeze blows across the water, bringing with it the constant lingering odor of the pluff mud. To most it smells gross, like sulfur, but to me it smells like home.

"I did, and it's not going well." Unconsciously, his left hand reaches under the table and he begins to rub his knee. I noticed more so this week that he's been alternating ice and heat rather frequently, and I also spotted a pill bottle on the counter that's his.

My heart hurts for him at this admission. "I'm sorry. I didn't know, and you haven't said anything."

His eyes lower to the table and his shoulders droop. Seeing him like this, I'm again taken aback by how different he was at the party and Thanksgiving versus now.

"Yeah. It's been almost three months." He shakes his head. "I expected there to be some swelling, but not this much." He leans back in his chair and lets out a sigh.

"Nothing went wrong with the surgery, did it?" I hadn't considered the possibility that he wasn't put back together perfectly.

"No, they repaired it like they were supposed to. Sometimes there's just chronic swelling, and that's where I'm at. It makes it hard for me to rehab it when structurally it can't handle the stress right now."

"Why haven't you mentioned any of this to me?"

He shrugs his shoulders and his eyes find mine. "Because every day when I wake up, I pray it's finally going to be the day it's gone."

Hope. He's hanging on to hope, and I understand that feeling from seven years ago. When everything is uncertain and you're stuck in this limbo phase not knowing what's going to happen next, hope is really the only tangible emotion one can hang on to. You have to.

"Is there anything I can be doing to help you? Help you wrap it, help you more around the house so you stay off it, or maybe massage it?" I think back to how people offered to help me, but really, I wish they had just been proactive and done things. I should have been doing more for him, should have recognized that he needs more instead of steering clear while he dealt with it. Inwardly, I groan, and guilt assaults me as I think about him climbing trees to cut down flowers for me. I'm certain that didn't help.

It's then his eyes brighten a little and he chuckles. "Meg, if there's something on me that's going to be massaged, it's not going to be my knee," he teases.

And there he is—there's my cocky guy. An instant blush burns up my neck and into my cheeks as my jaw drops.

He laughs and reaches across the table for my hand, my heart fluttering at the contact. I know it shouldn't, but the tiny connection between us feels nice and I realize I kind of needed it. I need him to be his sexy, charming self. The Jack from before our night together never would have hesitated to touch me, and since then he has.

"Sorry, I couldn't resist." He grins, and his dimples make a tiny appearance. "You set yourself up for that one."

Unable to speak over my emotions, I just shake my head at him, and we both smile.

"You are beautiful," he says, his eyes trailing over the details of my face. My soul sings at his kind words.

"Thank you. You are too," I tell him, and he is. He's so beautiful.

Maybe it wasn't just him who needed a night out of the house. I'm thinking I did too.

We continue talking about his knee and all the things that happened at the restaurant this week, but our conversation is now lighter, warmer, easier. When the waitress brings our dinner, we reluctantly separate our hands and go about eating our food. It's a meal with him I know I'll remember for a long time.

Afterward, we cash out and wander over to the outside bar. Although we're facing the east, the view still makes for a pretty sunset, and he holds up his phone to take a selfie of us. I'm staring off into the distance while he's staring at me, and he captions it: **Such a beautiful view.**

Finding my hand, his fingers thread through mine, and he gently closes them together. I've held his hand plenty of times over the last couple of months, but this feels different. Good different. Scary different. Gray area different. Maybe it's that we need this after the last couple of weeks, or maybe this is just how we always were; I'm not sure, but I do know I don't want to let go, even if I should.

"Thank you for bringing me here tonight. You were right about getting me out of the house. I know I haven't been myself lately . . . I'll try harder."

Turning to face him, I look up at him as he looks down at me, and my free hand falls to his waist. "Jack, no one is asking you to be one way or another. Just be you, okay?"

Different emotions coast through his eyes before he clears them and finally says, "Okay."

"And don't shut me out. Talk to me." I take a step closer to him, hoping he acknowledges that I'm serious. I want to hear what's on his mind, on his heart.

"I will. I promise," he says quietly, his gaze dropping to my mouth.

I should move back, I know I should, but I just can't.

Slowly, he reaches up and wraps his hand around my face. His thumb sweeps back and forth across my cheek and my lips part as my eyes flutter shut. I know he wants to kiss me, and I want to kiss him just as much, my body telling him so as it sways his way. Hesitantly or just slowly, I'm not sure which, he lowers his head and kisses me so sweetly. With his lips lightly pressing into mine, the vulnerability and intimacy behind it feels real, like real on a whole new level I'm not sure what to do with but don't want to turn away from.

He brushes another kiss against the corner of my mouth, his cheek rubbing across my skin as he moves to rest his forehead against mine. He lets out what feels like a long, slow, overdue exhalation, and his warm breath fans across my chin just before he wraps his arms around me and folds me into the tightest embrace.

Frogmore Stew

Ingredients:
- 2 medium onions, peeled and quartered
- 4 garlic cloves, smashed
- 1 lemon, halved, plus extra lemon slices
- 1/2 cup seafood seasoning, such as Old Bay
- salt if needed
- 2 pounds of small red potatoes, scrubbed and cut if preferred
- 1 package turkey kielbasa, cut into pieces
- 8 ears of corn, husked and halved (we used 4)
- 2 pounds of shrimp, unpeeled
- melted butter optional
- garlic bread optional

Directions:
Set a large roasting pan or stock pot over two burners. Add three quarts of water, onions, garlic, seafood seasoning, lemon halves (squeezing their juice into the water before adding the shells), and salt (if needed). Bring to a boil.

Add potatoes and kielbasa; return to a boil.

Cover with foil which lets some of the liquid evaporate, reduce the heat, and simmer until potatoes are just tender (20 minutes).

Add corn; increase heat to medium-high and cook, covered, until tender (5 minutes).

Top with shrimp; cover and steam (3 minutes).

Turn off the heat; stir shrimp into broth and let stand, covered, until cooked (2 minutes).

Serve with melted butter and lemon wedges. Serves 8.

Chapter 25

I'm All In

Jack

DINNER WAS AMAZING. She did the right thing by dragging me out of the house, out of myself, and the place couldn't have been more perfect. We were outside and away from the touristy scene, it was casual and uncrowded, and in a way we felt like we were in our own little bubble, the only two people in the world. I hadn't realized how low I'd gotten, but I did realize tonight how vital she is to me. No, I'm not even close to being my old self again—I'm not sure when that will happen—but I am significantly better than I was just a few hours ago, and that's all because of her.

I know they say happiness can't come from others, it has to be found within, but well, she is in me, and if we're off, I'm off. There's nothing I can do about it.

"What are you thinking about?" she asks, looking over at me from the driver's seat.

"Not much. Just enjoying the ride," I tell her, reaching over to lay my hand on her thigh. Usually I'm a stickler for driving, but I like her behind the wheel of my truck. She's so tiny, and she has the seat pulled way forward. She's wearing a cute little dress that shows off her legs, and there's something about those high heels on my pedals that turns me on. Granted, most things she does turn me on. I can't help it; I'm insanely attracted to her and I'm not ashamed of it. She's beautiful inside and out.

She frowns at my response, and I crack a smile, shifting in my seat. She asked me to talk to her more, and I will, but I don't think she wants to know about this. Maybe I should tell her I'm thinking about the hushpuppies. That'll satisfy her curiosity; after all, they were damn good, and we'll be returning soon to get some more.

On the radio, a song sung by Will Ashton from the Blue Horizons band comes on. It's a duet where he is singing with his wife, Ava, and the lyrics speak to me. They describe a love between two people who are each walking their own path in life, but at the end of the day they know how to find their way home, to each other.

Does Meg hear the words? Does she see that this can be us? Over the last nine months, she's become my home, and it's why I ended up here in Charleston with her. She grounds me, and she's my safe place. When I'm with her, I don't have that itch to be thinking, doing, going somewhere else. I like when she's standing in front of me and my world stops moving. Doesn't she like it when I'm standing with her? In hindsight, when she asked me to talk to her, I should have put that back on her as well.

Pushing the skirt of her dress away, my hand finds her skin, and I lightly squeeze before sweeping my thumb back and forth. She glances over at me once, but she doesn't push me away, and I settle more into my seat with my hand never leaving my girl. Man, do I love to touch her, feel her, smell her, and her legs—they drive me crazy.

By the time we get home, my fingers have explored more of her leg, from behind her knee up to the inner thigh. Mostly it's all just innocent, but given the state we've been in for the last two weeks, it's easy to see it's affecting her as her chest is moving up and down and she's gripping the wheel tighter than normal. Her presence alone is certainly affecting me.

Silence falls over us after she parks the truck and turns it off. We're both looking at each other, and I know I'm not crazy when I say the air around us feels charged. Without even thinking, I lean toward her, and she does the same to me. My hand moves from her leg to gently wrap around the side of her face, and I bring her lips to mine—right where they belong.

This kiss is not like the one earlier on the dock. That one was more of an apology, a reunion kiss after an extended period of distance that said *I need this connection between us to right itself.* This one, however, is slow, deep, and deliberate. I want to drown myself in the taste of her and never come up for air.

Over and over I kiss her. I kiss her lips, her jaw, the spot under her ear, and when I finally reach for her arm and gently pull in my direction, she simply follows, understanding me. Climbing around the center console, she straddles my lap, and my hands slide up her thighs, under her dress, and around to her ass, where my fingers easily slip under the soft edge of her underwear. Her skin is so smooth as I lightly grip and drag her closer to me.

No one can see us here. The road is mostly empty, rarely are there pedestrians, and the windows are super tinted. Even still, part of me is surprised she's allowing this since she's been so adamant about just being friends, but the other part of me isn't surprised at all. I know she doesn't want to admit it, but we are good together and good for each other. She feels so much more for me than she's allowing herself, but I have to believe she'll eventually come around. She's worth the wait, and so am I. I'm worth it, too.

With her hands on my shoulders, she shifts so she's seated exactly where we both want her, and involuntarily, I roll my hips against her. She groans at the friction, the sound getting lost between us as her mouth returns to mine.

Why does this feel so perfect? Why does she feel so perfect? It's like she was made for me, and that's the only way to describe it.

With my fingertips digging in, I rock her back and forth across the length of me, swallowing the gasps she's giving me and dying a little each time she does. I know I'm getting ahead of myself, but I can't think of anything else other than having this, having her like this, every single day.

Moving my hands out from under the dress, I slide them up her ribcage and wrap them around her breasts. The plumpness of her flesh pushes up over the neckline, and as she tips her head backward with her eyes closed, my lips and tongue find their way, painting a trail from one side to the other.

I breathe in, the lingering scent of her citrusy floral perfume filling me. It's an added aphrodisiac that makes my head fuzzy and the desire for her even stronger.

"Just . . . once more." She breathes heavily as my forehead rests against her shoulder.

I pull back to look her in the eyes and say the truest statement of the night. "You know as well as I do it won't be just once." My voice sounds rough, deep, and even I can recognize I'm sitting at the point of no return.

"Jack . . ." she says, sounding pained.

Why she fights this, fights us, I don't understand . . . but at the sound of my name, my resolve cracks even further. I need more, more from her.

Gripping the back of her head, my fingers hide themselves in her hair as I pull her mouth back to mine. Taking her bottom lip, I roll it between my teeth as my willingness to not have my tongue wrapped around hers dissolves. Diving back in, I immerse myself in the taste, feel, and smell of her. These kisses are wet, bordering on rough, and if I could consume her, I would.

Feeling her hands slide down my chest and stop at the button on my jeans, I briefly hold my breath to see what move she is going to make next. After all, she's the one who has to make the move. When she hesitates for only a second and then undoes it, everything in me from the chest down shudders with a fierce need.

"Meg." I say her name in warning; she has to know she's crossing a line I'm not prepared to go back from, and her eyes fly up to find mine. The longing in them nearly undoes me, and instead of replying with words, she does so by pulling down the zipper, shifting my pants out of the way, slipping her hand in, and wrapping it around me.

I am hers.

One hundred percent hers if she'll have me.

As I lean my head back on the headrest, my eyes fall to half-mast and I take in the gorgeous mess that is this girl. My girl. Wild hair, flushed skin, swollen lips, dress halfway unzipped—perfect, just perfect.

"Would you rather go inside?"

She knows what I'm asking her, and I need to know if it's now or later.

"No," she says breathlessly just as her hand moves up and down me.

Groaning, I slip my fingers under the front of her dress and find the place we both need.

Yes, we could slow down. Yes, we could take our clothes off. But no, we don't want to or have to. Sliding her underwear to the side, my fingers gratefully find that she is more than ready for me, so I pull her forward, positioning myself, and she sinks down.

Perfection. So much so I damn near black out from the feeling—that is until she starts moving.

I am thirty-two years old. I have lived my life to the fullest for as long as I can remember, and only now, here with her, do I finally feel complete.

Fuck my life.

I have a sinking feeling this isn't going to end well for me, but I can't stop the direction I'm heading. It's too late. After tonight, after this, there's no going back. She's either mine or she isn't; there's no in between—not for me, not anymore—and I can't pretend there is.

I'm all in with this girl. I just hope she's all in with me.

Hushpuppies

Ingredients:

1 ½ cup self-rising flour
1 ½ cup corn meal yellow ground, medium-coarse
1/4 cup sugar
½ tsp baking powder
½ tsp Kosher salt
½ onion finely chopped
1 cup buttermilk
¼ cup beer
1 egg lightly beaten
3 dashes hot sauce
Peanut oil or vegetable, for frying
Tartar sauce for dipping
lemon wedges for garnish

Directions:

Heat the oil to 350°F.

Mix the flour, corn meal, sugar, baking powder and salt in a medium bowl.

Mix in the onions.

In a separate bowl, combine the buttermilk, egg and hot sauce.

Add the dry ingredients with the wet, and mix with a large wooden spoon. Don't over mix! Its okay for there still to be some lumps.

Mix enough beer until batter just comes together, about 1/4 cup.

Use a spoon to scoop a small mound of batter, just large enough to cover the spoon.

Drop the dough into the hot oil. Continue with more, but don't overcrowd. You will most likely fry in batch.

Fry until golden brown on the outside…about 7 to 8 minutes (varies depending on the size of the puppies!). Use a metal slotted spoon, or spider, to remove the hush puppies to a plate lined with paper towels.

Repeat process with remaining batter.

Serve warm with lemon wedges and tartar sauce.

Chapter 26

Not Written in the Stars

Meg

WHITE: THE COLOR that stares down at me as I lie in Jack's bed looking at the ceiling. Yes, I know ninety-five percent of ceilings are white, but it's this whiteness that has my thoughts racing from one thing to the next. The ceiling fan is on medium speed, and as the blades blur into a circle, I realize here in the early morning light that although I wanted things to go back to normal, now I'm certain they never will. I find I'm mourning what we used to have, not dreaming about what might be.

I told myself just once, but now that's turned into twice. Even I am logical enough to know there's not really such a thing as friends with benefits, so why I crossed the line again, I just don't know. I allowed myself to get swept up in the moment, in the reprieve of the emotional distress we'd been skirting for days, but I know this is going to do more damage than good. No matter how great it felt, no matter how wonderful he feels, no matter how much I'm beginning to wish things could be different.

Turning my head, I continue to lie completely still. Jack is sleeping, and I don't want to disturb him. His face is so relaxed and his features are so familiar to me that I could get lost in them, but I won't. I can't. I also don't want him to wake and see the emotions I know are present on my face. Regret. Longing. Admiration. Fear.

Fear, like the white ceiling, spurs on a memory, one I do my best not to think of daily.

It's funny how different moments alter and shape people's lives, and it's also funny how some moments shine clear and bright while others fade. I remember when my high school boyfriend broke up with me after we left for college, I remember the moment my parents told me they were moving to Florida, leaving this life behind, and I remember my acceptance email to culinary school. These are just a few, but with each of them, I don't remember very much else. The time of day, what I was wearing or ate that day, or even what style my hair was in—I went through phases of highlights, purple strands, and even an attempted keratin treatment to smooth it out and make it straight.

However, I do remember just about everything from when I was told I had cancer.

First of all, I had gone to see the doctor at the student health complex. That's where we went for flu shots, gynecological exams for birth control, whatever. It was after I explained my symptoms and she did a routine exam—you know, where they have you lie back on the table and they push around on your stomach—that she recommended I see an actual gynecologist. The staff scheduled the appointment for me. I was to have blood work taken first thing in the morning, stop by imaging for an ultrasound, and then see this new doctor afterward.

It was at this appointment I was told there was a mass on my left ovary and they needed to do a laparotomy to see what was going on. I didn't ask the question I should have and they didn't mention what I suddenly feared, so I blocked it out of my head and went about making plans for the surgery.

Three days later, my aunt came with me, and she was the one holding my hand when the doctor came in and said cancer. I think I was expecting bad news, but I didn't think it would be cancer. Cancer is one of those things you know happens and affects people, but you never think it'll happen to you. Did you know only two percent of ovarian cancer sufferers are under the age of thirty?

The room was bland and beige with a dark green chair. There was a generic sailboat picture on the wall, and I was wearing a red shirt. I remember as my aunt started asking questions about what happens next, a blanket of realization came over me: *I'm going to die.*

Having actually verbalized the words, the doctor assured us that since we had caught it early, survival rates were high. Apparently, the type of ovarian cancer someone in their twenties gets is likely to be one of the more uncommon but more treatable types. While they stared at me, waiting for me to ask more questions, the only other one I wondered was, *Does this mean I won't be able to have children?*

Children.

It's not normal to think about having children at twenty-one—if anything the goal is prevention, to not have them—and now there I was, being forced to talk about my potential future, one I wasn't sure of, one I now didn't have any control over.

With my world spinning, I felt out of control, and I desperately needed something to hang on to. So, that night, while lying in bed, I decided I would determine how I reacted to this, to life, to my life, and how I pushed through. Several times over the next couple of months, I made heartfelt promises to myself, and so far, years later, I haven't broken any of them.

For breakfast, my aunt made my favorite blueberry scones with lemon glaze. I've never worn a red shirt again, my hair was too long so I kept it braided, and the ceiling was white just like this one now.

Closing my eyes, I run my hand over my face to block out the whiteness and the memories, and I breathe him in. His room smells so male, like dryer sheets, a sporty body wash, and sandalwood. I love this smell, and as for him, my heart aches for the conversations I know we're going to have later today.

Slipping quietly out of the bed, I head upstairs to my room and then into the shower. The warm water eases the soreness of my muscles, and with my forehead resting on the wall and the steam surrounding me, I allow myself to replay images of the night.

Large warm hands, which he whispered he couldn't keep off of me, sweeping the length of me, gripping when needed and tender when not. Embraces so tight and so intimate I'm certain I could hear his heart whispering to mine. Ownership as we each handed over our most exposed selves, knowing the vulnerability in this was met with complete trust.

In a different world, if I were a different person, it would be so easy to let myself fall. But I haven't and I won't, because we're just not written in the stars. I've had to make hard decisions before, and I can do it again. He'll see reason, if he hasn't already, and I'm not going to waver. We can only be just friends.

With a renewed sense of purpose, I dry off and dress to go to work. Distance this morning will be good for us, and it'll give him time to clear his head. I'm prepared to deal with the fallout later, but what I'm not prepared for is having to answer questions now. A look of betrayal from him and what I'm certain will be a wounded heart is not something I can handle.

A need to see him one more time before I head out rises inside me, and although I shouldn't, I tiptoe down the hallway to peek into his room. What I find is him awake, facing my side of the bed, with his arm stretched out where I was not too long ago. Dark tired eyes stare at me as I stand in the doorway, and as he processes what I'm wearing, his brows pull down and his forehead wrinkles.

"Where are you going?" he asks, his voice deep and rumbly with sleep.

"I need to run over to the restaurant for a little while." It's a lie—I don't really need to go in—but the space will be good for both of us.

"Now?" He doesn't need to look at a clock to know it's still very early in the morning.

"Yeah. I was awake, so I figured why not." I shift my weight from one foot to another; the floor is cold.

There's a long pause as he considers what I've said. He's replaying in his mind how I told him last night at dinner that I wasn't needed at the restaurant today as it's a slower day and I was certain Taylor would have it covered.

Frowning, he reaches up to run his hand through his hair, and the blankets slide down his torso. Dark gorgeous strands stick up perfectly all over his head, the scruff from last night is longer and thus appears darker, and inches and inches of his bare skin call out to me. He is so handsome.

Letting out a deep breath, he contemplates what to say to me, and then he says the thing I dread the most. "Don't go. Stay here with me." He lowers his arm, rests it on the bed just in front of him where I should be, and watches me.

Why is this so hard when being with him is easy?

"I can't. I've got to go." I shake my head and lightly shrug one shoulder.

His perfect pouty lips press into a line, which turns down into a frown.

Blinking at me, he finally sees my emotional walls are up, and in that one second his open vulnerability is gone and his are slammed in place. The muscles tighten around his eyes and jaw and seeing the transition in his facial expressions kills me, but this is for the best. He shifts to his back, no longer looking at me, and says, "Then go."

"Jack—"

"Don't, Meg. Not right now." He rolls completely over, giving me his back, and my eyes well with unwanted tears.

I was wrong—it isn't the betrayal that's trying to break me; it's his disappointment. I've hurt him, again, and the pain of this is almost unbearable.

It isn't supposed to be like this.

We aren't supposed to be like this.

But I don't know how to be any other way. I made a promise to myself, and standing behind that, I quietly slip away.

Blueberry Scones with Lemon Glaze

Ingredients:
Blueberry Scones:

    2 cups all-purpose flour
    1 tablespoon baking powder
    1/2 teaspoon salt
    2 tablespoons sugar
    5 tablespoons unsalted butter, cold, cut in chunks
    1 cup fresh blueberries
    1 cup heavy cream, plus more for brushing the scones

Lemon Glaze:

    1/2 cup freshly squeezed lemon juice
    2 cups confectioners' sugar, sifted
    1 tablespoon unsalted butter
    1 lemon, zest finely grated

Directions:

Preheat the oven to 400 degrees F.

Sift together the dry ingredients; the flour, baking powder, salt, and sugar. Using 2 forks or a pastry blender, cut in the butter to coat the pieces with the flour. The mixture should look like coarse crumbs. Fold the blueberries into the batter. Take care not to mash or bruise the blueberries because their strong color will bleed into the dough. Make a well in the center and pour in the heavy cream. Fold everything together just to incorporate; do not overwork the dough.

Press the dough out on a lightly floured surface into a rectangle about 12 by 3 by 1 1/4 inches. Cut the rectangle in 1/2 then cut the pieces in 1/2 again, giving you 4 (3-inch) squares. Cut the squares in 1/2 on a diagonal to give you the classic triangle shape. Place the scones on an ungreased cookie sheet and brush the tops with a little heavy cream. Bake for 15 to 20 minutes until beautiful and brown. Let the scones cool a bit before you apply the glaze.

You can make the lemon glaze in a double boiler, or for a simpler alternative, you can zap it in the microwave. Mix the lemon juice with the confectioners' until dissolved in a heatproof bowl over a pot of simmering water for the double-boiler method, or in a microwave-safe bowl. Whisk in the butter and lemon zest. Either nuke the glaze for 30 seconds or continue whisking in the double boiler. Whisk the glaze to smooth out any lumps, then drizzle the glaze over the top of the scones. Let it set a minute before serving.

Chapter 27

Either Fish or Cut Bait

Jack

I KNEW THINGS were not going to be good the moment I woke up this morning and she wasn't in the bed next to me. Last night I was certain we were finally turning a corner to exploring a new part of our relationship, but as she stood in the doorway wearing work clothes with a pair of heels dangling from her fingers, it was clear nothing had changed, at least not for her. If anything, I could see things were going to get worse for me.

She didn't have to go to the restaurant today. She said so last night, she knows she did, but the minute things got too intimate for her, she decided to bolt. I couldn't look at her, couldn't watch her walk away after everything I gave of myself last night, so I rolled over and let her leave.

After the first time she made me feel like she was blowing me off, I had a shame-on-you mentality, but now, after the second, I've shifted to shame on me.

I'm not sure how long I lay there after she left. I also had no idea when she would be back, but I did know what I had to do next, no matter how hard it was going to be for me.

I have no regrets. I gave her all of me, but in the words of my father, it's time to either fish or cut bait, and I know I have to cut bait. She isn't going to change. I'm a nonfactor in the equation of her life, and it just sucks. You can't make someone want to be with you, no matter how hard you try or wish it to be otherwise.

So with that in mind, I got up, got ready for the day, and headed off to work out with Eddie. I know if I stay busy, I'll be able to ignore the emotional anxiety this is causing me—until it comes to a head with her later tonight.

Of course, Eddie took one look at me and decided it was best to keep his mouth shut. I hate that others can see my emotions on my sleeve, but this is the longest I've gone without saying what's on my mind, just hoping she would meet me in the middle, and she hasn't. It's like the emotions are trying to bleed out of me. I'm used to being honest with people about how I feel, but she's completely resistant to acknowledging our actions or taking responsibility for this situation we've found ourselves in, and I'm at a loss for what to do.

Eddie works me harder than he has before, and I tell myself the sweat pouring out of me is the tears of my heart. It's purging because I will not cry over her. I just won't.

By the time I get home, my knee is just as angry at me as I am with myself, and with my decisions solidified, I do what I have to do.

How did I get here?

And why did I let any of this happen to me?

This isn't me.

Just after three o'clock, Meg walks in and finds me on the couch. She's a little dirty, and she also looks like she's worked herself hard. Aside from the worry that lines her eyes, she mostly looks determined, and any hope I had for us fizzles away.

Stopping next to the couch, she puts her hands on her hips and lets out a sigh. "So, we're back here, are we?"

Back here? We both frown, and I ask her, "What do you mean?"

"This." She waves her hand at me. "You . . . on the couch."

"Would you like me to sit somewhere else?"

In this moment, I feel like I have officially worn out my welcome. Could this day get any worse? First she makes it clear that I'm not what she wants, and now she's made me feel like she doesn't want me here at all.

"You know that's not what I mean."

Reaching for the remote, I turn off the television and turn to face her more. "No, I don't. Tell me, Meg, what do you mean?"

She stares at me as if she's not so sure how much she wants to say. I can see this is hard for her; I mean she's the queen of deflection. Anything to turn a conversation away from being uncomfortable or confrontational.

"The black cloud is back, the one that hovers around you. It was just starting to go away, and here it is again." Breaking eye contact, she walks into the kitchen and pulls out leftover chicken, mushroom, and spinach lasagna she made two nights ago. I'm certain she's not hungry; she's using the kitchen island as a buffer between us.

I stand so she has to face me and finally get what she's been thinking off her chest. I cross my arms over mine. "Black cloud?" I ask her.

Her eyes briefly come up to find my face as she pulls two bowls from the dishwasher then goes about scooping some lasagna into them.

"Yes, black cloud," she says, lowering her head to watch what she's doing. "The depressed mood, the sulking—it's been months. It's time to snap out of it." She then lifts her eyes once more and again waves her hand at my face then pointedly at my knee.

She thinks my mood is about my knee, and yes, some of it is—that just kind of lingers there constantly—but today . . . hell, the last couple of weeks, it hasn't been. It makes me sad that she can't recognize that it's her. I don't respond to her—what is there to say?—but she feels the need to continue.

"The Jack I know . . . he's full of life. He's enthusiastic, optimistic, and loves adventure. I mean look at your social media feed—it's like the world is a candy shop for you and you're all wide-eyed as you experience one great thing after another. How do I help you find that guy again?"

"Help me?" Yes, she's right—I do love adventure. I've always been a happy, carefree, spontaneous, in-the-moment kind of guy, but sometimes I'm this guy, too. My feelings can get hurt just like the next person. It's okay to slow down, think, process.

"Yes, help you." She wraps the dish up and puts it back in the refrigerator.

"Last night you told me it was okay for me to just be me. I'm sorry today I'm not who you want me to be."

My lips pinch together and my arms drop as I look away from her, feeling more defeated than I have in a long time. I guess I can add a third thing to the list: I'm not wanted, she's tired of me being here, and now I'm getting lectured because she doesn't like who I currently am—or, apparently, who I've been.

"I just don't get it. Why—why are you still so down? You're better than that, and this is stupid."

I go back to watching her while I let her words sink in. She covers both bowls with plastic wrap, puts them in the microwave to warm up, and then turns to face me again, leaning forward with her elbows on the counter.

Heat burns under my skin as anger pushes its way to the surface. She just insulted me, and I don't like the way it tastes as I swallow it down. "Stupid? You think the end of my dream career is stupid?" My voice dips, and her eyes widen as she hears the change in inflection.

"That's not what I meant and you know it." She stands back up, almost like she's challenging me, and stares at me.

Well, bring it on, sweetheart. Two can play this game, and I can guarantee I will win.

"Do I? Because think it, speak it, and you just spoke it. If fact, you've spoken a lot lately." I move around the couch and come to stand directly across the island from her.

"Stop trying to turn this around on me. All I'm saying is that you don't have to be so negative all the freaking time. It's depressing, and I don't want to live a life surrounded by this. I also don't want that for you."

"I'm sorry if you think me being depressed over the last couple of months is an inconvenience to you. I didn't realize Little Miss Perfect-Sunshine-All-The-Time lived a *do it my way or no way* kind of life."

Her jaw drops at the sharpness in my tone and then she snaps it shut.

Moving away, I lean over the back of the couch, grab the ice pack I was using, and return it to the freezer. Her gaze follows me as I move into the kitchen, and then she turns, which blocks the way to my room. The microwave dings, but neither of us moves to open it.

She's directly in front of me, and she's so small, yet she's making me feel like I am. I don't like it, and I don't understand what I did that was so wrong.

"Jack, I understand—" she starts, and all this does is make me angrier, because now she's patronizing me.

"No, you don't understand. I get it, I do—you experienced something traumatic along the lines of life or death—but is it not in you at all to realize I did too? Traumatic things happen to people in different ways. Tell me, how long did it take you to get over what happened to you?"

"Losing your life and losing a job are two different things." She tilts her head to look up at me defiantly, and my eyes narrow as I stare down at her.

"You think football was just a job to me?" The muscles across my shoulders twitch at the insinuation.

"Well, it is just a job, and no one said you had to give up football, just that you have to give up playing. There are plenty of other things you can still be doing with the sport. I guess what I just don't understand is why you're still making it so tragic. You got to play, and for a long time, might I add. Be grateful and figure out your next move."

She doesn't get it.

She doesn't get me.

And it's clear she doesn't want to.

There's no point in continuing this conversation. I've heard enough of what she has to say on the matters of my mood and my career. I expected our conversation this afternoon to come to a head where we were frank with each other, but I didn't expect this, and my anger transforms back into hurt.

Pushing past her, I move down the hall and head to my room. Honestly, I don't know which is worse right now: the way she made me feel this morning, or the way she's making me feel right now.

A startled noise escapes her; she's followed me and is taking in the changes to my room. I turn to watch her as her eyes trail over the empty closet, the sheets that have been pulled into a pile to be washed, my backpack sitting on the edge of the bed. Earlier, I packed up my room, and the rest of my belongings are in the truck.

"W-what are you doing?" she stammers, a slight hysteria pitching her words.

With my left hand, I rub the back of my neck, trying to find the words to proceed. I never thought I would be here with her, and now that we are, every bit of fight I usually have in me has died and I'm left feeling like an empty shell.

There's always that one person you've had feelings for since the moment you first met them, and for me it was her. It's always been her. I lived for the moments she would respond to my photos (it's why I put up so many), and I counted down the days to when I would get to see her, her beautiful face. With my right hand, I grip the handle of my backpack, and I drop my other arm to look her straight in the eyes. It's now or never.

"I love you, Meg. I needed to tell you that. Just one time." Relief, terror, and the absolute truth flood through me all at once.

She takes a step closer to me, and I take one back. Her skin pales as she acknowledges the distance I'm putting between us.

"Of course you love me—we're friends. And I love you, too." She starts twisting her fingers together in a way I've never seen her do, but it's obvious she has done it before.

"No. I'm in love with you, and I feel like I'm suffocating under the weight of it. It's not just my knee, or football. It's you too. Every day I want to tell you and show you, but you've pushed us into this place where I'm not allowed to, and it makes me feel like shit."

Her eyes widen. "I don't think you're in love with me, Jack. It's all just circumstantial and you're confused." She shakes her head, firmly planting herself in the camp of team denial.

"I am not confused, and it is not circumstantial, so don't tell me how I feel." My voice gets a little louder. "I mean, that's all you've done for the last twenty minutes, and I'm over it. Yes, internally I am dealing with the uncertainty of my career, but lately, I have been considering alternatives to playing, and surprisingly I'm okay with it. Although I've never been a believer in love at first sight, I'm pretty certain I've loved you since the first moment I saw you standing in Zach's house. That was nine months ago. Just because I haven't shared things with you, that doesn't mean they are any less real."

And there it is, the whole truth. I've laid it out there, and now she knows.

"But . . . but that's not who we are." Her chin trembles and my heart sinks.

"Why? Why can't that be who we are? I'm not blind to the way we are with each other, and I know you aren't either."

The ache to pull her into me is so great it's hard to breathe. I desperately want to bury my face in her hair and have her tell me she loves me too, but I know she won't. All of this, from the moment she walked into the locker room at the Super Bowl until now—it's devastating for me.

"We're friends. You're my best friend." She says this as if it's the answer to everything.

"And you are mine, but friends don't know how their friends taste, and, Meg, I know every flavor you have."

"That's not fair," she says, just barely over a whisper.

"You're right, it's not."

The air turns heavy between us. This is it, her last chance to change her mind and decide. I would be lying if I said I wasn't holding my breath and internally pleading for her to pick me, choose me, but as she utters the words, "I can't," the last string holding me up breaks and I crash, shattering into a thousand pieces.

"Neither can I."

Her eyes turn glassy and fill with tears, which slowly drip down her face. It's a direct punch to the gut and one that tells me it's time to go. I can't stand here and watch her cry, and I won't allow her to see what she's done to me.

Walking toward her, I pause to bend and kiss her one last time on the forehead. My nostrils flare at the citrus scent of her hair, and for just a split second I squeeze my eyes shut. Her hand reaches for my waist and clutches my shirt, but I pull it free to move past her.

Without another word said between us, I grab my keys from the hook by the front door and leave.

Chicken Mushroom Spinach Lasagna

Ingredients:
- 2 1/2 Tbsp. olive oil
- 1 cup chopped onion
- 2 Tbsp. minced garlic
- 8 oz. white mushrooms, *thinly sliced*
- 1 tsp. dried basil
- 1 tsp. dried oregano
- 1/2 tsp. red pepper flakes
- 1 1/2 tsp. kosher salt, *divided*
- 1 (6 oz.) bag fresh baby spinach
- 2 cups shredded cooked chicken
- 2 1/2 cups low-sodium chicken stock
- 1 1/2 cups milk (I used whole milk)
- 1/4 tsp. nutmeg
- 1/4 cup all-purpose flour
- 1/2 cup shredded Parmesan cheese
- 8 no-boil lasagna noodles
- 1 1/4 cups shredded mozzarella cheese

Directions:
Preheat the oven to 375 degrees F.

Heat a large sauté pan over medium-high heat. When hot, add oil and then the onions, garlic, mushrooms, basil, oregano, red pepper flakes, and 1/2 teaspoon of salt. Sauté for 5 minutes or until the mushrooms soften while stirring occasionally. Make sure all of the liquid has evaporated from the mushrooms before going to step 3.

Stir in spinach and cook until the spinach wilts. Then remove the pan from the heat and stir in the cooked chicken. Set aside.

In a small saucepan, combine the chicken broth, milk, nutmeg, and remaining 1 teaspoon of salt. Bring to a slow simmer over medium heat. Once the mixture starts to bubble up around the edges, gradually whisk in the flour and let simmer until thickened, about 5-10 minutes. Stir in Parmesan cheese and then remove from heat.

Pour 1/2 cup sauce into bottom of 10X10 square baking dish, top with 2 noodles, 1 cup chicken mixture, 1 cup sauce, and 1/4 cup mozzarella, making sure noodles are covered with sauce. You can even press them down lightly. Repeat 3 more layers with noodles, chicken, sauce, and cheese. Last layer will have slightly more sauce and remaining cheese on top.

Cover baking dish with aluminum foil and bake for 25 minutes. Uncover and bake for 15 minutes longer. If desired, broil for 2-3 minutes for golden brown top. Let stand 5-8 minutes before serving.

Chapter 28

My Soul Mate Might Be Carbs

Meg

I HAVEN'T TALKED to Jack in days.

He literally told me he loved me, walked out of my house, and never looked back—not that I blame him.

I followed him to the porch, watched him climb into his truck, and then sat down on the steps as he drove away. I actually laughed at myself at one point, because me in this scene was straight out of a country song, red tail lights in the distance and all, but then that laughter turned to tears. It had been quite some time after he left when I finally went inside.

It's not that I thought he was coming back, although I had hoped he would. It was more that I needed to stall instead of entering into the reality I had created.

The one where he was gone.

And I was certain he wasn't coming back.

Of course I know it's my fault, but I can't be what he needs me to be, no matter how I might feel about him.

With Jack in the house, it felt smaller, quainter. Now with him gone, it feels large and empty.

Looking around, now I notice things are missing, whereas before they seamlessly blended with my things to become ours. Sports magazines, a blanket he bought for the couch after claiming my throw blanket wasn't long enough to cover his feet, even the canister of protein powder he kept on the kitchen counter—all of it, gone. He cleaned his bathroom, too, removing any trace of him at all.

And being in his room . . . that's the worst of all.

Yes, it looks just like it did before he arrived, but now the decorations seem insufficient and the room seems bare. Instead of washing the sheets, I put them back on his bed, climbed under the covers, and cried. They smelled like him, they felt like him, and for the first time in years, I doubted myself and the promises I'd made.

I didn't expect it to hurt, not like this.

Why does it hurt like this?

I dated my high school boyfriend for two years. When he broke up with me, I remember being sad, but I don't remember being hurt. This hurts, and in ways I'm not equipped to deal with.

"What are you doing?" Taylor asks as she slides up next to me, breaking me from my thoughts.

Pulling earbuds from my ears, I do a once-over of the kitchen before turning to face her. The lunch rush has ended, there are a few lingering tables before we close for the day, and the staff is moving around me preparing to shut the kitchen down and prepping for tomorrow morning.

Everyone around me knows something is going on as I've been here at the restaurant essentially open to close since he left, but no one has approached me. I'm also sure they've noticed that Jack hasn't stopped by, which was our routine for weeks. I am one hundred percent inclined to avoid conflict, whether it's with others or even just myself, and by staying task-oriented, my mind redirects to focus on what's in front of me and not what is around me or inside of me.

Am I hoping these feelings will just fade instead of having to be dealt with? Yes. If the expression time heals all wounds is accurate, I should be well on my way. As for the wounds, I'm not sure which ones are worse: the ones he's given me, or the ones I gave myself.

"What does it look like? I'm testing this month's featured dish." I glance at her before sticking my spoon into the bowl of sauce and bringing it to my mouth to taste. It's got both the salty and the sweet taste with a slight twinge of tang. It tastes perfect.

"Testing? Sweetheart, you're doing a lot more than testing. Looks to me like you're drowning your sorrows in carbs and cheese." She points toward the four other bowls on the counter. Yes, I know I'm making a simple Southern macaroni and cheese, but there are lots of ways it can be made. For example, one might want to blend in butternut squash to hide a vegetable, or make it gourmet with a medium cheddar and a Gruyere. You can make it white with just a little cheddar and lots of mozzarella and parmesan, and don't even get me started on fillings and baked crusts on the top.

I think about what she said and again look at my workstation, letting out a sigh. She's not wrong. It's been so long since I've given in to the feelings of things like disappointment, and I'm not even sure what to do with myself. I've tried to tell myself it is what it is and this is for the best, and although my head thinks this, my heart does not match it.

"Maybe. Besides, my soul mate might be carbs, and mac and cheese is the ultimate comfort food. I need to make sure it's menu-worthy." I taste the sauce again; it's delicious. My secret weapon for making mac and cheese has always been cream cheese, and it's not failing me now. By just adding a little, it makes the sauce so creamy and so good.

"Everything you make is menu-worthy, but seriously, put the spoon down and step away."

Taking a look at myself, I look down to see what Taylor sees. I have made a mess, and I'm always very meticulous about cleanliness when I cook. I'm also wearing Converse tennis shoes and not heels, which is not the norm for me. Wearing heels has always made me feel empowered, like a source of strength and femininity, and well, right now I don't feel strong. I feel sad.

I put the spoon down, take a step back from the counter, and turn to face her.

"That's better," she croons, smiling at me as if I'm a toddler. I just roll my eyes.

"Do we have to do this?" I ask her, feeling somewhat defeated yet irritated at the same time. She doesn't understand, he doesn't understand, and there's no sense in trying to explain it to them.

"Yes, we do. I'm going to make us both an iced coffee, and then I'll meet you outside on the patio."

She's using the secret weapon, the iced coffee, and it has been like eight or nine hours since I last had a glass.

"Fine."

She grins, pleased with herself for winning this round, only she doesn't understand that I'm not fighting. I'm not doing anything.

Stripping off my apron, I toss it onto the counter and catch the eye of my sous chef. He pops one eyebrow up, confirming to me that everyone is onto me. Looking around, I see a few more of the kitchen staff is watching, and I can't help but feel defensive.

"What?" I call out to them, tossing my arms in the air, trying to look at least five of them in the eye simultaneously. All of them evade me, out of fear, of course.

"Nothing, Chef. You all done over there?" He tilts his head toward the mess I've made.

I look back at the counter and frown. It really is a big mess. "Yes, I'm done."

"All right then, we'll clean that up while you're out talking to Ms. Taylor," he says. It's subtle, but his words are enough to tell me the staff is uncomfortable around me and they're ready for me to go. I should have picked up on that; they've been tiptoeing around trying to keep quiet and not disturb me.

"Thank you." I nod to him. Tucking my tail, I make my way out to the dining room and then to the patio.

Sitting at my favorite table, I look around at the garden we've made. Last year, we made the decision to screen off the patio. We weren't sure the city would approve of the outside changes, but they did and we've never looked back. The mosquitos around here can be vicious at times, and with the herbs, vegetables, and flowers on the patio and outside down the sidewalk, this keeps the bees away from the diners.

"So, Jack left?" Taylor says before she even gets to her seat.

"He did." There's no sense in denying it; everyone seems to have figured it out already.

As she sits, she hands me my glass and asks, "When is he coming back?"

I take a sip before I reply. This coffee is hitting the spot.

"I don't know. Never?" I shrug my shoulders and frown. There's a twinge of humidity in the air today, and the outside of the coffee glass is quickly covered in condensation.

She leans forward in her seat. "So, him leaving is not about him just checking in with his trainers back in Tampa?"

"No." It didn't occur to me that people might think I was working extra hours just because he went out of town for a bit.

"What happened?" She looks genuinely concerned about this new discovery.

"Nothing." I shake my head then take another sip. Man, do I hate these types of conversations.

"Well, something had to have happened." Her tone is slightly animated and accusatory.

"Nothing happened. I just can't give him what he wants."

People on the sidewalk pass us, and I overhear one say to the other that they need to stop in and eat here again, that the food was delicious last time. It lifts my spirits a tiny bit, but Taylor keeps going, and she's a complete buzzkill.

"And what is it he wants?"

"A relationship. A forever. I don't know. We were just meant to be friends, and he wanted to change us. I can't do that."

Looking past her, my gaze catches on the magnolia tree across the street. It's in a random spot, in the corner of the lot, and there are a few blooms left on it, but not many as its flowering season is almost over. I can't help but wonder if Jack cut a few from this one too.

Jack. My heart twinges.

"I hate to break it to you, but for all your determination to say you're just friends, you're kind of wrong."

My eyes come back to hers, and she's scowling at me.

"You were in a relationship with him whether you want to admit it or not. Think about it." She leans back in her chair. "Y'all were living together, spending all of your time together, being intimate with each other, and don't deny it because I saw it firsthand the day of the brunch, and well, it's the significant other who always holds the title of best friend. Open your eyes, Meg, and see this for what it is. You were in a relationship with Jack. Jack Willett was your boyfriend."

Hearing her put it like that, the dull pain that's been simmering in my chest since he left intensifies.

How do I answer that? Because looking at it from this perspective, she's not wrong.

Guilt washes over me, because even more than before, this solidifies to me that this situation between us is my fault. I've been trying to put it on him, telling myself he's the one who changed us, but I allowed the change to happen. I gave in to it, and in doing so, I gave him false hope. I led him on, which makes me a horrible person. I did this to him; he didn't do it to himself.

"Maybe, but then that makes his decision to leave even more the right thing to do."

She takes a sip of her coffee, eyeing me over the rim. "And you're sure this is what you want?" she asks, lowering the glass.

I want to say no, but reality forces me to say, "Yes."

Her eyes get sad as she studies me. I know she's not going to share any more of her opinions with me, and we both know I don't want to hear them. This is for the best, it is, and the reasons for my promises come flashing back bright and clear.

Pulling my shoulders back, I raise my head higher than it has been in days. With a renewed sense of purpose, I say the things I need to say.

"I am grateful for the time we spent together. How could I not be?" I give her a small smile, hoping to reassure her that everything is going to be okay. "But in the end, he'll realize I'm right, and I know he'll think just as fondly of me as I do of him. Soon enough, we'll go back to being friends again, just like we were meant to be."

Pushing the chair back, I put a lock around my heart. I should have done this the day he left. It will only hurt if I allow it to, and I refuse to feel sad over losing him when I am happy I got to have him in the first place. There's always a silver lining, right? I must be positive about this, because if I'm not, then what am I?

Southern Macaroni and Cheese

Ingredients:
   3 cups elbow macaroni uncooked
   1 ½ cups milk
   1/2 cup heavy whipping cream
   1 cup Colby & Monterey Jack shredded (cheese blend)
   6-8 oz Velveeta cheese shredded (feel free to cut back on the Velveeta if you don't want it to be super creamy)
   1 cup sharp cheddar shredded (can use less if you don't like a sharp taste in your mac n cheese)
   salt & pepper to taste
   2 eggs
   1 cup smoked cheddar cheese shredded (a must)
   paprika optional

Directions:
   Preheat oven to 350 F.
   Cook macaroni until just al dente or a little under al dente. (Look on the back of the box to see how long you need to cook your pasta for it to reach al dente.) Be careful not to overcook.
   Drain pasta and set aside.
   In a large bowl, add milk, heavy cream & cheeses (except for the smoked cheddar).
   Stir to combine.
   Taste the milk mixture and add salt & pepper until it has a good taste. (You can also add in other seasonings like onion powder,

paprika, etc. Tasting will help avoid having a plain, bland baked macaroni & cheese.)

When you are content with the taste, add the eggs.

Stir well until combined.

Butter a 9 x 9-inch baking dish.

Add macaroni to the baking dish.

Pour cheese mixture over macaroni.

Make sure the cheese is distributed well.

Top with the smoked cheddar cheese. (I add a little more Colby jack as well.) Sprinkle with paprika and/or black pepper, if desired.

Bake for 35-45 minutes. Do not overbake. It may be a bit jiggly when you take it out of the oven. It will firm up as it cool.

Let cool for about 10-15 minutes or until fully set.

Enjoy!

Chapter 29

Man's Best Friend

Jack

IF MARCH IS my favorite month, I've now decided April most definitely is not. It doesn't matter how pleasant the sun is, how green the trees are, or how colorful the azalea bushes seem to be. What I will forever associate this month with is that the first girl I ever said 'I love you' to didn't say it back, and that my team drafted a wide receiver in the second round last night. If that's not telling of the future, I don't know what is.

Instead of heading home, I drove straight to Bryan's unannounced to pick up Zeus. She may not want to love me, but I know he does, and right then I just needed someone to. After being climbed on and kissed for a solid fifteen minutes, the clutching of my heart eased a bit.

Of course Bryan and Lexi didn't say anything; they knew well enough by the look on my face that I didn't want to be messed with. Instead, Lexi led me into the kitchen, where she served me a piece of strawberry pie, and then she showed me the downstairs guest bedroom. This is where I've stayed. I know I should go home—it's been almost a week and it's time—but maybe in another day or two.

Bryan left yesterday afternoon for the team's draft party. He encouraged me to leave Zeus with Lexi and come with him, but I wasn't feeling up to it. What man wants to come face-to-face with his replacement, especially if he's not ready to retire? I know it's not certain I am retiring, but I still have a ways to go before we will know for sure. Whether or not I'll be coming back to a starting position is an entirely different scenario.

"Look at how sweet this picture is," Lexi says, coming out through the sliding glass door and handing me her phone. It's Zeus and me just sitting, staring out at their property, with my arm wrapped around his back. It is a great photo, and after I forward it to myself, I put it up as a post with the caption: **A dog is the only thing on earth that loves you more than he loves himself. #truth**

It isn't meant to be a jab in her direction, but maybe it is. I know she'll see it, and I want her to know I'm not alone—unlike her. She has no one and nothing that keeps her company, except for her restaurant, but that's a business, and at the end of the day, you leave it. I hate that I'm angry and hurt, but knowing she's not going to be in my future, I now feel like I'm in another transition for my life, which adds to my overall frustration.

What a freaking mess this is.

What a mess I am.

Letting out a sigh, I stare out at the treehouse Bryan, Lexi, and her brother James grew up in. It's crazy to me that it's lasted all these years, but it looks maintained and seems to have recently received a fresh coat of paint. I didn't grow up with things like this in my childhood. Maybe it's why I seek out adventures—because I was denied them for so long—and right this second I'm kicking myself because I think maybe somewhere in the back of my mind I believed Meg and I were going to have a life together where there were treehouses and children.

Could I sound any more pathetic?

I'm thinking I even hate myself right now.

Sitting down next to me, Lexi hands me a glass of sweet tea, places a plate of cornbread between us, and lets us sit there in silence.

Lexi is a great girl. Bryan should count his lucky stars that he finally pulled his head out of his ass long enough to go get the girl. There isn't anyone out there who I think could put up with him better than her. She gets him, and on a whole different level than most people. I thought Meg got me, too, but I guess not.

There I go again, sounding sorry for myself.

Surprisingly, it wasn't as hard to leave her as I thought it would be. A man can only take being shot down so many times, and no one wants to be where they aren't really wanted. I don't actually think she didn't want me there, she just didn't want me the way I wanted her, and that wasn't going to change. So, after making the hard decision to pack up that last day, despite being slowed down with this injury, it didn't take me long to move around the house and collect the few things that were mine. I hadn't been a slob in her home, but it was things like my watch charger in the kitchen, my flip-flops outside the back door, that kind of stuff.

"Are you ever going to tell me what happened?" Lexi asks, breaking me from my thoughts.

I know Meg texted her once, asking if I had picked up Zeus, and Lexi told her I was here, said they would talk at another time. I know she is her friend, and quite frankly that's where her loyalty should be, but I appreciate her letting things lie while I'm here. They can gossip about me all they want after I leave.

"What's there to tell you? It's just not meant to be." I briefly think back to Meg's face when she saw that my room had been emptied. Shock and a little bit of panic had set in, and was it impulsive for me to leave right then, yes, but for me, sometimes when it's fight or flight, flight is the best option. I like choices, and I wasn't her choice, so where did that leave me? I was stuck; I had to go.

"What makes you say that?" she asks.

My brows pull down and I glance over at her like she's crazy. "Uh, maybe because she's told me so repeatedly since day one last summer." I've always appreciated being heard, by my teammates, my parents, my friends; I should have done a better job listening to her, or at least taken her more seriously. She told me.

Lexi smiles at me like she knows something I don't, and it throws me off. Between her and Bryan, he's been more vocal about how much this situation sucks. He's the perfect kind of friend, one who will stand behind you and will also push you when needed. I'm glad he hasn't pushed this week. I've needed time to process.

"I don't think you should give up on her yet." She turns her head away from me and takes a bite of her cornbread.

"You can't give up on something you never had." Intrigued, I snag a square for me. Usually I think cornbread is dry, but when I take a bite, this one is moist and delicious.

"That's not true and you know it. Shelby called me after the Wine and Food Festival brunch, and she shared a lot with me about our friend Meg."

I'm sure she did. Meg was becoming an expert at having her cake and eating it too.

I turn to face her more, and I would be lying if I said I wasn't desperate to hear these little tidbits from her, no matter how perceptively incorrect they are. "Like what?"

She meets my gaze. "You already know, Jack. There's no need for me to repeat it."

And I do know. That was quite possibly one of the best days of my life. To start it with her lips finally on mine and then to end it with her naked between my sheets after the hallway . . . I thought it was going to be our beginning. Turns out it wasn't.

"She doesn't want me the way I want her. It doesn't matter anymore." I shake my head and turn to look back out over the garden she has planted back here. She doesn't need to see what these words do to me, and I for damn sure don't want her pity.

I take in the details; it is immaculate, just like Meg's. Of course they are completely different—one is urban and one is rural—but the intent is the same, and now I feel even worse from just looking at plants. How long will this go on where the stupidest things make me think of her?

"Here's the thing—I know you know Meg, but you only know this Meg." She pauses to let that sink in. "You didn't know her before the cancer or during the cancer, and neither did I. I did meet her directly after, and she's a different person now than she was then. Things change us, they shape who we become. She's only let you see what she wants you to see, but for all her smiling and living like the glass is half full, there are still some very dark places in her that linger from the past."

Her past.

Just like that, the confusion I was already feeling over how I could have misread the signs between us so badly takes a different turn. I hadn't considered this to be a possibility. I mean . . . that was years ago.

Yes, I've been trying to figure out why she is the way she is, but I never once considered that she hasn't always been this person, this when-life-gives-you-lemons-make-lemonade type of person.

And yes, I do believe life experiences shape us into the people we ultimately are, but she had to have been born with this sunny personality; that isn't something that magically appears. I understand that she had cancer and survived it, but that doesn't explain why she refuses to commit or love someone. She gets to live a full life—why doesn't she want to share that with someone?

Then again, no. The more I think about it, I think Lexi is wrong. Her past doesn't have anything to do with this. It's about her not having the same feelings for me that I have for her. You can't make someone love you.

"Everyone has a past," I tell her, standing and taking my glass and the plate with me. "Some are good, and some are bad, but in the end that's what it is—the past. No one knows what tomorrow will bring, and Meg of all people claims she lives each moment to the fullest for that reason. So, no, I don't think her past has anything to do with this. It just is what it is."

She stands next to me, takes a long, hard look, and then shrugs her shoulders all nonchalantly. "If you say so." With that she leaves me standing there, Zeus next to me and my hands full.

I do say so.

I know what I'm worth. I know the type of man I am and how good of a partner I would have been to her. Do I have a high opinion of myself? Maybe, but there's nothing wrong with confidence and seeing your own value. It's just too bad she didn't see it, too. Will I think about what Lexi said a little more? Absolutely. I just guess my question to that is: What does that have to do with me?

Strawberry Pie

Ingredients:

1 box of rolled 2-refrigerated pie crusts
5 cups fresh strawberries, rinsed, hulled, sliced in half/quartered
1/2 cup granulated sugar, or more depending on sweetness of berries
3 Tablespoons cornstarch
1/2 teaspoon fine sea salt
Milk, as needed
Turbinado sugar, as needed

Directions:

Follow pie crust package directions for thawing. Place the first pie crust into the pie plate and firmly press it into the bottom and sides of pie plate. Trim the excess dough leaving about a 1/2-inch overhang all around. Cover with plastic wrap and let chill in the fridge.

Roll out the second pie crust until 10 inches in diameter. Cover with plastic wrap and let chill in the fridge for 5 minutes.

Meanwhile, toss strawberries with sugar, cornstarch, and salt in a large bowl.

Pour strawberries into the chilled pie crust. Cover with the rolled out top crust. Decorate the edges with a fork, or pinch together with your fingers to form crust. Chill pie while you preheat the oven to 450 degrees F, with a baking sheet inside to warm.

Place chilled pie on the heated baking sheet. Brush top of

the pie lightly with whole milk. Sprinkle with turbinado sugar. Use a knife to cut four slits/vent holes in the top of the crust. This is necessary to let the steam escape and prevent the top crust from exploding during baking.

Bake at 450 degrees for 10 minutes. Then reduce heat to 350 degrees and bake for 15 minutes. Rotate the pie and continue to bake for another 20-30 minutes until the pie is golden brown. Let pie cool on rack before serving.

Chapter 30

Keep Calm and Save Recipes

Meg

THE KITCHEN DOOR at OBA swings open and bangs against the wall as Taylor storms in. Every head in the back of the house pops up to see what the commotion is all about, until they see it's directed at me. My eyes narrow at the anger rolling off of her.

"What are you doing?" She barely spits the words out at me, her cheeks tinted a nice shade of pissed-off red.

"What do you mean?" I ask her, keeping my voice low and not liking that she's causing a scene in front of my staff.

She points to the dining room and pieces of her blonde hair follow, flying into her face. "Why is there a guy out there who says he's here to pick you up for your date? A date, Meg?!"

Behind me, a few of the line guys start to murmur, and I turn to look at them. Some heads are shaking with disapproval but immediately drop as they resume breaking

309

down the kitchen from today while others are prepping for tomorrow. I'm being judged, by all these people, and I don't like it.

Not wanting to continue this conversation in front of curious eyes, I drag her into the walk-in cooler.

With her hands on her hips, she glares at me, her breath coming out in visible puffs. "Please, explain to me why you are going on this date today."

"First off, don't talk to me like that in front of my staff. It undermines my authority, and I don't like it. Second, I don't have to explain anything to you. You are really overreacting. And third, why not?"

Her face falls at my admonishment. I hate that I needed to point that out, but she can't be yelling at me in front of them, although I do understand her motivation. Outside of Shelby and Lexi, she is my closest girlfriend, and we've always been very open and honest with each other.

It's been over two weeks since Jack left, and I still haven't heard from him. Wanting to be the bigger person, I did text him a few days ago to ask how he was, but he never responded. That stung a lot more than I expected it to and reaffirmed that I need to keep going. My grandmother once told me to keep calm and save recipes, and I've created a lot of new ones since he left. It's time to move on.

"Maybe because you should be a little considerate of Jack's feelings and at least let the paint dry before getting back out there. He might not mean that much to you, but clearly you did to him."

Her words are like arrows, and they hit their target, making my jaw drop. "That's not true at all. Jack means a lot to me—you know that better than anyone." Although I would argue that if I had meant that much to him, it wouldn't have been so easy for him to completely cut me out of his life.

"Really?" She crosses her arms over her chest and pops one eyebrow up. The cold has started to sink into my clothes, but it doesn't seem to be affecting her at all.

The thing is, no matter how much everyone seems to think we were dating, we weren't. Did we cross the line a few times, yes, and did we catch feelings, maybe, but the bottom line is that we were never going to be something permanent, and I can't just waste my days away. Time is precious, and I owe it to myself to keep living life to the fullest. I locked those feelings away; I had to.

"Look, I have to go," I tell her, not wanting to argue. She won't understand, no matter how much I try to explain why, even though I don't need to explain myself to anyone.

"I wish you wouldn't. You are making a mistake." Her arms and her shoulders sag.

Am I? Am I making a mistake? I thought moving on was what normal people did. Granted, my perception of normal was altered years ago, but this is how you do this—or at least this is how I do it.

People don't understand that a cancer survivor's definition of normal is a bit different than that of someone who has never faced their mortality. That doesn't necessarily mean it's bad, it just takes some time to adjust, and if I'm honest with myself, I'm still adjusting. That said, I've given myself parameters for what normal looks like for me, and I'm okay with them. I've always owned the promises I've made to myself, and although not every day is a good day, I've given myself grace to know that the next day will be. It has to be, and I have to keep going.

Yes, I choose to live a life that views the glass as half full, but do I still have moments when I'm by myself where I'm not strong and fearless? Of course I do. That's part of my normal, my unique version of what defines normal, and although I've had to give in to the fact that these moments will happen, I also use them to fuel me from day to day. That's exactly what I'm doing with the feelings I had about Jack leaving. I worked through them—I'm still working through them—but I also took a long look at what it must have felt like for him, and I'm doing my best to let go. I have to. It's for the best. For seven years I've worked very hard to maintain a sense of stability and a rejection of complacency, and I'm not going to stop now.

We only get one life, and each of us has to choose how we live it.

Letting out a sigh, I know there's nothing more to say. Not needing to explain myself any more, I push past her and exit the cooler. The staff is quiet as I grab my bag, thank them for the great day, and say good night. I hate that in the span of five minutes, I've gone from being excited about meeting someone new to feeling guilty. I'm not doing anything wrong.

Moving through the restaurant, I'm lost in my head as I approach the hostess stand, and then my eyes catch on blond hair, flawless skin, a lean build, and blue eyes. He is quite possibly one of the hottest guys I have ever seen—outside of Jack, that is. *Curses!* I don't want to think about Jack.

Jack.

My Jack.

My heart frowns at the inaccuracy of that.

Not my Jack.

That same Jack didn't look back. That same Jack dropped me like hot cakes. That same Jack is posting pictures of him with Zeus, and him out to dinner and laughing with his friends, and on a boat fishing with his shirt off and a large sun hat on. That same Jack told me he loved me then made moving on look effortless. That same Jack—if I'm being honest with myself—broke my heart.

Moving to stand in front of my six-foot-tall date, I feel his eyes take me in from head to toe. By the time they find their way back to mine, my frowning heart has filled with an uneasiness, and a wrongness settles in.

"Hi. You must be Jack—I mean Jason! Sorry." I hold my hand out for him to take.

He smiles at me and slides his hand into mine. It's warm, nice, but alarm bells start going off in my head that it's the wrong hand and I don't want him touching me.

Why is this happening to me?

Oh, I know—Taylor and her meddling ways!

"And you must be Meg," he says, his smile so large and kind. Immediately I notice he doesn't have dimples. Why am I looking for dimples? If I could slap my hand on my forehead and not look ridiculous, I would.

"Yep." It's the only word I can get out as my throat seems to have completely closed and my lips won't move. I feel like an inadequate idiot.

"It's nice to meet you," he says, so genuinely.

"You too. Are you ready?" I need him out of the restaurant and both of us out from under so many condemning eyes.

"You lead the way." He steps aside and lets me walk out the door first. I don't turn around, don't look at any of my staff's faces; I just can't bring myself to do it. I thought this was a good idea, but now I'm not so sure. I don't understand. Is there some sort of unspoken timeline about these things? Because if not now, when?

The word *never* floats through my mind, and I cringe.

Jason falls into step next to me. "OBA is a great restaurant. When you said to meet you here, I was kind of hoping we would be staying to eat."

I'm not sure why I'm surprised by this, but I am. "You've eaten at OBA?"

"I have. Do you work there?" he asks, keeping the conversation going.

I want to feel a sense of pride like I normally do, but images of Jack's face as he came to meet me for a late lunch, hovered over me in the kitchen while I was cooking, painted the ceiling, and worked magic with the magnolias flash through my mind. Pain ricochets through me as my heart trips in my chest.

"Yes. Actually, I own it. It's my restaurant." The words come out strained, and he hears it. His brows furrow just a little, but then my admission sinks in and his brows reverse and rise in surprise. Heck, I'm surprised, too—I never tell people this. I don't know why I'm telling him now, but he pauses on the sidewalk to stop and look at me.

"You're the owner of OBA?" It sounds like a question, but it's not; it's more of a statement.

A knot forms in my throat, and instead of answering him with words, my lips stay pressed together and I murmur, "Mmmhmm."

"Wow. That's great."

We start walking again and he proceeds to talk to fill in the awkward silence I'm creating between us. He tells me

314

where we're headed to eat, what he does for a living, and how it's his job that brought him to Charleston. He tells me it was his sister's idea for him to join a dating site to meet people but says he would kill her if she ever did. No offense to me, but he worries about her safety.

At that, an unwanted noise escapes me. The guilt that descended upon me at the restaurant now morphs into something so suffocating I feel like I can't breathe. Jack hated me going on these dates, and although I am free to live my life how I choose, the thought of worrying him or disappointing him even more has me catching my heel in a crack in the sidewalk and stumbling.

"Whoa. Are you okay?" Jason asks, quickly reaching out to steady me with his hand on my elbow.

I snatch it away instantly, and he holds his hands up in surrender as he takes a step back.

"Sorry," I say softly, turning to face him. "Yes," I mumble in response to his question, my eyes filling with tears. He sees them and lets out a deep sigh, his hands landing on his hips. That's when "No" is whispered from somewhere deep in my soul and passes through my lips. I'm realizing my feelings for Jack aren't as locked away as I thought they were.

"Oh, man," Jason murmurs, running one hand over the back of his neck and looking at the ground. "The moment I saw you, I knew this was too good to be true." He shakes his head.

What do I say? I feel so stupid, but Taylor was right—this is wrong.

"Okay, this date is officially over." He stands up straight and frowns.

"What?" I ask, my eyes flying to his face to meet his while relief takes over and I wonder if I somehow said those words out loud.

"Yeah, to be honest, I just got out of a long-term relationship, and I wasn't really ready to put myself back out there in the first place. I just did so to make my sister happy, but still, I'm starving, and I need to eat. This place we're going to is supposed to have an amazing carbonara dish, and I love hanging out with my friends. So, friend, are you hungry, too?"

He still wants to have dinner with me, even though I just gave off hot-mess vibes.

He wants to be friends.

We can be friends.

With this thought, the invisible ropes that were squeezing me tighter and tighter with each step loosen. I love making new friends, and as long as he's figured out that's all we'll ever be, nothing more, I can do this.

Aside from being my friend, the one thing he'll never be is my best friend.

Spaghetti Carbonara

Ingredients:

2 large eggs
1 cup heavy cream
2 teaspoons olive oil
1/4 cup fried and crumbled bacon
1/4 cup diced ham
6 ounces dried spaghetti or linguine, cooked al dente
6 tablespoons freshly grated Parmigiano
3 tablespoons shredded or shaved Parmigiano
Kosher salt and pepper to taste
Chopped parsley (optional)

Directions:

Combine eggs and heavy cream in a small mixing bowl, and whip together well. Set aside.

In a 10-inch sauté pan over medium heat, heat olive oil, bacon and ham until sizzling.

Add pasta and toss well.

Slowly pour egg-cream mixture over top while pulling up spaghetti with tongs until coated.

Add Parmigiano, salt, pepper, and toss well.

Portion into serving bowls and top with shredded or shaved Parmigiano and parsley.

Chapter 31

You Can't Live a Full Life On An Empty Stomach

Jack

"ALL RIGHT THERE, Jack. Let's finish today with bending over and letting your arms dangle so your hands can touch your toes. Then roll up to a mountain pose while inhaling through your nose and exhaling at the top."

I replay what she just said to me while staring down at the teal mat, and I feel a pulse of irritation thump at the side of my head.

That's right. She said . . . fucking . . . toe touches.

I feel Jeanine move from her mat to stand in front of me to help with balance if I need it, and to make sure I don't fall, which I won't—I'd rather die first. After all these years and all this time, I've been reduced to this: doing yoga. On top of that, I can't even hardly stand here with both feet on the floor and both legs locked out straight. Heat flares in my face as even more anger builds inside me.

Dr. Leffers told me both feet would be flat on the floor after six weeks and I would be able to do toe touches without any problem, and I was. It's a weight-bearing exercise where you use your body to rebuild strength in the leg. Hell, over the last couple of weeks, Eddie and I moved way past this to running in the hydrotherapy tank and doing both open and closed chain activities. We did seated leg extensions, hamstring curls, calf pumps, squats, deadlifts, lunges, power cleans, and leg presses, but with the swelling not really receding, this is all the trainers are letting me do.

Fucking yoga.

I get it; I do. There are plenty of studies out there that show how great this form of exercise is for all kinds of athletes, but I don't want to be doing this and this alone. I want to be out with my team, sprinting with a parachute, working drills with Bryan, and doing exercises like hop and switch, not a warrior pose. At this point, I want to kill all the warriors along with their downward dogs, and then I want to throw Jeanine off all the different planks to drown in the water.

I know it's not her fault. I just want my life back.

Then again, the sixty-four-million-dollar question is: What life is that?

When I open my eyes, there she is, just like I knew she would be, and she's frowning. Now I feel even worse. She's just trying to help me, and although I'm going through the motions, this really isn't benefiting me. I don't feel calm or centered. I don't feel as if I've just had this amazing workout, and I don't feel like I am progressing at all. Actually, I feel like I'm regressing physically, mentally—just all of the above—and it sucks.

"Why don't you hit the showers and I'll text you later with when we should get together again." She moves away from me to turn off the supposedly calming music she was playing.

"Sounds good. Thank you, Jeanine." I'm trying not to come off as a complete dick, but my voice is rough with frustration, and I know she can hear it.

"Of course. What medicine are you taking?" She moves to bend down and pick up the mats and blocks we were using. I wrap my towel around my neck and grab my bottle of water.

"I don't like medicine, so only naproxen as needed." I think about the last time I took some and realize I'm due. I need the swelling to be as minimal as possible.

"Perfect. Once you're showered, have them hook up the TENS unit for thirty minutes, too."

A TENS unit is a device that sends electrical impulses to a desired area to help manage pain. Although the pain is minimal at this point, it's more of an irritation because of the swelling that bothers me.

"Will do." I give her a brief smile then walk out of the activity room and into the weight room.

Noises I once loved assault my ears, and I cringe internally. The clanging of the weights, the loud thumping music blaring from the speakers, the laughter from guys scattered across the room . . . Of course as I pass them by I get head nods and a few brief greetings, but it's like now that I've been removed from this, the family atmosphere I once felt it was doesn't feel that way anymore. It feels tiring and monotonous, like I had been sucked into a vortex and now that I've been let out, it's not the same. There's so much more to life outside of football.

On top of that, since I've been back, more than ever I have noticed the age difference between the incoming guys and me. Since the draft last week, the rookies have descended, and to me it feels glaringly obvious that I am old as dirt standing next to them. When we are in our twenties, we all feel the same, but I'm thirty-two and they are twenty-one and twenty-two. I may have time and experience on my side, but they have significantly less aches and pains and a hunger for the sport that I just don't think I feel anymore. I want to feel that, but maybe I'm immune to it after all this time, or maybe it's a sign that it's time for me to move on. I just don't know.

Plus, they look like babies. I mean, the one dude I passed coming in today still has acne.

Acne.

Quickly making my way to the locker room, I shower, get dressed, and head to the training room. It's here that Reid finds me, having just showered himself. I'm hooked up to the TENS unit and staring at photos of Meg on my phone.

"You look like shit," he says, not sugarcoating anything.

"Ah, thanks, man. Love you, too," I say sarcastically. Looking him over, I see he actually looks great, but then again, why shouldn't he? He's in great health, and he has the girl.

He pops the spout on his water bottle, squirts some into his mouth, and then his gaze flits to my phone. Spotting the image, he asks, "You talk to her yet?" His New York accent is sounding more pronounced these days than it used to, or maybe it's just that I've become accustomed to hearing a sweet Southern one.

"No." I look down at the screen and run my finger over her face. The photo is one I took of her in the back yard at her house. She's wearing little shorts, a tank top, and these large rubber boots she keeps just inside the back door. She's got the hose on, she's watering her plants, and she's smiling at me.

She's so beautiful my heart constricts in my chest.

"Why not?" he asks, propping his hip against the end of the therapy bench I'm sitting on.

I look back up at him and shrug. "Honestly, I don't know."

It's been over two weeks, nineteen days to be exact, and every day feels longer than the last. She made the first move. She texted me, and I didn't text back. I know I'm being an asshole to her, but my feelings are hurt and I'm still licking my wounds.

"You know you're an idiot, right?" He frowns at me.

"Probably, but what am I supposed to do? She doesn't want me, and you know that." At least she doesn't want me like I want her.

"Then change her mind," he says, as if it is that simple.

Have we talked about Meg since I returned to Tampa? Yes. Most of the guys were curious at first because I had been gone, but once word spread that it had ended, they stopped asking, which I am grateful for. There's nothing like sitting at the dinner table with a bunch of dudes and having them ask you about your broken heart. No, thanks.

"Seriously, though, I have never known you to throw in the towel when it's something you want. From beating one of your previous records to raising money for a charity, you go above and beyond for everything—why not her?" He tilts his head to the side to try to get a better read on me.

"I don't know." I shake my head.

He's right. I've always done everything to the max. It brings me joy and excitement to know I've put a hundred and ten percent into everything I do, so why did I bail on her, on us, so quickly?

I know why: because she wasn't changing her mind. At least not then, not at that moment, and I refused to stand there and let her see me cry. Now, though, after a little time apart, she might think differently.

"What do I do?" I ask him, desperation most likely written all over my face.

"Why are you asking me that? I don't know her or anything about her. You do. I know she told you she didn't want a relationship, but did she ever tell you why? We all know you're terrible when it comes to listening—you only hear what you want to hear—but she had to have said or done something."

Did she? Did she say something? I agree with him about only hearing what I want to—it's what keeps me fun-loving and not so serious all the time—but maybe it's not about what she said. Maybe it's about what she didn't.

Perhaps I've been looking at this all wrong. Despite what she says, I know, I *know* she felt something for me. I know from the way she looked at me, how she held on to me a tad longer when her walls were down, and really the way she let me in when she doesn't let anyone in. No one. Not one person. Just me.

Randomly, I think back to a post she put up months ago of chicken country captain. In the text to go with it she said, **You can't live a full life on an empty stomach.** Now that I think about it more, that's exactly what she's doing. She claims she's living her life to the fullest, always drinking from a glass of lemonade, but is she really? Her glass-half-full mentality is just that, half full, and with the way she's going, it will never be full—at least not where love is concerned.

Yes, she's gone out with a lot of guys over the last year, but that's always seemed strange to me, and it also felt like she was completing a life to-do list she made for herself rather than really taking in what the experience was supposed to be teaching her.

Why?

Why does she do this? And why does she think like this? I don't get it. She meets all these people, yet she chooses not to get close to any of them. It's strange. She was loved as a child, and from everything she's said, her aunt adores her. Her friends do, too. Maybe Lexi is more right than I gave her credit for; maybe Meg does have dark places she's never shared with me, and maybe I should have looked harder for them. Maybe it's time for her to come clean.

She's going to hate this, but I think it has to be done. She's always shied away from uncomfortable situations or conversations, but she needs to be honest with herself so she can be honest with me. Instead of me reacting to the first thing she says that I don't want to hear, I need to remain calm and listen. I need to listen to it all, because I truly do believe deep down in my gut that this isn't an us problem, and it's always been a her problem.

Well, I guess that makes it an us problem, because I want her to share her life with me. I don't want her to deal with things alone, and that's exactly what she's doing—no thanks to me.

That's about to change.

When I glance back up at Reid, he sees that my eyes have brightened with an idea, and a small smile curves his lips.

"You wanna go grab a beer?" I ask him, feeling the first ounce of the hope I've been starving for knock its way in.

"Absolutely," he says, now grinning because he knows we're about to brainstorm.

Unhooking the TENS device, I grab my bag, and the two of us head toward the parking lot. Reid claps me on the shoulder and squeezes, and that's when I realize I'm smiling. He's smiling, too. He knows I'm finally on my way to getting my girl back.

She doesn't know it yet, but I'm coming for her.

She's going to talk, I'm going to listen, and I'm not taking no for an answer.

Chicken Country Captain

Ingredients:

$^1/_2$ cup vegetable oil
1 (3-pound) chicken, cut into 8 pieces
Salt and pepper, for seasoning
All-purpose flour, for dusting
1 tablespoon bacon grease or butter
1 medium white onion, thinly sliced
1 large bell pepper, thinly sliced
2 garlic cloves, thinly sliced
2 (28-ounce) cans crushed tomatoes
1 $^1/_2$ teaspoons white pepper
2 tablespoons curry powder
1 tablespoon chopped parsley, plus a few leaves for garnish
1 teaspoon dried thyme
$^1/_4$ pound slivered almonds, toasted
2 tablespoons dried currants
2 cups cooked rice, for serving

Directions:

Preheat the oven to 350°F.

In a Dutch oven, heat oil over medium-high heat. Season the chicken pieces with salt and pepper and dust with flour. Once oil is hot, fry the chicken pieces, turning occasionally, until browned on all sides, about 8 to 10 minutes. Remove chicken from pot and place on a plate, then tent with foil. Wipe Dutch oven clean.

Return Dutch oven to stove over medium heat. Melt bacon grease (or butter). Add onion, pepper, and garlic and cook until softened and starting to brown, about 8 to 10 minutes. Stir in crushed tomatoes and bring to a simmer. Reduce heat to low and let simmer for 15 to 20 minutes. Season with salt, white pepper, curry powder, parsley, and thyme and simmer for 5 more minutes. Return the chicken pieces to the Dutch oven and nestle down into sauce, spooning sauce over all of the pieces.

Using the lid as a guide, trace and cut out a circle of brown paper. Place the paper over top of the chicken and cover pot with the lid. Put pot into oven and cook for 45 minutes.

Remove pot from oven. Carefully remove the chicken pieces from the pot and place them in the center of a large platter. Stir the almonds and dried currants into the sauce. Spoon the rice around the rim of the platter surrounding the chicken. Pour the sauce over the chicken and rice. Garnish with parsley and serve.

Chapter 32

Can't Never Could

Jack

I THINK I'VE been living my life in limbo. Well, maybe not my whole life, but at least for the last several years. It's like I can't go backward to who I used to be, but I'm not going forward either, and I didn't even realize it. This makes me think of Newton's first law: An object at rest will stay at rest, and an object in motion will stay in motion, unless acted upon by an outside force.

Jack was the outside force.

No, I didn't expect my life to be the same once I was declared cancer-free, but at the time things were moving forward with change and I just went with it. My aunt and Shelby got us set up at culinary school, and off we went. We were so busy. Then we graduated and started the restaurant. Again, so busy. I've always been busy, always been moving, and now I'm wondering if I missed part of the healing because of it. I never stopped moving, I never took the time, and now look where I am.

In my room. In my bed. Under the covers.

Reeling from what will undoubtedly be the biggest mistake of my life.

And because of that single thought, I just don't know what to do with myself.

I've worked so hard to live my life a certain way, and now I just don't know. I feel like I don't know anything anymore, and with everything compounding all at once, I'm sad.

Like really sad.

It's a kind of sadness I've never experienced before.

I'm sad I've spent so much time trying to live my life when apparently I wasn't. I'm sad I might have missed out on opportunities just because I was convinced I needed to keep moving from one thing to the next, and because of this I'm sad I didn't give myself what I needed: time to stop, reflect, and heal. I glossed over anything that wasn't happy or positive, even though the scars are still there, and they're still shiny.

I should have known this was bound to happen. Cancer invades our minds, our bodies, and our relationships. There's a process, and I only allowed myself to give in to one of those three. I think I felt if I let it consume my mind or my relationships, it would win, and I wasn't going to let that happen. I was fighting it—I'm still fighting it.

Only right now I don't feel like I have much fight in me.

After what I'm forever going to refer to as my "awakening," I called Shelby, broke down, and told her everything that had been going on. Of course she had already heard from Lexi and Taylor, but knowing me and knowing I don't like to be pushed, she gave me space. Like Taylor, she was mad that I went out with Jason, even though I informed her it really wasn't a date, more of an un-date.

Poor Jason. He was really nice, he just ended up in the wrong place at the wrong time. I didn't share too much with him—after all, he's not the guy I need to be opening up to; Jack is—but listening to him, I couldn't help but think he would be perfect for Taylor. So, I invited him to the restaurant next week for dinner, partly because of her, but mainly as a peace offering for the failure that was our night out. I told him to bring whoever he wants, but I will be introducing the two of them. Who knows? Maybe they'll find love.

Love.

I do love Jack. I know I do.

Now that I've actually given in to the idea of it, something I swore I'd never do, it's easy to see how I was a goner from the beginning. It was completely out of my control. All he had to do was smile, and I freely gave him anything he wanted. Unknowingly, he had me wrapped around his finger, and in hindsight, I don't even mind. I loved making him happy, even when he wasn't.

My thoughts drift to his knee, and I wonder how he's doing. From the photos he's posted, it appears he's back with his team, and that makes me happy for him. It also makes me sad for myself, but deep down I'm happy he's where he truly wants to be. I do want the best for him, even if he decided that's not me.

Rolling to my side, I stare out my bedroom door and into the quietness of the house. With Jack here, I had forgotten how quiet it is when I'm by myself. I used to think it was nice after a long day at the restaurant, but now it's just so silent. I can hear my ears ringing, and I'm confused by the idea that this was something I liked before. This quiet is lonely and sad, like me, and maybe it's time I change that. Maybe it's time for a pet.

With that thought, I can see Shelby rolling her eyes and hear her saying, *"Get up and go get your man!"*

But is he mine?

I now understand where I went wrong, but what about him? He told me he loved me then five minutes later walked out the door without ever looking back. If you love someone, don't you fight for them? Then again, what am I doing to fight for him? And would he even want me to?

Feeling anxious, sad, nervous, and determined, I quickly pick up my phone and fire off another text to him: **Just checking in—how are you?** He didn't respond before, but maybe he will this time. I've extended the olive branch twice, and I just hope he'll grab hold of it.

Three little dots appear, and my heart does the high jump in my chest.

He's responding.

And then he doesn't.

Time passes, the dots disappear, and no text comes.

I feel kicked in the gut, and my eyes burn with more unwanted tears.

I was so close to having something from him, and then suddenly it feels so far. At this moment I feel every bit of the four hundred and forty miles between us.

More time passes, and nothing comes.

So that's that I guess.

At least now I know.

I squeeze my eyes shut and allow the heartache to consume me.

Being unwanted is the worst feeling.

From below, the front door opens, and for a split second my heart stops beating at the idea that it might be Jack—but then Taylor's voice calls up the stairs with a greeting. Who am I kidding? It's not him. It's been three weeks . . . it's never going to be him.

"Get up, get up, get up," she says in the most cheery voice, and I cringe.

"I don't want to," I whine, and although I sit up, I pull the blankets up higher around me.

"I know that, but it's time and you need to." There's a pounding on the stairs from her feet; she's headed my way, and I brace myself for what's coming. "I have a surprise for you," she sings out, and then she's in my doorway.

My eyes widen as I take her in. She's wearing a short black cocktail dress and heels. She's dressed up, and instantly I feel my hackles rise. "But I don't like surprises." I gawk at her like she's crazy.

"Yes, you do, and this one you will love." She moves into my room and opens the blinds, letting the light rush in. "Rise and shine!"

Gah, it's so bright I have to squint, and I flop back down, pulling the blankets over my head. "But . . . I can't." And I don't want to. Can't she see that?

She rips the covers away and glares down at me. "Can't never could, and that's not you at all. You are a fighter, you embrace all that life gives you, and you never ever pass up an opportunity for a good time. And seriously, have you seen your hair? It's like two cats fought in it."

Rolling onto my back, I defensively pat down my hair and groan at the ceiling, because she's right.

"Don't you even want to know what we're doing?" she teases.

"Sure," I deadpan, looking at her smug face, and then I change my mind. "Actually, no. You are way too dressed up." There's no way she isn't picking up on my lack of enthusiasm. I'm in my bed for the night—despite the fact that it's still daytime—and the thought of getting that dolled up to go out doesn't sound good to me at all.

"Well, you've been in this bed for two days. It's time. You could at least pretend to sound a little more excited, because a lot of work went into getting these tickets."

"What tickets?" Color me intrigued.

She now grins from ear to ear. "I might have scored us two tickets to a private home and garden tour with wine and finger foods. I saw a chardonnay shrimp dip listed, and you love shrimp, so there you go. I know how much you were looking forward to the Festival of Houses and Gardens twilight garden tour, and although we missed it, because we were so busy we needed to work, I'm certain this one will be pretty good, too."

"A private tour? I didn't realize they did those." I was disappointed I didn't get to do the festival tour this year; I love looking at the gardens.

"Yep. A patron came in and was talking about it, so I signed us up." She moves to my closet and starts rummaging through the dresses.

"Really? Well, I guess it makes sense if you think about it. People are still lingering around since we're in season, and the gardens are all immaculately maintained. Anything to make a few more bucks while they can."

"Exactly. So happy early birthday." She beams at me, holding up a dark blue dress that is not too short and ties around the waist, along with a pair of gold heels. "Get up, take a shower, and be quick about it. Tour starts in an hour."

"In an hour?" I sit straight up.

"Yeah, is that a problem?" She lays the dress on the end of the bed then makes her way to the door.

"No, it just seems kind of sudden. You could have given me more of a warning." I throw off the covers and stand. My eyes fall to my phone, which is on my nightstand, and I lament its continued silence with a frown.

"I just got them, and I just got done closing down the restaurant. Forgive me, your highness, for interrupting your very busy schedule." She glances toward the messy bed and pops one eyebrow.

I let out a sigh and she claps her hands together, because she knows she's won.

"Come on! This is going to be great. I'll wait for you downstairs." And with that she's gone.

Of course she had to go and come up with one of the few things that would actually make me happy.

"Aren't you so excited?" Taylor beams beside me as we walk down the sidewalk at a speed that shouldn't be normal in heels like the ones we're both wearing.

"I guess so." I haven't been excited by much lately, but the house the tour is at, The Cooke home, is one of my absolute favorites in the Battery. In fact, I'm shocked they are even open to do this private tour, and I find that my brain is excited to see how they've designed the back yard this year, even though my heart is not.

"You kill me," she says, her piercing hazel eyes looking at me as if I've lost my mind.

"I know, I know, and I'm sorry I'm a bit of a Debbie Downer." My gaze pleads with her to understand. "I really do appreciate you doing this for me. Thank you, Taylor. I know tonight will be amazing." And it will be, because how could it not? A beautiful home and garden, great company, and let's not forget the wine. There's only one thing that would make this even better, but I'm not going to think about him at all tonight. He's made his choice, and after him not replying to my text tonight, I know I'm not it.

"Don't thank me yet. Thank me after you've had the best night ever." She grins as we cross the street corner and come to a large stone wall that's covered in ivy.

"Best night ever, huh." A smile stretches across my face at my friend. It feels nice that it's genuine and not forced like so many have been these past couple of weeks. All I would have done tonight is stayed home and wallowed, and it's time for me to stop doing that. As much as I really don't want to, it's finally dawning on me that I need to find a new sense of normal, one he's not going to be a part of.

My throat tightens and I force myself to swallow down the loss. Taylor went out of her way to do something nice for me tonight, and I'm going to enjoy it, no matter what.

"Yep," she says, popping the P.

It's almost seven thirty, and the golden hour has made this night look nearly flawless. The ombre sky is splashed with sherbet orange and lavender, and sometime over the next half hour, the sun will say good night, lowering the temperature and humidity with it. It's perfect outside, and the perfect night for a garden tour.

"Look, there's the entrance." She points to an opening in the ivy in the wall.

"Wow, I didn't even know there was a door there. It's hidden underneath all the greenery like in *The Secret Garden*."

"Oh, I love that movie," Taylor says.

"Me too. Can you imagine having a garden like that all to yourself?"

"I have seen your back yard, or should I say garden. Don't sell yourself short—it's pretty amazing, too."

"Yeah, it is pretty nice."

I'm proud of my garden. It's a little high-maintenance, but I don't mind.

As we approach the door, I notice there aren't any other people around; it's just us.

"Are you sure this is where we're supposed to go?"

"Yep, positive."

She ushers me in through the secret entrance, past a wrought iron door to a cobblestone pathway. My eyes are flooded by the sights and sounds of a gorgeous four-tiered fountain sitting off to one side with a bench next to it, manicured hedges around the perimeter that are designed to look like a maze, trellises arched over the walkways with blooming flowers, and the twinkle lights hanging inside a very romantic gazebo perfectly placed in the center.

In my bag, my phone dings with a social media notification, but I ignore it and stand there blinking. My eyes must be playing tricks on me, only they aren't. Waiting on the steps, cast in a shimmering light, is Jack.

Chardonnay Shrimp Dip

Ingredients:

2 cups frozen cooked salad shrimp, about 7 oz, thawed, drained
1/2 cup Chardonnay wine
1 package cream cheese, softened
2 tablespoons mayonnaise
3 tablespoons finely chopped green onions
1 teaspoon Dijon mustard

Directions:

Coarsely chop shrimp. Place shrimp in a small glass bowl. Pour wine over shrimp, toss to coat. Cover. Refrigerate at least one hour to blend flavors. Drain shrimp, reserving wine.

In another small bowl, mix cream cheese, mayonnaise, 2 tablespoons of the onions and the mustard with spoon. Fold in shrimp. If a thinner consistency is desired, stir in small amounts of the reserved wine.

Spoon shrimp spread into a serving bowl. Sprinkle remaining onions over the top.

Serve with crackers.

Chapter 33

Food is Love

Jack

THE CREAK OF the wrought iron gate is the giveaway that they have arrived. Immediately, my heart rate doubles, and I'm flooded with nerves prickling my hands, roiling in my stomach, and just making me jittery all over. It feels like it has been a lifetime since I've seen her, and my anxiety about this moment is a solid mixture of excitement and dread. There is the possibility that she doesn't want to see me, even though her friends and mine all assure me that isn't the case.

From my vantage point, I watch as she moves into the garden looking like the angel she is with her brown curly hair down around her shoulders and back, a short dress perfectly molded to her body, and tall shoes that make her legs look a mile long. One by one, she takes in all the details while I take in the details of her I've so greatly missed. Sheer delight spreads across her beautiful face as she moves to take in the lit-up gazebo, and then she sees me. The smile drops, she falters in her steps, and she stops walking, her hands flying up to cover her mouth. Moments pass as I continue to drink in the sight of her being so close to me after what feels like so long.

"Jack," she says, her voice barely above a whisper, her eyes large with what could be shock or fear.

Behind her, there's movement as Taylor slips out to leave us alone. I don't even think Meg remembers she's there, much less acknowledges it, all thoughts of anything else vanishing.

"Hi," I say, my voice sounding more sturdy than I feel, and I slide my hands into the pockets of my slacks to wait and see how she reacts once the surprise has worn off. Yes, I chose to forgo my standard attire of jeans and dressed for the occasion in a black button-down and gray slacks. I don't think she's noticed, though; her eyes haven't strayed far from mine.

Damn, she looks so good.

Beautiful. Just beautiful.

And then her face crumbles. "I'm sorry," she says just before she starts to cry.

As she raises her hands a little higher to cover herself so she can't be seen, panic shoots through me at her sudden distress. In just a few strides I'm down the steps, standing in front of her and wrapping her up in my arms. I didn't expect her to cry, at least not like this. This isn't like her at all.

"Please don't cry." I drop my head so my face is pressed into her hair. She smells so good, every muscle in me instantly soothed by just this one sensation.

Pushing up to her tiptoes, she presses herself closer like she's trying to melt into me, and she buries her face in that sweet spot just under my chin and over my collarbone.

"I'm sorry, it's just . . ." She lets out a strangled noise that vibrates into my skin, and my poor deprived heart thumps hard at the sound. My arms tighten even more around her.

"No, I'm sorry. I'm sorry I left like I did. I'm sorry I didn't text you back the first time, and I'm sorry it took me so long to make my way back to you." And I am—I am so, so sorry. I know I was caught up in how that last week I was here made me feel, but I didn't really stop to consider her feelings and how I made her feel.

She leans back, her beautiful face tear-stained, and she shakes her head. "No, this is my fault. I never should have let you go. You were right the whole time, about me, about us, and I'm so sorry."

More tears drop from her eyes, and with each one, she steals another piece of my soul. I pull her back against me, and she wraps her arms around me, holding on for dear life.

I read somewhere once that human touch can be stronger than any verbal or emotional contact, that physical touch can promote a sense of security and belonging in any relationship, and they weren't wrong. Every time I touch her and she touches me, I feel like all is right in the world, feel we belong to each other. I can feel my blood pressure coming down and my heart rate slowing as it seeks to fall into sync with hers. It's the best feeling, and I hold on a little tighter.

"You smell so good." She breathes me in. "You feel so good." She snuggles closer. "And I'm so happy you are here." She lets out a deep, long-overdue sigh.

Not as happy as I am.

Mine.

My girl.

Next to us, Zeus whines. I had forgotten he was here, and just like me, he doesn't like the distress that's been rolling off of her.

Pulling back, Meg looks down and spots him. "Oh, hi, buddy." She sinks to her knees to hug him and buries her face in his fur. "I missed you, too."

He looks up at me and glares. If I didn't know any better, I'd say he was pissed at me for keeping them apart for so long. *Trust me, pal, I'm pissed at me, too.*

Standing up with her fingers still lingering in his fur, Meg glances behind me at the setup underneath the gazebo. "What is this?" she asks, wiping her face and under her eyes. As if I care about smudged makeup.

"I owed you a date, remember?" I place my hand on her lower back and guide her up the three steps to the center.

"A date?" she asks, confused. "I thought this was a private tour . . ."

"It is, private just for us. You mentioned in passing on the carriage ride that you loved this house and garden, and I never forgot, so I reached out. And yes, it's my turn for a date with you. Taking a play from your playbook, instead of going to a restaurant, I made the food for you. Food is love, right?" The corner of my mouth rises just a little.

"It is," she whispers, dropping her head and suddenly appearing shy.

Pulling out her chair, I guide her to sit then push her in before taking my own seat. Zeus settles in next to her feet, and she runs her hand over his head and back one time before she draws the napkin into her lap and pierces me with steel gray. There's anger and accusation in her gaze, which

I can't blame her for; I did barge into her life and then exit without so much as even looking back.

"You didn't text me back. I texted you like an hour and a half ago. I saw the dots and then you stopped. Why?"

"Yeah, about that . . ." Fidgeting, I pull my own napkin into my lap and pick up the bottle of white wine I had chilling to pour her a glass. "The first time, I have no excuse, other than my feelings were still hurt and I wasn't ready. Today, I started to, obviously, but if I had, I never would have stopped, and I had a to-do list a mile long to get ready for tonight. I know it doesn't look like much, but you'll be happy to know I did prepare all of this by myself." I glance down at the charcuterie board, the tureen of she-crab soup, the shrimp dip, and the other finger foods like stuffed cherry tomatoes.

"You made all this?" She looks at me with wariness and awe.

I nod, feeling slightly concerned that she won't like it. She looks down at the table, at the different dishes laid out in front of her.

"Where? Where did you prepare it?" She glances at me quickly then looks back at the table.

"Actually, at OBA." I open the lid to the tureen and ladle some soup into her bowl then mine.

"What?" Her eyes widen. "When? How come no one told me you were there today?"

I shrug my shoulders and grin, hoping this doesn't get Taylor in trouble. I can't imagine that it will. "From what I heard, you haven't been in much the last couple of days."

She frowns. "No, I haven't."

Picking up her spoon, she dips it into the soup and tastes it. Her eyes light up at the flavor, and a flash of heat sears me upon seeing that she's pleased. I didn't realize how nervous I was for her to eat the food I made until she sat down at the table.

Deciding I need to let her lead the conversation between us, I load up a few items on my plate and start eating. She does the same, and I watch closely as she tastes different things. It's quiet between us, but it's not an uncomfortable silence, more like a regrouping about what's to come next. I know how I feel about her and she knows how I feel about us, so really, it's her who needs to break the ice and explain what she's thinking and how she feels.

Fortunately, she doesn't make me wait long before she blurts out, "I made promises to myself."

Promises. I'd like to make a few promises to her, ones that begin and end with us and forever.

"Like what?" I ask her, setting my spoon down and giving her my full attention.

"Like . . ." She stops talking, frowns again, and starts pulling apart a piece of bread. I don't say anything, just watch her, and piece by piece, she unknowingly builds a pile of crumbs.

The sun has now dropped enough that it's more night than day. Although I do have a few small candles lit on the table, the lights strung up around the gazebo have cast her in a mixture of brightness and shadows. I could stare at her indefinitely, and I'm certain I would continuously discover something new.

Letting out a sigh, she tucks a stray piece of hair behind her ear. She's struggling and I hate this, but she needs to talk; she needs to tell me. There's no way to move forward without her opening up to me. Then she drops the bread, straightens up tall in her chair, and meets my gaze eye to eye.

"I made five promises to myself, only five so they could be manageable and obtainable, and easy to remember. I needed them, and I've held onto them because they've fueled me, shaped me, and given me strength to get through the day."

I want to ask her when she made these promises and what they have to do with me, but I don't. I'm patient, and I wait, lifting my glass and taking a sip of the wine.

"The first is that I would not let the cancer fears get to me, and there are a lot of fears. The second is that I would eat healthier, exercise, and practice mindfulness. Third, I wouldn't freak out every time I felt tired or got a fever. Fourth, I would embrace each day as if it were my last and do my best to live a full life. And fifth . . ." She pauses and looks at me nervously. "I promised myself I wouldn't inflict this on anyone but me."

Leaning back, I remain silent as I watch different emotions wash through her eyes. Pride, because she's proud of who she's become over the last couple of years; sadness, I think because she finally knows she's missing out on some of the really great parts of life; and then disappointment because she thinks that's what I feel about her and her promises. She's completely wrong about that, though.

And then she does the thing, this thing where she shakes her head and then smiles. I've seen her do it before and have never given much thought to it, but now I think it's because she's trying to shake away bad or negative thoughts, and by smiling she's reminding herself that she must be grateful, must be happy—even when she's not. It's a mask, and for us to work, she's going to have to take it off.

I continue to stare at her as I replay these promises, considering how they impact her and how they might impact us, and other than the last one, which she'll need to explain, they all seem like nice things to work toward. I've also concluded that she made them to herself sometime during or after when she was sick.

"I went out with a guy—"

"What do you mean you went out with a guy? When?" Jealousy and betrayal slip in, and I scoot my chair back a bit to cross my right ankle over my left knee.

Her eyes drop to the table, which tells me she went out with someone recently and she knew it was wrong. Even so, she wants to tell me anyway, so I do what I told myself I was going to do: I keep my mouth shut and listen without overreacting.

"Sorry," I tell her, shaking my head. "Keep going."

Her eyes come back to mine, only this time the emotion present is loud and clear: fear. She's afraid to tell me, afraid of what I might think of her.

"Three days ago." Her cheeks tinge pink.

Pursing my lips, I feel my jaw clench. I'm not necessarily angry at her as we both know she wasn't looking for a relationship or to hook up with anyone; it's that she did it anyway knowing if I found out about it, it would most likely hurt me.

"Don't worry, I knew it was wrong—and everyone told me it was wrong." She smooths out the napkin over her lap. "But I saw the pictures you've been posting and it looked like you were moving on with your life, so I wanted to do the same. I just wanted things to get back to normal."

"Did they?" I ask her, needing to know if she's looking to regain her version of normal from before me, or if she's wanting to make a new normal with me.

"No. Within five minutes, I was openly crying on the sidewalk, and I ruined the poor guy's night." She reaches for her wine and takes a sip.

Part of me wants to be happy about this because she wanted me and not that guy, but the larger part of me—the part that wants her to just to be happy—has my brows pulling down.

"Meg," I say softly. "I don't want you crying. Not over this, not over me."

"I couldn't help it." Her eyes turn glassy behind the candlelight, and she sets her wine down. "I can't help it now. I didn't want him—I don't want anyone but you. I missed you. I missed you so much."

"And I missed you." Dropping my leg, I lean forward and lay my hand over hers on the table. The contact between us is nice, and she flips her hand over so we're palm to palm. My fingers trace the inside of her wrist. "Trust me, there was no moving on, at least not like you're thinking."

"What does that mean?" she asks, looking genuinely curious.

"Nothing." I shake my head. I want to tell her about my time back in Tampa, how utterly miserable I was, and then the interesting turn of events that occurred over the last week, but not yet. "I hear you when you tell me you've made these promises to yourself, but I need you to explain where and how I factor into all of this."

I do want this, more than anything, but only if she wants me in the same way.

And that is what I need to hear from her tonight.

She-Crab Soup

Ingredients:

1/4 cup butter
1/4 cup onion minced
1/4 cup flour
3 cups seafood stock
2 cups heavy cream set out for a few minutes to prevent curdling when added to hot stock
1/2 tsp Worcestershire
1/2 tsp lemon zest
1/2 tsp mace
1 tsp Old Bay Seasoning
1/4 tsp cayenne pepper
1-1/2 tsp salt divided
1 lb lump crab meat picked through and divided
1/4 cup dry sherry

Directions:

Melt butter of medium heat in large stock pot. Cook onion until soft (about 3 mins)

Add flour and combine to make roux.

Add seafood stock to roux. Reduce to low heat and stir until thickened (about 5 mins)

Add cream and bring to a boil.

Reduce heat to low. Add next 5 ingredients, 1 tsp of salt, and 1/2 of the crab. Simmer 5 mins.

Combine remaining crab meat, salt, and sherry in a small bowl. When you divide the soup into individual bowls, top with a scoop of the crab mixture in the center of the bowl.

Chapter 34

Seal the Deal

Meg

WHY IS THIS so hard?

For weeks, I have been dying to talk to him, to pour my heart out to him, and now that he's here in front of me looking like the best thing I have ever seen, I'm nervous.

It's not like I think he's going to judge me. When it comes to me, he's the most open and accepting person I know. It's just that these are my inner thoughts, the places I rarely go to, because if I do, I'm not keeping promise number one. I'm letting the cancer fears get to me.

Staring down at our hands, I ask him a question I'm certain I already know the answer to.

"Have you ever known someone to die of cancer?"

The words linger in the air and he doesn't respond right away; instead his fingers tighten on my arm and my eyes rise to find his. Warmth and love shine from them—they have since the moment our eyes collided across the garden—and it's this, having him here, openly wanting to know me that makes this easier than I ever thought it would be. Don't get me wrong, it's still so hard, but for the first time, I want to talk to him. I want to tell him.

"No, but I imagine you have," he says quietly.

I nod and think about the three funerals I went to within two years of my diagnosis.

When you are going through the experience of treatment, support groups, and counseling, it's comforting to be surrounded by a community who understands and is there to help. You meet people and make friends, but as much as it's embraced and discussed, the aftermath of surviving and the guilt that comes along with personally knowing those who don't is something I'm certain I'll struggle with for the rest of my life.

As for the funerals, the poignancy evoked by being so close to what could have been and still might be my reality . . . it sits too close to the heart. Mortality stares you in the face, and there's no escaping it.

"I'm sorry you lost people you cared for," he says as he leans forward and slides his hand up my forearm, his thumb swiping back and forth over the crease in my elbow.

I nod again and swallow to try to hold onto my composure. It's not just because of the topic, but because I'm discussing it with him and he's displaying empathy in the way that I need versus sympathy. It's easy to see when people feel sorry for you, but he wants to share this with me, and that's what I keep reminding myself.

Echoes of the water fountain pick up around us as he allows me to get lost in my thoughts. I glance around at the beauty of the garden, smell the fresh dirt and fragrancy of the plants from where they are perfectly placed around the gazebo, and it's through them I see flashes of people and the permanent etch of a lasting broken heart.

"It's not just the loss, though." I look back at him and do my best not to imagine what that expression would look like on him. "It's what each of them left behind. Yes, I've struggled with the 'why me' questions, like why did I get cancer and why did I survive, but the greatest struggle I've had is watching the friends and family members of those who don't, the ones who are left behind."

Letting out a deep sigh, I let my shoulders slouch in defeat at the injustice life delivers sometimes. These people, the ones I met . . . so young, so loved, taken too soon. He doesn't say anything, just watches me; after all, there's nothing to be said. I know he wants to understand, but there's no way he can.

"I know I'm not making any sense to you, but I can't be the reason others suffer, Jack. It's too much." I pull my hand out from under his and tuck it into my lap. Looking down at the place where his fingers just were, I can still feel the heat of them, as if they were tattooing my skin, and pieces of my hair fall around my face. I'm not hiding, really I'm not, but when Zeus shifts on the ground next to my chair, my hand falls to weave into his fur, and I turn my head so even more is covered.

Standing up, Jack moves his chair from the other side of the table to next to mine. The table wasn't that big to begin with, but now the only thing separating us is Zeus. Reaching up, he tucks the loose hair behind my ear and runs his hand over the side of my face to my shoulder then down my arm. He leaves his hand in my lap; he's not allowing me to pull away from him.

"Who? Who are these others you're worrying about? And why would you be the cause of them suffering?" he asks quietly.

"The families. The loved ones. Spouses, siblings, children, parents, friends . . . you. It's too much." My eyes again fill with tears. The thought of hurting him one day when it can be prevented—it nearly breaks me.

His brows pull down at my apparent distress as he studies the features of my face. "I thought you were cancer-free?" he asks, almost nervously. And that tiny shake in his voice, right there—it's what I fear and what I never want him to experience.

"I am . . . but . . ." I'm pleading with him to understand. This is all so hard to talk about, and quite frankly, scary. Scary because voicing it makes it real, scary because I'm allowing myself to imagine a time in my life I never want to revisit, and scary because I don't want this life for him.

"But you think it's going to return," he states more than asks the question.

I nod, rolling my lips in between my teeth. Two tears escape and roll down the sides of my face.

"Let me get this straight." He leans back in his chair, taking his hand with him, and he runs it over his head before dropping his arm back to the table. "You've denied yourself one of the greatest gifts of life because you think yours is still ending?" he asks, almost incredulously.

So, I lay it out there for him, the black and white. "With ovarian cancer, there is a seventy percent recurrence rate."

"So?" He shrugs his shoulders and shakes his head. He keeps his voice low, but there is an edge underneath his words. He's always been a very boisterous person and I can feel that he wants to argue with me, but I can't, not with him. He's frustrated, I get it, but I can't tell if it's with me or because he's finally grasping why I am the way I am.

"What do you mean, 'so'?" That one statistic should explain everything to him. There is a really high probability that it will come back, and then what? In fact, I feel like for the last seven years I've been a sitting duck, just waiting for it to return, and I never want to hurt people the way I saw people grieve during and after those funerals.

"Exactly what I said—so? If it does, it does, and we'll cross that bridge then," he says, as if what I just told him means nothing and we're talking about something as simple as the common cold.

"But that's just it—I never want you or anyone else to have to go through it. You didn't see them, Jack. It was awful. Death is awful, and not to the ones leaving, but to those who are left behind."

My chest tightens at the thought of this and a sob escapes me. The tears come out more, faster, and I raise my hand to cover part of my face. For the first time in a long time, I allow the fear to take over. Not only do I now worry about what would happen to him should I die, I have to face the reality that he would move on with his life without me, and that hurts, too.

Reaching for my elbow, he pulls me so I end up standing, and he slides me over onto his lap. I lay my head on his shoulder, and he holds me as I cry and drain my poor bruised heart.

"Meg, I'm not afraid of what might or might not happen," he says, speaking so calmly. "You could die in six days, six years, or sixty years, and no matter how short or long our time together, I wouldn't trade that for anything. Certainly not over an uncertainty, over the possibility of losing you. We all lose loved ones eventually. You know this."

His hand moves up and down my back; it's warm, affectionate, and I want to stay curled up here with him for forever.

"Well, I am afraid. It's why I have the promise." My hand slides up his chest to the highest button he's done on his shirt. Just above it a few hairs make themselves known at the split to his collar, and I run my fingers over them to the dip at the base of his throat. I love his skin, the way it feels, the way it smells, the way it tastes, and I can't tear my eyes away from this one spot.

"I hate to break it to you, sweetheart, but that's a promise you're just going to have to break." He pulls me away from him, and I want to protest until his hands cradle my head and the deep brown color of his eyes bores a hole into my soul, taking my breath away. "It's too late, because I'm not going anywhere. I'm in love with you. You know this, and you are stuck with me."

His fingers dip into my hair at the base of my head, and he prevents me from turning away. He wants me—no, needs me to look at him as he tells me this, but what he doesn't understand is I never had any doubts about him. The doubts have always been about me and what I can give him, what I could possibly take away.

"I do know this, and that's why I'm trying to tell you all these things. I want you to live your best life, one that's so amazing and fulfilling, the kind dreams are made of." What I leave off but he hears between the lines anyway is that I believe him living his best life won't happen with me.

"But, Meg . . ." His thumbs swipe across my cheeks to erase the tears that just won't stop. "What you don't realize is I'm already living my best life. It's already amazing, and you by far surpass any dream I've ever had. You are beyond a dream come true to me."

My chin quivers at the sincerity of his words. I believe him, I do, and that's why these words so effortlessly slide through my lips. "I love you."

Slowly, his eyes crinkle in the corners, and then his mouth turns up into the most magnificent smile, dimples and all. His reaction to my words has my pulse picking up speed, and I can't help but smile along with him.

Crushing me to him, he hugs me, and it's the best hug I've ever had in my entire life. It's one that says, *I've got you, and together we've got us.*

Sliding my eyes shut, I take in the moment and brand it to memory: the slight roughness of his cheek against mine, the clean body wash that's a permanent part of his unique scent, and the strength of his hold that, with no uncertainty, tells me I am his and he is mine. I always want to remember this incredible man, this perfect man, my best friend.

Loosening his arms, he eventually releases me, and I lean back, instantly missing the heat of his body.

"How about this," he says. "How about you start from the beginning and just tell me all of it. I've done my best to respect the boundaries you've put up in regards to this part of you, but I want to know. I need to know. The good, the bad, the ugly—all of it, all of you." His eyes implore me.

Can I do that? Can I share these last few parts of myself that I've never shared with anyone? Just then, Zeus's head finds his way onto my leg; I look down to see his big sweet eyes, and that's when I know I can. I don't need to worry about upsetting these two or be worried they will somehow think less of me. They love me for me, and despite all my fears, that isn't one of them.

"Okay, Jack. I'll tell you all of it."

He graces me with another smile, and it takes my breath away. When he looks at me like this, there's no way I can deny him anything, and I don't want to. So, I move back to my seat, and as we sit and nibble on the food he prepared for us, I pour out my story, leaving no detail unmentioned. Is it freeing? No, as I don't think I'll ever be free of that time in my life, but it is nice to share with him the burdens of my heart.

After some time and many more shed tears, he asks, "Do you want to get out of here?"

"But what about the rest of this food?" I stare down at the remaining no-bake chocolate oatmeal cookies. "I love that you made it and I want to eat it all."

"Already taken care of. I just have to text Taylor—she's going to come clean it up then drop the rest in a cooler on your porch." He pulls his phone out and fires off a message to her.

"You really thought of everything, didn't you?"

"I tried." He grins at me.

Standing, he takes my hand, and together we move to leave the gazebo with Zeus following. We walk down the steps, and he turns once he reaches the bottom, coming eye to eye with me.

"I can't leave here without kissing you first. It's been too long, and quite frankly, since you walked in, I can't stop thinking about it." His eyes drag down my face to my lips.

Butterflies flutter against my ribcage, neither one of us moving. The only sounds are those of Zeus as he walks around the garden exploring and my heart, which has started working overtime.

"Why do I feel like this is a first kiss when it's not?" I ask softly. One of his hands wraps around my lower back to pull me against him while the other moves up to cup my face.

"I don't know. Maybe because deep down you know this time it has a clear meaning. It's not fleeting." He tilts his head. "Or maybe because you know it's no longer forbidden by your self-inflicted standards. You've succumbed to my charms, and it's now allowed." There's a glint of mischief in his eyes. "Or it's because you know this kiss will finally seal the deal." His gaze drops to my mouth as his thumb rubs across my bottom lip, pulling it down just a bit. "There's no turning back now."

No, there sure isn't, not that I could even if I wanted to, which I don't. I close the distance between him and me and proudly break my fifth promise. I'm proud because what I realized tonight—and, well, if I'm honest with myself, what I've been realizing for months—is that my life and the things that happen to it are not a burden to him. To him I am a reward, a cherished gift fate bestowed upon him, and he is a gift to me as well. He is the best thing, and together we are worth it.

Rising up on my toes, I drape my arms over his shoulders and fall even more in love with him. His lips are demanding that I grasp what this means, but the way he moves is gentle and echoes the word cherished. I didn't know so much could be said by just a kiss, but when one heart is speaking to another, things are expressed in a different way, a way that's binding, everlasting. We get lost in the moment and in each other.

Taking a breath, he presses his forehead against mine. His eyes are still shut, and I revel in the closeness of him, even though I'm not sure if I'll ever be able to get close enough.

"Love you," he whispers on an exhalation, and I draw his words in as if they are life to me.

"I love you more," I whisper back, and he chuckles, rolling his head back and forth against mine.

"I don't think so. Not even close." Pulling back, he grins at me, and then I light up from the inside with anticipation as he says, "I'm ready to take you home."

No-Bake Chocolate Oatmeal Cookies

Ingredients:

1/2 cup butter
1 1/2 cups white sugar
1/2 cup packed brown sugar
1/2 cup milk
4 tablespoons cocoa
1 pinch kosher salt
1/2 cup creamy peanut butter (or chunky but is seems to make a more crumbly, dry cookie)
2 teaspoons vanilla
3 cups dry quick-cooking oats

Directions:

Add the first six ingredients into a 4-quart sauce pan.
Bring to a rolling boil and hold for 1 minute.
Remove from heat.
Add peanut butter into the hot mixture and stir until melted.
Add in vanilla. (almond extract is good also, but I only use 1/2 teaspoon almond extract with 1 1/2 teaspoon vanilla extract).
Mix in the dry oats until they are completely coated.
Drop cookies by tablespoonfuls onto wax paper.
Let cool until set.

Chapter 35

Tastes Like Forever

Jack

MOONLIGHT SEEPS IN through Meg's bedroom window, lighting it up enough that we don't need to turn the lights on but still keeping it dark enough that we feel hidden from the world. We're under her covers, completely naked and sated, and it's these moments I love the most. It's silent other than our breathing and the slow syncing of our hearts, and we feel so damn close to each other that nothing, not even the ghosts of her cancer, can separate us.

I learned a lot about Meg tonight. She shared way more than I thought she would, and for that I feel honored and grateful. I already knew she was an amazing woman, but by voicing her fears, which were really just her selflessness, she moved herself to a whole other level. It's not that I didn't already have her on a pedestal, but now the base is wider and made with titanium. It's sheer strength, just like her.

I also learned a lot about myself, too. I know I was in flight mode a few weeks ago. Leaving was an impulse decision because I couldn't bear the thought of being rejected by her. I am a people-pleaser, the fun guy, and when I thought I wasn't enough for her just as I am, I didn't know what to do. I didn't know how to change her mind, but instead of trying to, I bailed. What I should have done is stayed and listened.

I failed on communication, the most important part of any relationship, and I know that now. I was so wrapped up in not getting what I wanted from her that I was blind to being able to acknowledge my part of the problem. I wasn't listening to her. Although in a roundabout way she was trying to tell me why we could only be friends, I just wasn't hearing past the hurt. I was more worried about me and what I was feeling than actually understanding her motives for why she was the way she was. I knew she cared for me, but I was too hung up on her words and didn't look close enough at her actions.

She was all in; her body told me that in the hours and hours we spent together tangled between my sheets. I knew it deep down, but I didn't listen to her touch; I listened to her words.

So, what will I work on to make us be better than before is patience. I will listen with my heart and not my ears. I will remember that Meg hates confrontation and worries about upsetting me so she'll say whatever she needs to say to keep the peace. I know even though we've moved to this new place for us now, I still need to continue to slow down and not barrel ahead. I can't have her withdrawing, not ever again.

As I slide my hand up her thigh and over her hip, she lets out a contented sigh. We're both on our sides and her eyes are closed with exhaustion, but I am wide awake.

"I think we should buy one of those houses," I tell her, breaking the spell.

"Mmmhmm," she mumbles against my chest as she lies halfway on top of me, her leg thrown over mine.

"I'm serious." I squeeze her side to wake her up a little more. She stretches out, sliding her foot down and over my calf, the result being something else of mine waking up from its satisfied postcoital state.

"What do you mean buy one of those houses?" she asks sleepily, her curiosity piqued.

"You know, big, Southern, old, historic, in the Battery, with a gorgeous garden. You did say you were on the fence with your place, and well, those homes are larger. I'm a big guy. Trust me, over time, you'll want the space from me."

She tilts her head back on my shoulder and looks at me. Her lips are swollen, inviting, and dammit if that doesn't add to the arousal I already feel.

"You're not even going to be here half the time. I mean I know you'll only play for a few more years, but we don't need a huge house right now."

"Actually . . ." I'm nervous to tell her this, and I don't know why. "I'm not going to be playing anymore."

"What? What do you mean?" She sits up, the sheet and the blanket slipping down to her waist. My eyes drink her in because—well, how could they not? Complete perfection.

"I retired."

Her jaw drops as she takes in what I've just said to her. "Why? And why didn't you tell me sooner?"

I brush her hair over her shoulder; I just want to be touching her. "Because . . . because it was time. Because once I got back, I realized I didn't love it as much anymore. Because you're here."

Her eyes lock onto mine, and even through the darkness, they hold and search for the truth.

"Jack, I don't understand. All of this"—she waves toward my knee—"the last couple of months . . . it was all to get you back to playing caliber. You're going to give that up?"

Taking her hand, I thread my fingers through hers. "See, I don't feel like I'm giving anything up. The way it was in the gym, how young the new guys are coming in, and last week, Billy took a few of us out on his new boat—"

She turns her head away from me and looks out the window. "Yeah, I saw. I was here miserable and pining for you, and you were off having a grand old time."

I grasp her chin so she's forced to look back at me. "That's not how it was at all. They dragged me out of my condo after calling me a sad sack of shit then dumped me on the boat where I couldn't leave. Yes, the boat and the day were nice, but I was with Billy and Missy, Bryan and Lexi, and Reid and Camille. Tell me, how much fun do you think I had that day?"

"You love being with your friends." Her tone is sympathetic like she's worried, but she still doesn't get it, even after tonight.

"I do, but I love you more. I was miserable, and no matter how hard they tried, my heart was here, not there."

"But are you sure you are ready? Football is your life. Tampa—that's your home."

"Home has never been a place. You know I've lived in a lot of different cities. Home to me are the people. It was my parents, then my teammates, and now you. You are my home. It doesn't matter if you live in Charleston or Anchorage—wherever you are is where I want to be."

"But . . ."

"Look at your phone." I point to the bag she carried this evening; it's over on the nightstand.

Skeptically, she reaches over, grabs it, pulls it out, and sees the social media notification from earlier. She gasps as she opens the tagged post and it lights up the room. There, front and center, is a picture of her from the moment she first walked into the garden. I knew she was everything to me before then, but right then—that's when I knew for sure.

"I can't believe you took this picture of me." She glances at me then back to the phone.

"I had to. Did you read the caption?"

There under the photo it says: **The first and the last. My only.**

It already has over forty-seven thousand likes and over eight hundred comments. She double-taps it, hugs it to her chest, and then leans over, lightly placing her lips on mine for the sweetest kiss. It's not passionate, but it does hold so much promise and so much feeling. I can't help but tangle my fingers in her hair and pull her closer.

She lets me, of course, but then jerks backward as she asks, "What will you do now?"

"Well, you were right," I tell her, running my fingers down her arm.

"What do you mean?" she asks as goose bumps chase me.

"Just because I'm not playing football, that doesn't mean I can't still have it be a part of my life in another way. Three days ago, the day I decided I was coming here for you and not taking no for an answer, I got a call from Brick."

"The head coach at The Citadel?" Her forehead wrinkles with confusion.

"Yep. He said he knew it was a long shot, but considering my age and the injury, if I was ready to retire then they were interested in speaking to me about being their new offensive coordinator."

She tosses her phone to the side, her hand flies to my arm, and she squeezes it with shock and excitement. "No. Way."

"Yes way. I met with them this morning and accepted the job."

She gasps again then scrambles onto my lap, straddling me, still naked, but now pinning me down.

"You were that sure of me? Of us?" she asks, the enthusiasm still present but now accompanied by caution, too.

I sit up to be closer to her and take her face in my hands. "Without one doubt in my mind."

"Jack . . ." She exhales my name, and between her legs, she can feel what that sound does to me, what she does to me. "How did I get so lucky?" she whispers.

"Funny, I've been asking myself that same thing for months now."

Her chin trembles and her eyes shine, but I can't have her crying again, so in one swift move, I have her flipped over on her back and I settle between her legs. She squeals at the quick motion, but that turns into a moan as her back arches against me and my mouth finds that tender spot just under her ear.

That moan . . . I swear it's one of the best sounds in the whole world, at least it is until I slide inside and listen to her come undone for me.

Me.

I always knew we had chemistry—that came easy to us, from the friendly banter to holding her hand—but now knowing I get to spend an indefinite amount of time lost in her soft skin and her sweet smell . . . well, that tastes like forever, our forever, and I am the happiest man to ever walk this earth.

"So, back to the house talk," I mumble against her shoulder sometime later. I know she's exhausted and I am too, but I'm also excited.

"You're not going to let this go, are you?" She shifts to lie more on her side, reaches up to run her hand through my hair, pushes it off my face, and then trails her fingers down over my jaw. Just that simple move from her has my heart tripping in my chest, and I hope she'll touch me like this always.

"Nope, because I might have put in an offer on one of them." I also am having a hard time keeping my hands to myself, and I reach around her to pull her closer to me. My hand settles on her ribcage, and my thumb slowly brushes back and forth underneath the swell of her breast.

"You did not," she whisper-shouts, her whole body tensing.

I blink at her through the early morning light and can't help the smile that creeps up on my face. "Yep, I sure did."

"Which one?" she demands. Her dark curly hair is spread out all over her pillow, and her eyes narrow suspiciously.

"The Cooke house."

It takes her a second to register what I've just said, and then she shoots up to sit on her knees. Damn, the sight of her naked is something I will never get tired of, and I can't help it when my eyes drag down over her.

"Stop it for a second." She shoves me over onto my back, and I laugh. "Are you messing with me?"

"Why would I do that?" I interlace my fingers behind my head and grin at her.

"I don't know, but I love that house. I didn't even know they were wanting to sell it."

"I don't think anyone did. When I spoke to them about renting the garden for the night, he teased that the house was also for sale if I wanted it. He might have only been partly serious at the time, but I told him to name his price, and he came back to me yesterday with one."

"How much?" She leans forward, putting her hand on my thigh.

"Don't you worry about it." I shake my head and watch as she goes from excited to angry. Her fingers dig into my skin, and I yelp.

"Of course I'm going to worry about it! Those houses are insanely expensive. Jack, what were you thinking?" She gets out of the bed and starts pacing around the room. Again, she's still naked, and I'm loving every second of this.

"Did you forget that I played in the NFL for ten years? I have money—plenty of it."

She stops at the foot of the bed and glares at me. "You know I don't want your money."

"I know that, but I want you and me, together, forever. Like you said, you love that home—you've told me so repeatedly— and we'll need the space."

"Forever can be a long time."

Sitting up so my feet are now hanging over the edge of the bed, I reach for her and drag her back over so she's standing between my legs. Running my hands up her hamstrings, I squeeze her tiny little ass before I settle them on her waist. She's looking down at me as I look up at her, and she sees that I mean it when I say, "Forever will never be long enough."

"Sometimes you really do know how to say the perfect things," she whispers, wrapping her hands around my face to tilt my head back even more.

"It's easy when I have the perfect girl," I tell her, staring into her gorgeous eyes.

Pressing her forehead to mine, she rolls her head back and forth then slides her cheek next to mine before she seals our mouths together in the most delicious, appreciative kiss. She ends it too quickly, but at least I know there will be more, and soon if I have anything to say about it.

"What am I going to do with you?" she murmurs against my lips.

"Well, it's really pretty simple—I mean I am a simple guy." I suck a little harder on her bottom lip while running my hands up and down her back, and then I stop them on her ass, pulling her a little closer. "I told you on the day we met, don't you remember? The two Fs, food and fu—"

"Stop right there." She jerks back, covers my mouth with her hand, and I chuckle.

"Why? It's the truth," I mumble behind her fingers just before I lick her palm. She attempts to snatch it away, but I grasp her to me and lock my legs around her.

"Wanna know my truth?" she asks, gray eyes flaring, attitude present with each word.

"Always, sunshine. Always." I'm still grinning; I can't help it.

She then surprises me by smearing her wet hand across my face, and this time I openly laugh.

Lying back, I pull her down on top of me. Her elbows frame my face as she glares down at me, but my affection for her has expanded so much when I didn't think it possibly could any more.

"I love you," I tell her, and the glare drops only to be replaced with tenderness and reverence.

"And I love you," she says, threading her fingers in my hair.

"Do you love me enough to make me some breakfast?" I ask hopefully.

"What do you want?" She drops down so her face is buried in my neck, and I wrap my arms around her to hug her.

"Biscuits and gravy?" I mean, if I don't ask, I'll never get it, and doesn't that just sound so good right now?

"Always starving for Southern, aren't you?" She shakes her head, and I hug her tighter.

"I can't help it. You've bewitched me. I can't get enough of your Southern food, or my Southern girl." I kiss her temple and she sighs.

"I like it when you call me yours." Her breath is warm against my skin, and I force myself to stay focused on what I've just asked for—her feeding me food instead of herself.

"Well, you are mine. You've always been mine."

She rises up, her hair tickling my face, and she smiles down at me. "And for that—for not giving up on me—I will make you your breakfast, even though I'd rather be sleeping."

She climbs off the bed and finds my shirt on the floor. I watch, completely enamored as she slips it on and rolls up the sleeves. It's so long on her she could put on a belt and wear it as a dress, but that doesn't change the fact that it's sexy as hell.

"We can sleep after that. Just think about how much better it'll be with a full stomach." I stand and rub mine animatedly.

Her eyes travel down the length of me, and I watch as she tightens her hands into fists before she turns for the door. "If you say so."

"I do say so." Grabbing my boxer briefs off the floor, I tug them on while telling her, "Listen to your best friend—he knows what he's talking about."

With those words, she stops moving and turns back to look at me. "You are my best friend. That hasn't changed." If she's nervous about this, she shouldn't be.

"I'm glad, because you are mine, and so much more. I should warn you . . . I do plan on taking every title."

"Every title?" Her brows have risen.

I don't even need to answer her; I just give her a look that has her face smoothing out and her cheeks flushing pink. I do plan on it, every title: best friend, lover, boyfriend, fiancé, husband—you name it, it's going to be mine. The only question now is how fast I can make it happen.

"All right, handsome. I hear you. Let's go get you fed."

Of course I follow as she walks out of the room, and not just because my stomach is rejoicing at what's to come; I would follow her anywhere. She is the piece of me I didn't know I was missing, and now that I've found her, there's no going back. We're going to be teammates for life.

Sausage Gravy for Biscuits

Ingredients:

1 (16 ounce) can refrigerated jumbo buttermilk biscuits
1 (9.6 ounce) package Jimmy Dean® Original Hearty Pork Sausage Crumbles
1/4 cup flour
2 1/2 cups milk
salt and pepper to taste

Directions:

Bake biscuits according to package directions.

Meanwhile, cook sausage in large skillet over medium heat 5-6 minutes or until thoroughly heated, stirring frequently. Stir in flour. Gradually add milk; cook until mixture comes to a boil and thickens, stirring constantly. Reduce heat to medium-low; simmer 2 minutes, stirring constantly. Season to taste with salt and pepper.

Split biscuits in half. Place 2 halves on each of 8 plates; top with about 1/3 cup gravy.

Epilogue

Lessons in Lemonade

Meg

One year later

EVERY TIME WE visit Wolff Winery, I find myself overlooking the vineyard and the rolling hills at the base of the Smoky Mountains. They are calming and serene in a way that can't be found in the city, and I feel rejuvenated and inspired each time.

"What are you doing out here all by yourself?" Jack asks, coming up behind me and caging me against the railing with his arms.

"Just enjoying the view." I turn my head to the side, and he leans in to steal a kiss. His lips are soft, warm, and yummy with the lingering taste of lemons from the frozen lemonade cake.

"Yeah, me too," he says, his eyes holding mine so I can

understand his meaning before he wraps his arms around me and pulls me back against his chest.

"Anything in there upsetting you at all?" he asks quietly, with concern. He's been worried about today for a while, even though I assured him that wasn't necessary.

"No, I promise you, it's not. I am so happy for them." And I truly am. My heart is full.

I've now been cancer-free for eight years. It might seem silly to some that I still count the months and years, but it's not to me. I am grateful for this time, even if sometimes I feel like it's all just borrowed.

One month after Jack returned to Charleston, we moved into the Cooke house, and it officially became the Willett house. Jack swept me up in his arms on the sidewalk outside the gate and carried me down the little path to the front door, but instead of crossing the threshold, he put me down and got down on one knee. To say I was surprised would be an understatement, but as he talked about how the rest of his life had already begun with me and he didn't see the need to wait to make it official, I fell in love with him even more. He was mine and I was his, and he wanted the world to know.

We didn't have a big wedding, instead deciding to elope. Of course, if we had wanted it, all of our friends and family would have been there, but these days everyone is so busy, our schedules are all so different, and well, it made sense to us. So, with our marriage license all set to go, we headed off to the city hall with Eddie, his wife, and Taylor as our witnesses.

Of course I found the most gorgeous little white dress and completed the look with a stunning pair of white Alexandre Birman heels. I wouldn't be me if I wasn't in heels, and I know Jack appreciated them too as he discreetly told me he expected me in the shoes and just the shoes later that evening.

It was a beautiful June night, the sky clear and the humidity low. We decided to take a carriage ride around the city and drink champagne, and although they weren't for our wedding but for the many others that were happening that Saturday evening, the bells from the churches of the Holy City rang so loud and joyously, they may as well have been for us.

It couldn't have been more perfect.

Jack settled into his new role at The Citadel with ease. The staff and the team love him—I mean how could they not—and he immediately switched up the playbook, changed how the practices are organized, and made it fun by bringing Bryan up from Tampa to do a mini clinic with his quarterbacks. He's loving his job, and this past season they finished with a record of 7-3, earning them a spot in a bowl game. They didn't win it, but they were so happy to be there they may as well have.

"Okay. Do you want me to stay outside with you?" he asks as he ducks his head down and drops his lips to my shoulder.

"No. You go back in and visit with your friends. You don't get to see them enough as it is."

He turns me to face him, his brown eyes warm and affectionate. He wraps his hands around my face, bends down to place his lips on mine, and gives me the most delicious kiss. I swear there is nothing I wouldn't do for this man.

Pulling back, he smiles at me, dimples on full display, and then he slides his hands down to my backside and squeezes.

"I'll never get tired of doing that." He grins.

"I hope not," I tell him. I do love those large hands on me, anywhere he wants to put them.

"Let me know if you need anything," he says lovingly.

"I will. I promise."

He studies my face for a brief second longer, gives me a wink, and then wanders back inside.

We're here at Zach and Shelby's this weekend to shower Bryan and Lexi as they are having not one baby, but two. Twins.

Lexi still laughs when she tells the story about them at the doctor's office in the ultrasound room. Bryan was standing next to Lexi, and she was on the bed. The technician was pointing out different things on the monitor, and then she showed them the second heartbeat. She said Bryan made a strangled noise, they both turned to look at him, and then he passed out—like knees collapsed and out cold on the floor. He also hit his head on the way down, splitting it open, and there was blood everywhere. The technician ran out for help, all these people swarmed around him in the little room, and there she was standing in the corner with no pants on because at eight weeks it's a vaginal ultrasound and not one done on the lower stomach. It was chaos, it was messy, and she said when he finally came to, he was so horrified and excited at the same time that he cried.

Lexi got her first set of black and white images of their babies, Bryan got a nice set of stitches, and hand in hand they left the office with their world changed.

As for me, I can't have children, at least not in the traditional way. I'm okay with this, and as much as I was nervous about telling Jack, which I did that night under the gazebo, he was okay with the idea too. That's why he's worried about me today, but he doesn't need to be.

At twenty-one, I had a full hysterectomy. They did leave the good untouched ovary to not send me into menopause, but as for the rest of my reproductive organs—gone. We did choose to freeze some eggs in case I should ever decide on third-party reproduction where someone else would carry an embryo from us, but I'm not sure I want to go that route. Instead, Jack and I have met with two different adoption agencies. We know no matter which path we take, it will be a long process and will most likely come with some heartache, but we're prepared for what life has to give us. With him by my side, I know we'll be just fine.

When life gives you lemons, you make lemonade, right? And that's life. With each glass, we're taught lessons about ourselves, about others, and ultimately about what matters most. It's why I've amended my five promises and dropped them to four. After all, I created them, so I can erase them, too, or drink them. Lessons in lemonade—it has a nice ring to it, I think.

Maybe I'll put it on my menu.

Silently, Shelby and Lexi slide up next to me, and instinctively we wrap our arms around each other. The three legs of the tripod.

"How are your feet holding up today?" I ask Lexi as we all bend down to look at them. She's had some swelling issues, but that's to be expected as she's now in her third trimester.

"If I could see them, I'd tell you, but I can't."

We all laugh. Her stomach is so large; it's strange to see, and I can't even imagine what it's going to look like by the end.

"Well, they look good to me," Shelby reassures her, and I think about our conversation earlier where Shelby all but said, *No babies, not yet.*

After the success of the southeast regional Food Network magazine, Zach and Shelby both were launched into a new place with their careers. For Zach, the winery is now booked most weekends with events, and distribution contracts have doubled. For Shelby, her pitch for a network show was picked up, and the pilot of her series will air in the fall. Aside from Zach, no one is more proud of her than me.

And at that thought, my eyes swell with tears.

I feel so lucky.

"It's been a pretty amazing couple of years, hasn't it?" I look at them, and they look at me.

"It really has," Lexi answers, each of us gripping a little tighter in our embrace with a clear understanding.

Maybe I'm feeling more sentimental today because we're all here together, or maybe I'm just feeling more blessed because with Jack I finally feel more hope than fear. Whatever it is, I'm finding it easier to admit to myself that I'm looking forward to seeing where we all are in five years. I've spent so long just trying to live in the moment, to not take each second for granted, that I never really made any long-term goals. Lately, though, I've been trying, and the future that once felt so bleak and scary now feels bright.

"Lexi." Shelby leans in and whispers so only the three of us can hear. "Now's your chance since Bryan isn't around—tell us the names." Her eyes are large and excited as she nods her head like this is the best idea ever.

"What? No!" Lexi tips her head back and laughs.

Lexi wanted to know the genders of the babies, but Bryan didn't. He wanted it all to be a surprise, but of course he caved to her wishes, and in return they made a pact to keep the names a secret so that would be the surprise when they arrive. One boy, and one girl—perfect for the two of them.

"Why not? We won't tell anyone," Shelby declares.

Lexi glows as she grins. "That's not how it works and you know it. I don't need him mad at me if he finds out. I need him to rub my back—daily."

I can't help the giggle that escapes me.

"Fine." Shelby takes a step back and flips her blonde hair over one shoulder like she's mad, although we all know she's not. "But it's his fault there won't be any monogrammed blankets or baby hats at the hospital."

"Not true. I ordered blankets, so stop worrying," Lexi tells her.

"You did?" she asks, surprised.

Lexi nods.

"Well that makes me feel a little better. I can't help it, you know. I love you and I want everything to be perfect," Shelby says so tenderly.

"I love you, and it already is." Lexi squeezes her hand.

"All right, if you say so." She lets out a deep sigh. "Okay, enough slacking on the job for me. It's time for me to get back to the kitchen and for us to break out the cupcakes! Either one of you need anything?"

We both shake our heads no, and inwardly I groan at the thought of eating more food.

"Wait, cupcakes? But we already ate cake."

"That was for the buffet, silly. This is the real deal. Just wait until you taste them." She rubs her hands together in excitement. The food has been overflowing today, but then again, that's just the way we do things. "All right, holler if you think of anything!" With her television-gorgeous smile and a spin worthy of a ballerina, she's gone.

"She really outdid herself today," Lexi says, glancing back inside.

"I think it was perfect," I tell her, smiling. And it was. Between Shelby, Michelle, Marie, Camille, and my aunt, not one detail was forgotten. That said, it's not the details that matter; it's the people, the laughter, and the memories.

Well, maybe the food, too.

Years from now, when we talk about this day—and all our important days—what we ate won't be remembered, but our time together around the table will be.

As chefs, we're taught that the most important thing to learn is how to create the magic of flavor, and once that is accomplished, the possibilities are endless. They aren't wrong, but I think that's only part of it. There's a secret ingredient, too, and not everyone knows it, but those who do understand.

"Are you ready to head back in?" Lexi asks.

"I am, although I'm not sure I can eat one more bite."

"You? I'm equally hungry and full at the same time. The twins say, 'Feed us,' and my body says, 'Really, you're going to put more stuff in me?' These last few weeks can't go by fast enough."

"You say that now, but soon you'll be begging for sleep."

"You're probably right." She smiles warmly and runs her hand across her stomach.

Together, Lexi and I move back into the tasting room, and as I think about that secret ingredient, I look around and know it was mixed into every snack, dish, cake, and pie. With my eyes on Jack's and his on mine, I move to stand next to him. He laces our fingers together then brings our joined hands to his lips, where he gently brushes a kiss across my knuckles, and my heart swells with joy and adoration.

See, that secret ingredient, the most magical part—it's love, always love, which is why I will forever stand by my declaration that food is love.

Sprinkle a little here, pour a little there, and I promise you everything will taste better.

Just try it. You'll see.

Frozen Lemonade Pie

Ingredients:
Graham Cracker Crust:
>2 cups graham cracker crumbs
>1/4 cup granulated sugar
>7 tablespoons butter, melted

Lemonade Filling:
>One 14-ounce can sweetened condensed milk, chilled
>One 12-ounce container whipped topping, thawed
>One 6-fluid-ounce can frozen lemonade concentrate, unthawed
>1 teaspoon candied lemon peel, for garnish

Directions:

For the crust: Preheat the oven to 350 degrees F.

In medium bowl, stir together the cracker crumbs, sugar and the melted butter until combined and resembles a wet sand mixture. Pour into a pie plate and press the mixture firmly along the bottom and sides. Bake for 7 to 8 minutes. Remove from the oven and let cool completely.

For the filling: In a large bowl, add the sweetened condensed milk and whipped topping. Fold the two together gently until combined, being careful to keep the mixture light and fluffy. Add the lemonade concentrate and continue to gently fold. Be sure to avoid letting the mixture get too liquid-y. Pour the filling into the pie crust. Place in the freezer to chill overnight.

Sprinkle with a little candied lemon peel and serve!

The End

Acknowledgements

I always have to start with my family, because it's the love and support that they give me, which makes this possible. Thank you for giving me the time I needed to work on these stories, for understanding why the kitchen is always dirty, and for loving dad's grilled food. Well, for loving food in general, which helped inspire this series. Forever my taste testers, I hope you know that if it comes from my kitchen, it was made with love.

Elle Brooks, thank you for always being my biggest fan. This series took four years to complete, but we did it! Thank you for sharing your insight for this story, I just hope I got it right. As with all finished books, I raise my glass to you and to us, forever my book bestie. xo

Kelli Bunton, I'm not even sure where to begin. You, more than anyone else, has had to listen to me ramble on and on about this story and all the others, day after day after day. The plotting, the ideas, the questions for Eddie, the feedback, I am so appreciative for you there are not even enough words. I love you, and I'm hanging on to dream that this will one day be our fulltime gig. You and me, we can do this, but until then . . . let's meet for lunch!

Megan Cooke and Karla Sorensen, thank you for being the best beta readers in the world. From line by line suggestions to overall story and character arc, I know between the two of you the story will turn out okay. Thank you for loving the story and for being my friend. Megan, this namesake was for you! xo

Thank you to my team who made my vision, words, and story sparkle: Julie from Heart to Cover, LLC, Caitlin from Editing by C. Marie, Emily from Lawrence Editing, and Elaine from Allusion Graphics, LLC. It's perfect.

To my reader group Kathryn's Krewe, thank you for the love, support, and patience you continually give me. One day I'll be able to write faster for you, but in the meantime, at least you know another one is always coming . . . eventually. LOL I love y'all something fierce. xoxo

To the readers, thank you for reading, loving, reviewing, and sharing my stories. It's because of you I continue to write and make this dream a reality. I will forever be grateful. This journey has been something else, and I'm so excited to see where we will go next.

Much love to all,
Until next time,
Kathryn xo

About the Author

Kathryn Andrews loves stories that end with a happily ever after. She started writing at age seven and never stopped. Kathryn is an Amazon Bestseller for her much loved Hale Brothers series, Chasing Clouds and is a chick lit, contemporary romance, and Southern fiction writer.

Kathryn graduated from the University of South Florida with degrees in biology and chemistry, and she currently lives in Tampa, Florida. She spends her days as a sales director for a medical device company and her nights lost in her love of fictional characters.

When Kathryn is not crafting beautiful worlds that incorporate some of her most favorite real-life places, she can be found hanging out with her husband and two boys while drinking iced coffee and enjoying the sun.

Follow Kathryn

Kathryn's Facebook Group

Come join in the fun in Kathryn's exclusive Facebook group, "Kathryn's Krewe". This Facebook group offers exclusive giveaways, cover reveals, sneak peeks, and is the best place to chat with Kathryn.

Kathryn's Newsletter

Do you want to be the first to know about new releases? Then join Kathryn's newsletter, link found on her website, for exclusive access to bonus chapters, author spotlights, giveaways, and more.

Website: www.kandrewsauthor.com
Facebook: Author Kathryn Andrews
Instagram: @kandrewsauthor
Twitter: @kandrewsauthor

Books by Kathryn Andrews

Starving for Southern series
The Sweetness of Life
Last Slice of Pie
Lessons in Lemonade

The Hale Brothers Series
Drops of Rain
Starless Nights
Unforgettable Sun

Other Titles
Chasing Clouds
Blue Horizons

Made in the USA
Las Vegas, NV
16 September 2021